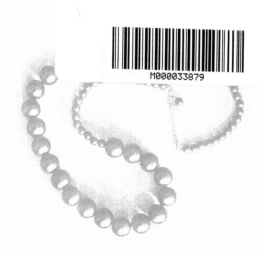

THREAD OF GOLD BEADS

Nike Campbell-Fatoki

BURTONSVILLE, MD

ISBN: 0988193205
ISBN-13: 9780988193208

Library of Congress Control Number: 2012946642
CreateSpace Independent Publishing Platform
North Charleston, South Carolina

Edited by Anwuli Ojogwu
Book cover design by Olawale Ajao

For information please write:
Three Magi Publishing
P.O. Box 239
Burtonsville, MD 20866

Printed in the United States of America

www.nikecfatoki.com

For Patience Modupe Coker
and
Frederick Douglas Sorunke Coker
Loving Grandparents
who sowed and watered my field of imagination
Your legacy lives on

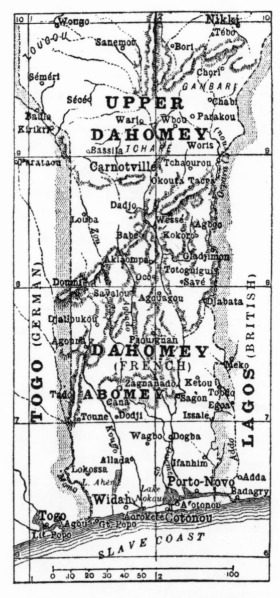

Published by The Probert Encycloapedia

OUTSKIRTS OF ABOMEY

Danhomè Kingdom

Circa 1889

RECOGNITION

The day I became the princess of Danhomè
Kingdom began like any other day. I tried to
dodge my task of sweeping the compound.
"Mama, I'm tired of sweeping! I swept just a day ago!"
I shouted.

Mama wagged her finger. "Amelia, what if I also
told you that since I made you breakfast yesterday,
then I don't have to make it today?" she shouted back.

"Mama! I am a growing child of thirteen, I need
to be fed!"

"Well then, the compound needs to be swept. You
have very little to do as it is. You'll probably disappear
for the rest of the day once you're done," she said
curtly and walked away.

I hurried off to get my broom behind our hut.
Akaba waved to me from the next hut.

"Come here," I whispered to him, pointing behind my mother's hut. In no time he was standing beside me, watching as I dug up from the soil our agenda for the day.

"What is it?" he asked, bending down beside me.

"Help me dig first and I'll tell you," I said quietly.

Akaba dug fast, shoving the dirt out like a dog burrowing in the ground. Soon, the object was in his hands.

"What are you doing with this?" Akaba asked, his voice trembling with anger, holding up the object.

"I found it. I need to know what it is," I said, tongue in cheek.

The object was a brown rectangular box spanning about the length of my hand. He looked at me in disbelief. "Amelia, you're lying. Tell me where you got this from," he said through clenched teeth.

"Amelia!" Mama sounded very impatient.

I turned to go, but Akaba pulled me back. "Amelia, tell me now!" He demanded, his voice getting louder.

I placed my hand over his mouth.

"Yes, Mama! I am coming!" I shouted, picking up my broom. "Let us meet at our usual place!" I whispered to Akaba. He rolled his eyes.

"Amelia, I am not going to be caught for stealing. Tell me now," he demanded.

"Shut up, Akaba! Just go and wait for me," I whispered back. I pushed him out of my way and ran to meet mama before she made up her mind to come looking for me.

∽

By the time I made my way to the back of the family shrine that stood at the end of father's property, I could tell from Akaba's face that he was ready to leave.

"What took you so long?" he asked. The box was not in his hands.

"Where is it?" I asked.

He sighed and reached under his wrapper tied around his waist. He shoved it in my hands. "Good luck Amelia. I will not be a part of this." He started walking away.

"Are you scared already?" I asked mockingly.

Akaba stopped in his tracks. "Scared? You know better than that. What I'll not be associated with is theft," he retorted.

We heard footsteps and ran behind the shrine. It was Father. He approached quietly, but did not go in. He seemed preoccupied. A man of average height, he exuded an authority that only royalty possessed.

Soon, we heard footsteps approaching the shrine again.

"Kondo," a female voice called out.

"You're welcome," Father said.

My heart beat raced. It was Kamlin. She had visited only a few days ago. Kamlin was one of the wives of my grandfather, Glele, King of Danhomè. She was an enigma in our land. She was tall and elegant. Her complexion was lustrously dark—the type that glistened. Her hair was woven intricately with beads down to her neck. Her eyes were shaped like a cat's—small and slanted, the type that could see into the soul. She was a commoner when she married my grandfather many years ago. Her influence had grown in the palace due to the favor she had with Grandfather. She glided silently over to where father stood and put her hand on his shoulder.

"It is almost time," she said, smiling.

Father nodded, looking at her.

"You must be ready anytime you are called on," she continued.

"I understand," Father said.

She undid the knot at the end of the wrapper tied tightly to her chest. "Here. Rub this on your body tonight," she said, handing something to him.

"Thank you," he said.

She nodded, and then suddenly, turned and looked in our direction. I hid back, pushing Akaba behind me.

"What is it?" Father asked.

My heart was in my throat. We would roast if father caught us eavesdropping. There was a long pause.

"Nothing. It must be your wife's chicken strutting around." Soon after, we heard them walking away and finally relaxed.

"That was so close, Akaba." I turned to my brother, breathing heavily.

"Forget that! What is this box?" he asked, lifting it from the floor, and opening it before I could respond. The top portion was glass, but the bottom was filled with white sand. It was the strangest thing we had ever seen. Kamlin had arrived with it a few days ago when she came to see father with Adandejan, father's cousin. I had been with him, like every other evening, when he told me stories about Danhomè. They had gone into his inner chambers to discuss some private matters when I took the box.

When I finished my confession, Akaba could hardly contain himself, jumping from one leg to the other. "You stole this from Kamlin? Are you crazy?" he screamed.

I had heard people say that Kamlin meddled in the supernatural and could not be touched. I was more interested in how she was able to wield so much power. This could be an answer to that. I shrugged, taking the box from him.

"I am not crazy, just curious. By the way, what was that all about?" I asked, trying to distract him.

"Oh, between father and Kamlin? Silly girl, like you don't know grandfather is dying, and the struggle is on between his sons to see who will be the new King. You remember Sasse Koka, who died mysteriously while trying to amass support at the palace?"

I shook my head.

"But you remember his mother, Na Vissegan, who heads the palace household. She is the Tononu," he said.

I shook my head again. Akaba sighed heavily in exaggeration. "Well, Kamlin is here to make sure Vissegan doesn't win and Father becomes King."

"How is Kamlin going to do that?" I asked, intrigued.

Akaba shook his head, looking pitifully at me. "For someone who thinks she knows it all—"

"Come on, Akaba!" I said quickly, the irritation oozing from my voice.

"Take it easy, Amelia. With the way you're behaving, one would think you wanted to be Kamlin."

I rolled my eyes to feign disinterest, but he was close to the truth. I wanted to be Kamlin. Besides the King, she was the richest and most powerful woman in Danhomè. I wanted to be just like her when I grew up.

"You know she's probably going to be the next Kpojito—father's reign mate? She's been the one gathering palace support for Father ever since we moved to this godforsaken place," Akaba said.

Every Danhomè King had a female companion who ruled alongside him. Often times, the Kpojito was the wife of the King's predecessor, just like Kamlin.

I looked at Akaba as he kept talking, wondering if maybe he would be the heir to the throne and I could be his Kpojito. I chuckled, realizing that was not possible. Our oldest brother, Ouanilo, was already showing signs of great leadership. It was obvious he would be picked as the next vidaho—crown prince.

"What's so funny?" he asked.

"Oh, nothing. Come, let us go and ask around, discreetly, about this box, Akaba." I pulled his arm, but he pulled back instantly.

"No way, you go and ask around. I'll wait to hear from you." He turned to leave, smiling mischievously.

"Not on your life. You will have to give me something to get any information about this box," I called to him.

He waved and ran off, leaving me to determine how to unlock the box's secrets.

❧

I was tempted to join my sisters playing in the compound as I walked past them.

"Amelia! Come and play with us! We need one more person!" Logbana—my immediate younger sister, Ma Doja's daughter—called.

"Yes! Come, Amelia!" my little sister—Francine, Ma Larame's daughter—called after me. I grinned at my sister of seven harvests. We had camaraderie between us since we both answered to foreign names. A whim Father had indulged mama and Ma Larame.

Holding my head, I turned slightly, calling out, "I have a headache. I need to go and lie down."

Our compound, surrounded by a tall mud wall, was fairly large. Comprised of ten huts, father's hut was strategically located in the center, and the others surrounded his in a fetus position. Today, I wished that the huts were organized differently to allow for privacy. I circled the communal kitchen wall to the back, pausing to look around to make sure I was not followed. As I bent to enter Na Zevoton's hut, I felt eyes on me.

"Amelia, is that you?" Her voice was low.

"Yes, Grandmother. How did you know?"

She cackled loudly. "You are the only one that visits," she said matter-of-factly, warming her feet by the small fire burning. She always complained of cold and aching bones. She grinned, happy to have some company.

"Come here. What trouble have you gotten yourself into? Are you hiding from your mother?" she asked, her black eyes twinkling in amusement. I could imagine her as a young girl up to some mischief, too.

I sat beside her and patted her hand. "I don't ever get into trouble, Grandmother! I'm here to see how you are doing," I said, hugging her.

She chuckled, giving me that knowing look. "Of course you are." She looked around the room. "Call me the help to get us something to eat."

I tried to explain that I wasn't hungry, but it fell on deaf ears. I had more important things to do.

"You're not? Well, that's surprising. You always ask for those little meat appetizers, but not today?" she sounded disappointed.

"Well—"

"Come here, Boy!" She called out. A slave boy of about seventeen harvests appeared. He had been selected for her, because of his physique. Grandmother needed to be carried around sometimes because of her failing health.

"Bring that tray of roasted meat for me," she ordered.

As he moved about to get the food, I watched him. He was expressionless, moving about almost in a mechanical manner. He placed the tray of roasted meat in front of us and left quickly. I immediately turned to Grandmother, feeling for the box under my wrapper.

"Eat, my child." She was already munching on a juicy piece of roast meat. I hurriedly dropped a piece in my mouth and swallowed. "Grandmother..."

"Yes, my child."

"I was wondering...have you ever come across something like this?" I laid the plain box on the mat between us. There was silence.

Grandmother stared at the object for a long time. "Amelia," she finally said.

"Yes, Grandmother?" I noticed she hadn't touched it.

"Where did you get this from?" she asked

"I found it."

"On whose body?" she asked. Her dark eyes shot up, flashing in anger. I sighed in resignation.

"Kamlin," I muttered.

Nodding, her eyes flashed as she patted the box. "This is a reading box. Kamlin is a sand reader."

I gasped. "She can read sand? What exactly does that mean?" I asked, my heart racing faster.

"She can read people's future using the sand," Grandmother answered softly.

"Like Father's? Can she tell he's going to be the new King?" I asked excitedly.

Grandmother grabbed my lips and held them tight. "Amelia, you talk too much." The quickness with which she had grabbed my lips gave me the impression her ill health was all pretense. She refused to let go.

I finally pulled free from her, holding my scarred lips. "Sorry, Grandmother." I grabbed the box, ready to run. She held my wrist.

"No, you cannot take this back with you. If anyone sees it, you will be in a lot of trouble."

"You will keep it for me?" I asked hopefully, happy to have a confidant.

"No, dear child, I will return it to the owner. I will tell her it was me that found it," she said curtly.

I thanked her, getting up quickly to escape.

"Amelia?" She called to me.

I turned from the doorway to look at her.

"You're not like most children your age…"

I nodded, stepping closer to her and knelt down.

"You are hungry for knowledge. Just be careful how you go about acquiring it."

"Thank you, Grandmother. Thank you," I said, leaving with more questions in my mind than I had come with.

෨

The high pitched wail woke me up. I jumped up from the mat where I had fallen asleep in front of the hut. It was now very dark. I struggled to pinpoint where the noise had come from. Mama had not returned from father's hut, even though she promised she would in time for us to retire for the night. Like many other occasions before, she had forgotten all about me and stayed closeted with her husband.

The wailing was coming from father's hut. It sounded like mama! I rushed across the yard, almost bumping into a large form at the door.

"Who are you?" a male voice inquired, holding me back. He was at least six feet tall and held a gun.

"And who are you? I want to see Mama! She's in there with my Father!" I yelled, pushing his hands off my shoulders.

"Go back to your hut!" he shouted at me.

By now, others were beginning to stir in their huts. A second man appeared from inside Father's hut. He was clad in a rich material worn mostly by chiefs.

"Leave her alone. Come in here, my daughter." He held out his hand to me, but I did not offer mine. I sidestepped him and walked into the hut.

Mama was sitting on the lion skin rug, weeping quietly. She looked up as I came in. Her eyes were red, her body shaking. I searched around for Father. Everything looked in place, but he was not there.

"Mama?" I called to her, kneeling down and taking her soft hands in mine. "What is it?" I asked.

She shook her head.

"Tell me!" I said.

She looked up at me, fear in her eyes. Looking around, I noticed disheveled clothing on the ground.

"Where is father?" I asked

"I don't know, Amelia. The last I knew we were fast asleep. When I woke up, these strange men were standing over me!" she shouted, pointing at the older man who stood watching us.

I sprang up.

The older man—who I later came to know as Meu, the second highest ranking official after the King, and one of two of the King makers, responsible for selecting the heir to the throne and the King's spokesperson—raised his hands calmly and smiled. "I was just about to tell you," he said and paused, smiling even wider. "The King is dead. Long live the new King!" he said

Mama and I glanced at each other and then back at him.

He bowed his head slightly before Mama. "Your husband has been taken to Abomey. He is privately being crowned the new King of Danhomè," he said.

The weight of what he said hit me and I found myself falling into Mama's lap. She caught me in time and pulled me to her chest.

"King?" Mama asked, searching his face. He nodded and smiled again.

Mama and I looked at each other, and then she started giggling. She carried me off her lap and stood up, thumping her chest proudly. "You mean Kondo is to be King now? You mean I am now *ahosi*, wife of the King?" she whispered, as though afraid of someone overhearing. Not waiting for a response, she began to strut around, her head held high, practicing the walk of a queen. I laughed, jumping up and down.

"What is going on in there? Is our husband all right, Ajo?" Ma Hwanje, Ouanilo and Akaba's mother, called.

Other voices joined hers. I glanced at the older man's face and he nodded his permission. I ran past him to tell my family the good news.

PALACE

Danhomè Kingdom

c. 1890 – c. 1894

2

UNFAMILIAR PATH

Circa 1890

"Now, tread slowly here children, this way leads to the soldiers' quarters to the left... no, no. You don't need to go in. It is off limits to everyone but the King and the battalion leaders."

We tried pushing past the older woman—our guide around the palace. Akaba, who was closest to the gate, peered in.

"I see them! What are they doing?" he asked, looking up at our guide.

I wiggled beside him, making a bit more room for myself. There were a multitude of women standing in orderly lines listening to someone. They each had a khaki colored cap on. Their backs were turned to us, but from where we stood, I could see their clothing consisted of a white-striped, round necked blouse that fell to their knees. Belts were tied around their waists with daggers dangling from them. Underneath their blouses were shorts. Each wore an anklet.

Our guide smiled proudly looking down at us, the new King's offspring. "They are receiving orders that will keep the King safe. Our 'mothers'—as we call our female warriors—have had the responsibility for thousands of years now of protecting our Danhomè Kings. They are skillful and fearless."

As if on cue, a shout rang out from the ranks, and the soldiers began stamping their feet, shaking the ground. Francine shivered beside me and grabbed my arm. I looked down at her and patted her plaited hair reassuringly.

"This way, children," our guide called to us, walking toward the next gate. We were immediately cut off by a short, stocky soldier gesturing wildly to the group of young girls lined up behind her.

"Will you come on? We don't have all day!" she yelled.

The first girl on the line up burst into tears, one hand on her head. She looked barely older than Francine. Her outburst prompted the others to do the same. As the next girl lifted her hand, the others followed suit, revealing a rope tied around each wrist.

"Why are they tied up?" I shouted, running forward. Immediately, the iron arm of our guide pulled me back.

"Don't disturb the kpakpa in getting these girls settled in their new home. They have a calling to serve the King. They are crying tears of joy," our guide explained, standing guard as the girls were escorted into the soldiers' quarters.

"They have been specially picked by the kpakpa from every village in the Kingdom to join the King's guards," she continued.

"But—" I pointed to the crying backs of the girls. Our guide gave me a stern look and I shut up.

She began walking ahead and we followed her quietly. "As you know, this is the King's inner court, it consists of the Kpodoji—the courtyard where kings have, from time in memorial, listened to songs and watched sacred dances." She pointed through the space in the iron gates. "You see the three buildings surrounding the courtyard?" she asked.

"Yes!" we said in unison.

She smiled, happy that we were paying attention. "The first one to the left—yes the white washed one on the left—that's the logodo, council chambers, where the King has his daily meetings with his council. The middle one is the legedexo, which houses the guards, and right next to it is another building, the tasinoxo, which is for the princesses who perform rites to the ancestors."

"Princesses? Those women I see look old!" I blurted out. Several of my siblings laughed.

"Yes, they look old. Princesses are supposed to be young and beautiful like us!" Francine shouted above the laughter.

Our guide laughed, her plump body shaking. "That is where you are wrong. I am a Princess. I may not be as beautiful as I used to be, but I have remained unmarried," she said.

We gasped, holding our breath. Her bushy gray brows rose up. "Yes, I am Princess Adandè, one of the many daughters of King Gezo, your great grandfather. Like my sisters there, I have dedicated my life to serving our ancestors and keeping their memories alive. I also live in there with them."

"You did not marry?" Logbana asked, moving closer, her shoulder brushing mine.

Princess Adandè shook her head. "No. It is my destiny to be here," she said simply, walking away. We followed her, talking quietly among ourselves.

The next gate led to our mothers' huts. The aromas coming from the various huts announcing lunch would soon be ready.

"I am sure you are already familiar with your dwelling places. Let us move on to the market square," Princess Adandè said.

"But, Princess, what is that over there?" I asked, pointing back at the lone hut with the oversized raffia covered roof.

"Oh, that is the sacrificial hut," she said quickly.

"Sacrificial hut? For sacrificing what?" Akaba asked.

"Enough questions. As time goes by, you will know more. Come, come, let us go," she said, resuming her steps.

Akaba and I glanced at each other. "I hear there is also the tonli—the secret hallways," he whispered in my ear.

"Let's go, everyone! Tonight there will be another celebration, so let's finish up here and go and get ready," the Princess said excitedly, causing us to clap and shout.

"Go home now, back that way, to your mothers' huts," she said in finality. Suddenly, she curtsied slightly as a woman walked up, followed by an entourage of women carrying loads of food stuff on their heads.

"Tononu," she said simply.

The woman was older. Her head was covered in a turban-like fashion with a black wrap. She was of average height, with coral beads adorning her neck and arms. A black wrapper was tied firmly around her chest, stopping just below her ankle.

"Well done," she said. Her gaze fell on us. "Who are these little ones?" she asked.

Princess Adande smiled proudly. "These are our King's younger children," she replied.

The older woman's eyes turned steely as they were fixated on me and Akaba. "Kondo's children?" she asked.

"Yes, they asked to see the palace," Princess Adandè said.

The older woman raised her hands, silencing her. "Enough, Adandè. Get these children out of my way, now!" she shouted.

We scurried off her path, leaning against the wall for her to pass.

She hissed loudly and walked off quickly, talking to herself.

"What's wrong with her, anyway? Why is she so angry with us?" Logbana asked, fuming.

Princess Adande turned around sharply, holding out her finger. "How dare you talk about our Tononu Vissegan like that?" She shouted.

We all grew quiet. I glanced at Akaba, who had a knowing look on his face. Princess Adande clapped her hands again. "Off you go children. I will see you all at the celebration tonight," she said.

We ran off toward the gate to our mothers' huts, shouting in one accord. "Hail to the new King Gbèhanzin!"

∽

I ran my hand down the soft fur, wishing I could lie on it all day. Pushing my face into it, I breathed in the animal scent, imagining how it must have been hunted down and killed. Rolling to my side, I leaned forward, placing my hand under my chin, and lookedg up at the wall. My eyes traveled to each carving. It was beautiful, the technique the artisan had molded the figures within the wall. The first one was the the figure of a man pointing a gun at a bird. My eyes moved to the next one. This one had a man hanging from a rope.

"Amelia!"

I jumped up, looking back at the doorway. Mama stood, looking at me sternly.

"I have warned you to stay out of this room! Only your father and close advisors can be in here."

I stood up and leaned against the wall.

"Why? It's not fair! Before we moved here, I could go into father's chambers anytime I wanted. Why must things change just because he's King?"

Mama clapped her hands together. "That is the very reason why things have changed! Because your father is now King," she said.

The tears welled up in my eyes.

"Don't cry. Now, your father has asked that his récade be brought immediately, but I must ease myself," she said, walking away.

"What is a récade?" I asked, watching as she climbed the steps leading to father's throne. This was one of the many thrones he had adorning his chambers. The throne was intricately carved with designs. Its base was thicker than triple the width of my arms. She knelt behind it and got up almost immediately, an object wrapped tightly in black cloth in her hands. She turned, almost bumping into me, not realizing I had crept up behind her.

"Hand this to Modupẹ his top guard. Your father and his council are in the council chambers. Do not disturb them. Just hand this over to Modupẹ. Please, hurry."

She handed it to me, but all I could do was stand and stare down at it in my hands.

"What is wrong with you? Will you please hurry? They are waiting on it!" Mama said impatiently.

I flew past her, holding the object under my arm pit. It was already dark out as I sprinted down the courtyard to the council chambers. As I approached the gate, there were two guards standing on either side, looking straight ahead. They held their guns in front of them, between their feet.

"How may we help you princess?" the one on the left asked, still looking ahead.

I looked down, remembering that the royal beads I wore gave away my identity. "I have something for my father. I am to give it to Modupę."

"Modupę is with our King," the one on the right said.

"I am supposed to give it only to her," I answered, my arm pressing down harder on the object.

They looked at each other and then at me.

"There she is," a female voice said behind me

"Are you sure?" another asked.

I turned around to see three girls walking past, attempting to talk in hushed tones. They looked a little older than me. Their short wrappers barely covered their well-rounded breasts. Their hips swung back and forth, unrestrained. Their strides screamed of entitlement.

My eyes clashed with the one in the center and I stepped back in surprise. Her eyes sparked with unbridled anger and hatred. Shifting my eyes quickly, I noticed a large circular birthmark on her right cheek. She immediately grabbed the arms of the others and walked past me quickly.

"Princess?"

I turned back to the guards. "What?" I asked.

"You can go in," the one on the right said.

They stepped aside for me. I walked only a few steps before entering the doorway of the white washed structure with an oversized thatched roof. Firewood was burning in the center of the room. On both sides sat the Council. The Meu—the man I had encountered in father's hut the night he was taken away—sat closest to the throne. The vibrant colors of the rich cloth he was adorned flickered in the light. His neck glistened with a row of coral beads, which were worn by all chieftains.

Beside him sat an older man who was dressed a little differently. A white wrapper covered him from his waist to knees. He was talking and holding something rolled up in his hand. "We must send the message back immediately, my King!" he said with urgency.

"Yovogan, we must at least know what message we are sending first," the man seating opposite them said. He was also dressed like a chief, with his oversized wrapper swung across his shoulder and the coral beads around his neck. Beside him sat Adandejan, Father's cousin and closest ally.

"We know the message we will be sending once you give us the word, my King!" a deep voice said. It belonged to a tall, muscular man in a soldier's uniform. His khaki shorts stretched tautly against his skin as he got on one knee, bowing his head to Father, who sat a few feet above everyone.

I took a step, and bumped into someone, and then I was grabbed by the arm and jerked back. "What business have you here?" a female voice asked harshly.

I gasped, pulling my arm free.

"What is it, Modupẹ?" I heard a familiar voice ask. The room became quiet.

A tall figure appeared and I looked up at Dossou with relief. "Amelia? What are you doing here?" he asked, smiling. Dressed in the same soldier's uniform, he looked very different from the Dossou who used to come around to our compound to see my older brother Ouanilo.

"I…er…I'm delivering something for Father," I said quietly."

He smiled. "Come in and deliver it." He beckoned to me with his hand and I followed.

"Who is it?" It was a female's voice this time. I approached father's throne, and noticed that some-one sat beside him—Kamlin.

"It is I, Amelia," I said, kneeling at the steps leading to Father's throne.

"Why have you come Amelia?" Father asked, his voice tinged with concern. I looked up.

"Mama told me to bring this to you, because it was very important." I pulled out the object—still wrapped firmly with the black cloth—as I got up. I paused, searching his face.

He held out his hand and smiled reassuringly. "Come my daughter," he said softly.

I smiled and ran to his side, giving it to him.

"Thank you, but next time your mother should not allow you to run the errands of a servant. You are now a princess," he said.

I nodded, my eyes traveling to the mysterious object still covered.

He turned and handed it to Kamlin. "You know what to do," Father said slowly. She nodded and turned back to the Council. She proceeded to uncover the object.

I gasped. It was beautiful. The staff was made of wood and metal. On top of its curved handle was a metal carving of a shark—father's royal symbol—the tip covered with the same metal. I squinted harder, noticing what appeared to be a trigger-like shape carved on the straight edge of the handle. The object glimmered like it had been polished innumerable times.

"Men of Danhomè." Kamlin stood up, holding up the récade.

"Our enemies have pushed us to this point. We have tried to communicate our wishes, but they have not heard. We have made sacrifices, even turning over Kotonou into their hands. Men of Danhomè!"

They all grunted in response.

"It is time for us to take them one final message with our King's récade."

"Yes!" they responded in unison.

"Where is the translator who will take the message?" Kamlin asked.

"Dossou?" the man in the soldier's uniform asked from where he sat.

"General, Alvarro will be here in the morning," Dossou said, standing to attention.

"Make sure he reports here upon arrival," the general said.

"Men of Danhomè," Kamlin continued.

"We will not back down. We will send the récade to them. This is enough confirmation that the message is from the King. They must send their troops back to where they came from. They will no longer take from our lands!" she screamed.

A shout went up. I looked sideways at father. His eyes burned brighter than the fire burning in the room. His hand gripped mine firmly and I smiled.

∽

Villagers walked with their heads bowed as Mama and I walked past their huts, muttering, "Our Queen, you are welcome."

"Mama, why don't they look at us?" I asked.

"They must not. It is forbidden to look upon the King's wives," Mama said smugly. Tall and skinny Awanatu—Mama's hand maid—carried a large bundle wrapped in cloth. Beside her was a younger girl, Yemisi, my own hand maid, whom Mama had given me upon moving to the palace. She was an orphan Mama had taken in two harvest seasons ago when we lived in the village on the outskirts of Abomey.

We were on our way to see grandmother, who now lived outside the palace walls. The huts outside the palace seemed to be in closer proximity with very little compound space. Mama stopped in front of a large hut—much bigger than the others that we had passed by. A dark, muscular boy-man appeared from behind the hut.

"Boy!" I called out, waving to him. He looked up, surprised, and immediately fell to the ground.

"Where is my mother?" Mama asked, looking around.

"I am here! I have been waiting for you all morning!" Grandmother appeared, leaning on her walking stick. Her eyes were dancing with mischief, as usual. Her eyes fell on me and she held out her hands. I ran to her quickly, almost pushing her down.

"Amelia! Do you want to break your Grandmother in two? See the way you just jumped on her?" Mama shouted, her mouth falling open.

Grandmother chuckled, patting my head. "Amelia! How have you been?" she asked , her voice light.

I looked up at her face. "I am well. I have missed you so much," I said, burying my face in her wrapper.

"And I, you. Come, let us sit," she said, taking my hand.

Mama waved her hands at the three who lingered. Boy was still on the ground. "Leave now!" she said.

Boy and Yemisi rushed away. Awanatu lingered.

"Are you deaf?" Mama asked angrily.

She pointed to the bundle beside her. "Where do I put this?" she asked.

"Mama, where should she put the food stuff?" Mama asked.

Grandmother glanced at it. "Take it to the back. Boy will tell you where to store them," she said.

Awanatu curtsied and picked up her load, making her way to the backyard.

Grandmother looked at me and smiled. I giggled and we hugged again.

"And why are you giggling Amelia? Oh, because you have now seen your Grandmother?" Mama asked.

Grandmother shook her head at mama. "Don't mind her. Sit down my child. It has been too long." We sat down on the bench.

Mama watched us thoughtfully. Grandmother looked up. "Well, are you going to sit down or stand the whole time you're here?" Grandmother asked.

Mama walked over and sat down beside her.

"Why are you so hard on this child Ajo?" Grandmother asked gravely.

"Mama! You know why. Amelia cannot be like other children. She is too carefree for my liking. She has to act like royalty! She—"

"Ssssh! Hear yourself, Ajo! This child is all of thirteen harvests. What does she know?"

"I already knew a lot when I was her age," Mama said flatly. Her eyes were unblinking as she stared through me at something unseen.

"Ajo, enough!" Grandmother snapped, slapping mama on the hand.

Mama blinked, waking up from her trance.

Grandmother turned back to me, plastering a smile on her face. "Tell me my child, what have you seen of the great palace?" she asked.

"A lot, Grandmother! You should see the court-yards. Father's council chamber is magnificent. And his thrones! Oh, have I told you about the female guards?" I jumped up to describe their attire. "I've seen three battalions so far. The antelopes, the elephants, and—"

"Amelia!" Mama shouted, clapping her hands again.

"Mama?" I asked, my hands raised in mid-air.

"You are *not* joining the guards, in case that crossed your mind," she said, crossing her arms across her chest.

Grandmother cackled. "But she never said that, Ajo," she said, cackling again.

Mama glanced at me knowingly. "Hmm, Mama. I know my daughter very well. Look at the way her eyes lit up when she started talking about the guards. No princess has ever become a guard and that will not start with you. Better start thinking of something else to occupy your time," she said and hissed.

"Yes, Amelia. I wanted to ask you what trade you want to learn. At least, until you get married." Grandmother cackled again.

"Mama, please, let's not start talking about marriage just yet. She still has some time," Mama said quickly.

"All right, all right," Grandmother said reassuringly.

"Greetings," a low raspy voice sounded.

I was not aware when this cripple came upon us. She was a woman, but her legs were so twisted around her that she crawled from her chest. She slithered over to grandmother, who appeared to have been expecting her. On her back was a single piece of folded cloth tied with a piece of string around her.

"Greetings, Low One. How is business?" Grandmother asked.

The cripple smiled, baring a gap in her front row teeth. "Business is moving. I have this for you," she said, and quickly pulled the string from under her, making the cloth fall to the ground.

I bent down to pick it up and handed it to her.

Her eyes warmed as they gazed on me. "Thank you, my child. Give it to your grandmother." She turned to grandmother. "I can see this one is yours," she said. The cloth weighed heavy in my hands as I placed it in grandmother's lap.

"Yes, this one is mine," Grandmother said, picking up the cloth.

"It shows." The cripple said again.

I watched grandmother open up the cloth and gasped. The cloth was an intricate tapestry design in hues of earth, blue, and white.

"Grandmother, this is beautiful. Is that the sea over there? What's this?" I asked pointing. Grandmother slapped my hands down hurriedly and rolled it up. She placed it between her and mama.

The cripple cackled. "Yes indeed, she is yours," she affirmed." I must be on my way."

Grandmother got up slowly with her stick and walked away with her companion. "I am most grateful, Low One," she said quietly.

"It is my duty. Another one will be arriving shortly," she said. Turning around, she looked at me and back to Grandmother.

"Amelia, stop eavesdropping," Mama said without looking at me.

I chuckled. "May I go and find Yemisi?" I asked.

"You may, but do not fraternize with the servants! Do you hear me?"" She asked, pulling on her ear.

"Yes mama." I skipped away happily, following the path Awanatu and Yemisi had taken to the backyard.

I found them standing together. Yemisi stood with her arms crossed, looking solemn. Awanatu was talking rapidly, gesticulating with her skinny arms raised above her head. Boy was sitting on a large stone, his face expressionless. He noticed me first and got up, his hands behind him. The two girls turned instantly bowing slightly.

"Princess! Do you need anything?" Yemisi asked, her voice shaking.

I smiled and planted myself between the two girls.

"No. What were you talking about?" I asked. I folded my hands and looked at Awanatu. Her nose flared instantly, and she immediately put a hand to her mouth.

"Tell me!" I demanded.

"The rituals to the Tohosu have begun, Princess. It is not wise to travel late at night, especially through the forest." Boy's voice was just as I had imagined. Flat and without emotion.

"Tohosu? Who is that?" I asked.

Awanatu chuckled, her hands still over her mouth. Yemisi looked shocked, hitting Awanatu with her elbow.

"The Tohosu are people…" Boy started to say.

"*People?* My Princess, they are not human beings like us. They are creatures. They cannot live among us," Awanatu said. "Some of them have two heads, others have twelve fingers or an extra limb."

I felt Yemisi shiver beside me. Boy shook his head slightly.

"You don't agree?" I asked.

"The Tohosu are human beings just like us. They were just unfortunate to be born into this world with deformed body parts. They took on the things we could not bear as theirs," he said, his voice rising as he spoke. His clean shaven head shone as it moved slightly. He looked up at me and then his head drifted back downward.

"How do you know so much about this Tohosu?" I asked.

There was silence. Boy clamped up, not looking up. Yemisi looked away while Awanatu placed her hand back on her mouth.

"Boy, how do you know so much?" I asked again.

His chin remained firmly pressed to his chest. I felt a throbbing on my temple. "Look, I will make sure you all get punished if you don't answer me right away!" I threatened under my breath, pointing my finger at them one at a time.

"Princess, *he* was going to be sacrificed to the Tohosu if not for Na Zevoton, your Grandmother, who saved him!" The words tumbled out of Yemisi's mouth as she fell to her knees. I gasped, fixing my gaze on boy. He looked up at me, and then down again.

"Is that true?" I asked.

He nodded.

"I will always be grateful to her," he said quietly, placing his hand on his chest and dropping it to the side.

"Mawu-Lisa," I heard myself say, forgetting it was forbidden to call on the deities on a whim.

"Amelia!" Mama called.

"Yes, Mama!" I answered. Turning to the three-some, I said, "I want to hear more about this later, do you hear me?"

Boy looked up at me.

"There is not much to tell Princess. Your grand-mother saved me from death, that is all there is to it," he said in his monotone voice.

"Amelia, come and let's eat with your grand-mother!" Mama shouted.

As I turned to run toward mama's voice, I caught the quick flick of the hand as Boy brushed a tear from his face, still looking down.

LABYRINTH OF SECRETS

Circa 1891

I had just finished having lunch with my siblings one lazy afternoon and decided to go back to my hut. As soon as I walked in, mama called me.

"Amelia, why don't you go and get me some salt? I forgot to buy from the market square. Just go quickly and buy it before they close for the night."

"Yes Mama," I said, heading straight to the corner of the room where she kept her cowries in the large pot.

As I passed by the palace help, they looked down and away from me. I made my way toward the guards' quarters with a plan to take a short cut through the side gate to the market square. I saw Ouanilo and Dossou approaching from the adjacent gate. They must have come from outside the palace where both lived across the Kana Bridge. I waved to them as I turned the corner, facing the building.

"See, our dearest Princess is passing by," someone said, followed by snickering.

I turned and saw the three girls whom I encountered many moons ago when I had delivered the récade to father. They looked me straight in the eyes. I paused for a second and kept on walking. Then I felt something wet fall on my right shoulder. I reached over and touched it. The slimey liquid wrapped itself around my fingers and fell slowly to the ground. They burst out laughing, clapping their hands happily as if they had accomplished an incredible feat. The anger kindled within me.

"Why did you do that?" I asked, walking back to where they stood. I planted my feet squarely in front of the one who appeared to be the ringleader. The large birthmark stood pointedly on her face. Her short-cropped hair framed a wide face. Her thick lips were curled up with disdain.

"What gives you the right to ask me?" she shouted in my face.

The others burst out laughing.

"Well, you need to be careful who you dare to disrespect. It may turn out to be the King's daughter!" I shouted back in her face. I crossed my arms and glared at her. I matched up to her in height and physique. Sizing her up quickly, I knew I could handle her. Her two other friends, however, would be a challenge.

They clapped their hands mockingly. The leader moved even closer, her nose almost touching mine.

"Well, point me to the King's daughter, because I know it's certainly not you, daughter of a slave!"

They laughed again, waiting for my reaction. I looked around to make sure it was me she had addressed.

"Are you all right?" I asked, touching my finger to my temple. "Is it me you called daughter of a slave?"

They all nodded, their hands crossed. I pointed at them one by one.

"You are the daughters of slaves, you wretched—"

They pounced on me before I could finish and began to beat me to the ground.

"Help me! Help me!" I shouted as loudly as I could from behind the half hidden wall of Ma Hwanje's hut.

"Shut up! Not only are you a slave's child, you dare to come from our enemy's land. What treachery! If you dare to shout again, we will finish you! Strutting around like your mother owns the palace, meanwhile, you're only the daughter of a slave! Shut up!"

Another blow fell to the side of my face, and I let out my loudest cry for help. I managed to grab a bushy lump of hair, and then plied my hand down one of the girls' face. I heard a scream, and felt an instant release on my shoulders.

"What is going on there? Who is that?" someone called out, and then I heard running feet. The girls scrambled off me and ran. I felt someone rush beside me and kneel. "Amelia!" It was a male's voice. A familiar face came into view, peering into mine. It was Dossou. He cradled my head in his hands. "Those girls did this to you?" he asked softly.

I nodded, wincing from the pain all over my body.

"Amelia? Amelia? Who did this to you?" Ma Hwanje appeared, breathing heavily. "Dossou, did you see them?"

"I saw them running in the direction of the gate, Mama," he replied.

Ma Hwanje turned around, arms in the air.

"Somebody help me! Help me! Stop those girls! They want to kill the Princess! Stop them!" she shouted.

I watched through puffy eyes as people began gathering and then fell into a merciful sleep.

∾

I opened my eyes to see father staring down at me. The frown on his face made him look even more formidable than he usually did.

"She's awake!" someone screamed and rushed forward. Mama's face appeared. She had been crying. Ma Hwanje and Ma Doja hovered behind her.

"My daughter, who did this to you?" Mama asked, touching my swollen face.

I couldn't talk. I could only watch father nod as if making up his mind about something. He walked back to his chair and sat down. I must have been carried to the honga—Father's private room where only his closest wives and ruling council were allowed.

"Amelia," Father called me from where he sat on his throne on an elevated surface. I shifted my head on the mat to look at him. "Can you tell me who did this to you?" he asked softly.

I nodded, and opened my mouth to attempt some form of speech, but Ma Hwanje came forward and knelt beside me, facing father. She pressed a finger gently on my lips to stop me from speaking.

"Our husband, it was the daughters of the Princesses. I heard them harassing Amelia. They wasted no time in beating her to the ground."

Ma Doja and Mama gasped. I nodded in confirmation. Mama held my head gently, tears running down her face.

"Hwanje, take the guards with you and pick those girls out. Instruct the guards to put them in the holding chamber," father said calmly.

She nodded and hurried off. He turned to Ma Doja who was kneeling down, her arms folded tightly across her chest. "You can leave," he said.

She rose to go, first touching me on the shoulder, and then did the same to mama.

Finally, it was just the three of us. We were quiet for some time. Mama was not crying anymore. She cradled my head in her lap. With my half-closed, swollen eyes, I tried to gauge Father's mood.

He was looking at the floor holding his long pipe and smoking intermittently. "Ajo, who did you tell?" His tone was icy. He hadn't looked up yet.

Mama raised her head sharply. "I did not tell anyone Kondo. I did not!" She held her hand to her chest.

Father looked up, his eyes flashing with anger. "Then how did they know?" he prodded.

Mama shifted her body, causing me to wince. "Sorry, Amelia." She slowly placed my head on the mat and went to Father. She knelt beside his chair. Moving her head close to his, they talked in hushed voices. Her hand went over his on the arm of the chair. His face softened as he listened to her, his eyes watching her closely.

Mama turned to me, and attempted to smile. "I will call the help to bring you clean clothes and a bowl of water to clean up." She excused herself quickly.

"Father?" I said in my loudest voice, even though my head hammered.

"Yes, my daughter. Do not trouble yourself by talking," he said

"Father, the girls that fought with me..." I spoke very slowly, with the left side of my face looking at him. "They said I was the daughter of a...of a..." The words stuck in my throat.

"Sssh. Do not bother yourself, Amelia. Whatever you heard were lies," he said.

A short mulatto man came in quietly and prostrated himself before father. "My King, I have arrived from Kotonou," he stated quietly, his face pressed into the floor. It was father's translator, Alvarro, the go-between with the French.

"Good, Alvarro. Let us meet in the outer room. My daughter is here and needs to be taken care of," Father said.

As he began to rise, his guards appeared from the dark corners of the room. But for the small moulds on their chests that slightly lifted up their jackets, I would not have known they were women. They stood emotionless with knives jutting out of their clothing. The four guards stood quietly, two on either side of him. They were of varying heights. One was tall and skinny. Another was short and stocky, while the last two were of medium height and weight. They were all dressed in sleeveless, white jackets and knee-length wide shorts; belts were clasped around their waists. They had their khaki caps plastered on their heads. One took Father's pipe from him.

"I will come and see you later tonight, Amelia. Rest well," he said, looking down at me as he passed by. He disappeared through the side door with his subjects.

Alvaro remained in the prostrate position until Father's footsteps faded away into the other room. He finally got up moved closer to where I lay. It was evening and already getting dark. I could barely make out his face.

"Amelia? I am so sorry. Whoever did this to you must be punished!" he said sharply. It took me almost two seconds after he spoke to understand him with his heavy accent. His small stature retreated quickly to join Father.

Soon, Mama returned with Yemisi behind her. Yemisi's fearful eyes were darting about as she approached. I smiled through my cracked lips.

"Yemisi, make the bed right here on the floor. We dare not move her for now," Mama instructed.

Yemisi proceeded to pad the floor with multiple pieces of clothing. Mama gently shifted me onto the padded floor. I winced. Finally, she wiped me down with a damp cloth, only pausing to wash out the blood from it into the bowl of water nearby. I stopped wincing when she finished. Yemisi packed up the dirty things and left.

"I hope she remembers to bring the food. You know how Yemisi is, a little scatter-brained," Mama said, and began to get up, but I held her hand.

"Mama, wait. Please." I gestured for her to sit beside me, not letting go of her hand. She was reluctant. "Am I Father's child?" I whispered.

Her eyes flashed angrily. "How dare you, Amelia?" she asked under her breath.

I smiled. "Good, so I am his child. If I wasn't, that would have been the worst thing you could have told me."

Mama looked down at the floor. There was silence.

"Please, Mama. Is there something else? I need to know," I said, pushing the words out even though it hurt.

Mama was mute, but her eyes were darting about as if for some escape. A long sigh escaped her and then she looked squarely at me. "I promised your father you would never know. He wants you to feel as entitled to everything you have, just like your siblings. He will not forgive me for this."

My eyes pleaded with her.

"I will tell you then…how I came to be in the Kingdom of Danhomè."

⚭

Father came to see me late in the night as promised. He came alone. The same brooding look was on his face. A guard brought in a wooden stool to place beside me and then he sat down. He smoked his pipe quietly, not looking at me. "I hope your meeting went well," I said, initiating the conversation.

He nodded and began taping his right foot slowly, and then sighed. "Amelia."

"Yes, Father?"

"You have made your mother very sad, and in doing so, you have made me sad too." He turned and looked down at me. "Why are you angry with her?" he asked.

"I'm not angry with her, Father. She did nothing wrong." Even as the words came out of my mouth, I knew it was a lie. I didn't understand why I felt the way I did. I felt tainted after Mama's narration of her story.

He kept tapping his feet and smoking. "I loved your mother the first time I laid eyes on her. She was fifteen." His eyes held mine, bidding me to listen. "She was…is smart. Do you know she taught me how to read some English?"

My eyes widened in surprise.

He nodded. His lips turned up at the sides in a smile. "She was…*is* so beautiful. You take after her. If you want to hate anyone, hate me, my daughter. I could not let her go back. Even though some nights, she would cry."

I felt faint as I listened. "It is all right, Father. I don't hate mama." I touched his hand and he opened it and held on.

"Good." He paused, and then said, "Another thing, your attackers, were they three girls?"

I nodded in affirmation, steeling myself to hear what must have happened to them.

"They have been caught," he said softly.

"Where are they now?" I asked, holding my breath. A flash of anger crossed his face for a second and disappeared. He patted my hand.

"That is not for you to worry about, little one. Just know that they will not bother you again."

My heart jumped for joy. Dossou's face came to my mind and I remembered. "Where is Dossou? Didn't he bring me here?" I asked.

Father smiled. "Oh, yes. He did." He smiled proudly. "He was here, but he had to go and rejoin the military training. He apologized that he did not wait to see you come around."

I nodded.

"I'm happy he was there to save you," Father said softly, patting my hand.

"Me too," I added.

"I am sure Akaba would have done the same, if not that he was away at his manhood initiation ceremony."

I chuckled, feeling the pain course through me again.

"Don't laugh, but he may not have been opportuned to be around at the time," he said seriously, the twinkle in his eyes betraying him. We sat quietly for some time, and then he looked around. A guard immediately appeared out of the dark. He waved her forward.

"Go to her mother," he said, pointing to me. "ask her to give you her bocie, immediately. She needs it with her." I felt my waist with my hand. It was no longer there. It never left my waist. That was probably why I lost the fight with the girls. The guard curtsied and went immediately.

"Do you want to hear another remarkable story of the warrior kings of Danhomè?" Father asked.

"Yes, of course! But this time, tell me the story of how Danhomè was created."

"Again?" he laughed.

"Yes, please. I want to be sure of the details so I also can tell my children."

He laughed again, throwing back his capped head. He leaned back in his chair and began.

"Many, many moons ago, there was a peaceful kingdom that lived in harmony. The King had a dutiful wife. She loved the King and gave all she had to him. They were happy, except when they dwelled on their bareness. He decided to have other wives, but there were still no issues..."

I nodded, wishing he wouldn't pause. There was a movement at the door.

"Come in. Do you have it?" Father asked the guard who had returned.

"Yes, my King," she answered, kneeling down and holding out the object to me. My bocie. Father dismissed her with a wave. I looked at the hand-carved, silver plated object in the image of a female—made by father's diviner, one of the many bokonons within the palace. This particular one, the head of bokonons, had made it for me a few moons ago when we still lived outside Abomey. Wrapped around the carving was a rope, a piece of my hair, and stones that I had picked myself and said prayers over.

"Keep it close to you, Amelia," Father said softly.

"Thank you," I said.

He began to get up from the chair.

"Father, you have not finished the story."

He smiled and patted my hand. "You don't give up, do you? All right, where did I stop?" he asked.

"The part of the King having no issues…"

He nodded and continued. "Yes…the Kingdom of Tado—that was the name of the kingdom—was without a prince or princess. That is, until one of the secondary wives mated with a Leopard and had three sons."

I stared at his face, in awe everytime I gazed upon the three imprints on his temple resembling the paws of a leopard. His voice floated around me, easing my tense nerves. My eyes fluttered down to rest.

~

The cold breeze danced slowly through the room. It had grown cold during the night and Mama had thrown a cloth over me. I opened my eyes slowly, surprised to see I was all alone. During the night, I had noticed Mama sitting in the corner as I tossed in pain. There was silence and then I heard footsteps approaching. I could not turn my head to see who it was. "Mama?" I called out.

"No, it is me." She came into view, a small older woman who diligently took care of Father's personal quarters every day. Her gray hair was cut close to her scalp. She had a wrapper tied around her almost skeletal body. She shuffled closer and looked down at me. My heart beat faster. "How are you feeling, daughter of the leopard?" Her toothless smile did little to warm my heart.

"I am a little tired, but I will be fine," I managed to say through my swollen lips. She nodded and smiled again.

"I cannot sweep while you are on the floor. I will come back another time." She began to turn around.

"Please...what is your name?" I called to her.

She came back. "It is Boma. What do you need, my princess?"

"Have you seen my mother?" I asked.

Her eyebrows furrowed for a second.

"Which one is your mother? Is it the one with the fair skin just like yours? She is one of the ahosi—high ranking wives of the great shark. She is called the King's favorite?"

I smiled at her lengthy description. "Yes, that is her. Did she pass by you?" I asked.

She nodded slowly.

"But she was not alone. I saw her with Tononu. They were...they were talking." Her voice wavered.

My heart skipped a beat. Vissegan's angry face flashed before my eyes. "Thank you. Please, if you see her on your way, tell her I need her," I managed to say, gripping the ends of my wrapper.

"I will," she said and left.

I waited quietly, staring up at the thatched roof. Nothing stirred. Then I heard voices approaching. "I must go and see my daughter, she is asking of me," Mama whispered.

"Of course, but this discussion is not over by any means," I heard a voice that sent chills running down my back.

"I have given you my answer. There is no reason for us to continue with this conversation," Mama responded, her voice rising angrily.

I heard a throaty chuckle. "So you think, Ajo, but it is not over yet." I heard footsteps walking away.

Seconds later, mama appeared, looking flustered. "Schewwww!" She hissed and then approached me, placing her hand on my forehead. "How are you feeling, Amelia? Better?"

"No, Mama. My head hurts so very bad," I muttered, closing my eyes from the pain. "What can you give me to get rid of the pain?"

She sat beside me, crossing one leg over the other. "I have called for the bokonon to come first thing in the morning. He will be here soon. He will also bring you a new bocie." She turned her eyes to the door, in deep thought, and then shook her head. "Stupid woman!" she muttered.

I gasped in disbelief. "Mama! Was that not Tononu, the head of the whole palace staff?"

She eyed me furiously. "And so what? She's a woman, just like me. How dare she talk to me like that?"

"How?" I asked.

"She..." Mama caught herself in time, clamping her lips together. "Do not worry about it. I will deal with the situation." She stared at me for a while, a sad smile on her lips. "ọkọ mi, my dearest" She whispered.

"Mama, no more!" I snapped.. "I won't speak *that* with you anymore."

A myriad of emotions washed over her face. "What do you mean?" she asked slowly.

"I am not speaking with you in that language anymore!" I shifted painfully, turning my back to her.

There were several moments of silence.

"You don't mean what you're saying, Amelia," she finally said.

I closed my eyes, willing myself to be silent.

"Amelia?" She touched my shoulder, but I shrugged it away. "Amelia!" she whispered. I knew her heart was breaking every minute my back was turned away from her. "I knew it was a mistake telling you. I don't think you can handle this burden," she said quietly.

She got up. The moments ticked by as I stilled my body, waiting for her next move.

"It is agreed then. I will no longer speak to you in that language any more. Maybe in time, you will forget," she said with finality—pulling the cloth around my shoulders to keep off the cold—and walked out. There was quiet again, and then I heard a shuffling noise.

"Mama, is that you?" I asked.

Footsteps hurried off and my heart gave way. I turned my body back slowly to the entrance, wincing in pain. There was no one there. "Who is that?" I cried out, feeling helpless.

"Daughter of the Leopard, what is wrong?" Boma reappeared, looking concerned. I felt the tears dart to my eyes.

"Was that you? Were you standing there listening?" I asked, my voice rising in anger.

"Me? I would not do that!" she said. "That would be wrong of me." She stepped back.

"Then who was behind there listening as mama and I talked?" My heart beat faster as I waited, watching her intently.

Her eyes held mine steadily as she replied. "I do not know. If I had seen anyone standing there, they would have been sent away."

I studied her for a moment, not sure she was telling the truth.

"May I go now?" she asked quietly.

I nodded.

There was a tap. "I am looking for Amelia."

We both turned to look at the stout man holding a long stick. His shiny head seemed too big for his small frame as he stood at the entrance. Behind him stood Yemisi. It was the bokonon—head of the diviners.

"You are welcome." The old woman bowed slightly and exited.

He came in, followed by Yemisi. "They dealt very well with you I see," he said dryly, touching my swollen face.

A scent wafted up into my nostrils as he drew nearer. He smelt of incense and dry sweat. His hands fell to my neck and the upper part of my chest. I pulled back, looking up in surprise.

"You must allow me to look you over," he said matter-of-factly.

I relaxed, and immediately, his hands undid my wrapper. I closed my eyes as his hands touched and prodded my skin. Finally, when his hands fell to my ankles, I pulled my wrapper over my body.

"Give yourself sometime to mend, daughter. Be patient," the old healer advised as he stepped back.

"Where is your mother? I want to give her some medicine to give you over a period of time." He looked at me from under his white bushy eyebrows. I glanced at Yemisi, who stood guarding the doorway. She shook her head and then looked down. I shrugged. This was Mama's way of showing how angry she was at the way I had treated her. The bokonon looked at me knowingly and held out something in his hand.

"Use this balm all over your body every night until your time of the month. When it comes, do not use it anymore," he said.

I took the small wrapped balm, and glanced up at him. "But it starts in a few days…"

He nodded. "Then use it until then."

"For just five days? Will I be healed by then?" I asked.

Yemisi's mouth dropped at my questioning.

He smiled as if expecting my response. "That is all the time you need, little one." He turned around and walked to the door, his walking stick making a thudding noise as he went. Yemisi followed after him, murmuring a salutation. He waved her back. "Stay with your mistress. Oh, here, take this to her." He handed Yemisi something. He disappeared behind the door mat. Yemisi walked over to me and knelt down by my head.

"What is it?" I asked, holding out my hand. She handed it to me.

I felt the object with my fingers and lifted it up. My new bocie. A sigh of relief escaped me as my eyes caressed the carved object in the shape of a girl stared back at me. "Please, help me up. I must go back to my hut." I said.

She shook her head. "No princess. I have been instructed to keep you here for the next few days."

"By Mama?" I asked, my voice rising angrily.

"By your parents. Nobody is allowed to come in except by permission," she added, straightening my wrapper. She proceeded to sit at my feet and stare into nothingness. I turned away from her on the mat, anticipating that the next few days would be the longest days of my life.

❧

"They are back!"

I pushed myself off the wall I was leaning on just as Yemisi ran in smiling broadly.

"It's the prince and his mates! They are back from the initiation!" she shouted, running back out.

"Where is she? I said, where is she?" I heard Akaba shouting as he drew closer. I slowly made my way outside the door just in time to see Akaba running toward me.

His head was clean shaven. His eyes looked different—older—as he stared at me.

"My goodness, Amelia! I was gone for only a fortnight and look what happened to you!" he exclaimed. I sat down slowly against the wall and he followed suit, roughening my hair.

I hit his hand, glad he was back. "Take your hands off me, Mr. I-have-now-reached-manhood! I don't need you to take care of me." I watched his eyes widen in disbelief and then he started laughing.

Yemisi cleared her throat and we both looked at her. "Would you like me to bring your lunch now?" she asked.

"Lunch? Has time flown by so quickly?" I asked.

"Yes, it has. Please, bring lunch that will feed two people. I have come from afar and I'm very hungry." Akaba said, pulling off his slippers. Yemisi nodded and hurried off. He turned to me, smiling gently.

"I heard everything that happened to you. So, how do you feel?" he asked.

I shrugged, glad to move my limbs without wincing in pain. "I'm surviving. This incident happened just a few days ago. I am almost healed," I said.

"Who were these girls that beat you up and why did they do it?" Akaba asked, his eyes flashing, reminding me of Father.

My heart skipped a beat and my mouth went dry. "They were insulting me," I said.

Akaba's eyes narrowed. "Insulting you? Why? Did you know them before?" he asked, his voice rising.

"Akaba, please let us forget this whole thing. They have been punished and that is enough," I said looking away into the courtyard where people were walking back and forth on their business. He grinned, leaning back against the wall.

"Yes, they received the ultimate punishment, I heard. I also heard that they were sent *by* someone high in authority to beat you up," he said.

My head jerked back to look at him. "What do you mean?" I whispered.

He moved closer and whispered in my ear. "I heard that when they were begging for mercy, they cried out that someone in the palace had sent them. Someone they couldn't refuse."

I gulped, feeling the sweat trickle down my temple.

Akaba grabbed me by the shoulders. "But don't you worry. I will make sure I get to the bottom of this," he said, laughing it away.

"Enough, Akaba. Why don't you tell me more about your initiation?" I tapped him on the thigh, waiting expectantly.

Akaba's shaved head moved sideways. "Absolutely not, woman! How can I divulge the secrets and essence of being a man to you?" He shook his head. "The beating must have destabilized your senses as well." He cackled, throwing back his head.

I leaned over and gave him a knock on the head, moving back quickly to avoid retaliation.

"I can see you'll never change," he muttered, looking out as someone approached. He immediately stood up. "Commander!" he shouted, his hands by his sides.

"Akaba, you may sit," Dossou said, standing before us.

Akaba nodded and sat back down.

Dossou stood towering over us, his eyes looking down at me. "Amelia...Princess, how are you feeling now?" he asked, lowering himself down beside me. I felt my eyebrows stand in surprise.

"I am fine. Thank you for your help." I smiled in appreciation.

"It was nothing." He sat down across from me, and smiled. "You look much better," he said quietly.

I nodded, and smiled again. "Anything's better than the way those girls left me," I said.

We all laughed, after which there was a lull. Akaba looked at me quizzically and I made a face at him. It was not lost on Dossou, who glanced at both of us and smiled again. He got up, saying, "I just got back from the ceremony with Akaba, I was in charge of the combat training, but I did want to see you before going home."

"Oh…" I said awkwardly.

Akaba jerked his head back and forth in agreement. "It was the best part of the whole initiation!" he chimed in.

As I rolled my eyes, Dossou caught me in the act and chuckled. "Akaba did very well. He will make a good soldier one of these days," he said.

Akaba was beaming brighter than the sun. Dossou turned to me again. "Please accept this in the meantime while you heal." He snapped his fingers and a young male soldier appeared with a pair of thick sticks and padded handles. He placed them beside me on the floor and left immediately. "They will help support you until you can get back on your own feet."

"How do I use them?" I asked, touching the polished wood.

Akaba sprung up and grabbed the sticks. "Let me show you!"

He placed the padded flat end of each under his arm pit and leaned all his weight on it. He then lifted one foot first, with the stick, and lowered it slowly.

He did the same with the other foot. Looking up, he smiled.

"That was perfect Akaba," Dossou said quietly, and turned to me. "Do you want to try it?"

I looked at Akaba, who looked at me like I was crazy. "What are you waiting for?" he asked, grabbing my shoulder and pulling me up, playfully. I winced, pushing him off just as Dossou sprang forward, pushing Akaba back instinctively. I felt myself lose balance.

"Amelia!" Dossu shouted. He reached out, grabbing the air as I fell to the ground.

"Amelia! Amelia!" Akaba was screaming as Dossou lifted me up gently, cradling me. Akaba fell down beside us, peering into my face.

"Princess! Princess!" Yemisi screamed as she ran towards us

I felt Dossou's breath on my cheek as he looked down at me. "Are you all right?" he asked.

I nodded, pulling back. "Thank you, Dossou."

"What happened? Where is my daughter?" Mama's voice was louder than the others as she approached. A crowd was forming quickly around us.

Dossou chuckled under his breath as he carried me to sit down against the wall. I caught his gaze and smiled. He winked and stepped back as my family clamored around me in concern.

"How did you fall like that?" Mama pulled me into her bosom and then held me at arm's length, touching me all over. "Are you sure you're all right?" she asked. Turning around, she fixed her gaze on the other two. "Akaba? Dossou? What happened to my daughter?" Her eyes were wide with fright, like nothing I had ever seen.

"It was an honest mistake, Mama," Dossou replied in his deep voice, looking directly at her.

"What happened?" Mama asked through clenched teeth.

"I just fell, that's all. I am fine," I answered quickly, pulling on Mama's arm.

"Shh! All I asked for was what happened. Finish!" Mama said angrily.

Akaba stepped closer, his hands behind his back. "It was me Mama…I…I pulled Amelia too quickly and she—"

"And what Akaba? And what?" Mama sprang up in anger, letting go of me, her arms raised.

"Don't you dare, Ajo!" The air was still as Ma Hwanje appeared from nowhere, as if she had been hiding and biding her time. The crowd grew thicker.

"Mama!" Akaba stepped in front of his mother, talking quietly to her. I pulled on Mama's wrapper, my heart beating fast. This could not be happening. Mama looked down at me, and then shook her head, her eyes clouded with rage. Pulling her wrapper from my grip, she stepped closer to mother and son.

"I will dare it and then some, Hwanje! What will you do?" she shouted. She eyed her senior wife from head to toe and hissed. I watched as Ma Doja and Ma Larame huddled together, their hands covering their mouths. Ma Hwanje pushed forward, her hand in the air. Akaba pushed her back gently. Dossou stepped in front of Mama. By now the crowd of junior wives, children, and slaves were cheering.

Yemisi moved closer to me, already crying.

"Mama, please! Ma Hwanje, please!" I heard myself screaming.

"Take her into the inner chambers, Yemisi," Dossou said quietly. He took Mama by the arm.

"Come, Princess." Yemisi pulled me up quickly and began leading me in. I turned around in time to see a shadow at the edge of the crowd. A feeling of foreboding washed over me as I stared at Vissegan. She had a snarl on her lips, her hair hidden under a cotton wrapper that she flung round her neck. Her eyes looked sharply at Mama and back at me. They met mine and immediately, she seemed to jolt. Turning around, she retreated into the crowd.

"If you dare touch my son, you will see!" Hwanje screamed, holding a finger up at Mama's face. The crowd began shouting.

"Hwanje! Ajo! My daughters! Why are you bringing shame to your husband? Come this way! Now!" Grandmother shouted. She walked up slowly through the crowd, her face lit up in anger.

Yemisi pulled me to the door of the honga. "Come, Princess," she said calmly. I put one hand on her shoulder, hoping on one leg into the inner chamber. Once inside, she placed me back on my mat. She immediately pulled the long bench in the corner to the door way and slowly used her weight to push upward, blocking the doorway. She came back to lie at the foot of my mat, reminding me of a dutiful dog. The voices outside began to quiet down. I moved forward. Yemisi looked across at me and then shook her head.

I lay back and waited. Finally, someone came to the entrance of the door and knocked. The bench moved slowly and then stopped.

"Amelia? Yemisi? Are you there?" Mama's voice called to us. Yemisi got up quickly and moved the bench again to the side of the wall. She knelt to the floor. Mama entered, followed by Grandmother. Their faces were stony and unreadable.

I sat up on the mat, leaning against the wall. Mama lowered Grandmother slowly beside me and sat down beside her. Grandmother touched my head. I could see the sweat trickling slowly down her temple. Her eyes seemed watery and tired.

"Grandmother, are you all right?" I asked, putting my hand over hers.

She smiled slowly, gripping my hand. "I should be asking you that my child. I hope you have not broken any bones."

I shook my head, glancing at Mama. She still looked very angry and seemed to be in deep thought. She caught me looking at her and mustered a tight smile.

"Is everything fine now? I mean, with you and ma Hwanje?" I asked, afraid of the response.

Mama hissed, looking down at the mat.

"Ajo!" Grandmother said sternly.

Mama turned to Yemisi who still stood, waiting. "Leave now."

Yemisi scurried off. Mama turned back to me. "You are not to speak to that woman or her children again!" she shouted almost maniacally.

Grandmother gripped my hand hard, making me look at her. "You will do no such thing! Hwanje is your senior mother. You will pay her due respect!" she said firmly.

Mama was silent, tapping her feet together.

"Mama?" I searched her face.

She looked at her mother, and then at me, and smiled a sad smile.

"Ajo, you cannot ask Amelia to stop speaking to her senior mother and her siblings. That is not the way I raised you!" Grandmother's voice rose indignantly.

I looked from one to the other as they stared at each other. Mama sighed heavily, finally looking away. Grandmother leaned forward and grabbed her by the shoulders.

"Mama, no! No!" Mama pushed her hands away, screaming. Grandmother refused to let her go. Finally, Mama burst into tears and collapsed into Grandmother's arms.

"Sssh. It is enough. It is enough. I understand how you feel. It will be all right, my daughter," she said softly.

I watched them whispering to each other—Mama lying like a child in her mother's lap, Grandmother patting her softly on the head.

I shifted slowly to touch Mama's cheek as she cried. They both paused and looked at me.

"See, you almost forgot your daughter in the midst of it all," Grandmother said, smiling. "You must never forget what is most important."

Mama nodded. I had a feeling this had been an ongoing conversation that had started long before today. She reached out and took my hand. "I am sorry, Amelia. I am ashamed of myself for acting like this in front of you...in front of the whole palace! Kondo will be so angry with me." She sniffed and wiped her face quickly.

"Don't worry about him. I will set his mind at rest," Grandmother said. "You stay here with Amelia tonight. Tomorrow, all will be restored." She scrambled off the floor quickly.

I watched in amazement. "Grandmother! Are you leaving us again? Please don't return to the village, stay here," I said on the verge of tears.

Grandmother had reached the doorway by now. She turned and smiled. "My child, I must. For the sake of..." She paused and exchanged a look with mama. "For the sake of all that we hold dear, I must leave. Good night." She disappeared through the doorway, leaving us to tend to our broken hearts.

ᖶᕒᕚ

T he next day, we moved back to mama's hut. The other mothers watched us from afar as we moved about the compound, not saying much. I did not see Akaba all morning, even though I sat outside, hoping he would come by. I poked at the sand with the long stick Dossou gave me in my hand, looking up occasionally as people passed by.

Mama came out of the hut with a large pot. She glanced sideways at me. "Amelia, I hope you are not going to be sulking all day?"

I squinted up at her. "I don't know what you mean, Mama. All I am doing is resting like you said." I hoped she wouldn't see the tear trickling down my other cheek.

She stood looking at me, and then shrugged and walked over to the logs of wood. "All I am saying is that it will do you no good to sit and think. You need to immerse yourself in some activity. Why don't I call Logbana to come and play with you?"

"Mama, no!" I shouted. "The last time Logbana and I played, she stole the one thing grandmother ever gave me!"

Mama looked up from blowing on the fire. "That remains unconfirmed. We searched her hut and found nothing," she said.

I shook my head, reluctant to talk. "Mama," I said softly.

"Yes, my daughter."

I smiled, knowing from the tone of her voice that now was the time I could ask for anything I wanted. "Can Yemisi go and see if Akaba is at home?" I asked.

Mama did not stop blowing on the fire. I waited, praying. I could see Logbana running toward us, like she had heard us talking about her.

"Mama...please?" I pleaded. Logbana would be upon us in another second.

Mama looked up at the approaching figure and nodded.

"Oh thank you!" I turned toward the backyard. "Yemisi! Yemisi!" I called, just as Logbana crouched down beside me.

"Amelia, how are you feeling?" she asked, touching me on the arm.

Yemisi appeared. "Please, Yemisi, go and call Akaba for me. Tell him to come and see me," I said breathlessly. I watched as Logbana's face darkened. Yemisi nodded and ran to deliver the message.

"Akaba? I thought you both had a fight yesterday?" Logbana asked, confused.

Mama walked closer, nodding her head, her hands across her chest. "Is that so Logbana? Did you see Akaba and Amelia actually fighting?" she asked quietly.

Logbana sprang up, putting her hands behind her. "N-no Mama. I'm sorry."

"You better be!" Mama shouted, stepping closer to the cowering girl.

Logbana knelt quickly and sprang up again. "I will be on my way. I think my mother is calling me," she said, her teeth chattering.

"I'm sure she is!" Mama called to her fleeing back.

I burst out laughing, clapping my hands in glee.

Mama joined me. "Good riddance!" she called out. Logbana rushed past Yemisi and Akaba, who were approaching. Akaba paused when he saw Mama.

I held my breath, not sure what he would do. Mama stood, and then slowly, she held her hand out and beckoned him to come.

Akaba picked up his pace again and walked confidently toward us. His wrapper now fit nicely around his widened shoulders, flapping slightly at the ends when the wind blew.

"Good afternoon, Mama." He bowed slightly when he reached Mama.

Mama stepped forward and touched his shoulder.

"Good afternoon, my son," she said softly. "How is your mother today?" Mama asked.

"She is very well. I will tell her you asked of her," he said.

"You do that. Will you have lunch with us?" Mama asked.

Akaba nodded, patting his flat stomach. "Mama! Why must you ask me this question to which you already know the answer?" he asked in feigned surprise.

We all burst out laughing. Mama turned to Yemisi. "Yemisi, you heard the Prince. Please get me some more tubers of yam from the back." She proceeded to the boiling pot, leaving Akaba and I alone.

Akaba sat down beside me, not saying anything. I glanced at him. He had a slight smile on his face.

"Why are you looking like that?" I asked, chuckling.

He looked at me, and smiled even more broadly. "You wouldn't understand," he said quietly

"Try me," I challenged him.

He sighed, and then shifted his body to face me. "*They* tried to break us."

"What? Who are *they*?" I asked.

He shrugged. "I knew you wouldn't understand."

"Then explain…"

He shrugged again. "There's nothing to explain Amelia. It's either you understand or you don't."

I watched him quietly, not sure if I liked this new Akaba.

"Akaba!" Mama called.

"Yes, Mama?" Akaba responded.

"Please come and help me with this hot pot. It is so heavy with this water."

Akaba walked over to her. I watched as they began to lift the pot from the fire.

Out of the corner of my eye, I saw something moving toward me. I turned to see a hen. Hens were all over the palace, scavenging for food. Their owners did not bother to feed them. It was barely a few feet from me and I chuckled at its bravery. The eyes seemed oddly familiar.

Suddenly, it sprang toward me. The next thing I felt was a sharp pain on my ankle. I screamed, grabbing hold of what seemed to be the wing of the hen. It let out a screeching sound.

"What is it?" someone shouted. I screamed louder, and then let go of the hen's wing, several feathers sticking to my hands. Blood trickled down my leg as I fell sideways to the ground.

"My leg, Mama! My leg! It was the hen, it bit my leg!" I screamed. The pain was becoming unbearable.

Akaba picked me up. "We must take her to the bokonon!" he shouted, leading the way.

"Yes! Let's go! Yemisi, please, let's go!" Mama called, already running behind us as we made our way across the palace courtyard.

∞

"**D**id you see the hen? Did you catch it in the end?" someone whispered.

"No, we were too busy trying to get her to the bokonon," Mama whispered exasperatedly.

I opened my eyes slightly, looking up into the thatched roof. I shifted my leg, immediately feeling a sharp pain and screamed.

Mama scrambled to my side. Next to her was Ma Hwanje. "It is all right, Amelia. I am here," Mama said.

"My leg, Mama!" I screamed again. The pain was wrenching as it danced sporadically up and down from my thigh to ankle. I tried to touch the source of the pain, but was held down by the two women.

"Just pass me the medicine. That's what he said I should give her once she woke up."

Sudden flashes of the hen running toward me appeared as I closed my eyes and I felt myself shaking.

"You will be fine, Amelia. Take this." A bowl was pressed to my lips and I felt the bitter liquid going down my throat. It immediately began rising back up again.

"Close her nose now!" Ma Hwanje shouted. Immediately, I felt fingers clamp down on my nose. My mouth fell open, gulping the air and inevitably, the medicine. The liquid moved down without hindrance and stayed there. After moments of imprisonment, I felt a release of my arms.

Mama leaned back against the wall. Ma Hwanje followed suit.

"Thank God. So, what were the instructions again Hwanje? I can't remember. Please, help me remember," Mama said tearfully, drawing me close as she looked across at Hwanje.

Hwanje took Mama's hand. "It is fine. I am here for you. He said we should keep giving her water,but no food. Not until her fever breaks."

Mama nodded and placed me back gently on the mat. Picking up a damp cloth, she began wiping me down slowly. I groaned, feeling the pain again. "Sorry, Amelia… sorry…but, Hwanje, it was just a hen! How can it have progressed to a fever like this?" Mama asked in a panicked tone.

There was silence.

"Hwanje! Did you not hear me?" Mama asked angrily.

"Hmmmmm." Hwanje sighed heavily, shifting her weight on the mat. "…Have you looked at her ankle?"

"What do you mean?" Mama asked.

"Hmmmmm." She sighed again.

"Hwanje, what is all this *hmmmm* you're making?" Mama asked angrily.

"Ajo, you said that the hen just pecked her on the ankle right?"

"Yes."

"So, how come her whole leg has swollen up like she was hit by a moving cow?"

Mama gasped. The hen's piercing eyes flashed before my closed eyes.

"This is not normal, Ajo. Something is amiss." Hwanje concluded.

There was a deadly silence until Mama cut in, her voice now controlled. "How do we protect her?" she asked.

"Good, that is the question I have been waiting to answer," Hwanje said almost contentedly, and continued. "There is a popular Nago priest just at the outskirts of the palace. He is the most powerful bokonon for miles and miles. He can look at you once and tell what ails you," Ma Hwanje said.

"Nago Priest? You mean he is from the Yoruba tribe—"

"Yes, yes, but that is besides the point, He can work wonders. My younger sister has been convulsing since birth. She was taken there just before the last moon and was finally rid of the disease. She had been suffering for thirty harvests since her birth!"

Mama exclaimed.

"Yes, and besides healing, he can also fortify you and your daughter."

"What do you mean?" Mama asked.

Hwanje's voice floated around me as my eyes began to flutter. "He can spiritually protect you from evil forces, Ajo. It looks like Amelia is going to need it."

"Yes, I agree with you my sister…"

I felt my head growing lighter again, as I drifted away.

❀

The days following the hen attack were a blur to me. I was so weak from the pain that I could barely sit up. My visitors were father, Hwanje, and Akaba. Mama and Yemisi never left my side. At some point, I think Dossou and Ouanilo also visited with me.

The night I knew I would survive, I woke up with a strong desire to take off all my clothes. The sweat trickled quickly down my back as I struggled on the floor. Mama stirred beside me.

"What is it? Are you all right?" she asked, lifting her head to look at me in the dark.

"Mama, it is too hot! Did you light the fire? No, it can't be. What did you rub on me? I feel too hot!" I squirmed, unable to bear the scorching heat.

She sat up, leaning away to pick up something in the dark. In a second, she put on the oil lamp and moved it close to my face.

"You....you feel hot, Amelia?" she asked quietly.

I pulled on the arm sleeve of the blouse, nodding repeatedly.

"Heee! It has finally happened!" Mama exclaimed, raising her hands up in awe.

"Mama!" I shouted impatiently, frustrated at how weak I was, unable to take anything off.

"Oh, sorry, let me help you," she said, quickly pulling off my blouse. Finally, I felt the cool air, and breathed slowly.

She laid me back on the mat. "I serve a living God. I serve a living God!" she muttered repeatedly, fanning me with the blouse. "A few hours ago, you were complaining that you were cold even though your temperature was so high. I serve a living God!" she muttered again. "Are you hungry? I can have Yemisi make you pounded yam, your favorite," she said.

I shook my head, trying not to chuckle. "Mm... Mama, I cannot have pounded yam even before the cock has crowed."

"Why not? You can have whatever you want, my daughter. You have only to tell me."

I shook my head. "Just water Mama. I just want water," I said, still feeling faint.

She immediately placed a bowl to my lips and I drank to my heart's content. We settled down again in the dark, and soon, were asleep.

HIDDEN TREASURES
AND SECRET PLACES

Circa 1892

Akaba and I made a dash for the palace gates when we saw no one was looking. They would not know we were missing until it was too late. Everyone was engrossed in the annual customs, which had been going on for almost thirty days. This was the final week and everyone was in a state of frenzy. We were on our way to the Nago priest who lived on the outskirts of Abomey.

During the endless days of lying on my back with nothing to do but recuperate from my wounds, I had thought about my life. I waited expectantly for Mama to take me to the Nago priest, but she did not. I decided to take my destiny into my own hands. "Akaba, please! Just come with me!" I had pulled on Akaba's arm as we stood under the banana tree.

He had shaken his head in disbelief, and then started laughing. "Why are you so interested in meeting this man?" he had asked, folding his arms over his now expanding chest.

"I'm interested because I finally realized something or someone is out to get me. Akaba, I must protect myself!" I had hissed in his ear, not sure if anyone passing by would overhear.

"Indeed! So you have finally been brainwashed by our mothers, ehn? So, how do you know someone is out to get you?" he had asked, sounding amused.

I had remained mute, watching as people bypassed us on the way to one of the many celebrations.

"Aren't you going to argue your way through as usual?" Akaba had asked, laughing

I had crossed my arms and waited. Suddenly someone bumped into my side.

"Oh, I'm sorry! Aah, it's you Amelia. Aren't you coming to the stream?" Logbana had smiled widely, grabbing my arm. I shook my head, pulling away.

"Logbana no! I will meet you there!" I had shouted, startling her and everyone else around. Her face transformed immediately to one of anger. Her young, budding breasts shot up under her wrapper as she tried to match me, shoulder-to-shoulder.

"What is wrong with you, Amelia? Have you gone mad? All I asked you was a simple question and you want to beat me up!" she had shouted in my face.

I lifted my hand, ready to defend myself. Akaba sprang in between us, holding up his hand. "It is enough, my sisters! Logbana, you know Amelia is still not feeling too well. Why don't you go on and we'll meet you there?"Akaba asked in an appeasing tone.

Logbana had eyed me up and down for a few seconds and then glanced at Akaba. He patted her arm reassuringly. She turned and looked at me again, hissed, and marched off. Akaba turned to me, shaking his head. "Amelia, if going to this Nago priest is what will calm you down, then we will go. We will go there."

Now, as we made our way through the crowd of excited villagers and visitors who came to enjoy the last week of the annual event, I pulled down the head tie that was my disguise. Over it was a veil. I was dressed in a long, flowing wrapper picked from Mama's abundant wardrobe. Glancing at Akaba, he looked quite different as well. Standing over six feet tall, and very slim, he wore a woven, multi-colored quarter sleeve shirt that looked like a bag on him, along with a pair of long white cotton pants, and a white cap with flaps on the sides, similar to the ones worn by the chiefs.

We looked like visitors from another region, making it difficult to remain unnoticed as we walked away from the palace when everyone else was coming in the opposite direction. A few people gave us curious stares, but we were not stopped. When we crossed out of the palace into the village, I finally heaved a sigh of relief. I was more afraid of what Mama would do to me if she found out.

We had been walking for sometime when Akaba stopped dead in the middle of the road and asked, "Do you know where we are going Amelia?"

"I do! We just have to make it to the market, and it will be less than a mile from there. He is a modern juju man, not like the ones we used to hear about that live far-far in the forest. I hear he'll even give you water to drink first and get you relaxed before you state your business," I said.

Akaba hissed, picking up a pebble and throwing it down the deserted road. We passed through the crowded huts of the villagers. We had grown accustomed to so much space in the palace, we had forgotten that people lived like this.

I skipped along, happy. We finally got to the market, which was scattered with large trees. There were a few traders and buyers.

"So, we are at the market, Amelia. Which way now?" Akaba asked.

The market women were beginning to stare. I smiled at the one closest to us, a large woman selling oranges. She had a child tied to her back with a wrapper.

I moved closer to her. "Well done."

"Thank you. Are you lost? You don't look like you're from these parts," she said, loking at us curiously.

I had made sure to remove all the jewelry that would single me out for questions. Today I looked like an ordinary villager. "I'm afraid we are. We have come from Ouidah for the annual customs. We hear that there's a very powerful Nago priest who can consult on our behalf. He lives not too far from here, right?" I asked.

She nodded her head. "Yes, you must be talking of the Yoruba priest from Ketou. He is very powerful, but have you not heard?" she asked, looking nervous.

"Heard what?" I asked, stepping closer to her.

"He has been warned by the King not to dabble with his powers anymore. He has become very proud."

"So, where is his place? Can you direct us?" Akaba cut in, sounding a little bit irritated.

"Well, just take the right turn after that baobab tree. Then make an immediate left. His hut is right there. You cannot miss it." Then she turned her back to us.

I touched her arm. "Thank you very much. Please, something for your child."

I dropped three cowries in her palm. Her countenance changed. She almost got on her knees to thank me. Her curious look returned. Girls in these parts did not own cowries. "Thank you—"

"Come, let's go!" Akaba said, pulling me away quickly. I turned to look back and saw her waving. We hurriedly made a right after the tree and then a left. It was deadly quiet. The hut was reddish. A deeper red than the others we had gone past. There was a long bench at the entrance of the hut. I glanced at Akaba who was looking a little bored. My hand crept to where my bocie hung under my wrapper. I hoped it would do its job today. We stood awkwardly for about a minute, not knowing if to go in, or even whom to call. Then we heard the sound of a wooden object strike the ground. The noise got louder as it came toward us.

"Children of Gbèhanzin, you are welcome," a deep voice called from within the hut. We both gasped and stepped back. He appeared from inside the hut. He was very tall and dark-skinned. He held a long cane, although he had a straight back, and stood erect. I had imagined he would be old and crooked with barely any teeth. He was draped in a white cotton wrapper. He had a cap similar to Akaba's with the flaps on each end covering his ears.

"Good afternoon, priest," we said in unison.

He laughed, exposing, perfect white teeth against his midnight black skin. "Call me Baba. Everybody else calls me that. What brings you here when the sun is so high in the sky?"

We stared at him, not knowing what response to give.

He smiled at us. "Come; take a seat on the bench."

"Thank you Baba." We sat down. He did the same. Akaba nudged me to speak. "Baba, thank you for seeing us. I am Amelia, and this is—"

"Akaba," Akaba interjected, flashing me a look of annoyance.

Baba flashed his white teeth again and nodded for me to continue.

"My brother was gracious enough to come with me. I came because I need your help." I paused as I retrieved my bocie. He held out his hand and I gave it to him.

"Aah, your bocie. You want me to make it stronger?"

"Yes, Baba."

He stared at me and then back at my bocie. He pulled back the rope that held the stone the sculpture carried on its back. Immediately, the stone fell to the ground.

"No!" I grabbed the stone and was about to grab my bocie when he shifted back. Akaba caught me before I landed on the ground.

Baba was laughing very hard, but still holding on to my bocie.

"Why did you do that?" I asked angrily.

He stopped laughing and looked very serious. "What audacity! Do you not know that I am the most powerful priest around? You bring this thing from one of your mediocre priests for me to give it power. Never!"

Akaba got up, pulling me alongside him. "Baba— or whatever you call yourself—give my sister back her bocie! If you cannot help her, give it back immediately!"

Baba eyed Akaba and spat on the floor.

"Here. Take your useless effigy!" He threw my bocie in the air. Akaba caught it quicly. "When you are ready to acquire power, be ready to give me something that is very, very precious to you." He got up to go, and then paused, turning to me. "Amelia, daughter of Gbèhanzin, you have the heart of the Leopard. It's a pity you did not come as a man." He turned to Akaba and shook his head. "Akaba, you take after your ancestor also named Akaba—strong and forthright—but the sun will set early on you."

Akaba hissed.

"Give this message to your father." He held us with his steely black eyes. "Tell him he must come and pay homage to me. Until he does that, he cannot find rest in his courts or with the white man." He began to walk away and then stopped, his back still turned to us. "Remember, if you want real power, make sure you bring something that is very dear to you as a sacrifice." As he disappeared into his hut, we heard him cackling.

"Stupid man! Can you imagine him challenging father like that? He is sure to hear about this!" Akaba shouted loud enough for Baba to hear and then stomped on ahead of me in the direction we had come.

I was silent for most of the journey while Akaba fumed with rage. We were nearing the palace walls when I grabbed his hand to slow him down.

"Father must not know we were there. He will not be happy," I reminded him.

Akaba looked around wildly.

"Akaba, what is the matter?"

He scratched his hair through his cap and looked toward the courtyard overflowing with visitors, and then back at me. "Did you hear what that soothsayer said about me? That the sun would set early on me?' Do you know what that means?" he asked.

"Don't mind him, Akaba. As you said, he's only a soothsayer," I reassured him.

He tapped his left foot and suddenly lifted his hand in the direction we had come. "He's nailed his own coffin. I'm going to make sure he doesn't get to say that about anyone else ever again," he said through clenched teeth and marched off again.

My body went cold. "Akaba, please think hard before you do anything stupid!" I shouted, running after him. He ignored me, taking off his cap and walking into the crowd. I realized that my veil and head tie were still on and discarded them before following him. The less Mama saw of my ensemble, the better. The music became louder as we got to the front row of the crowd. A parade was underway.

Dressed in flowing white wrappers and head ties, the women that made up father's harem danced by slowly. They looked happy as they filed past. I knew mama, Ma Hwanje, and Ma Doja would be seated behind father. He was smiling and speaking with guests, his pipe dangling from his left hand. A guard held an umbrella with drawings depicting his conquests over him, while another fanned him with ostrich feathers. We were in his line of vision. I prayed he would not see us from across the courtyard.

"Princess! Princess!"

I felt a tap on my shoulder. I had to look down to see Yemisi standing there, a look of relief on her face. "Princess, we have been looking for you."

"What do you mean, *we*? Who else was looking for me?" I asked, trying to subdue the panicked tone in my voice.

"The guards. I informed Modupę. She promised not to tell your mother though, because I would be in a lot of trouble!" she said excitedly, clasping and unclasping her hands by now.

I hugged her in reassurance. "Thank you Yemisi. I am fine, nothing happened to me. Come, let's sit."

We found a spot in the front row and sat down. Akaba was still moody, not saying a word. We watched the harem pass by and waited for the next form of entertainment. Beko, the town crier, came out.

"My King, honorable guests, and the people of Danhomè!" The crowd responded with a loud cheer. "As you all know, the annual customs present opportunities for the King to mediate in disputes. We have a few before us today, that—with your consent, my King—you can bestow your wise counsel in settling them."

Father signaled for him to continue.

"I call forth the girl they claim is a clairvoyant. According to her fellow villagers, she is evil. Everything she says comes to pass. According to villagers, she wields a lot of evil. My King, they are calling for her head!"

A loud cry erupted from the crowd as a figure appeared, pulled by a rope. As she made her way through the crowd, the people shrank back in fear. Finally, she knelt before Father. She stood all of five feet, not a day older than thirteen. She looked haggard—her head hung down, her shoulders slumped. Her hair had been chopped off and clumps of it framed her face in a mess. She faced Father, her back turned to us. She had been flogged. The marks were on her upper back and shoulders. Her wrapper was dirty, barely covering her thighs.

"What is your name?" Father asked. The crowd became quiet.

"Nasame." Her voice rang with the touch of innocence.

"Why have the people accused you of this crime of clairvoyance? Are you a witch?" Father asked.

She shook her head adamantly. "My King, I am not a witch. All I can say is that I have a gift of knowing things."

The crowd erupted with a defiant shout. "It is a lie. She's a witch!"

"Be quiet!" Beko shouted, holding up his hand. "If you have anything to say, you have to come out and speak."

Immediately, a woman came forward and knelt before Father. She pointed at the girl. "My King, this girl killed my child!" She burst out crying.

"Quiet, woman!" the town crier shouted. "Do not waste the King's time. Just tell us what the girl did!"

She wiped her tears and continued. "She is my neighbor. I gave birth three moons ago and she came to visit me. She looked at my child and said, 'This baby is only passing through.' Barely a day after, he passed away in his sleep! She killed him!" She pointed an accusing finger again. This time, a loud jeer burst from the crowd.

Father raised his hand and everyone was silent again. My heart was beating so fast.

"Where is your mother, Nasame?" It was as though the woman had been waiting. She was petite. Her daughter looked like her, pretty in a fragile way. Her eyes were large and beautiful. Large rows of plaited hair shaped her heart-shaped face. She sank to her knees before Father.

"Has your daughter always been this way?"

She looked down on the floor as was the custom when in the presence of the King. "Yes, my King. My daughter says what comes from her heart. She is not evil. She merely sees what others don't."

Father glanced at the pair, and I could tell he had made his decision. "Nasame."

"My King." She sounded prepared for what would come next.

"What would you like to do when you grow up?"

Her head shot up in surprise. "I...I...I would like to be a soldier. Just like them." She pointed to the body guard behind Father.

He smiled slightly. "And so you shall, my daughter. If that is what you want."

She nodded vigorously, her eyes widened with surprise.

"One thing, though. I can see this thing is part of you. To live happily amongst our people, you must silence the voice so that you are no longer feared."

"I understand my King." She spoke with such finality, resigned to her fate.

Father waved her off. "The King has spoken! You may go in peace."

The town crier shouted happily. Mother and daughter got up, hugging each other. The crowd clapped, some people jumped up. I watched them disappear into the multitude, wondering if I would ever see them again.

༄

It was the last day of festivities and I couldn't wait for it to be over. It had become tiresome having so many people in the palace. Everyone wanted to look around and greet the royal family. Today, Father would bestow gifts on those he felt worthy of them. I had helped Mama plait her hair last night so that I could be free to go and look for Akaba. I had not seen him since we returned from our visit to the Nago priest. Every morning since the start of the week, I rushed over to his place only for Ma Hwanje to tell me that Akaba had left. Today, I decided to get there at the crack of dawn.

As I neared the hut, Akaba came out. A guilty look washed over his face as he sighted me.

"Akaba, you have some explaining to do! Where have you been all week?" I crossed my arms over my chest and waited for his excuse.

"Look, Amelia, I don't have time for all this. Are you my mother?" He sounded abrasive and looked very tired. His hair was unkempt and his clothes looked slept-in. His eyes were bloodshot.

I backed down. "I'm sorry Akaba. I've just been very worried."

He shrugged.

"So where were you going?"

He paused. Akaba had never reacted like that before. "I was going into the village."

"Akaba, you know we're not allowed to go out of the palace like that. I'm sure Father doesn't know," I accused.

He laughed hysterically, throwing back his head. "Father knows this one. He ordered me to accompany the guards." He patted down his unruly hair and called out. "Brother! Let us go!"

Ouanilo appeared, followed by four male soldiers. They carried rifles on their sides. I ran forward and hugged him. "Brother, good morning. What is going on?" I asked.

He smiled, shaking his head. "Amelia, why don't you mind women's matters for once and leave the war faring to us?"

I smiled sheepishly. "So that means I can't come with you?"

Akaba shook his head. "No, you cannot. I will come back and tell you all about it. Don't worry; you will be happy when I tell you," he said with a wicked smile on his lips. I had a sinking feeling in the pit of my stomach.

Ouanilo turned to the guards. "Let's go."

The guards marched ahead.

"Akaba. Akaba!" I called to his retreating back. He ignored me, focused on the mission into the village.

"Amelia." I turned to see who had called me. Ma Hwanje stood beckoning.

"Good morning, Mama."

She walked up slowly, her ample hips rotating under the woven cloth. "Don't bother yourself with what they are doing. Why don't you go and join your sisters in learning how to dye cloth. Doja will be starting in a very short time."

I smiled politely. "Of course, Mama," I replied.

I felt her eyes on me as I made my way toward the usual meeting spot. They were all seated, waiting under the large oak tree.

"Amelia, we've been looking for you, come and join us," They called to me.

Ma Doja was bent over a large bowl of murky brown water. She looked up as I got closer. "Amelia, how nice of you to grace us with your presence," she said, eyeing me up and down. "I went to your hut earlier to ask you to join us, but you weren't there. I assumed you had run off with Akaba again."

I heard a chuckle and turned around to see Logbana cover her mouth.

"Come closer girls, so I can show you how it is done," Ma Doja said, bending down to immerse her hands in the blue water. She pulled out a cloth. A string was tied down its length.

"Come, one of you, and hold it on the other side," Doja said. Francine ran forward grinning, the gap in her teeth visible. Everyone laughed as she grabbed on to the end of the cloth, almost falling under its weight.

"Thank you, my daughter. Please, someone else help Francine hold the other end," Ma Doja called out. Dara, who was a harvest season older than Francine came forward and grabbed on.

"Very good. Now, watch girls, as I unwind the string," Ma Doja said. She swiftly pulled on the knot and slowly the string gave way and fell to the ground.

"Now, hold on to any edge you can lay your hands and watch the new colors come out." They all rushed forward, following instructions.

"How beautiful!" they screamed. I leaned to look over their shoulders and saw a myriad of rainbow colors all over what had once been a plain cotton cloth. My sisters were shouting excitedly, touching the cloth.

"Now girls, be careful not to touch the wet colors. See how beautiful it is? This is going to replace the old tapestry work we've had for centuries. You watch. Soon, we will be selling these everywhere."

I stayed as far back as possible, timing my escape. We were in front of the ajalala—the hall of many openings. There seemed to be no one else around. Along the passage way that linked the courtyards, I thought I saw some movement under the hanging plants. I moved slowly away from my giggling sisters. Someone grabbed my arm—Logbana

"Where are you going now, Amelia?"

Since our slight altercation, she seemed a little cold. I smiled sweetly, prying my hands free.

"I just need to ease myself. I will be back very soon," I stated quietly.

"Hmmm, Amelia!" She pulled on her ears, stepping back for me to go.

I glanced across the yard to catch any more movements under the hanging plants, but there was nothing. The person had disappeared, but to where? I had heard rumors from Akaba that there were secret passages between the courtyards for the King to pass unseen. I had never been able to confirm it until, hopefully, today. I would bide my time until nightfall and then return.

∽

Mama turned on her side again, muttering to herself. This was her third time shifting within a few minutes. Her eyes were moving so fast under her eyelids there was no doubt she was dreaming. Luck was on my side. I got up quietly, throwing off the three layers of cloth. I had fooled Mama into thinking I wasn't feeling well and came to bed early. That had prompted her to come in earlier than usual, too. Now that she was in a deep sleep, it was time to go in search of the secret hallways. I crept out, past Ma Hwanje's hut, and then Ma Doja's. I made a bee-line for the courtyard leading to the hallways. I crept forward, hiding behind the trees to avoid being seen. Then I heard voices. I ran quickly behind the tree a few feet from what I could almost swear was the hidden hallway.

A female with a shawl wrapped around her head and shoulders was limping slowly across the courtyard. She had her left arm supported by a cloth sling and tied at the back of her neck. The female's head was covered. There was something familiar about her.

A tall slender figure walked quickly toward her. It was the Kpojito. The two stood a decent distance from each other, making hand gestures. Suddenly, Kpojito Kamlin snapped her fingers and walked off. The other woman stood transfixed for some time, and then hit her free hand to her chest and raised it to the sky. I shifted my foot, stepping on the leaves beneath me. The woman looked in the direction I was hidden. I held myself still. When I heard nothing, I leaned over again slowly. In that moment, her shawl slid from her face, and in the dull light of the half cast moon, the woman was revealed. It was Tononu Vissegan.

Her eyes darted around. When she seemed satisfied that no one was there she turned around slowly. I waited for some time, listening to crickets chirping, and the distant noise of the villagers on the outskirts of the palace walls. A soldier passed by whistling as she twirled her knife above her head, making her way to her quarters.

Finally, silence.

I ran straight under the hanging plants, which I suspected covered the entrance way to the tonli. My hands felt a flat surface overgrown with moss and I pushed on it. To my surprise, it gave way easily. I stepped into a narrow hallway and the door swung back into place. I felt along the wall of what felt like a hallway. I counted ten steps. My eyes were now adjusted to the dark, and I could finally make out an arched door way on the other end.

I tiptoed past, praying that no one would emerge from the opposite end. I stepped into an empty room. I felt along the wall for about another ten steps, and then my hand fell on a round carved knob. I pushed on it and the stone wall began to give way slowly, revealing a dark hallway. I felt my way on the wall for what seemed an eternity, trying to stem the panic that began to grow within me. I counted ten steps, holding on to the wall as I went. I heard voices.

Then a girl crying. I could hear her short, muffled tones. It sounded like her mouth was covered. Moving closer, I saw a light burning around the corner.

"Shut up!" a sharp female voice shouted.

I crept closer to the light. When I got to the corner, leaned over. I was in the legedexo—the guards' quarters. There were about ten female guards there. Lying down on the floor was a girl. It was the clairvoyant, Nasame. Several of the guards began to insult her, raining curses on her. Some danced around her, laughing loudly. These were women who normally had blank looks on their faces. Right now, they looked like everyday women in their wrappers. A stocky, middle-aged woman stepped forward, a cap on her head. It was the kpakpa whom I had first seen when we had first moved into the palace many moons ago pulling young girls behind her.

"So, witch, you want to be a soldier? Were you not told that we do not allow witches into our battalion?"

Her foot slammed down on the girl's ankle and she cried out in pain. The women laughed.

"Please, leave her before she puts a spell on all of us!" someone cried out.

"We will kill her before she does!" another retorted.

Cackles rang in the air as more of them surrounded her. I had to do something or she would be killed. I ran forward, holding out my hands. "Well done, soldiers!" I shouted above their noise. The place went quiet.

They stepped back and made way for me. "Princess?" Kpakpa asked, squinting her eyes.

"Yes, it is I. Oh, are you with the clairvoyant girl?" I asked offhandedly, moving forward slowly.

Several of them nodded. I was now in the center of the circle, looking down at the girl.

"Princess, what brings you here?" Kpakpa asked.

"Father asked me to bring the girl to him," I responded calmly, even though my heart was about to jump out of my chest. They could not challenge the King's commands. Her eyes narrowed slightly. I was unsure of what to do next.

"The King wants her?" she asked, pointing to the body whimpering on the floor.

"Yes. Immediately," I stated sharply and moved even closer to pull her up. My hands were shaking slightly.

"But, are you sure?" she asked again.

I turned to her sharply, mimicking Kpojito Kamlin as best as I could. "How dare you challenge the King's order?"

She bowed slightly, looking downward. "I am sorry. Let me help you."

She assisted me in pulling Nasame from the ground.

"Pull off the cloth on her mouth," I muttered angrily. I was sure to tell father. He would not have authorized this.

The girl looked sideways at me, uncertainly.

"Come, Nasame. Come with me," I whispered. The leader made to follow us to the door way, but I blocked her way.

"No. Stay here. I can take care of this myself."

"Of course, princess." She sounded disgruntled, but obeyed.

I placed my hand around Nasame's waist and put her arm round my neck. They watched us silently as we left. I prayed they did not follow me as I led her to Mama's hut.

∽

I kept vigil the whole night. By the time mama woke up, I was ready to explain why there was a strange girl in our hut. She didn't seem surprised. In fact, she looked as though she had been expecting something like this.

"Mama, why aren't you angry with me?" I asked.

She was looking down at the curled up body on the mat. "I can't be. You did a good deed. You saved someone in need," she said. "Let me make us all something to eat. It looks like it's going to be a long day," she went out quietly.

I shook my head in disbelief. I had expected her to rant and rave and ask all the details of how I found her. I looked up to see Yemisi peering in from the doorway.

"Princess, good morning."

"Good morning Yemisi."

"Will you be going to the stream today for a bath?" she asked.

"Not today. Just get me a pot of water." Nasame could wake up anytime. I had to be there to reassure her all was well.

"Of course. I will be right back." Yemisi left quickly.

Someone ran past the hut, shouting, "Did you see it? Did you see the body?" It sounded like one of the new wives. Their shouting could wake ten giants.

Nasame stirred on the mat. I heard stamping feet as people ran past.

Mama ran in. "Amelia, you will not believe what happened," she said in hushed tones, her eyes round in disbelief.

"What is it, Mama?" I asked, jumping to my feet.

"The Nago priest's body was just found hanging on a tree with a rope around his neck in the center of the market place."

"What?" I heard myself scream. This time, Nasame woke up with a jerk, also screaming.

Mama rushed to her. "Sorry, my daughter. We didn't mean to frighten you." She held her shaking body. The poor girl was in shock.

"Mama, please look after her. I...I...I must see Akaba now!" I pulled my sandals on.

"But...what has Akaba got to do with this?" She sounded perplexed.

I ignored the question and pushed back the mat, almost falling out of the door. The palace compound was already overflowing with people who moved in the direction of the ajalala.

People were surrounding a man who was screaming at the top of his lungs.

"Come and see the Nago priest displayed in his entire splendor! He dared to defy our King by challenging him. See what becomes of one who defies the gods!" The man was a messenger of the palace. Like so many of them who delivered Father's messages to all the corners of the Danhomè kingdom, he was dressed in a peculiar manner. His hair was shaved on only one half of his head, a light cotton cloth swung across his shoulders and around his waist, as was common with most men. Even with the long distances he had to walk, he still went bare feet.

I ran through the crowd, making my way to the princes' huts, which was quite a walking distance from the main palace.

I found Akaba outside the hut with his friends. He had a smug look on his face. He walked over and slapped me on the shoulder. "I told you he would be taken care of," he whispered.

"Akaba...you had something to do with this?" I asked my hands over my mouth.

He put his hands in his pockets and started whistling. His friends looked in our direction and started laughing.

"Akaba, we don't pay evil with evil," I whispered to him.

His eyes turned steely. "No one threatens my family and gets away with it, Amelia. Remember that. Now, please go and see to your new friend."

"How do you know I have a new friend?" I asked, eyeing him.

He smiled knowingly. "I know everything that goes on around here little sister. Everything."

I shook my head and wagged my finger at him, "Be careful brother. Be careful." I cautioned. He walked away, laughing, his carefree attitude returning.

҈

Mama and Ma Hwanje were standing in front of the hut as I approached. Mama had a deep frown on her face, her brows knotted together in deep thought. She beckoned to me frantically as I drew closer. "You were gone for too long!" she said, out of breath. Sweat was running down her temple.

"Mama, what is the matter?" I asked.

Ma Hwanje touched my arm gently. She was out of breath just like mama. "Go inside now, quickly!" she ordered.

"Mama?" I asked.

Mama lowered her head down, hands on her knees breathing heavily. "Amelia, go in. I will be there soon," she said softly, looking down.

I pulled back the mat and entered the hut. Nasame was still sleeping. All was quiet, and then I heard them whispering. I crept closer to the doorway.

"Take. Make sure she uses it immediately! I knew we shouldn't have waited this long before going to see the Nago priest. Now he is dead," Ma Hwanje said.

"Well, I hope this will work, Hwanje. My daughter cannot be harmed again," Mama said.

"Just use it like Kamlin said. It *will* work," Ma Hwanje said.

There was silence, and then a rustling sound.

"It looks so small! Will this be enough?" Mama asked.

"You heard Kamlin. Just take a little with the tip of your finger and a rub. Watch it spread across her body. It is more than enough," Ma Hwanje said.

"Hmm, if you say so," Mama said.

"Not me, Kamlin did, and you were there too. I must go. See you at the meeting tonight."

Ma Hwanje walked away and I quickly stepped further into the room and sat down beside the sleeping Nasame.

Mama entered, holding something wrapped in leaves. "Get up," she said, already unwrapping the leaves.

I did.

She came closer, revealing the contents of the leaves—a lumpy dark substance no bigger than a newborn's fist. She pulled off my wrapper and dabbed the clumpy substance in little dots all over my body.

"Now, rub it all over yourself," she said quietly.

I did so without a word. She had a look on her face that forbade any questioning. When I finished, I looked up at her.

"Good. Now, stay in here with your friend. I will call you when food is ready. You hear?" She pulled on her ear. "Stay in here! Do not venture out," she said sternly.

"Yes, Mama," I said quietly.

"Oh, by the way..." Mama said, stopping at the doorway.

"Yes, Mama?" I asked.

"You will begin your apprenticeship with Low One in a fortnight," she said.

"Apprenticeship?" I asked.

"Yes, you have to learn a trade, Amelia. Low One is the most talented weaver in the whole kingdom. You will start going to her place in a fortnight."

I nodded.

Mama smiled, turned around, and left the hut.

INDOCTRINATION

c. 1892 – c. 1893

Low One was outside her hut as Yemisi and I approached. Her toes were tapping her forehead rhythmically. She smiled, her eyes traveling to Yemisi who held my stool.

"Must she be here with you?" Low One asked.

"She must," I replied, trying to keep from staring at her form.

She was quiet, and then finally looked at me. "Very well then, but she must stay in the front yard. There are things meant for only your eyes and ears," she said quietly.

My heartbeat quickened as I nodded.

She turned around on all fours and began to move. "Follow me," she said, not looking back. I held out my hand and Yemisi gave me the stool. "You will not need that. We work with a back strap loom," Low One said, her back still turned to us.

I looked around, realizing how quiet it was. "Where are the other students?" I asked.

She turned around, smiling. "There are no other students, Princess. I gave up teaching the art a long time ago." She turned back and began making her way to the back yard.

I gulped and paused.

"Come along, Princess. The day is far spent," she called to me. I hugged the stool to my bosom and followed her.

♋

The drumming was low and steady. I followed the sound, walking out of the royal wives' living quarters into the main courtyard. The sound was getting louder, tugging at my heart. People were going about their normal business, seemingly unaware of the noise. I bumped into a figure as I turned the corner that to the entrance of the tasinoxo.

"Oh, I'm sorry," I said, stepping back.

The figure turned. I was looking into the face of Princess Adandè. She smiled and touched my shoulder. "My child, how have you been? Princess Amelia, am I right?" she asked. Her body was moving slightly to the beat of the drum. Her eyes looked unfocused.

"Yes. Good morning, Princess Adandè. What is going on?" I asked.

"Oh, that? My sisters are paying homage to our ancestors. Will you join us?" she asked, already taking my hand.

We walked through the gates into the yard. There were a multitude of girls and women ranging from my age to at least one who looked a hundred harvests. They were swaying to the beat of an invisible drum. Their eyes were closed.

"Come, sit beside me," Princess Adandè said. I obliged, crossing my feet.

The swaying continued for some time. My companion was completely oblivious to me. She was in a trance. "Oooh yeee! Oooh yeee! Oooh yeee!" she said repeatedly, her voice rising every time the words escaped her.

"Oooh yeee! Oooh yeee! Oooh yeee!" the group repeated. They began to rise together without any utterance of command. I sat on the floor, not sure what to do. They began dancing forward, the drum beat getting faster and louder. They pushed past me. I felt a thump on the head.

"Yeh!" I shouted, trying to get up. The crowd pushed me back down.

"Princess Adandè!" I screamed, looking around frantically for the familiar face. I rolled myself into a ball, covering my head, screaming. She was gone.

"Amelia? Amelia! Is that you?!" someone shouted from over the gate.

"Yes! Get me out of here please!" I screamed as someone stepped on my ankle.

Kpojito Kamlin looked at me through the gate. I felt myself being lifted up by my arms and legs. I was carried over the heads of the crowd toward her solitary figure.

"Are you all right?" she asked as my feet landed on the ground.

I grabbed the folds of her flowing wrapper, still dizzy. "Kpojito…I…I don't know." I grabbed my throbbing ankle where the hen had scarred me. Her arms pulled me close and I inhaled her musky scent, feeling safe.

"It is all right my daughter. Did you not know this is the period for their ceremonies? No one goes in there but the daughters of neshuwe," she said quietly.

"I…I was with Princess Adandè," I stammered.

"Princess Adandè?" Kpojito Kamlin snapped, her eyes flashing.

I nodded. She fixed her eyes on me. "Now tell me, Amelia. Have you seen Princess Adandè with Tononu Vissegan before?" she asked.

My heart started racing, and I held on to her wrapper tighter. "Just once, and it was…it was by chance."

Kpojito Kamlin's mouth formed a line. "Nothing is by chance, child," she said dryly. Turning to the guards by her side, she said, "Take that traitor hiding in the crowd!" The guards ran through the gates, scattering the crowd of females. Princess Adandè was dragged out. Her eyes still remained unfocused, but she seemed to be coming around.

"Kpojito, what is the meaning of this? I was in the middle of a ceremony!" Princess Adandè cried out. Kpojito Kamlin chuckled and then raised a finger.

"Do you think I care? Do you think I am unaware of your plan to kidnap this child to Vissegan? I have all

the information right here!" Kpojito Kamlin clapped
one hand into the palm of the other.

Princess Adandè's eyes widened. She glanced
down at me, shamefaced. I felt the sweat trickle down
my back.

"You will confess now!" Kpojito Kamlin's voice
rose. Heads turned and steps faltered as we became
the spectacle of the courtyard.

"I am sorry, my daughter," Princess Adandè whispered, glancing up at me.

"Confess now!" Kpojito Kamlin shouted again.

Princess Adandè fell to the ground, whimpering.
"It was Tononu Vissegan. She made me do it!" she
cried out.

"What did she make you do? You are a daughter of
the soil. No harm can come to you," Kpojito Kamlin
said, moving closer. I followed suit, holding on to her
wrapper.

Princess Adandè looked up. Her face was drenched
with tears. "She...she said I would be avenged for my
daughter that was killed, because of...because of *her!*"
she screamed, pointing at me.

"Ah, your daughter. Is she not the one with her
two cousins who almost beat Amelia to death?" Kpojito Kamlin asked. My mouth was dry as the face of the
girl with the birthmark flashed across my eyes.

"But, that cannot be Kpojito, Princess Adandè is
not married!" I shouted, pulling on Kpojito Kamlin's
arm. She almost smiled as she looked at me. The two
guards behind Princess Adandè chuckled, looking
away.

"You have a lot to learn, my daughter," she said. Turning back to Princess Adandè, she said, "Continue your miserable confession."

Princess Adandè was crying quietly. "Vissegan said it was *her* son who should have been the rightful King, not Gbèhanzin. She wanted him out. She was angry and wanted to hurt him." She paused, gulping for air. "She said the only way to hurt him was through his favorite child. The child of his most loved wife." Princess Adandè's eyes suddenly turned to steel. "I just wanted her to hurt the way *I* hurt."

The crowd shouted, jumping around.

"Quiet!" Kpojito Kamlin shouted. Immediately everyone obliged. "Take her away!" she shouted.

The guards grabbed Princess Adandè and pulled her away.

"Have mercy Kpojito. I did not mean it!" Princess Adandè shouted.

"Now you ask for mercy when the deed has already been done," Kpojito Kamlin said under her breath. She turned to me, putting her arm around my shoulder. "You need not fear Vissegan anymore. See?" She pointed east. I turned to see Vissegan being pushed from behind by four male soldiers with whips in their hands. The crowd ran toward her, shouting, "Traitor! Traitor!"

She had a murderous look on her face as she was dragged pushed past us. Her arm was free of the sling.

"What is going to happen to her?" I asked, looking up at Kpojito Kamlin.

"She has been banished from the Kingdom. You will never see her again," she said. Leaning down into my face, she smiled. "You never have to be afraid of her again, Amelia. Do you hear me?" she asked.

I nodded.

"You never have to be afraid of anything or anyone ever again," she said, squeezing my hand. I watched Vissegan's figure disappear as the crowd moved forward pushing her to the palace gates. I finally felt relief.

◡◠

M y hands worked steadily across the loom. The strap pulled on my back as I threaded the warps. I pulled back and let go. My eyes traveled up to where the opposite bar was held firmly by strings tied to the large trunk of the baobab tree at the back of my hut. It had taken some time, but as each day passed, I got better at it. There, that was the symbol for the river finally completed. I pushed back the braid that fell to my forehead and refocused my attention on my work. I heard footsteps behind me.

"Amelia, you are still here working at this time of the evening? Will you not take a break?"

I straightened up and turned around, looking directly at the girl before me. Her rosy cheeks were glowing and her eyes danced with laughter. She was not the same girl who had stood before Father many moons before. She walked up to me, dressed smartly in her uniform.

"There is little time left," I whispered, looking around.

Nasame bit her lip, moving closer until she stood over me. "Oh, sorry, I forgot." She whispered. "Have you finished?" she asked.

"I only have to finish this part." I pointed to the small patch.

She sat down on the bench, watching quietly over my shoulder as I ran the thread across the length and width of the loom. I wove in the three black dots that had somehow become my signature woven into all my tapestry work. Finally, I was finished.

"You are done?" she asked eagerly.

"Yes," I said. "Help untie the strap from my back," I said. I felt the leather strap pulled off gently. I got up and stretched my legs.

Nasame fell to the ground, staring intently at the finished work.

"Amelia, this is excellent! You are quite talented. Just to think that you started only three moons ago." She clapped her hands over her head and laughed. I looked at her and shook my head.

"Well, I am still learning. Low One is the real talent," I said, standing up.

"Yes, but Low One can't make tapestry designs in three days. You can!" Nasame said excitedly, jumping off the bench.

I laughed at her comical dance. "Enough about me, how is your training going?" I asked. "Is the kpakpa treating you well?"

"She is treating me quite well now that she knows that I can go to the King if she doesn't," she said, smiling.

Footsteps were coming toward us. "Good evening, Princess." The voice was flat. Before us stood a royal messenger, his half- shaven head fell forward as he bowed. He was dressed in a long wrapper tied around his waist.

"Good evening," I replied.

"I have come to pick up the tapestry piece that was ordered," he said.

My heart lurched, as I tried to maintain my composure and remember everything Low One had told me. "Wait here," I said.

He nodded. I held up a hand for Nasame when she began following me.

"Just wait. I will return very soon." I walked casually back toward the front of the hut. As I entered, I saw it sitting right on my mat. I opened up the tapestry work, my eyes scrutinizing the hidden map in the art. Satisfied, I rolled it back up and went to join them. "Here," I said, handing it to the messenger.

"The client will be very happy," he said on cue, just as Low One had told me he would.

"Very good. Until we see," I said. We walked him to the front yard just as the kpakpa was walking across the courtyard with her new recruits. The messenger bowed again and left.

"Was that one of them?" Nasame asked.

"Sssh!" I said, putting a finger to my lips.

"I'm sorry, but I couldn't help it," she whispered.

"That was nothing, Nasame. It was just simply me completing a tapestry design for a customer," I said dryly.

Nasame's eyes widened, and then she nodded. "Of course," she finally said, a knowing look in her eyes.

"Come along, daughters of the palace. It is time to meet your mothers," Kpakpa's voice rang out. Nasame and I watched as the young girls hurried to meet their mentor, their faces lit up with smiles.

6

COMING OF AGE

Circa 1894

I rolled over on my side, trying hard to ignore the tapping noise. I opened one eye. *Tap, tap.*

I grabbed my bocie under my head rest, tied it around my waist and covered it quickly with my wrapper.

"Are you not there, this girl?" Nasame asked.

I hurried to the doorway and pulled back the mat. Nasame stood, demanding entry. My blood boiled as she stood there, grinning.

"Nasame, I hope all is well? Why are you here at this time?" I asked.

She pushed past me into the hut. "You must have forgotten, as usual," she stated, flopping down on the mat.

My hands went to my waist. "Forgotten what?" I asked.

"That we have to go earlier than usual to the stream today. We have to return in time for the female dance tonight," she said excitedly.

"Mawu-Lisa! Nasame, have I not told you that I will not be going for this dance?" I asked angrily.

"You are! Your mother has decided for you, so you must attend." She crossed her legs matter-of-factly.

I scratched my head sleepily, trying to wake up. "All right, let me get Yemisi," I muttered.

"Oh, don't worry, I already did. She will be here in no time," Nasame interjected. *Tap. Tap. Tap.* "That must be her. Come in!" Nasame shouted.

"Ssh! Do you want to wake up the whole compound?" I asked.

Yemisi came in, holding a large pot in hand. She averted her eyes from mine.

"Oh, so you planned this whole thing with Nasame?" I pointed at her.

She shook her head, but her lips were curling on the sides of her mouth. I raised my hand in the air. "Ehn! Ehn! Don't bother lying. Let me get my things."

Nasame clapped her hands in glee. "Please hurry before the boys who usually spy on us bathing get there," she said.

I slipped into my sandals and proceeded to get the first folded wrapper in the neatly folded stack.

"Let's go," I muttered, watching Nasame's back as she skipped away.

We didn't say much as we walked past huts. A few women were already up, either sweeping their yards or setting the fire for breakfast. We walked out of the palace gates and into the village just as the sun began to come up. Villagers turned and greeted us.

"Aah, Princess Amelia. Good morning!" a group of women called as they walked by us with pots on their head.

"Good morning!" I replied, watching their eyes sparkle at my response. "Good morning, Princess!" Ademola, the wine taper, called out as he stepped out from his hut. The heat rushed to my face when I remembered the jugs of palm wine he had deposited at the palace for me. I smiled slightly, trying not to encourage him any further. Of late, he was always standing outside his hut at the the exact time we walked by to the stream.

Nasame giggled as I finally waved at him reluctantly. "Your future husband! Ever since you came of age Ademola has been chasing you!" she teased, running ahead as I charged after her.

"Stop it, Nasame!" I shouted. I ran after her, disappearing as we sprinted down the winding path to the river. The trees were getting denser as we went further into the forest.

"Princess! Princess!" I turned around sharply to see Yemisi, eyes widened in fear, and doing her best to keep up.

"What is it?" I asked in alarm.

Yemisi looked wildly around and said, "Should we be in this part of the forest? Have we not gone past the stream already?" she asked.

I looked around, my heart quickening. We had gone into the forbidden area. If we were caught it could mean death. I breathed deeply and looked directly into Yemisi's eyes. "Don't worry Yemisi. Nothing can happen to us."

I placed her water pot on the ground and held her shaking hands. "But Princess, how can we get back? If we are caught, it is trouble!"

Yemisi could not be comforted. I looked out ahead and saw that Nasame had stopped.

"Come back Nasame!" I shouted out to her.

Yemisi had her mouth wide open, and gestured with her hands to her mouth, "Sshh! They will hear us!"

I knew exactly who *they* were. They were the spirits of the forest. It seemed an eternity before Nasame stood a few feet away. She was grinning from ear to ear.

"Are you so afraid, our Princess? Nothing can happen to us, you know. I have been in this forest countless times," she said, winking wickedly. Yemisi gasped, holding on to her chest. She looked like she was about to faint with fear.

"Don't worry Yemisi. You have nothing to fear," I said.

Nasame skipped behind as we cut through the trees, trying to find a shortcut to the stream.

As we walked slowly through the lush leaves hanging down from the branches, we almost stepped on a dead goat, its stomach cut open and blood splattered on the ground. I felt Yemisi's hand tighten around mine as we circled around it. A few feet away was a pot filled with blood. This time, Yemisi screamed, let go of my hand, and ran off.

"Yemisi! Yemisi! Come back!" I ran after her, with Nasame giggling and following behind me. Yemisi's hollering could be heard above the noise of our stamping feet. The thorns slashed my skin as I raced through the trees. I sighted her fleeing back, noticing that she was running a little slower. "Yemisi!" She had disappeared. I searched behind the tree I saw her last and then under the bushes. "Yemisi! Yemisi." I rushed forward through the bushes ahead of me. I heard myself screaming as the thorns pulled on my skin for what seemed like forever. I suddenly stepped out into what felt like an open space, and then blinding light. My hands automatically went to my eyes.

"Amelia!" Nasame's scream rang out as she bumped into my back. We heard a loud buzzing noise, and then silence. As I slowly opened my eyes, figures came into view.

Looming in the horizon was a male figure, and surrounding him were about fifty or more men. "I believe this place is off limits. What are you doing here?"

The voice was deep and harsh. I felt Nasame's arms around my neck. My eyes finally adjusted, and I could make out the faces of men. There was Dokpe—the challenger at tonight's wrestling match that would occur before the dance—brandishing a large sword, which was the source of the blinding light. They were all familiar, regular kinsmen—farmers, hunters, cattle rearers.

"Dokpe! Stop. Men, you can take a break, I'll take care of this," a familiar voice called out.

The men parted way as Dossou emerged. He was dressed like the other men—bare to the waist with a piece of cloth tied around his hips. Yemisi fell to her knees immediately upon seeing him.

"We're sorry for coming here! We won't do it again. It was a mistake, you see," Yemisi was blabbing on incessantly.

"Yemisi!" My voice rang out in a way I never liked — authoritatively. She shut her mouth and looked over at me. I looked at Dossou, who kept watching me. "Yemisi is right. We came upon this place unknowingly. We were on our way to the stream when we took the wrong path," I said.

Dossou had his hands behind his back and seemed to be holding something. It swung back and forth, and I noticed that it was a sword as well. Looking about at the other men, they also had the same. Some of the men were sweating profusely and breathing heavily.

My face must have asked the question, because Dossou shook his head slightly, without looking back, he handed his sword to the man behind him, who took it quickly. "Let me walk you back the way you came. I understand that this forest does get confusing sometimes." He stepped forward, and gestured slowly for the three of us to follow him. Nasame—who had not said a word since we got there—was looking around, noting the weapons of bows and arrows on the ground and long guns with wooden handles piled up. She walked ahead with Yemisi, two men on either side of them. I walked behind them with Dossou.

"Princess."

I stopped and looked up at him. "Yes, Dossou?"

I noticed how his muscular arms glistened as they moved by his sides. Dossou's brows were furrowed as he said, "I will advise that you don't come to this area of the forest again. It is dangerous."

"I know that. As I said earlier, we got *lost*," I said sharply.

We walked quietly for a while. I noticed the short glances he kept giving me. I looked up, catching him again. He smiled. "Little Amelia."

I smiled and shook my head. "I am not little any-more, Dossou. It has been over two harvest seasons since we saw each other," I said.

He stopped in his tracks, one hand going to his forehead and tapping it. "That is so true. How time has flown," he said softly. "Yes…I had to go away for a little while for some training." He held his hand out, stopping me from moving forward. He pointed to the ground just as a large snake slithered across. I gasped, stepping back and tripping on a stone. I felt his hands catch me, instantly cushioning me against his chest. "Amelia." He said my name too softly. I looked at him. He had a slight smile on his face and his eyes were twinkling in amusement.

"Oh, I'm sorry," I said.

"No, no…look, it's just going home," he said.

The huge creature disappeared into the back of a tree. I noticed that his hands still held mine and slowly slipped them out. Dossou stepped back as if regaining his train of thought. "I'm sorry for keeping you. I see your friends have already left for the stream."

I looked ahead to see that Nasame and Yemisi made it the stream just a few feet away. The two men who had accompanied them waited patiently. "Thank you for your help. I can find my way back." I nodded, stepping gingerly forward. I felt my left sandal fall off my foot.

"Your sandal's been cut...allow me to carry you," he said.

"No...please." I laughed, holding up my hand as he started to bend to pick me up. "Don't bother. I can see that you're...busy. Besides, I'm already at the stream," I said, pointing to the familiar shrub of trees, which were our only form of privacy when bathing.

He nodded. "All right."

"Amelia!" Nasame called, waving to me. "Come in now before these useless boys arrive! You know they like to peep! We have to get ready for the dance tonight!"

"Dance? You will be at the dance tonight?" His voice was laced with laughter.

I glanced up at him. "I have been forced to attend by my mother, so I must. Will you be there?" I asked.

His wide shoulders shook with laughter as he threw back his head the way I remembered and laughed. "Amelia, you? At the dance?" He threw back his head again and laughed.

"What's so funny about that? Do you think I can't dance?" I asked.

He shook his head adamantly. "Oh no, it's not that. I just can't believe boyish little Amelia is now turning into a lady," he teased.

I hit him quickly on the chest. He laughed as his hands fell on top of mine and held them there. I felt his heart beat thundering under my hand. Looking up into his face, I realized it wasn't just me that was transfixed. His eyes were serious as he stared back. Then, as suddenly as we touched, we separated.

I looked away, stepping back. "I...I have to go." I gathered my wrapper closer around me and began running toward Nasame.

"Amelia...your sandal..." he called to me.

I waved, not looking back, unsure of what had just happened.

❦

I could hear the drums from inside Mama's hut. It was beyond my understanding why she wanted me to come out this year rather than next year. One more year couldn't hurt my chances of getting married, but Mama would not hear of it. I was tired of her repeatedly saying she would not watch me become an old maid right before her eyes!

"Amelia, are you not ready?" Mama shouted impatiently.

"I'm ready, Mama. How do I look?" I asked stepping back, my beads jingling round my waist and ankles. The beads woven in my hair moved too, jingling back and forth.

Mama gulped, trying to hold back the tears. "Absolutely beautiful. You are your mother's daughter," she said softly.

Her reaction was surprising. I really did not understand it. She walked over and hugged me.

"I'm going to *try* and have some fun," I stated gruffly, brushing back my hair.

Mama cupped my face and stroked gently. "Make sure you do. I'm sure you'll have no problem doing your dance!"

I laughed aloud and walked out. Awanatu was waiting patiently outside the door. She carried Mama's stool as we walked slowly to the courtyard through little human traffic. Approaching the courtyard, there was already an overflow of people waiting excitedly for the dance to begin. The young maidens were standing to the side, dressed in new attire, their faces painted beautifully, and their hair woven on top of their heads. They sat or stood talking amongst themselves.

"Amelia!" Nasame walked up, looking pretty in her blue wrapper. "Good evening, Mama." Nasame knelt down, paying homage.

"Nasame, my dear, how are you? How is your mother?" Mama asked.

"She is well. Mama is over there." She pointed to her mother who stood waving.

"Aah, tell her I said hello. You know I must go and sit with the other wives," she said, pointing to the group of heavily bejeweled women sitting to the side Patting my shoulder, she moved on.

Nasame grinned at me and then grabbed my hand. "You are looking beautiful! I am sure you're going to catch a lot of eyes today!" She winked and started giggling.

"Please! I don't want to catch anybody's eye. I am doing this for my mother. I have not had any rest since she heard a dance was being held," I interjected, raising my hand to her face.

"But you will catch someone's eye!" she shouted above the drum beat that began. She pulled me toward the group of animated girls. She began shaking her hips as the beat increased in crescendo.

I shook my head at my crazy friend. As we reached the edge of the crowd, the way parted for us. I looked up to see several men looking in our direction and they bowed their heads slightly. I smiled back and looked away.

"Danhomè! You are welcome!" Beko, the town crier appeared in the middle of the crowd, wrapped in a fine woven wrapper that was thrust over one shoulder. The crowd shouted and started to clap. He beamed, raising his hands up for silence. Putting them down, he continued. "Tonight, I know we are here to see the lovely young maidens."

There was another uproar, cut short when he lifted his hand again.

"But before we begin, we have the much-awaited wrestling match between Ogba—our reigning champion—and Dokpe!"

"And unbeknown to most, a soldier of the Danhomè army," I added quietly.

Ogba stepped out. He was known for his catlike movements and quick steps. He was a small man. Rather, too slim, which belied his natural skill. Dokpe, on the other hand, was heavy set, stocky, but very light on his feet. Cries for both sides rang out as they made contact. The dust flew up in the air, and for several seconds, all we saw were tangled arms and feet rolling on the ground. The crowd screamed, moving closer.

I had always had little interest in wrestling. Looking away for a second, I noticed someone standing at the edge of the crowd looking my way. He had his hands folded across his chest, over six feet tall, his loin cloth that was tied across his neck flowing to his feet. He was looking right at me.

It was Dossou. *How long had he been there?*

He smiled slightly, not batting an eye even when he knew he had been caught.

I looked away, flustered for a second.

"Are you all right?" Nasame leaned over to ask.

"Hmm? What?"

"You just murmured something. Are you all right?" Nasame asked again.

"Yes, yes, of course," I muttered.

Glancing in his direction again, he had disappeared. The crowd shouted as Dokpe toppled the champion over, placing him on his back. The crowd went crazy. Everyone clapped, and jumped, happy to see the end of an era for Ogba, who had reigned as champion for too long.

The drums took on a slower beat, signaling the start of the dances. The young maidens sat up, their chattering finally easing.

"Who do you think will go first?" Nasame whispered into my ear.

I shrugged, not caring. From the past dances, the younger girls would have to stand together and come forward individually into the circle the audience had made. As if on cue, we all stood up and danced forward.

"Danhomè! Villagers! Here are the juiciest fruits in the land. Are they not beautiful?" Beko asked.

A shout of agreement went up in the crowd.

"We would like to know how well you dance, maidens. How well your mothers have taught you!"

Some of the girls giggled, already wiggling their waists. I couldn't help rolling my eyes. Was I really about to do this! Unlike the other girls whose main goal for dancing was to find a man to marry them, I did not need to dance to do so. I would dance for the fun of it. Listening to the beat, my feet began to move.

"Ehn, hen! Now you're moving!" Nasame said happily, glad to see me in the mood.

The first maiden was already in the circle, dancing. It was Didjou, the Meu's first daughter. No surprise, since she was always pushing her way into the spotlight. She bent low and came back up as the beat quickened. Her beads jingled loudly, her arms moved back and forth. The girls began to look at one another when the considerable time for Didjou to finish went by and she was still on the dance floor.

"Didjou! Thank you!" Beko called out. That was her cue to get off, but it seemed she was deaf. The next girl danced over, taking the floor from her.

"Aahh!" The crowd collapsed into laughter.

Didjou eyed the new dancer, and danced off slowly, unwillingly. Finally, the line was moving as each girl gave her best performance.

The crowd of girls was decreasing, and there were only two girls in front of Nasame and I. We looked at each other and Nasame winked mischievously.

I couldn't help but smile. We were going to be different. Then, finally, it was our turn.

"Ehhnnnn! Is this not our King's daughter?" Beko shouted.

The crowd shouted excitedly. I felt my smile widen. They had me undone. I loved these people who loved me regardless. The beat changed somewhat, moving slower. Nasame and I glanced at each other and stepped out in unison.

"It's a double delight! The Princess and her friend!" Beko screamed, his stocky body shaking in excitement.

We danced in response to each other's movements. Nasame moving her arms forward and back, and stopping, waiting for me to pick up the dance. I moved, pushing my feet back and forth, hips shaking from side to side. The drum beats quickened again and we moved together with it.

We were in a world of our own, enjoying the music, oblivious to the eyes and the voices. Finally, we completed the dance, our arms coming down from above our heads. A loud shout went out and I came back to earth.

Nasame laughed out, watching the excited crowd. She glanced across at me and winked again. My chest heaved up and down as I breathed quickly.

"That was wonderful!" Beko shouted above the noise.

Nasame looked across at the town crier, shaking her head. "That was my dance! Amelia just helped," she shouted above the beat and danced away.

The crowd erupted in excitement. Turning sharply to Nasame, I tried to control my urge to harm her.

"Our Princess must dance for us!" Beko demanded. The crowd went crazy, jumping and clapping.

Nasame had planned this all along!

Glancing across at my mother, I knew right away who had been her accomplice. Mama clapped along with the others smiling proudly. I shook my head in disbelief, and turned around to see Nasame walking off to stand with the other girls.

I lowered my eyes for a second, bringing it back up as I twirled around slowly, my arms flung out to my sides, hands cupped. The drum beat faster, and the crowd clapped along.

I moved within the formed circle. Swinging my beaded hips I felt a sudden impulse to twirl again, and did so, moving faster. The faces blurred before my eyes as I went faster and faster. Finally, I stopped, falling to my feet. The drum beat stopped and there was a quiet. Not realizing that I had closed my eyes while doing a twirl, I opened them to find out why there was such a deadly quiet. I had landed at a man's feet.

Everyone knew what it meant when a maiden positioned herself at a man's feet during a dance—it meant the maiden was interested in the man. I was afraid to look up. After what seemed like an eternity, I did. As my eyes climbed up the sandal-clad feet, and loin-clothed body, I knew who it was before the face came into view.

Dossou was staring at me, a strange light in his eyes. His hand appeared to help me up.

The drums began to beat slowly. He bent slowly and dusted the sand from my knees and then straightened up. Realizing he was still holding my hand, I slowly took it away. I heard myself say thank you. He bowed his head, placing a hand across his heart, and stepped back. The drums began again, and I turned around and danced off.

∾

D anhomè Kingdom must have talked about the dance for days. Every hut and gathering I visited mentioned how beautiful I was. I could not hear enough of how I had danced. Mama was beside herself. She pranced around the palace with her head up and chest out. She took every opportunity for me to accompany her everywhere—except to the Council meetings with Father. Those were out of bounds. Tonight was another grand opportunity for her.

"Amelia!" Mama pulled back the mat over the doorway and entered. I looked up from arranging the pile of clothing on the floor. "I have a meeting with the palace wives. Let us go together. You know, it will be good for you to hear how we run female affairs in the palace." Mama was the official *yovoganon*—female counterpart of the yovogan, the interpreter for the white man in the king's court. She was present at all meetings that father had with the white man. Ma Hwanje was also a member of this select group of the Kings Council, present at any meeting father had. She was the *miganon*—female counterpart to the migan.

I shook my head slowly, and then vehemently. "No, Mama! I don't want to go. You were the one that told me to sort my cloths. Why do I have to go with you?" I grumbled.

"Will you come with me now?" she shouted, her eyes flashing angrily.

I knew when not to argue. I sulked as we walked toward the ajalala. Awanatu walked silently behind us, carrying Mama's stool. The air was laden with the smell of fried meat wafting from the direction of the meeting spot. The full moon provided needed illumination as we walked. As we got closer to the courtyard, the sea of heads seated on the ground and stools turned.

"Our counterpart! You are welcome!" the wives shouted their greetings.

"My fellow wives, I hope I meet you well!" Mama responded, sitting down on the stool Awanatu placed quickly on the ground beside Ma Hwanje. I sat on the mat already spread on the floor beside Mama. I noticed no other child was there, except those that suckled at their mothers' breasts. I glanced up at Mama angrily. She patted my shoulder without looking at me.

"Is everybody here?" Ma Hwanje asked, looking around the sea of heads.

"All except the two best friends!" someone called out. There was chuckling in the crowd.

"Who are you talking about? Oh, you mean Doja and Larame?" Ma Hwanje asked. She shrugged her shoulders.

"Let us begin, please," Mama interjected.

Mama Hwanje cleared her throat. "As you all know, we have a new Tononu."

There was loud clapping as all eyes turned to a woman seated a few feet away. She was smiling broadly, her eyes twinkling with laughter. They reminded me of father's.

"Na Tama. We welcome you." Na Tama was father's immediate younger sister. Another clapping ensued.

"Thank you, my sisters! I am happy to be your new Tononu. As you all know, I have been away for some time." Some of the wives exchanged knowing glances. "But, I am now back, and I plan on taking on this new responsibility with all seriousness!" Na Tama said enthusiastically.

They all clapped—except for Mama and Ma Hwanje who had their heads together, talking quietly. I looked beyond the sea of heads to see a shadow lurking under the tree I had hidden behind not so long ago. My heart lurched in my chest. Hadn't she been banished?

"Amelia!" I heard Mama's high pitched voice and then noticed my fingers were digging into her arm. I immediately let go. "What is the matter with you?" Mama asked, looking down at me. The talking stopped as everyone turned in our direction.

"Awanatu!" Mama shouted.

I felt myself shaking uncontrollably. "Mama... Mama?" My teeth were chattering.

"What is wrong with her?" I heard someone ask.

"Mind your business please! Start the meeting, I will join you," Mama said.

"Mama..."

"Yes? What is it?" Mama's eyes searched mine.

"There's someone there! There's...there's..." I pointed to the tree.

Mama turned quickly, looking back at me, confused. "There's nobody there. Why are you acting so strange?" Mama asked, waving the women away.

"Ajo, what is wrong with Amelia now?" Ma Hwanje asked, crouching down.

"I have to take her home. She is not feeling well." Mama tightened her wrapper around herself, and began to get up. I held her back.

"No, Mama. Please. I will be fine. You stay, I'll go home," I said quietly.

She searched my face again, and seemed to believe me, because she nodded. "Fine. Awanatu. Take Amelia back to go and rest."

"I'm sorry Mama...I wish I could have..." I began apologizing, knowing she had wanted to showcase me once again.

"No, it is fine. I think you still need to rest. Just go home. Go," she said softly, cupping my cheek.

I was relieved to walk away from the crowd. Awanatu held my arm, which I tried prying away.

"But you are not well. I must make sure you don't fall," she argued, her nasal tones revealing her northern roots. Aware that Mama was watching, I stopped fighting against her hold on me.

We walked silently down the dark hallways.

"Amelia?"

I stopped in my tracks as we were about to go through the gates into the inner courts,

Dossou appeared. My heart skipped.

"Dossou? What brings you here?" I asked, pulling my arm free from Awanatu, who proceeded to pout.

In two strides, he was beside me, peering down in my face. "I had a meeting with your father and the Council," he said abruptly. "But, where are *you* going? I thought there was a meeting with the wives. Were you not going with your mother?" he asked, his eyes not missing the exchange between Awanatu and I. She had begun to fidget and grumble beside me.

"I was not feeling well...Awanatu!" I snapped at her. "Stop that noise you're making! Just go and call me Yemisi, I'll wait for her here."

Awanatu gasped and fell to the ground, rubbing her hands together. "Please, Princess. I am sorry! I was only making sure you didn't fall. Please! If your mother hears that I left you for one second, I am dead."

"Fall? Did you fall?" Dossou asked, his hand already at my elbow.

I glanced at him and back at Awanatu. "Don't mind this girl! Of course I didn't fall." I turned to Awanatu, I shouted, "Just go!" I was more irritated at her display than anything else. I clapped my hands at her. She burst out crying, burying her face in the earth.

"Awanatu, please there's no need for that. I will take the Princess to her hut myself. Nobody will know you left her alone," Dossou said, touching her shoulder.

Immediately, she stopped crying and looked up. Dossou gestured to her to rise.

"Princess?" she asked, unsure.

I nodded, happy for her to leave. She got up quickly and disappeared behind the wall into the inner courts.

I glanced up at Dossou who was watching me strangely, intently.

"Maybe I should have called for Yemisi…" I heard myself say.

A slight smile appeared on his lips. "You don't need Yemisi. I'll take you home," he said softly. A slight breeze danced around us, lifting up the edge of my wrapper. I instinctively pulled it down, feeling self conscious.

"Can I take you home?" he asked, holding out his hand.

Laughter rang out, and we both turned to see a group of women walk by us, toward the courtyard where the meeting was being held.

"Amelia, is that you?" Ma Doja and Ma Larame stopped in their tracks. They were dressed alike, with the same wrappers and matching necklaces.

"Good evening." I tried to smile.

They glanced at each other and then at us. "Why are you out at this time, and with a man?" Doja asked sharply.

"Ma Doja, it's me, Dossou." He put his hand to his half covered chest, his voice light with laughter.

Ma Larame folded her arms across her skinny chest and heaved a sigh. "I know it is you, Dossou, and that is why I have asked why our daughter is out this late with a man," Ma Doja said, clucking her lips and turning her gaze on me. Ma Larame did the same.

"Ma Doja, the meeting has started. They must be waiting on you," I said, tempted to say more. I felt a slight nudge, and looked up quickly to see Dossou wink at me. "Amelia! You and that mouth!" Doja sprang forward, but not fast enough. Her hand touched Dossou's brick chest. I felt his other hand on my waist.

"Ma Doja, we will be on our way now," Dossou said.

Ma Larame tapped Ma Doja on the shoulder, the latter glanced at her angrily. "Let us go, Doja!" Ma Larame grabbed her by the arm and began to walk.

"Come, Amelia," Dossou said in the same calm voice. We walked away, taking the exit toward the outer gate.

"I'll bring you back through the other way. Let's just leave for now," Dossou explained, noticing my quizzical look.

We walked, not saying a word. I felt ashamed that Dossou had witnessed my brazen behavior. I looked up high at the wall we circled made of mud, still in awe at the sacrifices put in to build this palace. I felt my foot slip and grabbed on to Dossou's arm.

"Are you all right?" he asked.

I nodded, closing my eyes briefly and then opening them. My ankle throbbed, at the same spot the hen and attacked me leaving an indelible scar.

"Yes. Just a bit…" I was carried up in his arms quickly. "What are you doing, Dossou?" Instinctively, my hands went around his neck.

He laughed, a low soft rumble coming from his chest.

"Put me down," I whispered, unsure why.

His eyes looked into mine and he smiled that disarming smile. He was silent, making his way assuredly through the labyrinth of huts. I buried my face in his chest, hoping that would deter him from staring at me. His heart beat slowly against my ear pressed close to his chest. He stopped suddenly and I looked up. We had arrived at my hut. He looked down at me, seeming almost reluctant to release me. He finally did, lowering me slowly. I stepped back, patting down my wrapper.

"Will you be all right by yourself?" he asked.

I nodded. "Yes, of course...thank you," I said, wriggling my hands, not sure what to do with them. My heart began beating faster. I felt the sweat trickle down my neck.

He stepped back, putting one hand to his chest in salutation. "It is my pleasure, my Princess."

I smiled, unsure of what was happening. "Dossou...is everything all right?" I finally asked.

His eyes lowered briefly and then looked intently into mine. "I've been asking myself the very same question for some time now," he said.

"If everything is all right?" I asked, not sure what he meant.

He turned to go, and then seemed to change his mind. He walked back. "Amelia..." His eyes held mine in a trance.

"Yes?" I blurted out.

"Would it be fine with you if I called on your father?" His voice trembled.

I gasped, looking up sharply at him. "You want to call on father?" I echoed.

"Yes. I must," he said softly, his lips barely able to get the words out.

The blood thundered in my ears as I realized my response could change everything, forever. A chiming noise rang out, signaling an intermission in the royal wives' meeting. I took a deep breath and looked into his eyes. "You may. When you call on him, make sure you bring his favorite thing—tobacco," I said softly.

His face was instantly transformed. His lips spread into a broad smile. "I will." He stepped back, for the first time, looking unsure of himself. "Will you be fine by yourself? I can call for Yemisi." He began to move toward me again.

"No. I will be fine," I said quickly. A strong urge to make him stay washed over me.

"If you say so," he said, not moving, his eyes watching me.

I twirled my braid around my finger, waiting.

"I will take my leave then," he said.

I nodded.

He stayed. "Good night," he said.

"Good night," I replied.

He turned to leave, and then swiveled back. "I had been meaning to tell you…"

"What is that?" I asked.

"You are an exceptional dancer," he said smiling. Before I could respond he walked briskly away, disappearing behind the next hut.

The smile lingered on my lips as I went into my hut.

ᘯ

"What possessed you to go into the forest, Amelia?" My mother was incensed, glaring down at me. It had been several days since this incidence and I was surprised that she was just finding out.

Besides being woken up from my afternoon sleep, the fact that this information had gotten to mama, after swearing Yemisi and Nasame to secrecy, had me fuming. I was looking everywhere else but at her.

"Are you dumb? I tell you, Amelia, do you think that you're still a child?" she hissed furiously and shook her head.

"Mama, I am sorry. We got lost, that was all," I muttered, standing up slowly.

She snorted. "Indeed! So, if I did not go looking for Yemisi—who you may or may not have noticed has been hiding for fear that the spirits will carry her away—you would not have told me. The girl is distraught!" Mama shouted, lifting her hands up in the air.

I shook my head. "It was nothing, Mama. We were fine. We came upon Dossou and his soldiers and he escorted us back. Moreover, I don't believe in all that. We did not offend the spirits, so there is no reason for them to come after us," I said. There was silence, and I looked to find out why Mama hadn't said a word. She stood transfixed. "Mama! Are you all right?" I asked

She blinked and then raised up a finger. "What did you just say? About Dossou? He was there?" she asked, trying to control herself.

"Well…" I murmured.

Mama sat beside me, her voluptuous parts following suit. "You did, didn't you?" She smiled sweetly, her mood changing instantly.

"Yes, he was practicing with some of his soldiers in the forbidden forest. There were a lot of them. Mama, are we finally going to war with the French?" I asked, changing the topic.

Mama sighed heavily, gesturing for me to sit beside her. I sat down quickly, tapping her on the lap quickly to continue.

"It seems that we must. The French are trying to gain control of our land, so we have to act fast. Your father is getting together his army. It will not be long before the war begins," she said calmly, like our kingdom went to war every day.

I grabbed mama's hand, unable to contain myself. "But the French—especially this man they call *Dodds*— he sounds heartless, wicked. Can our soldiers stand against them? Will we prevail?" I asked.

"Amelia, I don't know. We can only do our best. Your father knows what he is doing," she said.

There was a tapping on the raffia mat that covered the entrance. "Enter!" I called out.

A slave came in, carrying a large basket, followed by another who carried a similar large basket.

"What is this?" Mama asked.

"It is for the Princess," the slave answered, placing the basket down, as did her counterpart. They knelt and got up quickly, disappearing the way they had come.

I looked quizzically at mother, and then pulled off the cloth covering the items. The first basket was filled with the most colourful cotton and woven cloth materials. The second basket was filled with gold necklaces and beads, piled high, almost overflowing.

My heart was racing, not believing what was before me. Mama gasped, covering her mouth, and gazing at me. "Who? How?" she stammered, raising her hands in the air.

I sat back on my heels, my head reeling. I could hear Mama's voice buzzing in my ear, but was unable to focus.

"Amelia? Answer me! Who is sending you things without consulting with your father first?" Mama asked as she picked out the clothes, checking them one at a time. They were expensive and tasteful.

"Mama, I think it's—" as I was about to say his name, something fell out from the cloth Mama held. It was a pair of leather sandals. Sandals were not very common in our land, and only the well-to-do owned them. Traders often brought them in from their travels. Only one person could have known I needed sandals. Dossou had made sure to include them, so there would be no doubt in my mind who had sent the items.

"Well?" Mama demanded to know, now picking up the jewelry.

"It's Dossou. He sent them," I said softly, looking down on the floor.

Mama looked into my face and smiled. "Really? He finally did!" she shouted, clapping her hands in the air.

"Finally? What do you mean? How long have you known that he would?" I demanded to know.

She sat back, smiling contentedly. "My dear, ever since he was no more than your age, I knew he would marry you," she said.

I couldn't help but roll my eyes. "Mama, please!"

"But it's the truth. And then the dance confirmed it. Even the gods approve."

There was commotion in the palace courtyard. A sudden shout had us flying to the door way, pulling back the mat door and stepping out.

"Amelia, look!" Mama pointed.

A crowd of family members, court officials, and slaves were pushing closer into four men carrying large gift baskets. The crowd of people parted way for Dossou, followed by two men—one looked like father, and the other looked closer to Dossou's age.

The palace guards, in an attempt to contain the situation, formed a border around them.

"I am sure your father will be calling me soon. Let me go and change!" Mama said excitedly, disappearing quickly into the hut.

I couldn't move from the spot. According to tradition, I wasn't supposed to be seen by my suitor. Most likely he wouldn't see me, since they were backing my mother's hut. My eyes could not break away from Dossou, who towered over everyone. He was smiling slightly as he waited to be admitted into Father's presence. He slowly turned his head around, and over the top of every other head, he saw me. His eyes lit up. A slight smile broke on his lips, and he mouthed something. *I'll see you tomorrow.* I nodded slightly, as I watched him disappear into Father's chambers.

"Amelia! Come here right now!" Mama pulled me back in, lecturing on how I could not be seen. I tried to hide my smile, but couldn't. She adjusted her wrapper and then looked across at me. "Don't smile! I understand that he is the most eligible man at the moment, but you should know that you're also the most eligible maiden. Who wouldn't want to marry the King's daughter? So, don't make this easy for him. Remember that the wine tapper has been depositing palm wine as dowry for many moons now!" Mama collapsed into laughter when she saw my face.

"Mama!" I glanced at her face and couldn't help laughing as well. I could tell that Mama had prayed and waited for a day like this. She was brimming over with pride.

Awanatu arrived at the door. "Na Ajo...you are being called by our King," she said, kneeling.

Mama clapped her hands, and then patted her wrapper, trying to control herself. She cleared her throat ceremoniously and tilted her head up. "All right. I will be back shortly Amelia, stay indoors."

I watched her disappear behind the raffia mat, catching the slight smile on her face as she left.

✁

Kukuruku! The cock crowed. I jumped up from my mat, and realized that I had fallen asleep waiting for the introductions to be completed last night. It was not so very early, as I could hear people moving past the door.

"Good morning, Doja!"

"Good morning!"

"I can see you all did not sleep last night."

"Yes, oh! You know that the young commander has asked for our daughter's hand in marriage. It was a great celebration last night. You should have seen what he brought for the King! Not to talk of what he brought for each of us the wives."

"Eehn! You are all lucky, oh! What a fine addition to your family! Amelia will not want for anything."

"Are you telling *me?* That man has been in love with our Amelia since she was a mere child!"

"Tell me more."

Their voices faded away as I scrambled over to see them through the doormat. I shook my head at Ma Doja's show of familiarity. I waited impatiently, realizing that no one was coming to check on me. I decided to go and get my water for a bath. I picked up a clean wrapper and a pot, and stepped out of the hut. I walked down the hallway, going past my siblings who hugged and greeted me.

"Princess." I turned to see who had called me. It was Modupẹ. She marched over briskly. "Your father asks that you meet him in his chambers at lunch time."

A smile played on her lips. She knew as well as I did that Father wanted to discuss the august guest he had received the night before.

I smiled back at her. "Thank you. I will see him then."

She nodded and marched away as quickly she had approached. "Amelia! Amelia!" Akaba shouted, running toward me.

It was Akaba. He flung his arm around my neck.

"Well, well, if it isn't my dearest sister! So I hear that our Commander-in-Chief has been busy with things other than affairs of the Kingdom!" He said it quietly so only I could hear it.

"Akaba, you need to stop!" I warned, hitting him playfully on the arm.

He stepped back, avoiding my fist. "Am I wrong? Anyway, I just saw him at practice, and he seemed a little distracted. If you know what I mean!" He flung back his head and laughed.

"What do you mean?" I had walked straight into his trap.

Akaba stepped back. "Our Commander-in-Chief just could not hold his sword upright. When he wanted to mention someone's name, your name came out. Amelia this, and Amelia that!"

I shook my head, about to step into my hut.

"Amelia," Akaba said in sober tone. "I'm really happy for you."

I hugged him. "Thank you. But it doesn't change anything. We'll still do things together. Like go hunting and fishing like we normally do."

He shook his head. "You are so naïve. It changes everything."

Just then, a servant approached from the outside court carrying a large basket. "Princess," she said approaching me. "This is for you. Where should I put it?"

I knew who the basket was from. He was lavishing me with gifts.

I pointed to my quarters, watched her disappear briefly, and come back out, curtsying. With that she walked away.

My brother tapped me on the shoulder. "The change has already begun. I will see you later." He jogged away happily, calling to a friend.

"Akaba!" I called to his retreating back, but he just waved happily, and disappeared to the outer courts.

"Where is he going again?" Nasame approached, clad in her uniform.

I shrugged. "He didn't say. You didn't even stop by this morning," I said accusingly.

Her eyes twinkled. "Oh, sorry, my Princess, but I thought you needed sometime to refresh after yesterday's surprise event." She winked, hitting me on the shoulder playfully.

"Yes, it was a surprise…" I said, smiling shyly.

"Hmm! Like you didn't know that Dossou wasn't going to ask you to marry him ehn?" She said, chuckling

I placed my pot on the ground. "What do you mean, Nasame? It seems that I'm the only one who *didn't* know this," I said. She giggled.

"It was so obvious, even a blind man could see that! Didn't you notice the way he always hovered around you? He's always there whenever you need help. In fact, I heard that he went to warn Ademola the wine tapper to stop bringing kegs of palm wine."

I laughed out loud in disbelief. "You don't mean it? No wonder! Ademola stopped bringing the kegs for some time now," I said slowly, watching from the corner of my eye as Logbana approached a pot in her hand.

"My sister, are you going to the stream too?" She asked , smiling sweetly.

I glanced at Nasame who was looking steadily at Logbana. "Yes. Nasame, are you coming with me?" I asked, hoping she would hear my call for help.

Her knowing eyes looked at me. "Sorry, but I have to return for practice. Make sure you don't stray from the path to the stream. It is almost afternoon and you should not have any problems with those useless boys that try and peek. I must go now." She squeezed my arm gently and jogged off.

I took a deep breath and turned to Logbana. "Let's go then."

She smiled again, grabbing me by the arm. "This is so nice! Just me and you—sisters! Going to the stream. We haven't done anything together for the longest time you know." She kept rambling on as we passed by the huts, making our way across the kana bridge. "Do you agree? Amelia? Amelia?" Her voice screamed in my ears.

"What? What did you say?" I blurted out, unsure how we had reached the stream so soon.

Logbana's eyes flashed in anger, realizing that I must have ignored her all the way. "I was asking you if we should just take our bath since there doesn't seem to be any one around," she said.

I looked about the stream, which was shrouded by trees all round. "You know it's not wise to do that... early morning has been set aside for young maidens to bathe, and besides, this is not the fourth day of the week, which is the day assigned to us."

"Oh, stop that! You know that nobody comes here at this time. The men are already at the farms and the women at the market. Let's go in!" Logbana was already pulling off her wrapper. The next thing I knew, she jumped into the water, shouting in glee.

"Ssshh!" I stepped close to the edge, feeling the warm water on my toes.

"Come in!" She called, flipping backward in the water.

I put down the pot, glancing around again cautiously.

"Come in!" She called to me again.

"All right, just stop shouting!" I said in lower tones. Untying the knot on my wrapper, I quickly slipped out of it. I looked around again, expecting to see a head or two sticking out from the hanging trees.

"There's nobody there, Amelia," Logbana hissed and swam forward.

I stepped in, feeling the warm water up to my neck.

"Doesn't that feel good?" Logbana asked, watching the look on my face.

I smiled, pushing forward and going under. I came back up after what seemed an eternity, spitting out the water. Logbana giggled, standing up, revealing her growing breasts.

"Will you come back in?" I screamed.

"Oh, stop! You're always behaving like you're so prim and proper! You don't fool me one bit, sister!"

"I never tried to, Logbana. For the last time, get back in this water!" I swam after her, missing her at every turn. I gave up after about four attempts, and swam to the bank. I sat down beside my folded wrapper, watching as Logbana still played around. Shaking my head, I reminded myself she was still younger than me. There was a crunching noise like someone stepping on leaves. I froze, remembering my nakedness. Quickly taking my wrapper, I pulled it around me.

"What was that?" Logbana called.

I got up, holding out her wrapper and gesturing to her at the same time to come. She swam forward immediately. I threw her the wrapper as she stepped out of the water. She covered herself immediately, moving to stand by me.

"Who is there?" I shouted, looking into the woods.

There was silence.

"Who is there, I said?" I shouted. There was someone there. I could feel it. "You will be killed for spying on the King's daughters if you don't reveal yourself now!" I shouted again.

There was another crunching noise. A figure emerged, dressed in sandals and a wrapper tied across the chest that flowed to the ankles. He looked about my age, his hair was bushy. His face was dark. The eyes—I knew those eyes. They were the same dull eyes I remembered. I gasped. "Dare?" I whispered,

The young man moved closer, carrying a medium sized bundle over his shoulder.

"Yes. Is that you, Amelia?" His voice had changed. It was deep.

"Dare?" I started walking toward him.

Logbana pulled me back and I turned to her sharply.

"But, it is Dare!" I whispered.

She shook her head. "No! We do not know that for a fact. He could be a spy," she whispered in my ear.

I glanced across at the young man again. He had filled out. His shoulders had broadened and he was taller than me now.

"It is me, Dare. Look, look," the deep voice said. He held out something in his hand, coming forward.

Logbana picked up a stone. "If you come any closer, I will kill you," she said sharply.

He held up his hand, revealing an object that dangled through his fingers. I gasped. The coral beads looked so familiar. They used to adorn Ma Bolanle's neck all year round.

"It is Dare, Logbana. It's our brother!" I shouted, rushing to him. He held out his arms and hugged me.

ॐ

The morning went by quickly. The news of Dare's return had spread throughout the palace. Mama was the most excited. She was beside herself, not letting Dare out of her sight. He was now securely lodged in Mama's room.

Mama stopped by as I was preparing to go and see father. I was dressed in a long, flowing cotton wrapper. My neck was adorned with a gold necklace with matching earrings and bangles. Once she was content with my dressing, she said, "Now, do not go gallivanting with Nasame! You are now betrothed and need to carry yourself in a respectable manner."

"Is that why I have not seen Nasame? Did you tell her not to come around?" I asked in surprise, not putting anything past her.

"I didn't need to tell Nasame anything. She knows by now what is expected of you and of her," she said sharply.

My shoulders drooped in disappointment. If marrying meant I was going to lose all my friends, then I wasn't really sure I wanted it so badly. Mama came forward, held me by the shoulders gently, and tilted my chin up.

"My daughter, I am sorry for sounding so harsh. I am just trying to teach you what is expected from a princess and a wife. No one will teach you. Most girls learn from experience, but I want to teach you as best as I can." She looked me squarely in the face. I nodded. "Good. Now, go and meet with your father. He is expecting you to sit and dine with him."

I grabbed my wrapper, about to run off as I normally did, except, I saw the look on my mother's face. Dropping my wrapper, I stood up straight, and walked slowly away, but not before seeing the smile that lit up my mama's face.

೧৩

As I approached the doorway to father's inner chambers, a man's voice rang out. "And who told you they saw me in Kotonou? That coward needs to come forward! My King, they are out to get me!" I lifted the beaded curtain to watch the older man fall to the ground, his legs and arms outstretched.

Father looked unperturbed, smoking his pipe, but I could tell he was upset. His finger tapped lightly on his chair. Kpojito Kamlin glanced sideways at him, and said to Solo, who still lay prostrate on the floor, "Rise up, Solo. Rise up."

Solo stood up, trying his best to look dignified. He looked up almost pleadingly at Father, who had not said a word. He then turned to Adandejan, who sat quietly, observing. "You may go," Kpojito said.

Solo glanced quickly at father, who kept smoking. He stepped back, bowed and turned around to go. I stepped aside for him.

"Amelia! Is that you?" Solo asked, peering into my face.

I smiled at him. "Good evening" I responded. Solo was Father's distant relative.

"Amelia, come in, come in!" Adandejan gestured to me, dismissing Solo with another flick of his hand.

Solo disappeared through the door. Father was beaming from ear to ear as he patted the stool beside him. I moved forward to the three of them.

Kpojito Kamlin got up and hugged me. "My daughter, you are welcome. Let me call the servants to bring the food," she said, letting me go.

Adandejan got up as well. "I will take my leave now. You must have your time alone with your daughter."

I smiled at him and sat down on the stool beside father.

"Yes, let us talk later tonight," Father said. Finally alone, he placed his pipe down, and immediately a guard appeared to set it aside.

I looked up at him as he seemed to contemplate what he wanted to say. "I asked him how long he would have you as his only wife before he picked another."

My heart skipped a bit. It was only my father that could ask a question like that of anyone. "What did he say?" I heard myself ask slowly.

Father sat back in his chair—a strange smile on his face—and chuckled. "He said for as long as you would have him."

My heart melted.

Father sat up, and took my hand in his. "My daughter, I am happy that you are getting married to someone who I already consider my son…but I have a question to ask of you."

I waited for him to continue.

"Are you ready to watch him go to war?"

I took a deep breath and thought for a second. "Father, I don't know. I will have to get used to the idea," I answered.

He nodded and patted my hand. "That is fine. That is fine," he said softly.

There was a knock and the servants entered, bringing in a long table and others followed with steaming food heaped in large bowls.

"Is anyone else joining us?' I asked

"No, my daughter. This is a father-daughter lunch. Let us have our time together. Soon, you will be adorning your husband's table."

In the many moons and years to come, I would always remember that time I spent with him—just my father and me.

Nasame came by to see me later that evening after her training. I was happy she had stayed within the palace premises in the guards' quarters, which was not so far away from the wives' court. I was afraid Nasame's attitude toward me might change now that I was betrothed, but it seemed I had nothing to fear. She was still as crazy as ever. She gushed over all the gifts I got and even tried some on.

"But you know, this your brother that returned. What is his name again?"

I looked up, noticing Nasame was studying Dare, who sat across from us in the court yard, playing with my siblings. I could hear Akaba's voice the loudest.

"Dare. His name is Dare," I said quietly.

He looked up almost like he had heard us, and then looked away. Nasame kept her eyes on him. "Hmm…Have you found out why he returned?" she asked.

I sat up, turning my full attention on her. "Not yet. We're giving him sometime to get settled. You know he walked all the way from…from…" I paused.

"You don't even know where he's come from?" Nasame asked in feigned surprise. Her eyes told me she already knew that.

"Schewww!" I hissed, irritated at her show of insensitivity.

She got up from the stool. "I have to go," she said sweetly, her mood changing.

I pouted, getting up with her.

"Don't worry, I will come back tomorrow! We'll go to the stream together."

We started walking together, holding hands and sharing in a little gossip. As we walked out into the outer court, we saw Dossou talking animatedly with Ouanilo. They both looked up as we approached. Nasame nudged me, as if I hadn't noticed myself.

"I will see you tomorrow," she said, and then turned to greet and curtsey to the two men before she disappeared through the side gate.

"Amelia, I see congratulations are in order. I was just telling my brother here that he has made the *best* choice. I was afraid he had chickened out, seeing as how long it took him to finally make a move!"

Dossou smiled, touching his bare chest in mock protest. "Ouanilo, you don't need to give away all my secrets!"

I smiled up at both of them.

"I can and I will!" Ouanilo turned to me, grinning. "Sister, this man here has been pining away for you for a long time! I had to beg him to at least wait until you came of age."

I had to laugh, watching as Dossou playfully hit Ouanilo on the shoulder. Ouanilo stepped back, laughing. Dossou smiled, turning to me. "I'll have to say that your brother is right. I'm just saddened that he had to divulge my innermost secrets so freely."

I giggled, and Ouanilo burst out laughing again.

"You laugh, too? There I was thinking I had made a good show of myself," Dossou said.

"I'm sorry for laughing, but you know Ouanilo. He is something else," I said.

Ouanilo grinned, stepping back. "Let me leave you two alone."

He walked off quietly. Out of nowhere, male guards followed behind him, all of them disappearing behind the huts in the direction of outside gates. Ouanilo lived outside the palace gates, as was tradition for princes being groomed to be kings to live with a close relative. In this case, Adandejan. Dossou and I turned to look at each other, and a smile spread across my face.

"Shall we walk to the stream, Princess?" He held out his arm for me. I took it and walked in step with him.

The evening was serene. A cool breeze wafted through and we could hear the sound of the splashing water and the laughter of children. Everyone was going about their evening activities—the women setting fire to start the evening meals, the men sitting under the oak trees to drink and play board games. An old man sat under the large tree in the ajalala courtyard surrounded by children.

"My children, would you like to hear how our kingdom came to bear its name?" he asked, his deep voice a sharp contrast to his frail stature.

"Yes!" the children screamed excitedly, moving closer.

I stopped and touched Dossou's arm to stop beside the tree behind the children. "Let's listen for a bit," I said quietly.

He looked surprised.

"What? I like to hear folk tales," I said, giggling softly, turning my attention to the deep voice ahead. I felt Dossou behind me, quiet.

"Thousands of harvests ago, our King's forefather—King Houegbadja—ruled the kingdom. He had conquered many other small kingdoms, including the area called Gedevi. Prince Akaba, the son of King Houegbadja—yes, our young prince Akaba is named after him—visited the house of Gedevi. He ordered that a plot of land be given to him by the head of the house, Dan. He was given the plot of land. But he was not satisfied and asked for another, and then another, every request was for a newer and larger plot of land. Well, Dan got tired and shouted out, 'Soon you will be building on my belly!'"

There was a gasp among the children as they gazed up at the old storyteller. "What happened, Baba?" one asked.

"Yes, what happened Baba?" another joined in.

The old man raised his wrinkled hand.

"Prince Akaba did exactly that, he built the new palace on Dan's belly," the old man said quietly.

A deadly silence engulfed the small group. A child whimpered.

"Now, now, there's no need to be afraid," he said.

"But, is this true, Baba?" a child asked.

"Oh yes, why do you think our kingdom is called Danhomè? Homè as you know, in Fon, means belly. Danhomè means *on the belly of Dan*."

I looked back, and caught Dossou watching me. "You're beautiful," he said

"What?" I heard myself asking under my breath, feeling self-conscious.

"Come," he said, and we began walking away to the palace gate. We walked in silence, greeting passersby who kept smiling at us. We reached a clearing at the outskirts of the palace and right before us was a feast spread out on mats.

"Who did this?" I asked him wide-eyed, looking around for the servants who might be lurking around.

Dossou held out his hand. "Come, sit with me Amelia," he said.

"Did you arrange for this?" I asked, searching his face as we sat down.

"Well, we have to eat. What would you like to eat first?" he asked.

I stared down at my favorite dishes—fresh fish stew, vegetable stew, and pounded yam. He must have talked with mama, who gave him all my favorite dishes. I felt tears dart to my eyes, and blinked them away. My chest felt tight with emotion.

He washed his hands in the bowl of water placed on the mat and then poured out a little portion of each delicacy into bowl. I watched as he scooped a handful of pounded yam, rolled it in the stew, and then carefully brought it close to my mouth.

"Open up," he said softly. My mouth dropped open in astonishment.

"Why are you surprised?" he asked, and I slowly obeyed him. I kept reminding myself that I had to eat like a princess should—with grace. That was hard, what with the way he was watching. I lowered my gaze until the food went traveling down my throat into my stomach. Then looked up.

His eyes were twinkling with laughter. "That was a sight to watch, my princess," he said softly.

I smiled shyly. "Why do you say that?" I asked.

He sat forward, his head almost touching mine. "Because, it was obvious you enjoyed your first bite, but didn't want to show it."

I could feel my face getting hot. "I *did* enjoy it," I said quietly.

"I know, but you didn't show it," he countered

"Well—" Before I could complete my sentence, he had scooped up another ball of pounded yam and waited for me to open my mouth.

"Here, eat and show me you enjoy it," he said softly, his eyes held mine steadily as I opened up. I ate slowly, watching him. This time, I savored the taste of the crayfish in the vegetable and swallowed, feeling it slide down my throat. A little smile curled around his lips as he watched me.

"Now, that is a look of enjoyment on your face. Be *free* with me, Amelia. I want you to always be yourself." His other hand came up and cupped my chin softly. I nodded, wishing he would look away for a second while I collected myself. He chuckled, dropping his hand.

"What?" I asked, curious to know what he was thinking.

"You really want to know?" he asked.

"Yes, of course. You're laughing at me, so why wouldn't I want to know?" I asked.

He leaned forward to wash his hands in the bowl.

"All right then, but please, promise me you won't get shy again?" He leaned away from me in preparation.

"I can't promise anything, Dossou," I said, not yet sure of what he would say. He looked away for a second, his wide jaw twitching.

"Did you know you walk in a very interesting manner?"

I gasped in disbelief. "How would you know that?" I asked.

He threw his head back and laughed. It was a deep throaty sound. He finally stopped, holding his chest. I waited, placing one hand on my waist to show my mock indignation.

"Any observant person would have noticed that you walk with a lift in your heels—as though you were dancing."

My mouth went dry.

"See, you're shy again," he said softly.

I finally spoke up. "I'm not shy, really, just surprised that you would say so. Nobody has ever told me that."

He took my hand slowly. "I will always tell you how I feel. It will probably take you sometime…" His brown eyes stared at my face, not missing the way my hand pulled back my hair when I was lost for words.

We heard footsteps approaching. "Oh, my princess, I didn't know you were here."

It was Yemisi and a group of palace slaves. They had pots on their heads, on their way to the stream. They all curtsied, kneeling on the ground when they saw who was in my company.

"Good evening," Dossou greeted them, sitting up. I waved as they hurried off.

"Well, that should give the palace something to talk about for a few days," I said, chuckling.

He smiled. "Well, let them. Do you care?" he asked, getting up. He held out his hand and pulled me up gently.

"It depends ," I said slowly, as a curious look came over his face. "If you don't declare your love for me at every instance, such that everyone would think I have used *juju* on you, then I won't be so concerned." I pried my hand from his and ran, knowing he would follow.

I laughed, rushing through the branches, as he gained ground behind me.

"You better start begging before I get you, Princess!" he called out.

"Never!" I screamed over my shoulder. I felt his arm on my waist, and felt myself being pulled down to the ground.

"Oh, are you all right?" he asked turning me around. His eyes looked worried and I laughed.

"Of course. What, are you afraid?" I asked.

The worry disappeared. He sat up, pulling me beside him. "I have to be. You've had too many accidents in the past not to be worried," he said, brushing the leaves from my knees.

"That's sweet. Your mother must be so proud she has such a sensitive, thoughtful son," I teased.

"My mother's dead," he said quietly.

My hand went to my mouth in horror. "I'm so sorry, I didn't mean to sound heartless. I just never knew." I said quickly.

He smiled. "Not a lot of people know," he said.

"What...what happened to her?" I asked.

"She died in child birth," he said quietly, his eyes still holding mine.

There was quiet. "*Your* birth?" I whispered.

"Yes," he said. The pain still very raw in his voice.

I stood on my knees beside him, looking into his eyes. "I am so sorry, Dossou. So sorry," I whispered.

The tears appeared in his eyes and he nodded. I felt the urge to hold him. To make him feel better. My hands pulled him close and I cradled his head in my bosom. "I'm so sorry," I said again.

We held each other and cried quietly.

7

RITE OF PASSAGE

I watched mama pick up the heavy woven *aso oke* to inspect. Several had been woven in a competition to determine which weaver's designs would be selected as the wedding attire to be worn by Dossou and I.

I couldn't believe how three moons had flown by and in a day, I would be married to Dossou.

Preparations for the wedding had started the moment Dossou and his family had come for introductions. Kings, princes, and chiefs from as far as Mahi had already arrived. Father had built new huts to host them. The feasting had begun seven days before the wedding, and every evening, father hosted the dignitaries to all forms of entertainment. The most interesting for the guests, of course, were the female soldiers. They had heard brave and gory stories of these fearless women whom had placed fear in the hearts of men.

As I looked across the room at mama, my eyes caught her favorite, and only, book hidden beneath the sea of clothing. "You still have this book?" I asked

She looked up, her mind obviously somewhere else. "What?" she asked.

I pointed at it. "That."

She picked up the beaten-up book. "Oh, my Bible? Yes, of course." She smiled at it wistfully. "Aah, Kondo did not want to hear about the white man's religion. Not one bit! According to him, it was just a means for outsiders to gain access to our lands and goods," she continued.

I was surprised that father had allowed her to keep it. Father had banished all wandering missionaries— as he called them—from the kingdom. He didn't trust them the same way he didn't trust the French. I held out my hand for the book. She handed it to me and then picked up another cloth.

"But he still allowed you to keep it," I said, flipping through the book, wishing I could read the print.

"Of course. That was the one thing I asked of him. Having it close is comforting. The Bible says there is only one true God and all other gods cannot compare. I have called on Him many times, and He's heard me," she said.

"But you still pray to the other deities. Just last moon you still paid homage to Ifa," I blurted out.

She looked up sharply from scrutinizing the cloth in her hand. "I must, my dear, as the wife of the King,

I must obey him. But in my heart, God knows He is the only one I worship."

I searched her face, seeing sadness in her eyes. "Is that why you gave me the name, Amelia? Is it in this book?"

She laughed. "No. There is no Amelia in the Bible. I just liked the name," she replied.

"I like it too," I said. I leaned over and gave her a hug. It hit me suddenly that I was all she had.

"My dearest daughter," she said softly and hugged me quickly, pushing me back. She was always trying to hide her soft side, except when she was with father. She got up slowly, holding up a beautifully woven gold and bronze cloth. "This is what you and Dossou will be wearing for the wedding," she said, getting up. Then she turned back slowly, as though remembering something. "I have been keeping this for you." She placed something round in my palm. It was a simple thread of gold beads.

"Thank you, Mama!" I shouted, hugging her.

"I've had it for a long time," she said quietly, her eyes looking beyond me into the distance.

"Thank you. I will always wear it," I promised.

She smiled. "By the way, you must be ready for the priestess this evening. She is coming to perform the wedding rituals."

My heart skipped a beat. "No, Mama!" I shouted.

"Sssh! It has to be done. You know that. Without it, you cannot get married."

I scrambled up, grabbing her hand pleadingly. "Please, Mama! I have heard of the awful things that

go on during the rituals. I cannot do it. I'd rather die,"
I whispered.

She laughed, clapping her hands. "Indeed!" She
stretched out her hand, pointing outside at the women
who went by, some with babies strapped to their back.
"Do you see all these women ? Did they not go through
it? Are they walking corpses? Did I not go through it?"
She looked me squarely in the face. "If they can, and I
can, then you can too. Now, get prepared. Yemisi will
bring in your meal," she said.

I stepped back, realizing I had lost this battle.

"Daughter of Gbèhanzin."

I looked up. Her eyes lit up with joy.

"Yes, Mama?" I replied.

She smiled. "You must fear nothing. Whatever you
fear controls you, and that is not who you are. You are
your father's daughter." She nodded her head as if to
confirm it and left.

༄

I waited in nervous anticipation for the wedding rituals to begin. I couldn't help my eyes wandering to
the door as the sky became darker. Nasame came by
to keep me company. She tried to distract me—telling
me cooked-up stories that made me laugh and cry so
many times I had to beg her to stop.

"It will be fine, Amelia."

I looked at my friend, whose face had grown serious. "Do you think so?" I couldn't help whispering.

She nodded. "It may not be what you expect, but it
will all be fine," she said quietly.

I searched her face. There it was again, Nasame speaking out of turn. Her gift had surfaced again. She had a faraway look in her eyes as if in a trance. Then, she blinked, as though she had come back to the present, and kept talking. "My older sisters have gone through it. It is the same priestess that comes every time. I am forbidden to see the actual rituals, but I am told that she—"

"Silence, there!" A voice cackled.

We screamed, falling into each other's arms.

She stood all of four feet tall, clad in all white and black, her face as dark as night. The priestess had walked in upon us...or had she just appeared in the room?

"What do you know about the rituals, you silly child?" She cackled exposing missing teeth.

"I'm sorry, priestess! So sorry!" Nasame shouted as she got up, letting go of my hand.

The priestess snorted, her dark eyes appraising her. "Leave us! Call in my assistants as you leave."

Nasame didn't need further urging. She waved a quick goodbye—a poor attempt to encourage me—and then fled.

My heart hammered against my chest as I watched the small person before me. I had heard tales of her evoking incantations where foggy objects appeared to choke the life out of her victims. If I sensed any such thing about to happen to me, I would pull out the knife from under my bedding and aim for her neck. I'm not too sure how effective that would be, given that she was supposedly able to appear and disappear as she pleased.

Two girls came in, each carrying a large basket. The priestess gestured to them to lay down the objects from the baskets on the floor.

A large white hen and a reddish cock appeared, and then a calabash. Soon, the whole floor was covered. I could not recognize the rest of the items.

"Here, put this on," the priestess said, handing me a piece of white cloth. I took it slowly, unfolding it to make sure there was nothing hidden in it.

"Quickly, take off everything else including your jewelry. The waist beads and anklets must come off too," she snapped.

I turned away from them and did as told.

"Good. Now sit on this stool." She had placed a wooden stool at my feet. On one side of the stool was carved a masculine profile, and on the other, a feminine one. The carving depicted Mawu-Lisa, the creator deity of my people. Mawu was the female, which represented night, fertility, motherhood, and all things feminine. Lisa was the male—a representation of daylight, hard work, strength, and war.

I sat down slowly, making sure that not one part of my body brushed hers. She smiled. She probably knew what I was thinking. The priestess turned to her two assistants and gestured for them to begin. The two girls sank to their knees, closed their eyes, and began to chant. They seemed to go into a trance. She joined in the incantation. Picking up the hen, she came toward me.

I cringed, pulling my shoulders in.

"Get up and pull off your cloth," she said. She continued chanting, holding the hen by the feet and turning it upside down. "Now!" she shouted when she saw my hesitation.

I obeyed, covering my breasts with one hand and my womanhood with the other. The room began to spin. I felt the hen's feathers all over me, from the crown of my head, down my neck and back.

"Open your legs!" she barked.

I felt the hen brush between my thighs. She did the same thing with the cock. In one quick movement, she broke the necks of the cock and hen and drained their blood into the calabash. By this time, the two young priestesses were in a frenzy. One was shaking all over in silence, while the other began to speak in a deep male voice in an unknown language.

The priestess stopped all of a sudden, looking at the one who spoke.

"Say that again?" she asked.

The deep voice repeated what it had said. Her eyes darted to my face. "Put your wrapper on."

I did not need further prodding. She walked away to the corner, chanting again. I watched all three of them as they chanted, swaying from side to side. They kept at this for a long time. If this was all the ritual entailed, it wasn't so bad after all. Finally, they stopped just as they had begun.

"Get some rest, Princess. Lie down now. In the early morning, we will be taking the calabash to pay homage," she said.

"Pay homage? Where?" I asked. I heard the panic in my voice.

She shook her head, gnashing her gums in anger. "That is not for you to know right now. Sleep!" she shouted.

She rolled out a mat and slowly sat down. The young priestesses remained in their trance. I lay down. If it took every ounce of energy in me, I would stay awake.

∽

"Wake up princess." The priestess was staring down at me, holding the calabash.

How long had I been asleep? How could I? What had she done to me? I looked down, patting myself to see if anything was missing or added. She cackled.

The young priestesses were already waiting outside, carrying the baskets.

It was pitch black when we began the walk. It was the early hours of the morning and no one stirred from their huts. These were the hours the unearthly roamed and did as they pleased. The priestess gestured for me to go ahead of them.

"But I don't know where I'm supposed to go," I whispered, turning around to look at her while hoping I wouldn't have my face slapped.

"You know where to go. We will follow," was all she said. I stepped out in the darkness and just kept walking. We walked out of the palace, moving past one towering wall to the next until we made it past the tenth wall and into the village. Not a soul in sight. Finally, we entered the forest, and I kept walking, not knowing when to stop. Then, something moved in the dark. I stopped, holding on to the calabash on my head. It stood there, watching.

The priestess came forward and stood beside me, chanting under her breath. "What do you want?" she asked slowly.

The human-like figure shifted from one foot to another, but did not move closer. It was not very big. It stood only slightly taller than the wild plants that grew about the forest.

"Tell us what you want," she said louder

A sound came from it, and it pointed at me.

"Take the calabash over."

To that thing? I couldn't breathe.

She pushed me forward. The figure stood waiting. I took one step and then two. It stood there, still. Now I could see its glittering eyes. I couldn't move any longer, even though I tried. The figure made an impatient sound.

"Take it now!" the priestess' voice was tinged with anger.

The tears fell down my cheeks. My feet refused to move. I felt like I was giving away a part of myself if I gave that calabash away. An angry sound escaped the figure. It went down on all fours and made as if to charge toward me. The priestess pushed me back and knelt in front of it, chanting. Her two assistants joined her on the ground. By now, they stood on my two sides, as if protecting me. The priestess talked in a soothing manner to it and then gestured for me to hand her the calabash. I gave it to her quickly, stepping back behind the two priestesses. She went forward, placing the calabash just two feet from the figure. Her head touched the ground and stayed there for some time. The glittering eyes moved from the priestess to me. I could not look away. A sad sound came from it. The priestess looked up and began to move back.

"Thank you. Thank you," she repeated to the creature. She came back toward us. "Turn around and begin to go. Do not look back!" she said harshly.

I ran, stepping over broken tree branches and leaves. Tears streamed down my face. The priestesses ran after me. We finally made it back just as the darkness began to turn gray. The day was upon us.

The priestess stopped me as I began to go into the hut. "Princess…" Her face looked grim. "Your performance was not only immature, but disappointing."

I felt something heavy in my throat.

"The fact that you did not give the calabash to the tohosu with your own hands bodes something unpleasant. I just hope my appeal will lessen the punishment," she said. I nodded, wishing her as far away from me as possible.

Her eyes softened as she looked at me. "It is well with you, my daughter. May you have a fruitful and happy married life."

She turned around, shuffling off, her protégés behind her. They disappeared out of the palace courtyard.

THE UNION

"Is it tight enough?" The stylist asked me above the rustling of the head tie being wrapped around my head.

"Yes. Pull out my ears from under the head tie. After a while, it starts to hurt," I said.

She obliged.

"Ooohh!" my sisters exclaimed as they came into the hut and crowded around me. They were dressed in the same burgundy aso oke. Mama's choice of the gold and bronze aṣọ oke was perfect on me. The intricate design glittered as I moved. My neck, wrists, and feet were heavy with gold and red beads. It was quite a task taking steps.

"You look beautiful, Amelia!" Nasame exclaimed as she appeared at the door, dressed in beautiful pink attire.

I smiled, waving her over to me.

"So, how did it go last night?" she whispered in my ear. I shook my head, reluctant to think about my horrible night and morning.

"Did she hurt you?"

"No! I just saw something I couldn't explain. It was beyond my comprehension."

Her eyes widened, and she grabbed my hand. "Mawu-Lisa! Did you run? Did you?"

"Worse, Nasame, I couldn't move."

She gasped.

"My dear daughters, you all look lovely!" Mama called out. She was beaming with pride. She was dressed so beautifully in a heavily woven cloth tied to her chest with a head tie in a flamboyant style to match. Her neck was adorned with gold jewelry and beads on her brown golden skin. Voluptuous as I had always known her, she was still able to carry herself with grace as she aged.

My sisters giggled, crowding around her, clamouring for her attention, asking her opinion of their outfits. "Mama, you look beautiful too!" They sang, dancing around her excitedly. She laughed, hugging them to her chest and looking across at me.

"Come now, my dears, step on outside. The drummers are waiting for you to lead your sister."

They needed no further urging, waving to me and then going out one at time, making sure not to trip on their beaded feet. Nasame began to leave too, but Mama held her back.

"Not you, Amelia's sister," she said quietly.

Nasame's eyes welled up with tears. She held each of our hands and we stood around in a close circle.

"Amelia, my beautiful, sweet, intelligent daughter. You are the one thing that has made my stay in this land worthwhile." Her hand tightened around mine. "I pray that you have all that I never had…" Her voice was choked with tears. I felt something pressed into my hand. I looked down to see the gold beads glittering.

"Mama," I said quietly

"Don't forget these," she muttered and smiled, cupping my face. "You make me proud. From the moment I had you, you have brought me only joy," she said.

The tears flowed down my cheeks and I placed my hand on top of hers.

"So I wish you all the joy you deserve. God will keep you and make you great." She hugged me tight.

"I love you, Mama," I whispered,

"I love you, my daughter." She hugged me tight, and then turned and hugged Nasame, who was howling by now. She walked to the door. "We will be waiting for you outside."

I walked up to Nasame, who couldn't seem to gather herself.

"It's fine Nasame, my dearest friend." But that only made her howl louder. I hugged her, and then realized the only thing that could save the situation.

"Guess who I saw yesterday?" I whispered to her.

Her head was further buried in my shoulder, her body shaking.

"Ademola, the wine tapper."

She finally stood still, looking through her tears. I nodded, grabbing her hand.

"He asked after you," I said and winked. "He mentioned that since I was no longer for the taking, maybe he could come calling on you."

She threw back her head and laughed. "He must be out of his mind!" She hit me playfully and pulled me into a hug. "Come, Amelia, it is time. Can you hear the drums? I can't wait to dance the whole night!" she shouted excitedly.

She pulled me gently to the door and stepped out. I couldn't believe what was before me as I stepped into the yard. My sisters standing in ascending order of height, flagging me on both sides. They shook their waists as the drums sounded. Their faces shone with happiness as I danced up to them. They surrounded me. A large veil was placed over my face. No one could uncover my face now, except Dossou. My heart skipped a beat in excitement as I saw the palace court—Father's wives and slaves all danced ahead of me. We were on our way to the outer court already filled with guests waiting, and eventually, my husband. They sang a song that floated to my ears as I danced. A song just for me.

Viton do Alohluwèdo egbe
Gbèhanzin vi gnonnou
Azin kondo dahoton
Wa kponél

Agbazaton gnondèkpè din
Aliton wini
Kpon dé hè do hwédouègbonlè
Dèkpeton dounou

Kpon edo yiyi Houè la
Pkon noukou ton les non ta zo
Pkon noukikoton non nan djro
Houn mon ye

Our daughter weds today
Gbèhanzin's daughter!
Daughter of the Great Shark!
Come see her!

Her skin so fair,
Her waist so tight
See her regal dance
A beauty to behold!

See her go!
Her eyes so bright
Her smile, many a prince
Wish was theirs to behold!

The guards stood at attention, lining the road side. They were in the thousands, standing all the way down to where my husband's family waited. The crowd jumped and danced behind the warriors. Even in their excitement, they knew not to break the rank.

My heart swelled with such pride. I waved at them with the woven fan in my hand. As I approached the throne, I caught Akaba and Dare standing and watching. Akaba raised his hand up to catch my attention, a wide smile on his face. I raised my hand and waved at him excitedly, blinking back a tear. I gasped as my eyes fell on Dare. He looked almost angry. His hands were clenched firmly by his side as he stood stoically.

"What is it?" Nasame whispered in my ear, holding me by the elbow.

I shook my head, unable to talk. Her eyes followed mine, and I felt her hand tighten its grip. "I knew he was no good," she said under her breath. I looked sideways at her, tripping over my wrapper.

"Nasame! What are you doing? Your duty is to take care of your friend!" someone called from the back. I felt a nudge on my other side, and looked in time to see Logbana squeeze her way beside me. She grabbed my other elbow, eyeing Nasame in horror.

"If you can't handle this task, you might as well leave!" she said coldly, dancing to the beat of the music.

"It is fine Logbana. None of this was Nasame's fault." I glanced at my friend, who seemed more interested in staring Dare down.

Finally, I stood in front of Father, who sat on his golden high chair atop a podium. Mama sat beside him on the left and Kpojito Kamlin on the right. The courtyard, which normally could take over three thousand people, was overflowing.

Nasame's hand guided me gently to kneel in front of Father. My sisters disappeared into the crowd of onlookers. Through the veil, I watched Father smile and laugh with his three female advisors—Mama, Ma Hwanje, and Kpojito Kamlin. His cap, specially made for the occasion, was a perfect fit on top of his head. His heavy wrapper draped one arm, fit around his body, falling to the ground. In one hand was his pipe. His large umbrella, held by a soldier, protected him from the sun. He got up, and immediately, everyone fell to the ground. I knelt before him.

"My beautiful daughter." His hand rested on my right shoulder. I knew it was customary to look down, but I didn't. I pulled up a side of my veil and stole a look at him. His eyes shined brightly as he blessed me. I wrapped my arms around his feet, and his hand came to rest on my head.

Bless me father. And he did. He called on Olodumare, Mawu-Lisa and the earth and sky gods. He blessed me like he would a son. Finally, he sat down and gestured for me to sit at his feet. The drums began again and everyone rose up. A popular large woman who was known as the mistress of ceremonies and presided over all wedding ceremonies came forward. She called on my mates to come and parade themselves. They danced forward with happiness.

"Have a final maiden dance with your mates my princess—your last maiden dance!" the mistress of ceremonies shouted.

I got up and danced up to them. Immediately, they swallowed me up in their hugs.

We danced uninhibitedly for what seemed only a short while until the mistress called to us.

"Come. Sit, sit. We will be taking you over to your new family soon!" she shouted.

The ceremony continued with Dossou's family presenting my father with gifts of food, hot drinks, and clothing. I watched from under the shade of the large umbrellas held by a guard as they prostrated, lying flat on the ground and paid homage. Dossou's sisters, uncles, aunts, and cousins were many.

A band of acrobats jumped into the center of the courts causing an uproar. We turned back to watch the spectacle. They were soon followed by dancers, magicians, and even the little children who insisted that they would perform for their princess. I looked around for Dossou and had to remind myself several times that the bridegroom was not present at wedding ceremonies. He sent relatives to bring his bride home.

Eventually, I was called on to dance my final and solo dance. I did, like never before. From the corner of my eye, I could see father tapping his feet, and blowing smoke from his pipe. Mama swayed in her chair. My siblings joined me—Ouanilo, Akaba, my other brothers, and sisters. Nasame was by my side throughout. Akaba's cap was almost falling off his head as he did an acrobatic step, bringing the crowd to their feet, cheering. I shook my head, wagging my hand at him.

"Brother, this is my day, not yours!" I shouted above the drums.Everyone laughed. The celebration continued with feasting. Many came forward to congratulate father. Soon, he left with many of the dignitaries for the jononho, where he entertained foreign visitors.

I knew my new family would come for me. "Our bride, we have to take you now."

The mistress of ceremonies appeared with my mates to lead me back to my husband's house in a dance procession.

～

By the time I arrived my new home in the early hours of the morning amid dancing and joyful noises from the crowd, I was tired. Dossou's family accepted me warmly, washing my feet at the door as was customary. I was led away into the inner chambers where I knew Dossou was waiting for me. The two young ladies—whom I had come to learn were Dossou's younger sisters—stood at the door. One knocked on the mat that covered the doorway.

"Brother, your wife is here," she said.

I heard his steps, and then he pulled back the covering. "Thank you."

He smiled at his sisters who curtsied and walked away, smiling. They gave me a knowing look, and I flushed with shyness at what I knew they were thinking.

"Come, Amelia." He held out his hand. My eyes searched his in the dim light from inside his room. "Don't be afraid. It's just me."

I took his hand, and went in.

༉

I rolled over on to my side, and immediately, felt something shining in my face.

Opening one eye, I stared into a large rectangular object. My image was looking right back at me. I was staring into a large mirror. Father had one of these in his room passed down to him from his father. The French had bestowed it on Grandfather Glele when things were still cordial. I wondered how Dossou had acquired his.

Dossou! I gasped, looking down at myself. I was completely naked under the wrapper that draped my bosom and hips. There was a dull ache between my thighs. It was all coming back to me—his hands on my waist, his lips on mine. My wedding night had proved to be very enjoyable. I giggled under my breath as I got up to walk to the full-length mirror that stood against the wall. I pulled the wrapper around me and stared at myself. My neatly plaited hair was woven with fine beads into a bun at the top of my head. I threaded my fingers through the plaits that fell to my neck. I had Mama's hair texture—full and long. My eyes still bore the tell-tale signs of the kohl that had been used to line it. There was a mark on my neck. It was new. I felt myself getting hot.

My hand felt my flat stomach. Maybe a baby was already in there. My heart leapt at the thought of carrying Dossou's child. He would look just like him—the strong jaw, beautiful lips, and sparkling brown eyes.

"I hope I'm one of the reasons you're giggling."

I swung around, almost losing my balance. He was standing in the doorway, smiling in a crooked way. A good thing our hut was designed a little differently, else his whole family would have seen me in all my glory. The hut was built with an outer room to meet guests, while the inner room was separated by a raffia mat. Dossou was leaning against the mat, his arms folded. It reminded me of the maiden dance when he had stood watching me. I managed to hold on to the wall and not fall. "I… er… good morning."

I began to go to the floor, replicating the way I saw mama greet father. But he caught me, and lifted me up, pulling me close. "Don't do that, don't ever do that," he said.

I was surprised. "I just wanted to greet you."

He lifted my chin up, our eyes meeting. "You can do so by doing this."

He brushed his lips against mine and pulled me closer, and we became lost in each other, again. By the time I realized it, we were on the floor. There was a knock outside.

"Brother, brother." It was one of Dossou's sisters.

"Yes?" His voice came out rough. He cleared his throat. I couldn't contain myself. A giggle escaped me. Dossou smiled, and we waited for a response.

"A messenger has come from the palace. You are being summoned by the King."

We looked at each other in surprise. Father would not pull my husband from my side barely a day after our wedding unless something serious had occurred. Dossou sighed, and then touched my nose.

"You must go," I said, releasing him.

"I must," he said quietly.

I watched him undress before me and felt no shame. He was beautiful He pulled on a pair of white cotton pants, his ribs rippling as he bent to put on his sandals.

"Will you wear your buba, or just tie a cloth?" I asked, getting up.

"You pick one," he said softly.

My heart fluttered, and I smiled. "All right."

I walked over to the pile of neatly stacked clothes and sifted through them. I picked out a buba with a nicely woven patchwork on the front. "This will look nice on you," I said.

He took it, and put it on. It fit his muscular torso perfectly. "Thank you my love," he said softly, crushing me to his chest.

"You'll be back soon?" I asked.

He held my face for a moment longer. "Don't worry, everybody loves you here. I've told my sisters to bring your food in for you. Don't bother yourself with anything. I'll be back before you know it," he said. I nodded.

"Don't be too long," I said, walking with him to the outer door. I watched him leave the compound. He was met at the gate by two tall muscular men just like him. One looked like Dokpe. Soon, they were only dots before my eyes as they disappeared in the direction of the palace.

༄

He came home as I was getting ready to go to bed. I had stayed indoors for most of the day, but eventually stepped out of the hut to greet my new family in the evening. They were so happy to have "our wife" with them. I sat with Dossou's father— Papa, as he was fondly called by everyone. He was a much older man in his eighties.

We talked about the wedding and how grand it had been. Dossou's stepmothers had come by as well, encouraging me to eat, but I firmly told them I was waiting for my husband to come back. I excused myself when I saw the sun had gone down and walked back to the hut.

My mind traveled to the palace. Father would be meeting with his council of advisors. I got up from the stool, ready to go in, when Dossou appeared in the distance. He waved at his younger siblings who called out to him as he passed by, but his eyes were glued on me. I felt the smile spread across my face, and waited for him.

"Welcome home," I murmured in his ear as we hugged.

He smiled and pulled me into our private abode. "Thank you my love." He pulled me on to his lap.

"Aren't you hungry? Your food is ready," I said.

"I'll eat later. Let me look at you," he said. His eyes looked worried.

"What is wrong? What happened Dossou?" I asked. He paused, and then held my hands.

"Alvarro," he said quietly.

"Alvarro? Father's interpreter? What happened to him?" I asked.

"He was killed," he said.

"By whom? The French? Where?" I pulled my hands free, trying hard to comprehend what he was telling me.

"Yes. He had gone to get some information in Kotonou and was caught," he said.

"Is that why Father summoned you?" I asked.

He nodded, pulling me back to him.

"So what do we do now?" I prodded.

He laughed, throwing back his head, exposing his thick strong neck.

"We? Amelia, you talk like a soldier."

I smiled. "But you forget I work just like a soldier," I said, tapping my finger to my temple. His eyes traveled to the wall where my tapestries were paraded.

"How can I forget," he said, pulling me close.

We played for a while, forgetting the imminent danger closing in on us.

"So what does this mean? Are we going to war?" I asked

"It hasn't come to that yet, my wife. It was only an outsider that was killed this time, not one of us."

So did that mean if one of us was killed, then war would be declared? I held my tongue from asking. I didn't want Dossou to think I was more interested in the affairs of the kingdom than in him. "Let me bring your food, we can talk about this later," I said, getting up.

He was happy with that. We ate together, discussing everything except the threat of war. The day would prove a foreshadowing of the many nights I waited up for my husband as he held war strategy meetings with father and his troops.

WAR IS UPON US

I listened to the light conversation from the inner room and smiled. Dossou had invited a select group from the troops he commanded to our home. They came a few evenings in the week to discuss everything under the sun. I was included in the conversations, making it easy for me to communicate news through my woven tapestries to our spies over in Port Novo and Kotonou.

From conversations within the palace and in our home, it was evident that we would be going to war. It was only a matter of time. Father had written a letter to the French, asking them to stay within their boundaries in Port Novo, and if they did not desist from what he called a threat to the kingdom, he would ensure that many would fall.

Tonight, there were four of them. Ouanilo was also present. For a few weeks now, he had become a constant fixture at the gatherings.

I was happy to have my brother around. He reminded me of home. Then of course, there was Dokpe—Dossou's right hand man who commanded a thousand soldiers under Dossou. Kodjo—also a commander of a thousand—was a very knowledge-able marksman. He spoke quietly, but with such confi-dence that it was very hard to question his judgment. Ahomadegbé was not nearly as tall as the others, nei-ther was he as well built. Initially, I wondered what was so special about him, until I watched him draw out an attack on the enemy. He had the uncanny ability to plan out an attack in seconds, a skill that was needed in the heat of battle.

The final guest was my favoite—Şosan. His fam-ily was from Ketou, but since he had been born in Abomey, he was considered a son of the soil. He could recount the wars fought by generations of Danhomè kings. He was walking history. He could sit and speak for hours on the legendary feats from Gangnihessou, the first King to Glele, my Grandfather. The troops needed someone who could boost their morale, and hearing even one tale from Şosan made me feel invin-cible. I hoped that soon, father would be added to Şosan's tales.

I stepped out from the room, my long dress float-ing behind me. I greeted them warmly, signaling for Yemisi to bring the trays of food.

"Our Princess, how are you this evening?" Dokpe was the first to speak and rise from the mat.

"I am very well. How is your family? Please sit, everybody," I said. I walked over to Ouanilo and hugged him. "Brother, how are you? How is everyone doing?" I asked.

"Everybody's fine. We miss not seeing our Amelia running all over the palace."

I punched his arm playfully, as they all laughed.

"Well, get used to not seeing her so often my dear friend," Dossou said. He held my waist for a moment and let his hand slide down to my hips.

Ouanilo shook his head, feigning a look of tiredness. "Look, Dossou, we know you are in love, and we have given you our flower. Let us hear something new," Ounailo said, sitting down on the stool set for him.

Ahomadegbé raised his clasped hands in a pleading gesture, turning to Ouanilo. "How is that possible, my prince? The troops are happy that our second in command is in good spirits even in these dark times! If this were before he married the princess, we would not even be able to talk with him. He would be all business or on some far away, covert operation."

The others nodded their agreement. My heart skipped a beat as I looked up at Dossou. I had a feeling that would be ending soon. Behind all the show, Dossou was an unrelenting, hardened soldier who had proved his worth many times over in battle.

"Thank my wife for that," Dossou interjected, sitting back down. He tried to pull me beside him, but I shook my head. I felt urgency in the air and wanted them to talk freely

"Wife of our commander, please come out!" Nasame called out from the doorway.

"Nasame, I am coming," I called to her, hurrying past the group. She was grinning from ear to ear. Her slight frame wrapped in a multicolored tie-dyed cloth.

"What happened? Why are you smiling like that?" I asked.

She sat down on the bench, waving excitedly at me to sit beside her. Turning to me, she grabbed my hands, our fingers interlocking. "I'm being dispatched!"

"Dispatched? To where?" I asked, my heart already sinking.

Her large eyes sparkled. "To the war!" she whispered in my ear.

I pushed her back in shock.

Her face fell. "Are you not happy for me?" she asked.

"Congratulations, Nasame. I am truly happy for you. Really, I mean it."

She stared at me for some time to be sure and then smiled. "Thank you."

We laughed and hugged.

"So, when do you leave?" I asked.

She shrugged. "It depends on how soon we get ready—in a few days at the most, but I'll be back before you know it. Why are you even that concerned? Your husband..." Her voice trailed off, when she realized that my husband might not even be here tomorrow or the day after. She grabbed my hand again. "Let's not worry about that. Come, did you hear about Didjou? She got married a fortnight ago, but the marriage is already over."

"What? Why?" I asked.

"Her husband did not find her 'at home'. He threw her out the same night. He said she should go and find the man who made her a woman." Nasame giggled, throwing back her head. I did not revel in others' misfortunes, but Didjou was an exception. She deserved what came to her.

We talked about village rumors like we had always done, enjoying each other's company. I studied Nasame's face, storing it in my jar of memories. I knew the time would come when the only means of seeing her would be by opening up that jar.

◦◦

My premonition that Dossou would be summoned to war became a reality few days later. He had gone to the palace as usual that morning and had come back almost immediately. I hurried out of the inner room when I heard his footsteps.

He smiled slightly and nodded his head, confirming my unspoken question. I flew across the room and hugged him tight. "May the gods go with you," I whispered in his ear.

"It will be only a few days, Amelia. I'll be back before you know it," he said solemnly.

I looked around the room quickly and saw it. My bocie was in the corner, behind the stool. I walked over and picked it up. "Take this with you Dossou. It will protect you, as it has always protected me."

He placed it in his pocket. "Thank you, my love. I know how much it means to you."

I nodded. He picked up the gun hidden behind his clothes—a long strapping metal object. We heard footsteps outside.

"Those are my men, I must hurry." In one step, he was looking down into my face. He crushed me to him, for what seemed an eternity and a moment at once—and then he was gone. He didn't look back. Not once. I watched him disappear as the tears washed down my face.

∽

Father was surrounded by his advisors in a deep discussion. I walked quietly past the door. Tiptoeing back to the door way, I leaned forward, looking through the holes in the door mat.

"My King, the French army has killed many of our soldiers. Can you imagine what they did in Oueme?" someone asked.

"I cannot believe it! Our sacred trees?" Agasunon said.

"Do you know who the traitor was? Solo!!" Someone shouted.

I gasped, placing my hand quickly over my mouth,

There was an uproar. Kpojito raised her hand and it stopped. She stood up amongst the group of men. "Must you get agitated like this, sons of the kingdom? We are known for action, not for arguments!" she shouted, the bones in her neck protruding.

They all agreed with nods. "The second in command just told us…"

My head reeled. *Dossou was here?* Why had he not come to me? It had been two moons since he had gone on a mission with his troops. I hurried away to find Mama.

"Mama! Mama? Where is Mama?" I screamed, running between the hung clothes. I demanded to know from everyone I came across in the courtyard.

"What is the matter, Amelia?" Ma Hwanje asked, grabbing my hand, looking very concerned.

I shook my head. "Have you seen my mother? I need to speak with her," I said, out of breath.

"She is in the garden. Have you any news?" she asked.

I was already gone, waving my hand in thanks.

Had I heard wrong? Was it that Dossou had updated the Council before he left? Could he be in the vicinity and I did not know? Dossou had not returned since he left that fateful day two moons ago. Now, I ached for him. How cruel life was. It was as though fate was teasing me— giving me a taste of love only for it to be snatched away again.

I found mama digging in her vegetable garden. She stood up swiftly when she saw me running toward her. "What is it?" she demanded to know.

I grabbed her hand. "I think Dossou is back," I whispered, afraid someone would hear us. Maybe there was a reason he was in hiding. Mama's eyes grew wider as I explained to her what had just happened.

"Really? Are you sure this is what you heard?" she asked.

I nodded.

"I will have to ask your father!" she said quickly.

"No! Please don't. I don't want him to think that I was eavesdropping."

She nodded, understanding. "I will tell him that I heard it," she said. Her eyes traveled down to my bosom and lower down—her eyes questioning.

I shook my head. "No, Mama. I have no news yet." I murmured.

She had asked two moons in succession now. "But, I wasn't asking you about—" she began to say, but I held my hand up,

"You don't have to make an excuse, Mama," I said.

She shrugged. "Anyway, don't worry. If he is here, he will make sure to see you before returning," she hugged me.

"You think so? You really think so? I am afraid he might have already left. I just have this feeling," I whispered into her ear.

"Forget that feeling! Trust me," she said and patted my face. "Now, get down here and do some work!" she yelled at me.

I laughed with her, helping her back to the ground, and setting myself beside her.

∾

The day dragged by painfully. I stayed in the palace, hoping to catch a glimpse of him. My family was happy to see me, but they knew I was distracted. I would often look around, expecting to see Dossou. I finally made up my mind to go home. Mama had insisted that I stay, but I refused. It hadn't felt right sleeping under father's roof when I had a home of my own, especially tonight. I couldn't explain it, but I needed to be at home.

"Amelia!" Akaba ran up to me. He was not happy being left behind while his older brothers went to war. As it was, five of the princes were gone, and it would be devastating if not even one survived. Akaba was the safety net here. "Mama told me you were going back to your house?" he asked.

"Yes, I said, picking up my cloth bag.

"Why not stay here with us?" he asked.

"No. Don't try to change my mind. Mama already failed at that," I said, watching as Dare approached. He was half naked, his upper torso glistening with sweat.

"Fine, let me walk you home then," Akaba said, taking my cloth bag from me. "Dare, where are you coming from?" Akaba asked.

I didn't notice the gun in Dare's hands until he thrust it under the folds of his wrapper.

"What—" I began to say.

Akaba's hand dug into my shoulder. "Yes, Dare, where are you from this evening?" he asked.

"From the forest. I went to catch some game," Dare replied, wiping the sweat from his face.

"With *that?*" I asked, feeling Akaba's hand dig deeper into my shoulder.

He chuckled, pulling me away. "We will see you later, Dare. I just need to walk our sister back home," Akaba said quickly, pulling me away toward the palace gate. He stopped in a sudden halt and looked around quizzically.

"Amelia, where are your body guards? And where is Yemisi?" he asked.

I rolled my eyes. "Please! I dismissed them a long time ago. I do not need body guards. As for Yemisi, she is staying for the night, because she has to be at the market early tomorrow to buy me some food items," I said.

My brother sighed, shaking his head. "Are they at least waiting for you at your place?" he asked.

"They refused to leave permanently. They said something about father killing them if they dared do that," I said.

"You can bet your life on that! It's bad enough that they are not walking with you," he said angrily. We walked quietly for some time. " Amelia, why can't you just leave Dare alone?" Akaba asked, as I had expected him to.

I rolled my eyes. "Akaba, all I wanted to ask, dearest brother, was how he expected to kill with accuracy with such a small gun. You are a skilled marksman, you should know better than that!" I said angrily.

Akaba sighed heavily. "I can't place my finger on why you have to be so mean to him. What has he ever done to you?" he asked.

"Absolutely nothing, Akaba. That's the problem. Ever since he returned, he has refused to tell us what happened to Ma Bolanle or where they were. You know how Mama especially was beside herself when that mother and son stole away in the middle of the night," I replied.

"But that was so long ago, Amelia, when we lived in the outskirts of Abomey, just before father became King" Akaba interjected.

I nodded. "Yes, and how can I forget? Mama cried for many moons over the fact that her best friend had disappeared," I said.

We could see my home and my guards. Two tall dark-skinned women were standing outside the door of my hut. Akaba held me back, turning me to face him. "That is not good enough reason to just stop talking to him. He is more like a blood brother to you than even me," Akaba said quietly.

I sighed, placing a hand over my brow. "I really don't want to talk about this anymore, Akaba. Just because Dare's mother and mine were very close doesn't automatically mean that Dare and I should be. He made his bed, so why should I lie with him?" I walked toward the guards, leaving him behind.

"You are welcome, Princess," the guards said in unison.

"Thank you," I replied.

"Prince, you are welcome," they said.

He flashed them his brilliant smile. He was obviously taken by them. They were young and virgins, devoted only to the King. Untouched and sacred. My dear brother found this very tempting. He went up to them, nodding at each one. "I have not seen your faces before. Have you just joined the army?" he asked.

The one on the left glanced sideways at him. "No, Prince. I have been a guard for six harvest seasons," she replied.

"And I, eight," the one on the right answered.

Akaba stepped back in mock amazement. "You don't say! How could I have missed such lovely faces and walked by them?" he asked.

I could see the guards tried to remain business-like, but a smile played on their lips, and then disappeared again. I walked past them.

"Akaba, meet me inside when you are done," I said. Turning to the guards, I asked as I had every night since they had become my personal guards, "Will you join us for dinner?" They declined, as they always did.

Akaba remained for a few hours, and finally left when he had had his fill. He made me laugh all the while. He had wanted to stay, but I told him I was fine. I couldn't sleep, though. My mind kept wandering back to the conversation in father's court. Dossou had been in the palace? I could feel my heart bleeding just thinking that he had been so close and I had not been able to see or hold him.

ᕦᕤ

The gentle shove became more forceful. Something warm touched my face, then slowly went down my neck.

"What? Who is that?" I murmured, my eyes opened slowly, and a face came into view. I gasped. My beloved was before me! I burst into tears and fell into his arms. "I knew you would come! I knew it!" I murmured, touching his face.

"Amelia, my love, I missed you so much. How are you?" he asked. He held my chin up, staring into my face.

"I am fine. How are you? Are you all right?" I asked. I sat up, touching him all over.

He chuckled, sitting back. "Yes, now that I can see you and hold you, I am fine, my love."

I laughed, jumping all over him. My excitement was short-lived. "You're not here to stay are you?" I asked.

He shook his head, pulling me to sit beside him. "No, I must leave before day break. No one must know I've been here."

"But the guards…" I began to say.

He chuckled. "I taught them what they know. They will never know I was here," he said.

"Are you hungry? Do you want to eat something?" I asked, starting to rise, but he held me back.

"No, my heart. *You* are what I came for. I don't need food. I just need to be with you," he said softly.

Falling back into his arms, we sat gazing into each other's face.

"Amelia…" he said softly.

I looked up at him.

"Are you?" He glanced at my stomach.

I felt the tears welling up in my eyes and shook my head.

"Why do you cry?" he whispered, wiping my tears.

"Because I want to carry your child," I whispered.

"I love you regardless if you carry my child or not. I will always love you."

I smiled through my tears, feeling his hands on my face, and wishing that time would stand still.

"I love you, Dossou, like I have never loved anyone in my life." The words tore from my throat.

He gulped and I only then knew how much he had waited to hear me say those words.

"I love you with all of my being," he said, touching his lips to mine. He drew back, looking somber. "Amelia, I came to tell you something very important."

I looked up sharply at him.

"You, Mama, and your younger brothers and sisters must *leave* the palace."

"Why? What has happened?" I demanded to know.

"The French are gaining ground. They have burned down the sacred trees. They are killing at will. I don't know if our armies can hold up much longer."

"What? That cannot be! Our armies should be able to handle them! I mean…" My mind was racing. I got up and started pacing back and forth. I paused and looked at him. "But where will we go?" I asked

Dossou got up, taking my hand. "You must go to Abẹokuta. You must go as fast as you can," he replied.

I searched his face and knew he had seen plenty.

"What of you, my love? What happens to you?" I asked, knowing the answer already.

"I have vowed to protect our land with my last breath, Amelia. I must stay and fight. I must protect my King, your father."

I nodded, trying my best to keep calm. "Of course, you must…do your duty," I said, broken, stepping away from him. I began to pace again. "You must fight for the land as you said, protect everyone, make sure we are safe. I mean, to do any less would be unheard of!" I glanced at him and kept pacing.

"Amelia…" he said softly, holding out his arms.

"Of course, I understand," I snapped back, pushing his hands away.

"Amelia."

"I said, I understand. You have been a soldier for so long; you couldn't possibly not be for once. You—" I choked on my words as the tears ran down.

"Amelia!" he snapped, turning me around.

"What, Dossou? What do you want me to say or do? You must go, mustn't you?" I asked, searching his face. I felt drained and beaten. I couldn't win this battle. Duty to land had won over the heart. We stood looking at each other. My eyes began to follow my bocie that swung gently on the string tied around his neck.

"I must. I wish I could leave with you, but I wouldn't be a man if I left and didn't perform my duty," he said calmly.

"So you want us to head to Abẹokuta? But we know nobody there," I said.

"Your father knows the Alake, the King of Ẹgba land. Let him write a letter to him to give you shelter," he said.

I sat back down, pulling my legs to my chest, and wrapping my arms round my knees. Dossou knelt beside me, taking my hands.

"Please, just do as I say. *Please,*" he said softly. "Amelia? Will you do that tomorrow? Go to your father and get the letter?" he asked.

I stared up at him, blinking away the tears, and finally nodded. He hugged me closely.

I stared up at him. Letting the tears trickle. Would I see him again? Would we hold each other again? We stayed clinging to each other for a long time, talking about nothing, and then letting our bodies do the talking. At the back of my mind, I knew this may be the last time I saw him.

᭟

I smiled even before my eyes opened. Dossou's voice still lingered in my ears. I opened my eyes to see an empty mat where Dossou should have been. I rolled over, my nose pressing into the raffia where his body had rested. I could smell him. It wasn't a dream. Dossou had been here. I burst into tears, pulling on my hair in agony.

"Princess! Princess!"

I sat up, wiping my face. "What do you want?" I shouted, hiccupping from the tears.

"What is the matter?" the guard asked, appearing in the doorway. Her eyes widened at what she saw. I pulled my clothing around me.

"Leave now!" I screamed, pulling at my hair again. She rushed out.

The silence was short-lived. Soon, I heard feet rushing toward my doorway again.

"Our wife! Our wife!" They were hitting on the mat over the doorway.

The tears flowed freely. This was my pain alone to carry, they must not know. I stood up slowly, wiping my face. I went to the door and pulled back the mat, staring into the concerned faces of my two mothers.

"Good morning, my daughter. Is everything all right?" senior mother asked, her bushy white brows knotted together as she held on to her walking cane.

Second mother nodded, watching me closely. I forced my lips to make a smile.

"Aah, good morning, my mothers. I am so sorry for waking you. Everything is all right. I just had a dream, that was all," I said.

"A dream my child? You could wake three villages with that scream we just heard. I hope all is well?" second mother asked, her eyes searching the room. I remember Dossou telling me she was the troublesome one.

"I apologize again," I managed to say.

"Well, if you say so my child. But, if there is anything you need, please, I beg you, let us know," senior mother said, already turning around to leave.

"Anything at all," second mother added.

"Thank you," I said.

A thunderous stamping of feet was heard. The two mothers pushed themselves into the hut as something approached from afar.

"What is that?" second mother asked.

I squinted, trying to determine what the figure was.

"It is our senior!" one of the guards shouted, standing to attention, her gun by her side.

"Halt!" The moving apparition stood before us—a group of six guards, fully armed. One came forward, tall and muscular. She bowed before me. "Princess, you are needed by your mother immediately."

"Mama wants me now?" I asked, looking at each one of them. "Is all well?"

"You can ask your mother when you get there. She needs you now," the same guard said.

I turned to my mothers. "I must leave now, my mothers," I said quietly.

They both nodded. "The gods go with you, Amelia. The gods be with you," they said repeatedly and began walking away.

"I will be back soon!" I called after them. They waved and kept walking.

I turned to the guards, "Let's go."

"You won't take anything with you?" one asked, looking surprised.

"Everything I need is in the palace," I said, walking ahead of her.

We walked quickly through the sleeping village. I could see the kana bridge that would lead us to the palace gates ahead, but the two guards in front of me made a detour to the right.

"Where are you going?" I asked, running after them.

"We are not going to the palace, Princess," one of the guards behind me said. "We only said that to deceive the old women. No one must know your whereabouts. Keep going."

As I followed the beaded feet ahead, my mind clouded with all kinds of thoughts. I realized this was the way to Grandmother's place. Two guards were also waiting outside her hut when we approached. A solitary figure sat down on a stool, with head on the knees. Upon hearing our footsteps, the person looked up.

"Dare! What are you doing here?" I whispered, looking down at him.

He looked up, his eyes round with fear.

"What is wrong with you?" I asked.

He opened his mouth to speak, but no words came out. Mama appeared at the door, beckoning.

"Amelia, come in here right now." Her voice was shaking as she grabbed me by the hand. I heard a shuffling noise as we entered the darkened room together.

"Is that my Amelia?" the crackling voice of Grandmother called out. Her huddled figure was in the center of the room.

"Grandmother!" I walked over slowly, making my way in the dark. She grabbed my hand and pulled me down.

"What are you doing?" I whispered, peering down to look at what she was covering. It was a small bundle tied neatly. My eyes now getting accustomed to the darkness could make out grandmother's face. I gasped, dropping down beside her.

"Grandmother! Why are you crying?" I whispered, taking her damp hands.

She smiled through her tears, patting my hands. "Do not mind me my child. I fear only for my son," she said.

I chuckled, gripping her hand, as if that would stop the madness that I saw coming upon her.

"Grandmother, what son? Your only child is mama." I chuckled again. There was silence in the room. I raised my head to look at Mama. She stood, looking straight at me, shaking her head.

"Grandmother?" I whispered.

Her weary old eyes fixed on me. "Your father is my son," she said flatly.

I dropped her hand, my head reeling. "No!" I whispered.

She grabbed my hand to her flat chest. "You will listen to me, Amelia, because there is no time to waste," she said sharply. The tears still fell, but the determination in her eyes shone through.

"Your father, Gbehazin, is my son—my natural born son. Your mother *is* my daughter. She has told you how she came to be in this kingdom, has she not?" she asked.

I nodded.

"She is the daughter I found. Your father is the one I gave birth to," she said. Her eyes looked like it was seeing into a different realm as she continued. "Unknown to most—except your father and a few who have since been banished from the palace—" she paused, her eyes flashing, "—I come from Abęokuta, which is across the Ogun river. Like most kings of Danhomé before him, King Glele preferred to choose the woman who carried his heir from the young girls captured from Abęokuta. These kings mated with them, impregnated them, and then tore their offsprings from their breasts the moment they were born. They were then sent back to their homeland. And so, King Glele did the same."

I gasped, gripping her hands tighter.

She smiled bitterly, looking at me. "But I endured, little one," she said quietly.

Something brushed my shoulder, and I realized mama had sat down beside me, putting her arm around my shoulder. I turned back to grandmother.

"Before I handed over my child, on my birthing bed, I marked my boy so that when the time came for me to tell him, he would know I was truly his mother."

I began shaking uncontrollably.

"It is all right, my child," Grandmother patted my hand and continued. "I was soon banished from the palace—this very same palace that lies across the kana bridge," Grandmother pointed. "But I didn't lose hope. I set forth on foot away from here, begging in the villages along the rivers, scavenging for food. I did not have a permanent place to put my head. That is the way I lived for countless harvests...until I met Low One," she smiled. "My good friend, Low One, found me, fed me, clothed me, and brought me back here to this village."

I glanced at the two women.

"But how did you tell father? Did he believe you?" I asked hoarsely.

She chuckled. "I told him after he married my Ajo. It would have been death for me if I had said it before. No one can touch the Prince's mother-in-law. At least, that is what everyone knew me as," she said and shrugged. "Of course he didn't believe me! He wanted to throw me to the dogs...that is, until I told him where his scar was," she whispered. "Only a mother and wife could tell you where that scar is."

Mama nodded, smiling.

"Then it became our secret. I would be known to everyone as his wife's mother, but he would know me truly as his mother," she became quiet, watching me.

"Amelia?" Mama said softly.

I blinked, my mouth dry.

"But, my child, that is but half the reason you have been dragged from your husband's house this early morning," Grandmother said gravely.

I felt my chest tightening. Her wise old eyes gazed at me.

"War is upon us and you must flee now!" she whispered.

I jumped back, clinging to Mama. "No!" I whispered.

"Amelia, you must listen to us! We cannot lie to you. You must leave now with your brother," Mama said.

"Akaba? Is he here?" I asked, looking around.

Mama shook her head. "With your other brother— Dare! No one has seen Akaba since yesterday when he walked you home," Mama said impatiently.

I struggled to stand up, breathing heavily, even as both of them pulled me down. "Where is Akaba? Where is my brother?" I screamed. A hand fell on my mouth, muffling my shouts. Their hands held me down until I stopped struggling from fatigue.

"Are you finished?" Mama asked angrily.

I remained still, looking up into the roof and crying silently. Grandmother's hands wiped my face gently. She pulled me up to sit beside her. "You must run now, Amelia. The kingdom is about to fall. We may fall with it, but *you* cannot. You are all I have fought for. To see you run free is for your mother to finally run free...for me to finally be free. You must go, now!" she whispered in my ear.

"Grandmother...I can't leave you...Dossou... Mama...Father..." I began to say.

"You must. For our sake, you must go," she whispered again.

I turned to look at mother. She was holding the bundle, her face stoic.

"Mama," I said softly, holding out my hand for hers. She placed the bundle in my hand, her fingers barley touching mine. "Mama," I pleaded, but she kept her eyes averted.

Grandmother turned my face back to her.

"You must safeguard what is in that bundle. It holds your future. In it is your father's letter to the Alake of Ẹgba asking for his assistance to take you in. Your mother wrote the letter in Ẹgba herself. It has your father's seal on it. When the King reads the letter, he will know that your family also comes from there. He cannot turn you away," she said. "There are gold pieces for you. Only spend them if you must. Otherwise, beg for food before spending what you have. Under no circumstance must you reveal who you really are until you get to Abẹokuta. Do you hear me?" Grandmother asked, pulling her ear.

I nodded, glancing at Mama, who still had her back turned to us.

"Take this off now!" Grandmother said quickly, pulling on the gold beads on my wrist.

"But, Mama gave me these. I promised never to take them off," I said, my voice shaking as she untied the knot on the thread that held the beads together. She gathered the beads and placed them in my palm.

"Mama," I called to my mother's back. This time she shifted her body on the wall, leaning her forehead on it, her chest was heaving.

"Your mother is in agony. She is losing a child and she may lose even much more before the day is over," Grandmother said, shaking her head. She got up slowly and pulled me up after her.

I brushed my tears out of my face and took a deep breath.

"Take the forest path. Yes, Amelia. You must," Grandmother said when she saw my eyes widen. "Go past the stream where you take your bath and don't look back. No matter what you see, do not make a sound. Trust no one, only yourself," Grandmother said, touching me where my heart raced. She pulled me to her where we stood head to head for some time, breathing each other in. Then she pushed me away, walked by mama, and out through the doorway.

Mama straightened up and turned to me. She held out something in her hand.

I gasped when it gleamed. "Mama, father needs his récade. He will know its missing," I whispered.

She smiled sadly. "You do not have any idea how much your father loves you do you?" she asked, pulling my wrapper open in my bosom and shoving the récade within its folds. "His symbol goes with you. Use this *only* if all else fails," she said, her eyes narrowing.

I gulped and nodded. She pulled me close. "My Father go with you. The one I truly ever worship, go with you," she whispered in my ear, choking on her words.

"Mama," I whispered, holding on to her.

She pushed me to the door. "Run! Run far away!" she shouted, pulling the mat open, revealing Dare standing at the entrance. He did not look surprised. There was no one else about.

Mama looked him in the eyes. "Go now," she said calmly and walked back into the hut.

"Mama!" I shouted as Dare took my hand and pulled me after him, running for the forest. The drum beat feverishly over the palace walls, followed by the female voices screaming in defiance and amidst thundering of feet.

Wa do France gbé nou mi
Mi so awouannou
Sounou Huè gnimi, mignignonnou au
noudé na do dji djo houè yo
Mi na wa

Give us the French!
We are ready for war!
We are men, not women,
Whatever the obstacle
We will overcome!

THE UNKNOWN PRESENT

The forest was dense and dark. There was an ominous silence around us. We crouched, almost crawling.

Boom! The sound came from far away. We had traveled for what seemed a day, from sun up to sun down, past all the familiar places. We were now in distant parts of the kingdom. It had grown dark again.

"Dare? Dare!" I whispered, looking from under the large plantain leaves. My heart was beating hard. "Where are you? Please, where are you?" I whispered again, feeling around me.

He appeared beside me, grabbing my hand, and pulling me under a large shrub. "You must be quiet! You must! Someone's coming!" he whispered back.

I could feel my mouth getting dry as I tried to breathe. A foot stepped on a branch close by. Someone was close. The sound seemed slow and cautious as the person drew closer, crunching on the leaves and branches as minimally possible. I wrapped my hand tightly round Dare's and closed my eyes tight. They were dressed in uniforms and metal hats. Wielding rifles under their arms, they came closer. They spoke a foreign language—very similar to what Alvarro spoke. A pair of sandal-clad feet appeared next to the shrub we hid. I felt faint. Dare had his hand over my mouth, the other holding down my shoulder. They were shouting at each other.

The one close to where we hid in the shrubs was pointing a little further down, speaking angrily. His feet remained planted, and then the tip of a rifle appeared right between me and Dare though the shrubs. He was searching! The other soldier spoke angrily too.

Suddenly, I felt something slide between my feet and the tip of the gun hit it. A large rabbit jumped out and ran off. The soldier spoke gruffly and walked off amidst laughter from his comrade. They talked briefly for a while and then marched off.

I searched for Dare's face in the dark, my teeth gnashing in uncontrollable fear. He had his head down, still holding my hand tightly. I put my other hand over his until his stopped shaking.

He opened his eyes, and I could see the tears. Breathing in deeply, he said, "We must go east, Amelia, through Ketou and Cové. That's the fastest way I know."

I nodded.

"Aren't you hungry?" he asked, sounding concerned.

I looked up sharply at him, surprised. "Yes, but—"

"I have the bean cakes Na Zevoton gave me," he said quietly, pulling the bundle I just noticed was tied to his back. He opened it, revealing an interesting assortment. The bean cakes were wrapped in banana leaves of about twenty or more. There was the shot gun he had held just the day before. That seemed like an eternity now. I picked up Ma Bolanle's coral beads and twirled them around my fingers.

I looked up at him. His face was emotionless again. Asking after his mother would be futile. I dropped the beads, my eyes moving to the wooden handle that peeked out from under the banana leaves. "What is that?" I asked, pointing at it.

He picked it up. "This?" he asked, pulling out the dagger.

"Stop joking. Do you even know how to use it?" I asked.

He raised his eyebrows. "Well, you have to wait to find out," he said quietly.

A branch snapped, and we froze.

"I thought they left!" I whispered, watching Dare pack up the contents of his bundle quickly.

"Let's go!" he whispered.

"Who is there?" a male voice asked as a figure approached our hiding place.

I leaned forward. Dare pulled me back. "Stop! I know who it is," I said, loud enough for the intruder to hear. The person stopped and I stood up.

"Princess?" the man asked, moving closer.

"Boy? What are you doing here?" I asked, looking into grandmother's slave's dark face.

He almost smiled. "I am running away," he said softly, looking down at the ground.

"Where are you running to?" I asked.

He shrugged. "Away from my mistress. Away to be free," he said in his emotionless manner.

Dare came out from hiding to stand beside me, towering over Boy and I.

"You cannot leave my Grandmother!" I said furiously, imagining her all alone.

Boy looked up at me, his eyes lifeless. "She does not need me anymore Princess. I would have stayed if she did," he said.

"Did she tell you that?" I asked, clenching my fists.

"Amelia…" Dare began to say as I lurched for Boy. Boy caught my fist in midair and pushed it backward.

"I do not wish to harm you Princess," he said quietly, stepping back.

"Amelia, enough!" Dare said, his voice rising. I glanced at him in surprise. He waved to Boy. "Come here and eat with us. You must be hungry," he said.

Boy stood for sometime, sizing Dare up. His naked chest was rising and falling slowly. He glanced at me and then back at Dare. "Thank you," he said softly, and followed Dare. I stood, waiting.

"Amelia, please join us. We must eat quickly and rest for a while," Dare called to me. I sighed heavily, and marched over to join them.

Dare opened his bundle of possessions again and brought out three banana leaf rolls. Placing one each in front of us. "We must ration our food," he said quietly.

I glanced at Boy, who wasted no time in unrolling the banana leaf and biting into the bean cake.

"Amelia," Dare whispered. I looked at him. "Leave him. He is fine," he said, looking into his bundle, and pulling out the dagger. He stood up to tear off a piece of his wrapper as Boy and I watched.

"What are you doing?" I asked. Finally, Dare had lost himself to madness.

He ignored me, pulling up the wrapper to reveal the pants he wore underneath. He leaned down and rolled the pant leg up to his thigh. Placing his dagger on the side of his inner thigh, he bound it with the torn cloth and rolled this pant leg down, covering it with this wrapper. He straightened up and looked at me.

"You do not need to know everything, Amelia," he said, and sat back down.

I picked up my banana leaf and unrolled it. Dare watched as I bit into the moistness of Grandmother's bean cake. Then I realized Boy must have prepared it. I felt the shame wash over me, and looked down on the ground. We ate in silence. The forest crickets and frogs our only companion.

"Let us sleep here tonight. We will resume our journey tomorrow morning. That is, unless you have other plans of your own?" Dare asked, turning to Boy. Boy stared at him, and then shook his head. "All right then. Just help me cut off some of the leaves off this tree to cover the ground. At least, enough for the Princess to sleep on," Dare said, getting up. Boy followed. I heard them some distance away, pulling down leaves. They returned almost immediately, laying them on the ground beside me. "Amelia, please sleep now. We will stay just some distance from you. You have nothing to fear," Dare said.

I looked into his face, lost for words. "Th...thank you Dare," I said, swallowing hard. I lay down slowly on the leaves, placing the bundle under my head. They each sat down at my feet, facing outwards, reminding me of two mother hens protecting their off springs.

"Good night," Boy said.

"Goodnight," Dare said.

I cried, aware that they could hear me no matter how softly.

∽

The boots crunched down hard on the tree branches close to where I lay. I smelt their sweat as they approached. I sprang up only to be pushed back down again by strong hands. Dare's face peered into mine. The gray skies were beginning to appear—day break.

"Be quiet," he whispered in my ear, laying close beside me.

I held my breath, listening for the feet. It got closer. The soldiers were back and they were combing the area. A loud angry voice spat out something.

Boy sat up and looked at us.

"They will find all of us very soon," he said flatly.

"Lie back down!" I whispered to him angrily, afraid of discovery.

"I have to turn myself in so you can go," he said, getting up.

The footsteps stopped and turned in our direction. The angry voice spoke. Boy stepped out of the shrubs and walked toward them. I lurched forward.

"Let him go," Dare whispered, holding me down to the ground. We heard a slap and someone being pushed against something hard.

"I am a slave! I was running from my mistress, please don't hurt me," Boy shouted. There was a harsh response from the soldier. He whistled, and immediately we heard footsteps approaching. It sounded like three or more soldiers converged.

A shot went up and they began shouting.

"Do not make a noise, whatever you hear, do you understand me?" Dare whispered in my ear. I nodded, shaking uncontrollably. We listened as they began to throw objects together. Soon, we smelt burning wood. Light and smoke appeared overhead. They had made a fire. Shouts went up again, and someone was pushed back and forth between them. They laughed as Boy's groans grew louder. Then there was silence.

"Aaaargh! Aaaargh! Aaaargh!" the agonizing screams came from Boy. Then I smelt the burning flesh. My head reeled from the odor. The men started laughing, patting themselves on the back. Dare's hands covered my mouth just as a scream from my throat. He need not have bothered—Boy's excruciating screams camouflaged mine.

The torture went on until the sun appeared in the horizon. By then, Boy was silent. We heard them pick him up, talking among themselves and laughing. The fire was killed and then they began walking away, one at a time. Flies buzzed around us under the shrubs, probably looking for fresh burnt flesh to consume.

I shifted under Dare, but he held me down still. "We must wait and make sure they have left," he said firmly. I gazed up at him and then closed my eyes. We would wait.

◌◠◡

"Amelia! Amelia!" Dare called, shaking me.

I opened my eyes and glared up at him. He looked surprised, but quickly collected himself. "We have to go. You slept off. It is now almost afternoon and we have to hurry," he said, picking up his bundle.

I sat up, looking down at myself. For a moment, I was afraid I had lost it.

"Boy? Where is Boy?" I asked, the tears springing to my eyes.

Dare glanced at me, his eyes stony. "You already know what happened to Boy, Amelia. Let's waste no more time," he said impatiently.

I turned away from him, pulling my wrapper closer around me to hold the recadé firmly.

"Come now!" he said gruffly, stepping out from behind the shrubbery. I picked up my bundle and got up, following him.

We walked silently for a long time, keeping just off the well-worn path to avoid people. The only passersby we encountered were rabbits and deer. My hands itched for a bow and arrow.

"Here," Dare said, handing me another banana leaf. I took it, not talking. We kept walking as we ate. "We must go further into the forest, Amelia. Let's not risk meeting a human for a while," Dare said, turning his head before pushing through the thick branches of the trees, making a path. "Enter, Amelia," he said.

"In there? Dare, we don't know what we'll meet. There could be lions," I said.

"Then we will kill them," he said.

"Dare—"

"Go in now before we meet another soldier," he said, his voice rising.

I entered the shadows of the deep forest, clutching the bundle to my chest. Dare followed, getting back into position in front of me.

"We will walk for as long as our minds and bodies will permit us, as far away from Danhomè as we can," he said, not faltering in step. I tried to keep up.

"Even at night?" I asked.

"Yes." His eyes went to my neck.

"Take your royal beads off," he said. My hand went to my neck.

Grandmother had even forgotten to take that off. I struggled to untie the knot.

"Dare?" I called.

Dare pulled at it too for some time. "I must cut it," he said.

"All right," I said.

I felt his breath on my neck as his teeth cut into the thread holding the beads. I felt the release on my neck as the beads fell around me. "My beads!" I shouted, trying to save them as they scattered to the ground. "My beads…" I said again, the tears falling.

"Don't worry about the beads," Dare said, already walking ahead.

I cried silently as he led the way.

∽

"Did you hear that?" he asked.

"What?" I asked.

He held up his hand. It sounded like water. A lot of it. We walked slowly toward the sound. There was a clearing in the forest ahead of us. After walking in the deep, dark forest for days, I lost count after day seven. It was obvious we had reached a new territory.

"Mawu-Lisa!" I murmured, watching the waterfall. It was taller than twenty men standing on each other. The large expanse of water flowed outwards, probably to the river.

Dare walked forward and touched the water. He turned to me. "Do you want to bathe?" he asked.

"Are you crazy? Aren't we supposed to be fleeing?" I asked, angry and confused at his attitude.

He frowned for a moment and then it disappeared. He shrugged. "Suit yourself. You don't know when next you will get the opportunity," he said quietly, walking away.

I stood, staring into the wonder before me. Dare stood watching me.

"Turn around! Don't look until I tell you!" I shouted. He shrugged and turned around.

I put down my bundle and undid my wrapper, holding on to the recadé to avoid it falling. Glancing back, I confirmed that Dare's back was still turned away. I folded my wrapper with the recadé within its fold and placed it under my bundle, keeping them as close to the bank as possible. I walked into the warm water. The movement of the water was almost comforting. I looked across at Dare again. He was still looking away.

I pushed myself under the water. My tears fell freely as I swam under the water fall. My beloved's face appeared as I closed my eyes and wondered where he was. I stayed under the water for as long as I could and finally had to swim up for some air.

"Ẹyin taniyẹn?" someone shouted. It sounded from above me, so I swam back, away from the waterfall, to see two men standing on the rock above where the water cascaded down.

My heart faltered, as I looked to the bank for Dare. He was already running toward me. "Leave her alone!" Dare screamed.

I gasped in disbelief, realizing Dare had responded in Yoruba—Mama's native tongue. The two men gazed down at us and then turned to speak with each other. "We mean no harm, brother," they shouted back.

Dare swam into the water and stood in front of me. I gasped, looking down. The midday sun had managed to reveal my nakedness and not even the gushing water could hide it. The men were staring, unabashedly.

"Amelia, stay in until I get your wrapper," Dare said.

"No!" I shouted, swimming ahead of him. Grandmother's words rang in my ears. *Trust no one.*

My feet touched the bank and I breathed in deeply. I pushed back my shoulders and stepped out. There was silence as I picked up my wrapper carefully. I covered myself quickly, tying it firmly with the recadé in its folds. I turned around to see Dare still in the water, staring at me. "Dare!" I shouted. He blinked and then began swimming toward me. I looked up at the men again, but they were gone. Dare emerged from the water, dripping.

"Let's go, Amelia!" he said, grabbing my hand and pulling me toward the trees.

"Your things!" I shouted, pointing at his bundle lying a little distance from us.

He scampered to pick it up, almost falling. "Hurry!" he shouted, holding out his hand.

"This is no way to greet the chief's son when you have wandered onto his territory," a male voice said.

Dare pushed me behind him as two men approached—the same ones I suspected had been standing over the waterfall. Three men appeared behind them, holding sticks and rocks in their hands.

The speaker—clad in a simple cotton buba and pants—had his hands behind his back and kept moving closer to us until he was but a few steps away. His companion was richly dressed in a flowing cotton wrapper. He had a plain cream cap on his head. His neck was adorned with beads.

We remained quiet, holding our hands tight. By now, the three other men had circled us.

"Who are you and where have you come from?" the same man asked.

I looked at Dare. We had not discussed what we would tell people. He looked stonily back at the man, and I realized he was not going to say a word.

"We are from—" I began to speak in Yoruba. It had been so long, I was surprised the words still came out with the intonation mama had taught me.

"Ketou!" Dare shouted, gripping my hand tighter.

The man's face wrinkled up. "Ketou? What are you doing in these parts?" he asked.

The richly clad companion took two steps around me. His wrapper grazed my arm.

"We went to visit our Grandmother in her village close to Parakou," Dare said.

"Parakou? Hmmmm…" the man said, his eyes studying us. He turned to his companion, whose eyes had not left me since the conversation began. "Your eminence," the man said, bowing slightly.

I felt his eyes on me still as he began to speak. "What is your name?" His voice was low.

"Dare."

"Not you boy! The girl!" the first man said sharply.

"Oh…" Dare chuckled nervously, gripping my hand tighter still.

"Leave her hand for once. Or are you her husband?" the first man asked. Everything stood still as they waited. "You cannot just have been struck dumb, because I heard your sweet voice but a second ago." The one I could only guess was the prince said in his low voice.

I looked up into a young man's smiling face. His beard was tangled up and touched his chest. "Your name?" he asked curtly, sounding impatient.

"Yemisi," I said, naming the first name that came to mind.

He smiled, stepping back to look at me from head to toe. "Ah, Yemisi! That was my mother's name," he said.

The first man smiled too. "This is a good sign your eminence!" He said.

The prince nodded and stepped back. "You will return with us to my village," he said.

"But, we were on our way back home," Dare said.

The prince smiled again. "Were you?" he asked and then turned and began walking toward the trees.

The first man turned to us. "The prince will host you for a few days. This will give you some time to rest before you continue on your journey," he said, smiling, though it did not reach his eyes. Dare and I looked at each other. He turned and followed the prince. "Come along, the prince cannot be kept waiting," he called to us.

Dare shrugged and I inhaled deeply.

The three men moved closer, pushing us from the back. We followed the path close to the rocks, which had been hidden by the trees and shrubs.

"The village is not far, just beyond the water fall!" the prince called to us and he walked ahead, holding on the rocks. We walked silently behind with the two guards behind us. True to his word, we made it through the rocky paths and uphill. "We are just beyond the trees over there!" the prince said excitedly

I looked up to see a splattering of huts in the horizon.

"Where is this?" Dare asked behind me.

"This is the unknown village with no name," the prince said, laughing.

Dare turned to look back at me quizzically even as the laughter grew louder. The first man hurried forward to the prince and put his hand on his back.

"You must rest, your eminence," he said calmly.

The prince stopped laughing and looked around, his eyes focusing on me. "Take Yemisi to the visitors hut, but do it through the back way," he said. One of the guards took my arm. Dare moved closer. "No, not you. You will come with me," the prince said, waving Dare forward.

"Please, where are you taking my brother? We have to be together!" I shouted, panic washing over me.

The prince smiled. "Just as I suspected. You are siblings. This is wonderful. I feared I would have to sever a husband from his wife." He chuckled, looking at his companion who did the same. My heart pounded against my chest.

"What do you mean?" Dare asked.

The smile disappeared from the prince's face as he turned to Dare. "What I mean is, you slow witted boy, your sister is to be my wife in a few days. The oracle foretold that my wife would come from another place. I have been waiting for some time now. I will wait no longer," he said. Turning to his companion, he said, "Make sure she is given all that she needs."

Suddenly, something was placed over my face, almost covering my nose. I shouted, only to have my mouth stuffed with cloth. I felt myself lifted up.

"Don't worry Am...Yemisi! I *will* find you!" Dare shouted.

The prince and his companion laughed, followed by a sound like someone being hit repeatedly.

I cried, holding on to my bundle tighter. Suddenly, I was thrown over a guard's shoulder and he sprinted away. His harsh breath reached me as I felt myself transported over some rocky terrain. Then he stopped and stooped. Something creaked open and we entered an enclosed space.

"Yemisi, when I take this blindfold off, you must not go crazy. You will sit down on this floor quietly, or else," a male voice said in my ear.

I nodded, grasping my bundle close to me.

He pulled at the back of my head and the cloth fell off my face. I gasped, stepping back. The second guard was there, hands crossed over his chest, watching me. He came closer and grabbed the bundle from me.

"Leave it!" The guard who had carried me said.

The second one looked angry, but pushed it back to me.

"He said to give her what she needs, not take from her. Let's go!" the guard who had carried me said. He beckoned to the second one to follow him to the door. The latter glared at me and went out, making an indistinguishable noise and flinging his hands about. He went through the wooden structure, closing it firmly behind him.

I heard them standing outside, one talking angrily while the other kept making the same grunting noise. They were not going anywhere.

I looked around the room. This was not a visitor's room at all. The ground was muddy and infested with insects. In the corner was dry grass piled high to about the middle of my legs. I looked down at my feet, noticing something shining in the mud. Beside it was the cloth that had been used to cover my eyes. I picked up the shiny object and the cloth. The shiny object was a gold earring. I was not the first guest to occupy this hut. My heart beat faster as I realized what needed to be done immediately. Glancing quickly at the door, I pulled out the recadé tucked deeply in the folds of my wrapper. I pulled up the wrapper, which fell around my knees up to my waist and quickly tied the recadé with the cloth to my thigh just as I had seen Dare hide his dagger and covered it quickly with my wrapper.

I moved back to the wall and crouched down, pulling my legs around me, I opened my bundle, for the first time, seeing what grandmother had placed in it. There was the letter to the Alake, three sets of gold earrings that I knew were family heirlooms passed down from generations, silver bangles, a medium-sized pouch that held cowries, and there were my thread of gold beads from mama. I had forgotten about those. I dropped my gold beads and cowries into the pouch and hid it and the letter in the enclaves of my thigh with the recadé. It would be safe there…for the moment.

I sat back, leaning my head against the wall. The men had grown quiet now behind the wooden

structure—my only means of escape. The only remind-
ers that they were there was when they shifted their
bodies. I sat staring into the roof, crying silently for
help.

ᧁ

I counted seven sunsets while imprisoned in the hut.
My only visitors were the two guards, who brought
me one meal a day of watery garri in a dirty wooden
bowl. I felt safer with the guard who could speak than
with the dumb one. At least I would not catch him
watching me and biting his lips. The one who spoke
would not allow me to talk. He would raise his finger
at me and say "Sssh!" then immediately walk out. On
the eighth morning, the one who spoke came in, carrying a larger bowl with hot steam coming out of it.

He was smiling. "Yemisi, Good morning." He
placed the bowl on the ground and stepped back.
"Tonight, you will be wed to our chief's son," he said.

I sprang up. "Please! I cannot marry your chief's
son!"

He laughed, shaking his head. "It is already
done! The rituals have already been performed. The
only thing left is the consummation and that will be
tonight!" he said, beaming. The room spun around
me and I staggered back.

He grabbed my arm. "You must not get too excited.
I know this is all a lot to take in, but see how fortunate
you are—marrying the son of our chief. He will very
soon become the new chief of this place you know?
Come, sit." He sat me down gently and did the same.

"Look, you have caused me no problems while I have watched you, so I will do you this small favour before your brother is killed."

I gasped, placing my hand over my mouth.

He nodded. "Yes, your brother will be killed tonight. The very moment of your consummation with your husband he will be sacrificed as a token gift."

I broke down crying.

"Sssh! If you don't stop those tears, I will change my mind," he said quickly.

I grabbed his hand. "No! I am sorry. Please, let me see him one last time," I said through my tears.

He stared at me, as if trying to make up his mind.

"Please," I whispered.

He nodded. "All right. It will be just before the chief's son comes. I will have my second stay with you while I get him. No one must know I have brought him here, except my second," he said, wagging his finger at me.

I nodded. He got up.

"Now, eat your food. It is almost midday." He left immediately.

❧

The wooden slab opened and the dumb guard entered, carrying another steaming bowl of food. I looked down at the one brought in the morning. The rice still remained untouched. He looked down at it and frowned. Pushing it to the side with his foot, he placed the steaming bowl down— pounded yam and vegetable stew. The tears welled up in my eyes as I thought of Dossou. A sound escaped his throat as he pointed to his mouth. I shook my head and looked toward the door.

He came closer and I looked up to see his face contort in anger. He grabbed me by the throat and lifted me. I clawed at his head, struggling to breathe. He squeezed harder. I felt life leaving me and I dangled from his hand.

"What?" I heard a shout as someone entered. I felt a release on my throat, and then I was on the ground. A scuffling ensued between three bodies as I gasped for breath. Two bodies slammed into one on the floor, hitting away with an object. Soon, one body stopped struggling and lay still.

"You must run now."

My eyes finally focused and the two figures stood before as clear as day. Dare stood over the dead, dumb guard with a dagger in his hand dripping with blood. My guard stood at the foot of his former colleague, a rock in his hand. Dare looked across at me, his face expressionless. His hair had grown out and was unkempt. "Did you hear me, boy?" the guard said, leaning over and shaking his shoulder.

Dare blinked, looking down at his bloodied hand.

"We must run," I said softly.

The guard looked at me and nodded. I got up slowly.

He rushed to me and helped me up. "I will tell them you escaped. Take the path leading back to the stream...your brother knows the way. He has been here for seven days without blindfolds. Go!" He walked me to the door. Dare walked slowly behind us, still looking down at his hands.

"Wake up! Boy, you have become a *man* tonight! Take care of your sister here." He pushed us out pointing in the dark . "Run that way, he will be here soon."

I grabbed Dare's hand and ran.

❧

The days merged into each other. We trekked down deserted paths when we could, hiding when we heard footsteps drawing close. I had no idea how long we had been on the run. Dare confirmed that the last settlement we had sneaked through in the dead of night was Iboro. The village was small. They were friendly people that opened their homes to us. They didn't even have a mat to demarcate their entrance ways. We had gone into village once during the day, disguised in order to trade for some food. Dare had done all the talking while I stood back. That was when we heard of the devastation that had hit the palace.

The old woman bestowed on us a toothless grin, accepting the silver bangle I placed in her palm.

"These look expensive," she said, lifting her eyes to look at me.

"It is," Dare said.

"Where did you get these?" she asked.

I looked around at her stall, laden with flies perched on dried fish. "Mama. This was our late mother's," I said, silently asking my mother's forgiveness and wading off evil with my hand behind my back.

The old woman nodded. "Aah, your mother's. I can believe that. She must have been a very fashionable woman," she said, putting the bangle up in the sun.

Sounds of admiration came from her fellow traders who turned on seeing the reflection from the sun.

"We want fish, garri and—" I looked around, "—also, I need a new wrapper and buba," I said.

Her eyes traveled down my torn wrapper. She nodded. "That is fine," she said. Immediately, she called to a young girl sweeping the ground. "Bring a bag of the smoked fish and a satchel of garri. When you are done, go to Iya Posi and ask her to give you two yards of the adirẹ I picked out yesterday."

The child curtsied and went to the display table to begin picking out the fish.

"Please sit down on the bench over there. She will soon be done," the old woman said.

Dare and I looked at each other, unsure if to believe her.

She laughed. "Oya, take. Hold on to it. When she brings the food stuff and adirẹ, you can give it to me," she said, handing the bangle to me. I glanced at Dare again and he nodded. We sat down on the bench she had pointed to and waited.

People walked by us, talking loudly in good spirits. A man approached the old woman's stall. His cap was in his hand, flapping it intermittently around his ears and neck to wade off the flies.

"Mama, you have not retired from this job?" he asked, laughing.

The old woman turned around, her laughter joining his. "Folusho, mi! How is your mother?"

He prostrated, getting up quickly. "She is fine. She sends her greetings," he said.

"That is good. How is her business?" she asked.

"Well, you know with the war erupting in Danhomè, it has been hard for her to get to Kotonou to sell her wares."

My hand gripped Dare's thigh.

"What is going on thereabouts?" the old woman asked as she steadily built a pyramid from her dried fish.

"The French have finally infiltrated the great Danhomè. The great Gbèhanzin has fled into the forest."

I gasped.

Both of them looked at me. "What is wrong, my daughter?" she asked.

I shook my head, unable to speak.

"She is faint from hunger, Mama. Have you anything for her to eat?" Dare asked.

"Poor child! Yes, here, give her some of this garri I was soaking to eat for lunch." She passed a bowl to Dare. "Continue, so what is the situation now?" the old woman asked.

Dare fed me the garri with his hand. It tasted like wood as it passed down my throat.

"Gbèhanzin set fire to his palace so that the French would not gain control of it. He is waging war from the forest. I hear his family is also there with him," the man said.

"What a pity! Gbèhanzin is a great King. His father was great too. Why this must happen in his time, I do not know," the old woman said, shaking her head.

I nodded my head in affirmation, feeling an immediate nudge from Dare.

"Mama, here are the food stuffs and the cloth," the young girl said, standing before us.

"Good. Please give it to these people," the old woman said, walking toward us.

Dare took the items and I handed the bangle to her. "Thank you," we said quickly.

"Where will you be staying?" the old woman asked, her wise eyes fixed on us.

"We will be on our way back to our home," Dare said, already dragging me behind him.

"Where is that?" the old woman asked after our retreating backs.

∽

"A melia." Dare shook me awake.

"What is it?" I grumbled. It seemed like only a short while ago when I laid my head down.

"Sshhhh! Did you hear that?" he asked. His eyes had doubled in size as he crouched next to me under the tree. We were deep in the forest, just stopping for the night to rest. Tomorrow, we would be on our way again. Hopefully we were going in the right direction to Abẹokuta. If the directions given to us by the old man in Iboro were right, we should be.

I sprang up, listening for anything, but it was silent. I was concerned that Dare was going senile before my eyes. I peered at him and saw him gesture for me to be quiet and wait. That was when I saw it—a figure which was about a quarter of my size walking with sticks in its hands. Its tiny waist was covered in a raffia skirt to the ankles. Its tiny feet were bare. I looked at Dare to make sure he was seeing the same thing. His body was shaking uncontrollably, just like mine. When I looked back at the caricature, they were now two. This one had raffia leaves covering its breasts in addition to the lower torso. They were talking in low tones.

"Dare! What are they?" I whispered.

"I think they are the forest spirits. We mustn't fight them, Amelia. If we don't harm them, they will leave us alone."

One was approaching us, its eyes glittering in the dark. We heard its feet on the leaves and waited breathlessly. It was very small. It came very cautiously and at last stood a few inches away.

It peered into our faces and made that noise again. The shrillness rang straight into my ears, and I flung my head back in surprise, as did Dare. Instantly, the others appeared, brandishing bows and arrows. We scrambled close to the tree and clung to it.

"We didn't mean any harm! Please, please!" I was screaming at the top of my lungs, tears cascading down my face.

I felt Dare's hands clamp down on my mouth. The silence was deafening. I closed my eyes, unable to watch anymore. They moved closer. I could smell their odor—it was a distinctly pungent smell of people that lived in an enclosed place without much air. Then I felt something warm on my cheek. It was a hand. I opened one eye. The thing had its hand on my right cheek. It felt my tears with its fingers and peered at me again. It turned and made a noise to the others. They responded with similar noises. They were communicating in those same low tones. Finally it turned back to me and touched my face with both hands. It talked in lower tones now, as though placating me.

My eyes searched for Dare in the dark. He was stunned. The thing stepped back and beckoned to both of us to follow.

"Dare? What do we do now?" I asked, breathing very hard,

"Do as they say," he said.

It waited. I got up, at the same time searching for Dare's hand in the dark. I finally found it and held on. The thing walked ahead, still gesturing for us to follow. The others were now in full view, and they followed us. It was walking toward a rock. Certainly, we could not enter into a rock. It leaned forward and brushed back the large leaves that had covered the large entrance. We stood waiting. A hand pushed me from behind. We looked back to see female looking up at us, holding a pointed stick.

The entrance was pitch black. I held on to Dare's hand as he followed the little creature. It was making those noises again. The underground entrance was leading somewhere. We followed in the dark. I could feel the little frames of two or three more creatures pressed against me as went further. We kept walking. I dared not speak to Dare. This close together, they could harm us very quickly if they wanted.

The darkness began to give way to orange light from afar. There were about a hundred of them, lying in small clusters. A central fireplace was burning. We had reached their commune. The entourage behind us reduced as they went to their homes. The first creature that had found us kept going, waving to us to continue following him. Behind us were two others who had been instructed to watch us. A few of them had looked up from their sleeping positions when we walked by, but most just turned around and slept. It seemed seeing beings our size was a normal occurrence.

Soon, we stopped in front of a figure that was sitting, as though waiting for us. It watched us steadily, its yellow eyes lighting up. It spoke to the one that had brought us, and it replied. The one that brought us stepped back behind us and waited. Finally, the seated one came forward, its animal odor was overpowering. I began to shake, falling backward.

"Amelia! Amelia!" I heard Dare's voice from afar. I wanted to answer him, but couldn't. I felt my eyes closing, and fell back into nothingness.

When I opened my eyes, Dare was staring down at me, calling my name softly.

I looked beside him and there was the creature too. It was a little bigger than the others. It had human features, but very dark, like the earth. It moved back when it noticed I was awake. "You are now awake. Good," it said in Mama's tongue.

I sat up with Dare's help. The creature had sat down on a stool, its short stumpy legs crossed at the ankles. "You are Fon," it said.

I grabbed Dare by the arm in horror.

"It is all right, Amelia," Dare said, patting me on the back, "I told him."

The creature stared at me. "I know you must be scared, Princess Amelia, but I want to put your mind at rest. We do not hurt people, unless they plan to hurt us," it said. "We travel deep within the forest and the rocks where men fear to go. We hear the deep dark secrets. Things planned in the dead of night. We know of the war waging in your land," it said.

I breathed deeply.

"Where are you headed?" it asked, its yellow glittering eyes fixed on us.

"Abẹokuta," Dare and I said.

It nodded. "If you wish to go to Abẹokuta, you will be led there," it said.

We kept watching each other. Suddenly, it got up and came forward. I was paralyzed with fear.

"There's no need to fear. I keep to my word. I will let you go. You have caused me and my people no harm, why should I?"

I nodded, not quite believing that it would let us go. I watched it call the same creature that led us in. They spoke quietly. The leader returned. "Sleep in my space tonight. Tomorrow, you will be taken to Abẹokuta."

"Thank you," Dare said.

It nodded, and walked away. Immediately, three of its kind arrived with large plantain leaves to place on the ground. They gestured to us to lie down.

"Come Amelia," Dare said, pulling me. I lay down, feeling the ground around me.

"Dare, we forgot our bundles!" They were still out there in the forest.

Dare shrugged. "We can still get them on our way tomorrow."

I felt under my wrapper. The most important items were still there. We lay down side by side, taking in the smells, happy to be alive.

༄

We were already awake and waiting when the one that had brought us arrived, stretching itself awake. It walked ahead of us, leading us through a labyrinth of rocks. We passed by more little creatures who were just waking up. They looked at us with curiosity, and then continued with their activities. The creature held lighted firewood as we made our way through a labyrinth of stone tunnels.

I hit my head on what looked like the roots of a tree that had grown into the earth. Dare stumped his toes several times on stones that poked out of the ground. We walked for over an hour in silence, except for the few times the creature would look back, calling for us to hurry. Eventually, we reached an opening. The creature climbed out and waited for us as we did the same.

"Dare, this is not the way we came in through!" I shouted, noticing the change in greenery. The forest had given way to shorter grass and trees. The air seemed dustier. I felt that we had reached foreign soil. It was something in the air. My heart mourned for home.

"You are right!" Dare said, looking around.

"Our food was in our bundles, Dare. What do we eat now?" I asked, shaking my head.

"We will soon be in Abẹokuta. We can survive until then," he said.

There was a rumbling noise and I looked down at my stomach, the source of the sound. The creature chuckled, its stubby fingers touching its stomach. Dare laughed and I joined in. It held out its other hand, a small pouch dangling from it.

"What is that?" I asked. Dare went forward and took it.

It made a noise, gesturing to Dare to open it.

He opened the pouch, lifting it to his face. His hands disappeared into it.

"What is in there?" I asked, moving closer.

He opened up his palm. "Kola nut," he said. I glanced at the creature who was watching us. "Thank you," I said.

The creature stood to the side and pointed toward the trees. I nodded and put my hands together to show gratitude. Its yellow eyes glimmered again, and then it disappeared back into the opening.

We walked quietly for some time. The sun came out, and we kept walking through the short trees, saying little. I glanced up at Dare's long, lean back. He had filled out since coming back to the palace. We had grown even farther apart now than before he had disappeared with Ma Bolanle.

I felt a sharp pain in my ankle—a reminder of my hen attack. Ever since that fateful day, I experienced sudden sharp pains, sometimes as frequent as twice a day, and other times not until the passing of two moons. "Dare!" I called out, stopping to massage it.

He turned around. "What is wrong?" he asked.

"I have to stop...my ankle has started hurting again. Look, let's stay under that tree over there," I said, pointing.

He looked down at me. "All right, but just for a little while." He took me by the arm and almost carried me to the tree. We sat down, looking out into the dusty horizon. We were nearing the end of our journey. I could tell by the narrow trail which looked well traveled. Dare untied the pouch and handed me a kolanut. I squeezed my face in disgust. He pushed it into my hand.

"You better eat something! Your stomach will continue to sing if you don't." He chuckled.

I hissed, biting into the hard nut. The bitter taste dissolved into my mouth and began to quiet my stomach. "Dare," I said quietly, my heart beating faster.

He looked across at me, silent.

"Where is your mother?" I asked.

He did not look surprised. "She is dead," he said flatly. I gasped, dropping the kolanut, my hand grabbing my chest. I burst into tears. "There is no need to cry. She has gone to a better place. This world did not treat her well."

I stared at him through my tears. "What happened to her? Did you tell Mama?" I asked.

He nodded, looking away. "Mama knows what happened to her friend...her sister."

"But...they just called themselves sisters, right?" I asked, holding my breath.

He chuckled, his eyes becoming serious as they burrowed into me. "Your mother kept too many secrets from you, Amelia."

"What are you talking about?" I asked, getting angry.

"Why do you think I can speak the *secret* language, and you never knew until we were imprisoned by that crazy prince?" he asked.

My mouth suddenly went dry.

He chuckled. "Have you asked yourself why our mothers were the closest in all the wives? Always spending time together?"

I shook my head. He tapped his knee. "Your mother came from Abẹokuta, and so did mine," he said quietly.

I laughed drily. "Dare, you are crazy! Your mother came from Ketou that is why her name is Bolanle! She named you after her father, that is why you are called Dare!" I hissed at him.

He shook his head. "Then how do I know exactly how *your* mother came to be in Danhomè? How do I know about the gold beads she gave to you, and which you wore until recently? My mother was there too."

My mouth fell open.

"Let me tell you how both Ajo—Ajokẹ to be precise—and little Bolanle came to be in the Kingdom of Danhome."

My mouth moved along with his, reciting the very experience Mama had gone through.

"Ajọke mi, ọkọ mi!" The woman called out in a sweet voice to her daughter who was coming down the grassy path-

way to their home. They lived about five miles from Abẹokuta in a little township. Their home consisted of three huts that were shrouded by tall trees.

Ajokẹ's mother was waiting, as she usually did every afternoon, waiting for Ajokẹ to return from the missionary school. Ajokẹ knelt down before her mother, almost bursting with excitement. "Mama, I am back! How was your day?"Ajokẹ asked.

"It was fine. As usual I went to the farm," her mother said, pulling her up. "Don't dirty your uniform! You know this is the only one you have. Come inside. Let me get you some food."

The hut was fairly large, with two mats, two wooden stools, and a section for their clothing piled one on top of the other. Ajokẹ glanced at her mother. who was looking into the pot. She couldn't contain herself any longer. "Mama, do you know what I learned today?" Ajokẹ asked, beaming from ear to ear.

Her mother turned around and smiled. "No, tell me."

"I learned the Lord's prayer. Everything! Do you want me to teach you?"Ajokẹ asked.

Her mother nodded enthusiastically, hands on her waist. She watched with admiration at her little miracle. Ajokẹ was her only child. After several painful miscarriages, she had finally had Ajokẹ at an old age. During her years of waiting, her in-laws had knocked on her door several times, accusing her of being a witch and eating up her unborn children. In a desperate move, the in-laws found a second wife for Ajokẹ's father. The second wife had also not been quick in having a child. Her first child, a girl, was born four years after Ajokẹ. She had her second child, a girl too, a year later. Ajokẹ's mother was vindicated. Ajokẹ's father did not interfere in raising Ajokẹ, giving full rein to her mother to raise her. She was not male and would soon take on someone else's name.

Ajokẹ was enrolled in the missionary school established by the Church Missionary Society—CMS. Ajokẹ's mother wanted to ensure that her daughter was literate. Her friends had shaken their heads, telling her she was throwing her daughter to the wolves. **What would happen when she started growing breasts?** *They had asked.* **The only girl in a school of boys!** *Ajokẹ's mother had laughed at them. That would never happen in a Missionary school.*

Ajokẹ pointed to the stool. "It's better if you sit down, this will take some time. Now, repeat after me," she said.

Her mother sat and looked up expectantly.

"Our father, who art in heaven,"Ajokẹ began to say slowly.

"Awa fada...Who...who...who..."her mother said hesitantly.

"Who art in heaven, Mama!" Ajokẹ shouted excitedly.

Heavy footsteps sounded outside. "Iya Ajọkẹ!"

The male voice called out. They glanced at each other and ran to the doorway. Like all the huts in Abẹokuta and its towns, the door was demarcated with a wooden gate that reached the waist of an adult of average height. On the other side of the gate stood a panting, lanky man—the male version of Ajokẹ's mother. It was Lanre, her twin. He was sweating profusely. His woven cap was in his hand.

"Lanre, what is it?" Ajokẹ's mother asked. She opened the gate for him, and he rushed in.

"Have you not heard what is going on?" Lanre asked. He looked around as if searching for someone.

"Heard what, you numskull? I swear to God, you must have dropped from the sky the way you behave!" Ajokẹ's mother shouted in anger.

Ajokẹ stifled the giggle with her fist, watching their interaction. They made her wish she had a twin.

"Hmm, Iya Ajokẹ, Abẹokuta is upside down! The Danhomè people are on their way to destroy us!" Lanre shouted, jumping from one foot to the other.

She moved closer to the jumping jack before her. His eyes protruded with fear. "Lanre, take it easy. Take it easy." She finally made him sit down on the stool, using the end of her wrapper to blow some air on him. "Ajokẹ, go out and play, please. I will call you once your food is ready," she said, glancing at her daughter.

Ajokẹ left without complaining, knowing that her usual spot for eavesdropping awaited at the backyard under the window.

"Iya Ajokẹ, I overheard the missionaries talking about it when I went to drop my usual tithe offering of yam tubers. They say that the Danhomeans are already crossing the Ogun river and will be here tonight!"

The Dahomeans were a crude and barbaric people. Tales of their ritual killings held the Ẹgba people in a grip of fear. A few years before, they had attempted to ambush and take over Abẹokuta, but had failed. Villagers lived in constant fear that they might return.

"Lanre! Lanre! I have warned you to mind your business! How can you be saying something like this to alarm us?" Ajokẹ's mother asked in exasperation.

He swore by all the gods he knew, starting with Olodumare, Ifa, Sango, and Ogun.

"Stop swearing. You call yourself a Christian and you still swear by these fetish gods."

At least Ajokẹ's mother had been true to herself about why she associated with the missionaries—to give her child an education. No one was sure why Lanre had decided to convert to Christianity. It certainly wasn't evident in his actions.

"Reverend Forbes was in Danhomè and saw it all during the annual customs. You know the annual customs, don't you?"Lanre asked.

Reverend Forbes was the resident head Missionary in Abẹokuta. Ajokẹ shook her head, almost hitting the mud wall. She had forgotten where she was hiding.

Her mother must have shaken her head too, because Lanre went on to explain. *"The annual customs are held every year by the King of Danhomè to pay homage to the gods and also to showcase his power and wealth to the people and visitors. A lot of human sacrifices are made and the poor people are sent off to become messengers to the dead royalty. It is a terrible thing to watch. He saw the popular female army—about two thousand of them! They were screaming **Give us Abẹokuta! If we do not take it down, bury us in its ruins!** That is how he learned that they were coming. In a day or two, they will be at our walls!"*

Ajokẹ's mother clapped her hands in amazement, unsure of what to do. *"Lanre, thank you for telling me. First, why don't we eat, and then we can talk more about it?"* she asked.

He looked up at her in amazement. *"Eat?"* He pulled on his right ear. *"Have you not heard what I've been saying? Danhomè will be upon us in less than a day. Carry your things and move to Abẹokuta proper. You will be safer there. Take Ajokẹ into the school where they can watch over her.*

When it is safe, you can both come back. By the way, where is your husband and the other wife?"

A hiss escaped Ajọkẹ mother's lips as she looked toward the window where her daughter crouched.

*"**That** one? He has gone to his usual three-day sacrifice to Ifa, and as usual, that follow-follow wife and her two children have gone with him. She will do anything to be in his good graces."*

Lanre stood up and said, "Very good then, the more reason for you to leave, now-now!" He looked around. "Ajọkẹ! Where are your things? Please pack them and let's go!" he shouted.

Ajọkẹ rushed into the house. Her mother pulled her to her side. "Irọ, no! Why don't you go and get your two wives and children and we will meet you in Abẹokuta," she said.

Lanre eyed his sister suspiciously, and seemed to give up, shrugging his shoulder. "Oda, very well. Don't say I didn't come and warn you o! I have done my duty as a brother and a twin. You have always been very headstrong, Iya Ajọkẹ, very headstrong." He began to walk to the door.

"Lanre, don't start again. I am still older than you by five minutes! Thank you for coming. Don't worry, we will see you later!" Ajokẹ's mother waved, dismissing him.

He placed his cap on, and shook his head. Looking down at his niece, he smiled that special smile reserved just for her. "Ajọkẹ, ọkọ iya. Take care of your mother," he said.

"Yes, Uncle." She waved to him, but still held on to her mother. There was a sad look in his eyes. He turned and walked out, whistling a tune.

༄

The evening passed, and nothing happened. Lanre had raised a false alarm, it seemed. The next morning, Ajọkẹ prepared for school. She had put on her uniform and was just about to have breakfast.

"Ajọkẹ, let me go and warm your stew to eat with your yam in the backyard. I will be back," her mother called to her, rushing out immediately. Ajọkẹ sat down quietly, waiting, Suddenly, her mother ran back in panting. "Ajọkẹ, we must leave! I just saw our neighbor, Iya Adamu, running. She said she saw a stranger hiding in the forest as she went to fetch firewood. We must hurry!" She did not wait for Ajọkẹ to respond. Gathering a few clothes, she rolled it up into a cloth bundle and placed it on her head. She then grabbed Ajọkẹ's hand. "Don't worry, I have put some food in here, we will eat once we get to Abẹokuta."

She pulled the child after her out of the hut. Ajọkẹ's heart thundered wildly against her chest, feet barely touching the ground as they made their way through the trees to Abẹokuta.

It took them half the day, but they made it unscathed. Abẹokuta was overcrowded. People had come from other townships, scared and full of news of an army of fetish cannibals advancing. Mother and daughter made their way to the missionary house, a large hut built with corrugated iron roof—the first of its kind in Abẹokuta.

Reverend Forbes was there in the midst of frantic people. "My children, please be calm. God is in control. The One who made it possible for the enemy to reveal his plans, will also fight for us. Please, be calm!"

The room—which was a classroom during the week, and converted into a church on Sunday mornings and Wednesday evenings—was now filled with worshippers of all religions. .

Ajọkẹ's mother walked up to the circle in a determined manner, holding on to Ajokẹ's hand tight. "Reverend!" she called out. Her honey-toned shoulder shimmered with sweat, her neck stretched long to ensure she was seen by the reverend.

"Iya Ajọkẹ! It is good to see you. Your brother had reported that you refused to leave yesterday," Reverend said.

She ignored the comment. "Reverend, are you very sure that the Danhomè army is upon us? Is it true what we hear you saw in Abomey?" she asked.

Everyone waited breathlessly. The reverend—a tall, white man, with thinning gray hair—looked directly at Ajọkẹ's mother above the other heads. His eyes were steady behind the thick glasses. "Yes, everything you may have heard has some truth in it. I cannot go on about everything, but I will tell you that the threat is real and they are advancing. We must be very prayerful."

The noise began again as everyone wanted to ask a question. Reverend Townsend—the resident missionary in Abẹokuta—came in, and gestured for quiet again. He was Ajokẹ's teacher at the missionary school. She enjoyed hearing his stories about England and his family. He had a Grand-niece named Amelia. She wrote him letter,s which he some-times read to the entire class. Ajọkẹ often imagined changing her name to Amelia. A portion of the crowd left Reverend Forbes and rushed to Reverend Townsend, talking nonstop.

"Come, Ajọkẹ, let us sit down. You must be very hungry," her mother said.

They sat on a bench beside a family of five. The chil-dren were small, between the ages of one and six. The mother sat beside them, holding the baby who was sucking noisily. Ajokẹ's mother gestured to her to turn her back to them before she handing her the roasted yam. "Eat quickly, Ajọkẹ!" She

*said desperately, her eyes darting around. People were filling
up the school. There was hardly any room to move.*

"Please ma...please ma..."

*The woman holding the baby was looking at Ajoke's
mother pleadingly. One of the children started crying.*

*Ajoke mother was looking everywhere except at the
woman. Ajoke nudged her, very embarrassed at this display
of indifference. "Mama, she is calling you!" Ajoke whispered.*

*She looked at Ajoke, and then at the woman. "Oh, sorry,
my mind was elsewhere," she said.*

*The woman looked very tired, as though she had traveled
a long distance. "Can you please give my children some food?
We left our village in a hurry and did not pack anything to
eat."*

*Mama sighed heavily, as though she had expected the
request. "I barely have enough to feed my daughter...but—"
She paused and dug into the bundle, bringing out half a
slice of roasted yam. The woman thanked her profusely, and
then proceeded to cut the piece into four parts, keeping none
for herself. They all ate in silence. Once in a while, the little
girl who sat closest to Ajoke would flash her a mischievous
smile, and Ajoke would smile in return. Often, Ajoke would
play with the gold beads on her wrist, wondering where her
father—who had designed the beads—was with her sisters
and second mother.*

*The day wore on with people moving in and out of the
building, some milling around the compound. As the sun set,
there were sounds of heavy marching in the distance. Everyone got up, rushing to the doorway.*

*"No, Ajoke! Stay here with the other children. Do not
move!" Ajoke's mother said before running outside to see
what was happening. Ajoke and her new friend glanced at*

each other. They appeared to be thinking the same thing. They watched their mothers disappear into the crowd and followed.

Crouching between the legs of the adults, they made their way forward until they could see the soldiers marching past. They wore the recognizable warrior attire with cowries sewn into the front and flat whitecaps. They were singing war songs, their faces stoic and eyes unblinking. There were thousands of them. Ajọkẹ felt herself being pushed along by the crowd. She held on tightly to her friend, wishing she would not let go.

"Get out of the way! They are at our walls! Get out of the way so we can hold them back!" the commandant shouted, his blood-red cap bobbing up and down. The crowd pushed back. The push broke the grasp Ajọkẹ had on the little hand. The little girl let out a faint cry, which was immediately overshadowed by the crowd's screams. Ajọkẹ looked about wildly, and finally saw what looked like a little foot through the sea of legs. She followed, pushing through the frantic crowd. She realized she couldn't even call her if she needed to. She didn't know her name.

By now, Ajọkẹ had run through the thick crowd, past the huts, and now was running toward the rocky path leading to the rocks. She saw the little girl hiding behind some rocks. Ajọkẹ gulped. They had had gone farther than she had thought. It had gotten dark. Evening had crept up on them. It was eerily quiet.

"Little girl, let's go! Our mothers will be worried. This place is not safe," Ajọkẹ called out.

They had reached Olumo rock. It was a place that symbolized a safe haven for the people of Abẹokuta. During times of war, villagers had hidden in these same rocks. However, tonight, it loomed ominously over the two girls. Ajọkẹ saw a small figure about ten feet from her scuttle further into the rocks. It was rumored that there were spirits in there. Rituals were made and the spirits were brought sacrifices here. Ajoke lingered at the entrance. "Little girl!"Ajoke called out again.

She heard a step behind her and turned. There was nothing. She hurried back to the path to lead her back to town. The little girl screamed again. Ajoke tripped in her effort to run faster and fell to the ground. Footsteps sounded behind her, and then a strange language was spoken between two indistinguishable voices. It was hard to tell if they were male or female. As Ajoke turned, she felt a sharp pain on the back of her head, and then darkness.

It was still dark, when Ajoke opened her eyes. She struggled to raise her hand, and then realized that it was bound to her sides. Her feet refused to move, it was bound to something heavy, like wood. She couldn't scream. Her mouth was filled with what tasted like cloth.

Someone move, and then several footsteps were heard approaching. Ajoke began to shake. The evil was porous. It was sucking the breath out of her. Ajoke could feel eyes on her; and then the same strange language was muttered. Someone else replied. It dawned on Ajoke—she was not in the missionary school, and these were not her people. They were the enemy and they had taken her. She began to cry. Soon, another cry was heard close by. It was a little child—the little girl.

"Is that you little girl? Are you all right? Are you hurt?"

Ajoke shouted out to her. The little girl only cried louder. The stranger's voice said something sharp over Ajoke. Though she couldn't understand, Ajoke knew it was a warning to shut up. She lay there listening as they moved around. Intermittently, high pitched cries came from bodies lying all around. They all sounded like children.

Gun shots were fired immediately, followed by movement around them . They talked harshly as they approached the bodies. Ajokẹ felt the rope between her legs untied and was pulled up into a standing position. She staggered backward, and then hit against what felt like a tree trunk. The faceless captors moved about quickly and untied the others. One came back and shoved Ajokẹ forward, talking harshly. She took a short step and then another. They were being taken away. Ajokẹ felt the tears falling down her face. This was one time she wished she had listened to her mother.

༄

I gasped, leaning forward to grab Dare's hand.

"Your mother was the little girl wasn't she?" I asked, not believing it until I saw him nodding. "How... how did they meet again? Mama was bought by Na Zevoton...how?" I asked, my voice trailing off.

"By chance. My mother was already working as a slave in the palace and your father took a liking to her."

My eyes fell to the ground in shame. "You don't have to continue," I murmured, knowing how difficult this must be for him.

He smiled wearily. "I am used to being called the bastard child of Ma Bolanle. The fact that I am not the child of the great King Gbèhanzin has been my greatest reproach in the kingdom of Danhome." His voice was cold. "My mother did not force herself on your father. He never asked her if she was seeing someone before he took her. She was already pregnant with me... when he took her. It was *not* her fault."

I gripped his hand tighter. "Is that why she was never really accepted by the other wives?" I asked. He nodded. My mind traveled back to the fateful time both had left and come back. "Dare," I whispered, wishing I did not have to ask this question.

"What else do you need to know?" he asked stonily.

"Why did you run away that first time? Who was the man you both ran away with?"

He was quiet, looking into the distance. Finally sighing heavily, he looked at me. "That was King Glele's personal servant...and my father."

I was quiet, my mouth twisted in shock. That was when Dare had come back withdrawn, never himself again.

"You obviously know what your father did to my father. He was found with his eyes gorged out, and his arms and legs amputated."

I looked down. "I'm so sorry Dare, for everything... for treating you the way I did," I whispered.

He withdrew his hand from my grip. "You were only being your *true* self, Amelia. I can't blame you, beloved daughter of the great Gbèhanzin."

His eyes flashed with anger for a second, and then disappeared. I froze in fright. He glanced at my face and laughed, throwing back his head. He stood up. "Come, we have wasted enough time. We must never talk of this again. The past is the past, all right?" He held out his hand.

I gazed up at him. His face was smiling now. "Come, my sister. You are still my sister, Amelia. I will always take care of you, just like your mother took care of mine."

I took his hand and he pulled me up, engulfing me in his arms. We began our journey again in a comfortable silence.

❦

"Wait for me a moment, Dare. I have to ease myself," I said, already walking away. Satisfied that there was enough distance, I crouched down behind a tree and opened my legs to feel my inner thigh. I touched the letter and pulled it out from under the tied cloth holding my possessions. The letter was tucked back firmly into my bosom under the folds of my wrapper.

I had my head down as I walked out to meet Dare. We fell in step, sharing the trodden path.

"Amelia, I think we need to talk about what to do once we arrive Abẹokuta. How do we go about seeing the Alake?" he asked.

"What do you mean? I thought it was as simple as walking into the Alake's palace and stating who we are," I said.

He shook his head. "Are you sure he will believe us? Even if he does, what if his councilmen don't and they influence his decision? I'm just trying to make sure we have another plan if this doesn't work."

"But it has to, Dare. It has to," I said.

"Remember what Na Zevoton said. We cannot trust just anyone," he said firmly.

I nodded, stopping as we approached the looming rocks ahead. We looked at each other, and then began walking faster, tripping at times over the rocks beneath our feet.

"We are here, Dare," I whispered, gazing up at rocks which were now just a few feet away. We had reached Abẹokuta. The creature had kept its word. It had brought us right to it. We stood staring for a while, unsure of what to do. Then we heard movement behind the rocks.

"Who is that? Who goes there?" The voice came from behind the rocks overhead. "I said who goes there? Are you both deaf?"

"It is me and my brother," I shouted back.

"And who are you? Are you from these parts?"

"No. We are from Abomey."

"Abomey? Is trouble not brewing there? How did you make it here?"

"We left before the trouble started," I shouted back.

By now, we could see the heads of men peeking through the rocks. "How are we sure you do not bring the trouble with you? Confess who you are and what you want, now!" This was a different voice, more authoritative.

I gulped. "I am Princess Amelia, daughter of the great shark, Gbèhanzin. I come in peace, and bring with me a message from my father to the Alake." Dare hit me on the arm, but I shoved it off, determined that we would be granted access.

A long pause ensued and I could feel our fate being debated behind the rocks. Finally, a tall man clad in a dyed red top that was covered in cowries and feathers appeared. He walked confidently toward us— he appeared to be walking on air. His head was covered with a red cap. "Are you who you say you are?" he asked, finally standing in front of us.

I nodded. His eyes narrowed. "Because if you lie, you pay with your life."

I looked him straight in the eye. "Yes, as I said, I am Princess Amelia, daughter of the great shark, and this is my brother."

He looked at me, then even longer at Dare. We looked tattered and worn out, and obviously could not harm a fly.

"Why is it that you speak Yoruba? And even the Ẹgba dialect too?" His eyes narrowed suspiciously as he waited for a response.

"We had a servant from Ketou who taught us how to speak it," I said, not batting an eye.

He seemed to be satisfied with the answer. He turned to the rocks and shouted, "Let them come through!"

"Ake, how are you sure they speak the truth?" One asked.

The one before us turned, and held out his hand. "Give me the message," he said.

My hand went to my chest. I pulled out the letter, Dare's eyes widening in disbelief. I moved forward to give it to the man. Dare grabbed my hand. "No, Amelia!" he whispered urgently.

The man threw back his head and laughed. "What? You, little boy, dare to stop her!"

He held out his hand and waited. I dropped the letter in it. He broke the seal, his eyes consuming the contents of the letter. Finally, he looked up from the letter his eyes devouring us as though seeing us for the first time.

ABẹOKUTA

South-Western Nigeria

c. 1895 – c. 1897

SOJOURNERS

Circa 1895

We had not met with the Alake yet. The
red-clad chieftain—Ake, whom we had met
at the gates—was a major in the Alake's
army. He was feared greatly for his physical strength
and juju. When we talked with the villagers, and told
them our story, they claimed that we were fortunate.
Ake normally did not give trespassers a chance to speak
before wielding his cutlass upon their necks. Villagers were used to him bringing severed heads back to
the palace rather than what they saw—two youngsters
trailing after him.

"You will follow me to my home for now. My wife
will take care of you while I gain audience with the
Alake," Ake had instructed us as we entered Abẹokuta.
Dare and I glanced quickly at each other.

Ake had turned back, as though reading our minds. "I cannot take you to the Alake. He is too busy right now. Be glad you have a place to stay in the meantime."

"We thank you," I stammered while Dare bowed his head slightly. As we followed after him, pushing past sweaty bodies in the market, I realized how slaves must have felt as they came into Danhome—bound, alone and frightened.

Ake's wife had welcomed us well. She was a tall, heavyset woman with little to say. A look from her sent everyone scampering around.

Our first nights were spent in the children's hut. There were twelve children in all, ranging from the age of six to twenty. They watched us with curiosity as we ate hungrily in the corner, day after day.

On the fifth night, the eldest approached us. He was nothing like his parents—barely five feet tall and stocky. His rotund body jiggled as he placed one foot in front of the other.

"You people, how long are you staying in our compound? Isn't it time you were on your way?" he asked.

Dare and I looked at each other.

"You!" he shouted, kicking Dare in the thigh. Dare scampered up, bracing himself.

"Are you deaf? I asked you how long are you here for?" he had asked.

The other children had drawn closer by now.

"Tope, leave them alone!" A taller female version of the boy came forward, hands on her hips—his sister, Kemi. She had never said a word up until then,

I suppose satisfied just watching us from across the room.

"Hmm, if no one else talks, I know you will! Look, mind your business!" he scolded.

"You mind *your* business! What have they done to you to deserve such treatment? Shameless boy! Better go and find someone else to harass!"

He ignored her and turned to us again. "I hear you are from the royal house of Gbèhanzin? Is that true?" he asked.

A gasp came from the group gathered.

"Answer me!" Tope stamped his feet, his voluminous stomach bounced with each movement.

"Yes," I said, standing up, ready to defend Dare this time.

"Does that mean you are a princess?" This voice was younger, but very strong. It came from a girl of about fourteen.

"Yes, I am Princess Amelia, daughter of the great shark." The distinct feeling of pride swelled in my chest as I spoke of my father.

"I don't believe you. Why would a Princess come this far without her guards?" Tope asked, circling us and glaring. He reminded me of a lion about to pounce on his prey.

"You are so daft, Tope! Have you been living under a rock, or have you not heard of the war going on between Danhomè people and the French? The Princess barely escaped capture!" Kemi said.

Tope hissed, tapping his feet. "I don't believe that you're a Princess! Why aren't you at the Alake's palace? Why here?"

"We are sorry if we are bothering you in anyway, I am sure it will be for only a short time," Dare said curtly.

I tried to stay calm, but could feel the anger rising up within.

Tope hissed again. "I don't care, I just want you out of here by tomorrow morning! This hut is already too crowded for all of us!"

The other children began to speak all at once, some agreeing with him, others not.

"What is all this?" A harsh deep voice broke the noise, and they all huddled together. Ake appeared, his cowries jingling all over his body.

"Baba, Tope started it! He doesn't believe that the princess is who she says she is, so he asked her to leave!" It was the fourteen-year-old again. She spoke boldly.

"Is that right Tope?" He turned to the now crouching boy. "What gives you the right to insult or harass anyone I bring into this compound?" Suddenly, Ake's fist slammed into his son's jaw. The children scattered, leaving Tope squirming on the floor. Ake turned to Dare and I, anger flashing in his eyes. "Both of you be ready tomorrow. I will be taking you to someone who can be of help."

"Who? Will this person take us to the Alake?" I asked.

"Do not ask questions. When you get there, you will know!" he shouted and walked away.

The children stood together, watching us, except Kemi who kept glancing over. Dare and I walked over to sit under the tree outside the hut. Soon, we heard footsteps coming toward us.

Kemi smiled, looking down at us. "Amelia, I'm about to go and take a bath at the bathing shed. I already fetched the water. Do you want to take a bath too?"

"A shed? What is that?" I asked.

She looked surprised. "It's a wooden shelter father built for us, for privacy when bathing. Come, let me show you." She reached down and took my hand. I got up with her. Dare held me back.

"Dare, your sister will be all right," Kemi said, laughing heartily.

I laughed along. "I won't be long, Dare," I said.

He released my hand and turned away.

Kemi made a comical face and then pulled me after her. "This your brother! He is too protective," Kemi said as we walked to the back of the compound. There it was. The wooden structure I had walked by a few times. There was an opening in the back. I peered in and saw two pots of water.

"Why don't you have your bath first? I will wait out here," Kemi said.

I glanced at her, unsure of what to do.

"Just use the bowl on the ground beside the pot. I have some black soap inside the bowl," Kemi said as I walked in slowly.

I took off my wrapper, the sight of the récade a reminder of a mission unfulfilled. I untied the torn piece of cloth that held my worldly possessions. There was now an indelible mark on my thigh. The gold beads made a rattling noise. I held my breath, waiting for Kemi to speak. She moved about, playing with an object on the ground. I folded my possessions in my wrapper and placed it on the ground.

"You can't leave your wrapper there!" Kemi shouted, appearing in the door way.

I grabbed my wrapper to the chest in surprise. "Why?" I asked.

"It's going to get wet, silly!" She sounded surprised.

I looked down, feeling the objects. Kemi laughed again, raising her hands.

"All right, all right! Just put it down just outside the door. Nobody will steal your precious wrapper," she said, turning and walking away behind the shed. I tiptoed to the doorway and placed the heavy wrapper just outside the entrance of the shed on the left hand side.

I dropped the black soap on the ground and then poured the water in the bowl over my head. It felt cool as I splashed it over my head. I closed my eyes, enjoying the pleasure of a much-needed bath. It could not have been that long, but when I opened my eyes, there was Kemi again, looking at me wide-eyed. "Amelia! I have been calling you over and over! Are you all right?"

I blinked, cleaning the water from my face. "What? I'm sorry, I didn't hear you," I said, walking toward her.

"You've been in there for sometime now. I must have my bath too!"

I picked up my wrapper, feeling its contents, my heart beating faster.My mouth went dry and tears sprang to my eyes. "Kemi!" I grabbed her.

"Yeh! Amelia! What is it?" she asked, pulling my hands off her.

"Who came here? Tell me!" I whispered.

"No one! I was here, except when I just went to ease myself."

"You went to ease yourself?" I whispered. The shed spun around me. Kemi's arms reached out to steady me. "Amelia!" she shouted.

"I'm all right," I whispered, leaning against the shed.

"Are you sure?" she asked.

I nodded. "I'll put on my wrapper now. Thank you," I whispered, holding my wrapper close, feeling the objects that remained.

Kemi stared at me for some time, and then shrugged and disappeared behind the demarcation again. I quickly pulled out the pouch to make sure the jewelry was still in there. There, my gold beads. I tied the pouch back on my inner thigh, my wrapper firmly around me. I blinked back the tears, walking out to meet Kemi. "Are you all right?" she asked, touching my arm.

I attempted a smile, nodding my head. "If you don't mind, I will go back to the hut now. I'm not feeling too well," I said.

"Of course, I'll see you when I'm finished," she said.

My heart bled as I realized that the most important symbol of my father had been stolen from me.

❧

"Can I just thank your wife for taking care of us for the time we've been here?" I asked Ake. He had arrived early to take us away.

"Make it fast!" he growled. I quickly went looking for her. She was not far away, tending to some skinny hens behind the huts.

"Mama, Mama," I called to her. It seemed fitting that I call her that.

She turned around, stopping in midair from throwing dried corn on the ground for the hens. "Yes, Amelia?"

I knelt down on my two knees. "Mama, thank you for your hospitality. My brother and I are leaving now, and I just wanted to show my appreciation."

Her face softened. "Please get up."

She put down the bowl of corn and held me gently by the shoulders. "I know the time here has been hard for you. My husband is still trying to get you audience with the Alake. However, whatever else I can do to speed it up, I will do."

"Thank you," I knelt down again and departed. That was the last I saw of Ake's wife for several moons.

❧

We followed Ake, leaving empty-handed, the same way we had arrived. Villagers stared as we went by, some even calling to others in their huts to come and see the strangers. Ake waved them away. The walk took us further into the village, until we came across a hut hidden far behind tall trees.

"Ẹgbon mi, my elder!" Ake shouted as we stopped outside the hut, waiting for a response. Almost immediately, the woman whom we later came to know as Ake's older sister, *Iya Alata*—the peppers seller—came out. She was as dark as the night. Her head was wrapped in a patterned cotton cloth with a matching wrapper tied to her chest that flowed to her feet. "Ake. You are here already?" She glanced at us "Are these the ones you mentioned?"

He grunted, tapping his hand on his thigh impatiently.

"What are your names?" she asked.

We told her.

"Ake said you need a place to stay. Well, I can give you that, but in exchange, I need you to help me at the market," she said, pointing at me. "I need you to help me at the farm," she said, pointing at Dare.

Ake nodded at his sister. "It is settled. Once the Alake grants me audience, I will take them." With that, he turned around and left. Iya Alata gestured for us to follow her. We came to find out that she lived alone, unmarried, and childless.

It had been four moons since then. Our days started before dawn, when I prepared the fresh peppers in a large tray, stacked on top of the other. Ours was a very competitive market, with over thirty other women selling only peppers. However, Iya Alata got the most patronage. Our stall would have five people haggling over the produce while other stalls stood empty. The women would glance our way, jealously.

I picked up the peppers and set them on the tray as quickly as I could, with Iya Alata still glaring at me.

"Bye, Ma. See you at the market," I said, walking past my benefactor on that fateful morning. Hurrying, I hoped to meet up with Bimpe—a young girl about my age who managed the stall next to ours for her mother. I had asked her once what was so special about Iya Alata's peppers. It was almost as though people were compelled to flock to our stall.

Bimpe had given me a knowing look. "You will know soon enough," she said.

I caught up with Bimpe and we greeted ourselves.

"You know today's the start of the Oya festival?" she asked.

I shrugged, uninterested in the Oya festival. "I don't have to go, do I? Does Iya Alata stay for the festivities?" I asked.

"Who knows with Iya Alata? As long as she is able to make her money, that is all that matters," Bimpe said.

"Oh no!" I shouted, halting in my tracks.

"What is it, Amelia?" Bimpe held on tight to her tray, frozen in fear.

"I forgot to bring the spicy peppers, after all my work washing them. Iya Alata will kill me if she finds out!" I yelled, turning around. "I must go and get them before she realizes my mistake!" I shouted as I ran, holding on to the heavy load on my head.

"All right, don't be too long!" Bimpe called to me.

I rushed down the path back to the hut, pushing past tree branches. I walked into the quiet compound. Dare had left an hour before me to the farm and Iya Alata was probably getting dressed in her hut. I rushed to the back yard, almost falling over a crouched object.

"Yeh! Yeh!" Iya Alata rolled over, clutching her head. Something fell out of her hand.

It looked like a gourd. Red liquid spilled from it to the ground. White feathers went scattering around her. A headless chicken lay beside her. I began to scream, unable to take my eyes off her murderous gaze.

"Stupid girl! You have destroyed my homage to the gods! Let me get my hands on you!" she screamed.

I didn't wait for her to get up. I threw down the tray, scattering all the peppers, and ran. My heart raced as I cut into the trees to hide. Iya Alata was putting a spell on her peppers to make sure people bought from her. Where would I go now? I couldn't return to Ake. First, I had to go and get Dare. I wove through the trees for what seemed an eternity until I came to the farm.

Dare was speaking with one of the hired hands when he noticed me running toward him. He dropped his cutlass and ran to meet me. "What is it, Amelia? What is it?"

"We must go, Dare! She is after me. We must run!"

He dropped his cutlass and grabbed my hand.

I shook my hand. "There is no time to explain. Our lives are in danger!" I screamed.

He searched my face for a second and nodded. We ran past the laborers and disappeared into the woods. We stayed hidden in the forest for hours behind large tree trunks when the hunters and other villagers went by.

"Where do we go now?" Dare hissed in my ear as we hid behind the tree trunk.

"Let's just stay here for the night," I whispered back

"You must be stupid. Don't you know the hunters can be prowling around and mistake us for game. I don't want to die out here."

"All right, let's just wait until the sun goes down," I said, biting my nails.

By sunset we were starving. There were said to be dangerous animals wandering these forests. Tales of lions attacking had filtered through the town one time too many.

"We have to decide what to do!" Dare's voice was getting frantic and I felt like shouting back at him. I closed my eyes for what seemed like forever...and then Ake's wife's face appeared to me, just as she looked the last time I saw her. We would go to her.

∾

"Psssst! Pssst!" My heart thundered against my chest as I hid behind the large hut, hoping and praying that Ake's wife—bending over the large cooking pot—would hear me. She stopped stirring the large spoon in the pot for a second and then continued.

"Pssst! Psst! Psst!"

She looked back in my direction.

"It is me, Amelia! Please come!"

She dropped the spoon and watched me curiously for a second. In three strides, she was behind the hut. "You have some explaining to do. What do I hear about you and Iya Alata?" she whispered, looking calmly at me.

"I don't know what you've heard, but please understand that I speak the truth. I forgot a portion of the peppers at Iya Alata's place and went back to get them this morning. I walked into the compound and caught her conjuring! *Casting spells!*"

Her eyes narrowed. She stood still for what seemed forever before she finally heaved a sigh. "Iya Alata has told the whole town that you stole from her. I cannot tell my husband that you are here. He believes everything his sister tells him. You must remain in hiding." She laid her hand on my shoulder. I began to stammer and explain, but she silenced me with a hand on my shoulder. "Of course I don't believe her. I have been a victim of her occult ways. Do not fear. I will make sure she pays for this." A spark lit up her eyes. She immediately went off and returned with some food wrapped in a cloth. "Come with me. I will take you to a safe place."

"Please—" I held her hand pleadingly, "—my brother is with me. He cannot stay behind."

She nodded. "That will not be a problem. He can come too."

I turned to the tree where Dare hid and waved to him.

"No! Go back to him. I will return shortly, and then we will go," Ake's wife said. I nodded and ran back into hiding.

෧෧

T he safe place proved to be her sister's, right in the middle of town and very close to the palace. Her home from the exterior looked common-place, but once we stepped in it was another world.

A young girl let us in. She knelt down before Ake's wife. "Ẹkalẹ *ma*, Good evening ma!"

"Where is my sister?" she asked, already pushing past the girl

"She is in her room," the girl said.

Ake's wife turned to us. "Wait for me. I will go in and talk to her." She disappeared into the dark hall-way.

"Won't you sit down?" the girl asked, smiling.

"No, thank you. We will stand," Dare said quickly.

She looked surprised, but then shrugged and walked away. We stood quietly, taking in the room. Her home was filled with all types of merchandise—cloth-ing, leather slippers, beads, and carved artifacts. The walls were lined with soft, beautiful cotton cloth, the benches were beautifully carved, and the floors were clad with soft, lamb rugs. Everyone knew Madame Tit-ilayo was unmarried, but extremely wealthy. She was a trader by profession with ties to the Hausa, Ife, and Benin Kingdoms.

The two sisters came out of the inner room. Madame Titilayo was petite. She had her hair wrapped in a head tie, emphasizing the delicate features of her face. Her almond shaped eyes stood out immediately. She had honey-colored skin, just like Ake's wife. She was dressed in an aso oke, which was worn only on special occasions. Her arms were glittering with gold bangles and coral beads, her fingers piled with rings. Her eyes sized us up immediately.

"Amelia, Dare, meet my sister, Madame Titilayo. You must know of her already," Ake's wife said.

I knelt down, and Dare prostrated on the floor.

"Get up, children. Sit down, please," she said, her voice was soft, gentle. We did as she said. "Jumoke, my sister, has told me what you have endured. Please, you do not need to fear anything anymore," she said.

Ake's wife nodded, turning to us. "Dare, Amelia, I must hurry before my husband gets home. My sister has been briefed. Trust her. She knows what to do."

I walked over to this woman—who had turned out to be an ally—and hugged her. She hugged me back. "Do not be afraid. God is with you." She stepped back, and touched Dare gently on the head. "I will not be seeing you again until everything comes to light. I am sorry that I did what I did—" She stopped abruptly, looking quickly at her sister, who had signaled something to her. She walked out, leaving us alone with our new benefactor.

"Sit down please." Sitting across from her on the stools, she looked at us matter-of-factly, her almond shaped eyes unblinking. "Amelia and Dare."

We looked back at her, waiting for her next words.

"I took you in not just because of my sister—I trust her, and will help her anyway I can—but I have survived so many years on my own because I relied on my *intuition*. I can tell you are not what the whole town had been gossiping about. You're definitely not thieves who stole a bag of cowries from Iya Alata."

A gasp escaped me and I quickly covered my mouth. *A bag of cowries?* What would I use that for? Especially when I have no idea where to go? Madame Titilayo broke into laughter, holding her sides and throwing her head back. I realized I had spoken the words out loud. "You are so right, my dear. Exactly what I said! You are a smart one." She laughed, clasping her dainty hands.

"I'm so sorry. I just can't believe the things being said about me. I came to Abẹokuta at the request of my father with a message from him to the Alake. Ake met us at the gates and promised to help us gain audience with the Alake. It has been many moons without success. I fear that all our efforts are futile. The letter is no longer in my possession and I have no evidence proving that I am the Princess!" I broke into tears, burying my face in my hands.

"It is all right, Amelia. It is all right. Wipe your tears," she said calmly.

The sobs rocked my body and I couldn't stop for what seemed the longest time. "I apologise, Madame Titilayo."

She waved her hand in dismissal. "It is fine. Are you better? Do you need some water?" she asked, getting up.

"No, I am fine," I said, clearing my throat and wiping my eyes with the back of my hand.

Madame Titilayo did not return to her stool. Rather, she stood facing me. "Princess Amelia." She paused, making sure she had my attention. "I know for a fact that you are the Princess." She nodded and smiled. "Why do you think my sister brought you to me? She knows I've traveled far and wide, and yes, I have been to your kingdom."

I held my breath.

She smiled. "Are you not Gbèhanzin's favorite daughter? The only daughter that can freely enter into his inner chambers?"

"But, how did you know?" My voice trailed off as I watched her walk into the inner room and come out almost immediately holding up a familiar object. "Look at what my sister found in your belongings," she said softly, pulling back the cloth.

I gasped, covering my mouth. "Was that what she was apologizing for?" I asked. The récade looked like it had just been polished.

"How?" I searched Madame Titilayo's face.

She smiled apologetically. "Forgive us, but we had to be sure. My sister found it hidden in your wrapper when you were having a bath. She brought it to me late last night to find out what it was."

I glanced sideways at Dare, and as expected, he had a surprised look on his face. "I'm sorry, Dare. This was one secret I had to keep to myself," I said, feeling like I had betrayed him.

Madame Titilayo looked from Dare to me. "I know this object is a very important symbol of your father. It is a representation *of* him. Once the Alake sees this, he will know that you speak only the truth. Ake was never going to help you," she said matter-of-factly.

Dare and I glanced at each other in horror. I turned back to her. "What happens now? Will you help us gain audience with the Alake?" Dare asked.

"You don't worry. I will make sure *I* gain audience with him," she said.

I touched her hand hesitantly. "Thank you so much. How can we repay you?" I asked.

She smiled. "Only God can repay. I do it for God." She stood up. "I will hold on to this for now," she said, lifting the recadé again. I nodded. "Come, let me take you in to rest. You will have to stay indoors until I take you before the Alake. Do you understand?" she asked.

"Yes, ma," Dare and I said, as we followed her in.

"Good." She turned, almost bumping into us.

"Atinuke!" she called. The young girl who had met us at the door earlier appeared. "Have you set the bedding like I told you?" Madame Titilayo asked.

"Yes, ma! Atinuke said.

"Take the young man to his room then," Madame Titilayo said.

Dare turned and prostrated again.

"Thank you, ma!" he said, his voice choking with emotion.

She stooped to pull him up. "It is all right, my child. Go and rest."

Dare followed the girl, for the first time, not looking back to see if I would be fine.

"Come, my dear child," Madame Titilayo said. I followed her into what appeared to be her room. There were two mats laid on the ground with multiple clothing placed on top.

"Sleep now. Tomorrow's another day." She turned to leave, but I held her hand, falling to the ground to embrace her at the knees.

"Thank you Madame Titilayo. May the gods reward you for all that you are doing."

"The glory is the Lord's," she said softly, pulling me up. Our eyes met and I realized then that she was a Christian, just like mama. My heart warmed at the thought. I did not feel so alone any more.

LIBERATION

We were in hiding for a fortnight. Atinukẹ and Madame Titilayo were our only companions. We spent all of the time in our rooms listening as people trekked back and forth down the road. There was only one visitor who came by during our time in hiding. She was faceless—never venturing into the inner chambers where we hid. From her voice, I could tell she was boisterous and outgoing. Madame Titilayo often referred to her as Doyin.

One morning, Madame Tititlayo woke us up rather early. "It is time, Amelia. I have woken Dare. The Alake is ready to see you today. We must hurry before everybody is up and about. We do not want a mob on us even before we state our case."

I jumped off the mat, rubbing my face awake. "It is today? He has agreed to meet with us?" I asked.

She held my gaze. "He has agreed to meet with *me*.
I did not tell him *whom* I was bringing. It is better this
way. Once we get into his court, I will have the opportunity to state our case."

"Of course," I said simply.

Dare appeared at the door, a signal for us to be
on our way. As we stepped out to the outer chambers,
there stood a large woman. Her hair was woven intricately, her cheeks round. Her eyes seemed to dance
with mischief as she watched us approaching.

Dare and I greeted her, prostrating and kneeling.
"Good morning, ma," we said together.

"Get up, my children," she pulled us up, enfold-
ing us into her bosom. "My friend here has told me
all about your plight. I am so sorry!" she said, finally
releasing us to look into our faces.

"Children, this is my very good friend, Doyin
Oladele. Everybody calls her Mrs. Oladele. She is like
my sister. We grew up together," Madame Titilayo said.

She smiled. "Yes indeed, not too far from here, but
still close enough to Abẹokuta."

Madame Titilayo looked around. "We must leave
now, before everyone wakes up." She turned to Mrs.
Oladele. "So, you are off to Ibadan ehn?" she asked.

"Yes. I would have come with you, but you know I
have been waiting for these merchandise for a long
time. I will return in a few days," Mrs. Oladele said.

"I understand," Madame Titilayo said. "We must
go now children."

Mrs. Oladele laughed, clapping her hands together
in amusement. "Children? My dear friend, you see this
beautiful girl with wide hips and breasts like this and

call her a child? Look at this man before you!" She clapped her hands again.

Madame Titilayo looked at us like it was the first time. She hissed, grabbing both our arms. "Doyin, it is only *you* that will see all that. We must leave now. Have a safe trip!" She pulled us hurriedly after her, going through the front entrance. By the time we crossed the road, there were people milling around, already starting their day. I noticed that as we walked by them fast, they began to mumble. Some pointed.

"Madame Titilayo! Madame Titilayo!" a male's voice called out.

"Do not look back, my children. Keep walking, but do not run," she said under her breath.

We walked quickly, even as the footsteps behind us sounded like they were multiplying. The sweat trickled down my back as we walked in step with her. Soon we stood before a gigantic whitewashed wall. We had arrived at the Alake's place. I could hear hurried footsteps behind us accompanied with loud voices.

"Stop those people! Is that not the girl that we have been looking for? Is that not the thief?" someone shouted.

Madame Titilayo held our hands, beckoning us not to run. The mob surrounded us led by an angry looking slender man. "Madame Titilayo, why are you in the company of this thief?" the slender man asked. The crowd shouted and waited for a response. She looked at him calmly.

"As you can see, I am on my way to see the Alake. He has asked me to bring them with me. Will you stand there and waste the Alake's time with these questions?" Madame Titilayo asked angrily.

He shrank before our eyes, stepping back. "I… er…I did not know that you were on your way to see the Alake," he stammered.

The crowd began to shout again.

"Silence! Don't you have anything better to do this early morning? Clear out of my way this minute or I will inform the Alake of this disrespect!" Madame Titilayo spat on the ground.

They moved back, shamefaced, making way for us to continue on our journey. We followed after her, entering the palace through the gates.

Glancing back at the crowd, I noticed they still waited just outside the gates, watching. The guard greeted Madame and made way for us to pass. We walked down the long hallway, finally coming to a half open door. Turning to us, she said, "I will be called in soon. You both stay here. I will be gone only a short while."

A guard came to the doorway. "The Alake is ready to see you."

She went in.

We waited, barely breathing. By now, people were walking by, throwing cursory glances at us.

"Hold those two scoundrels!" someone shouted.

My heart jumped. It was Ake. We turned to see him rushing toward us, his blood red cap flying in the air. I grabbed Dare's hand and pulled him behind the guard. The guard blocked Ake's hand from grabbing me.

"You must be stupid! How dare you stop me?" he growled.

"These children came with Madame Titilayo. You cannot take them." The guard's anger couldn't be masked by the monotonous tone he addressed the crazed man before him.

Ake laughed wildly, pointing to us. "So, my Jumoke and her impetuous sister are behind this betrayal? I took both of you in, gave you food, and *this* is how you repay me?"

In an instant, he hit the guard on the chest with an object, and the younger man fell down dead. I screamed, scrambling to the door, pulling Dare behind me.

"You cannot escape me you little cockroach! If you think—"

"How dare you, Ake? How dare you?" Madame Titilayo's voice rang out. She appeared with two men in tow. They looked very important with highflying caps and flowing aṣọ oke. Ake turned on his sister-in-law, chanting some unrecognizable words at her. A sinister feeling crept down my spine. He began to raise his hand again.

Madame raised hers, pulling out a black book from under her wrapper. "You dare not, Ake! You dare not raise your hand to me. I am protected. You cannot kill me. Neither can you kill these children," she said calmly.

Ake laughed a sinister laugh, throwing back his head.

"*Ewọ Ake! Ewọ!* It is forbidden!"a female voice screamed.

The voice belonged to an older lady who appeared beside Madame Titilayo, clad in all white from head to toe.

"*Iya Lode*, don't get involved! This is between her and me!"Ake pointed at her and then twisted back to face Madame Titilayo, lifting up his hand again. By now, the crowd had thickened, and I could barely see what was going on.

"*Ewọ se!* I warned you, Ake!" the woman screamed again.

Suddenly, she pointed a short staff at Ake. He became paralyzed on the spot. His head hit the soft sand first before he passed out. The crowd screamed, scattering to the four ends of the courtyard.

"Come in, quickly." She beckoned to Dare and me at the same time, instructing the other guards to carry Ake into the palace. I grabbed Madame Titilayo and Dare's hands, pulling them into the King's court.

The room was quiet as we entered. The Alake sat on his throne. He was not very striking. He was of average build. He wore a white cap, his arms barely noticeable under the long flowing *agbada* he wore.

"Kabiyesi o!" Madame Titilayo shouted, falling to the ground.

We copied her, falling to the floor, lying flat, and then rolling from side to side.

"*K'ade pẹ lori, ki bata pẹ lẹsẹ.* May your reign be long," she chanted.

He gestured with his large white staff to rise up. Iya Lode sat on a stool beside the other three male advisors. Madame Titilayo remained kneeling, and I moved beside her, pulling Dare along. Four guards carried in the unconscious Ake and laid him to the side of the throne, opposite us. The Alake looked in our direction. "Are these Gbèhanzin's children?" he asked.

"Yes, my King. This is Princess Amelia and Prince Dare," Madame Titilayo said.

"I see—" he paused, "—Titilayo has explained your unfortunate situation," he said.

His stature had camouflaged his deep, strong voice that was filled with compassion. My heart sang with joy. I knew then that he would not turn us away. I nodded, and waited for him to continue. "How long have you been in my kingdom?" he asked.

"It has been four moons, my King," I answered.

His eyes flashed in anger. "Four moons! And this—"He pointed to the unconscious Ake on the floor. "This man who calls himself my *strongest* warrior decided to keep you a secret for this long? To what end?" his voice rose in question. He shifted in his seat, and then fixed his eyes on his advisors. "What have you to say, Balogun?" he asked.

Balogun—a heavyset man—scrambled to his feet. "My King, you know that we have not had a good relationship with Gbèhanzin and his forefathers. We have not had a good history with the Kingdom of Danhomè. We are *enemies!* Why should we now take in his children? How are we sure they are not spies?" He sat down, and began to tap his feet.

The advisor next to him got up. Folding the arms of his aṣọ oke, he cleared his throat.

"Gbadewale, you may speak," Alake said.

"My King, I do not agree with Balogun. They are just children. Of what benefit would children be to come and spy? Do they have any war tactics to use? And, if they are indeed spies, would they wait this long? Be held for so long and risk being caught, as they have been?" Gbadewale asked and sat back down.

Balogun rose again, turning to us. "That may be the case, but tell me, my children, what proof is there that you are Gbehazin's offsprings? That should clear up any doubt." He sat down.

Madame Titilayo raised her hand, requesting to speak. The King nodded. "I have all the proof you need. May I show it to you, my King?" she asked.

The Alake nodded. Madame Titilayo got up quickly, pushed her hand into the thick folds of her wrapper around her waist, and pulled out the récade. My heart jumped for joy. There was a unanimous gasp in the court. She walked forward and handed the object to a guard, who handed it to the Alake.

"This is the symbol representative of Gbèhanzin. You can see the shark carved in metal. There is none other like it in this world. These children brought it with them. If nothing else, this will prove that they are indeed the children of Gbèhanzin." Madame Titilayo pointed to Ake. "My King, this man has *wronged* these children! He must be punished!"

The third male advisor stood up, his small eyes seemed to miss nothing as he eyed us from head to toe. "My King." He bowed.

"Adesina, you may speak."

"I am not a clairvoyant. Neither do I possess the physical attributes to hold off an oncoming mob. What

I do know is that we, as a people, have never turned anyone away who needs help. Abẹokuta represents a place of refuge. Even if they are spies, let them in. Of what use is the spying now that the Kingdom of Danhomè has crumbled? Let them stay. They will need to rebuild their lives." He sat down.

Tears rolled down my eyes. Hearing about the demise of my home from someone else made the reality hit home harder—there was no more home, husband, or parents to go back to.

"Iya Lode, do you have anything to add?" Alake asked the only woman on his council.

She got up. "They are pure souls, my King. They can do you no harm. Let them in." Nodding in our direction, she sat down.

The King sat in silence, pondering. Finally, he looked up. "Someone call me Iya Alata. Let me hear what she has to say about the allegations she made." He gestured for us to sit opposite his advisors. We waited, listening as the King and his advisors discussed other affars of the kingdom.

After sometime, Iya Alata appeared. Her little frame scrambled up to the throne, where she lay prostrate. "Kabiyesi o."

He gestured for her to rise. "Tell me what allegations you have brought against this young girl before me."

She glared at me, and then turned back to the Alake. "My brother brought her and the brother to me. According to him, they were children of Gbèhanzin and had escaped capture. He said they would be with me for a short period of time, so I accepted." Iya

Alata turned to me, pointing a finger. "I had no idea I was harboring a *thief!*" Her voice could wake up a giant. Her brother began to come around.

"Lower your voice in the presence of the King!" Iya Lode snapped at her.

Iya Alata curtsied, apologizing. "I am sorry, my King. My emotions overtook me."

Alake held his hand up, silencing her. "How much did she steal?"

My heart hammered in anticipation. Iya Alata froze, unable to speak or move.

"I said, how much did she steal? You should know immediately, shouldn't you?"

"Emm, it was...it was about fifteen cowries," she said.

"You lie!" Adesina screamed, flying out of his seat, his cap falling off his head as he did.

"I speak the truth!" Iya Alata screamed back, hopping from one leg to the other.

"Then why are you not sure about the number of cowries? Where did you keep the money when it was stolen?" he asked. Adesina was even more excited than Iya Alata. He towered over her, waiting for her response like the rest of us.

"In my hut," she said.

"Where in the hut?" he demanded.

"In...er...in—" she stammered.

"You lie again!" he screamed. Adesina turned to the King. "It is obvious she lies, my King. She deserves death!" He sat back down.

"Me? Adesina? Me? What arrogance you have now that you have become the King's adviser. You forget so quickly that I was your mother's bosom friend? You show no respect?"

Adesina turned up his nose in disgust, and from the corner of his mouth, said, "You forget also that being so close to you, I observed your fetish and *wicked* ways. Iya Alata, *afẹfẹ ti fẹ, a ti ri furọ adiyẹ!*"

Iya Alata gasped, stepping back, almost falling. A groan escaped Ake who lay on the floor.

"Ake! Ake! Rise up!" Iya Lode shouted. She walked over to the body on the floor and tapped her foot on Ake's. "I said, get up! You and your wicked sister are being tried, here and now."

Ake got up slowly, holding his chest.

"Iya Alata, tell me now, did this girl *really* steal from you? Be slow to answer. If it is found out that you lied, your punishment will be irrevocable."

We waited for her response. Ake made a move to speak.

"Silence! The King was speaking to me!" Iya Alata spat out.

Ake shrunk into himself.

"Then speak!" Adeṣina interjected, stamping his feet impatiently.

"She did. She stole my fifteen cowries in my hut. I caught her red-handed."

I shook my head. "That—" I began to speak.

Madame Titilayo touched my hand gently, urging me to be quiet. She looked calm and confident.

Iya Lode rose, gathering her cloth around her in preparation. "Since you have refused to tell the truth, let all present be witnesses." She produced a small round cloth, and untied it. "Take this kola nut and eat. Make sure to repeat after me."

Iya Alata took it and waited for Iya Lode to continue.

"If I am telling the truth then nothing will happen to me when I eat this kola nut."

Iya Alata repeated, raising the kola to her mouth.

"But, if I have lied, may I fall down and die now!"

"But if I have lied, may I fall down and die!" Iya Alata began to drop the kola into her mouth.

I sprang up and rushed over to her, grabbing the kola out of her hand.

"Do not do that, Iya Alata! You know the truth. Do you want to die?" I shouted.

There was silence. Not a sound was heard all around the palace. Madame Titilayo pulled me back.

"That was brave of you, my dear," she whispered.

"You are indeed a fool!" Iya Alata turned on me.

"Silence!" the four advisors said in unison.

The King looked at me and back at Iya Alata. "From this one act of selflessness, the truth has been revealed," he said.

"Yes! As you can see, I was *about* to eat the kola nut and redeem myself, but this useless *refugee*—" Iya Alata screamed at me, pointing her finger.

"Be quiet!" The King's voice rose in anger. He pointed his staff at her. "You are a menace to this land—an evil woman. You were willing to kill yourself rather than to have this girl freed? You will be held captive for the remainder of your miserable life!" He beckoned to the guards.

"What? That is impossible! What will happen to my business? I will not accept this!" She screamed, falling to the ground. The guards moved forward and picked her up effortlessly, carrying her out as she begged.

"Ake," Alake called.

Ake looked down at his feet, his hands behind his back, unrecognizable from the burly giant that had met us at the gates several moons ago.

"You were aware of what your sister was doing and you remained silent. Even worse, you kept the existence of these two from me. For what purpose, to hold them captive forever? You are banished from this kingdom. All that you own will be transferred to your wife and children. Do not return or you face death."

Ake burst out in tears. "Forgive me my King! I have no excuse. I should have brought them to you, but my sister said it would be better if I kept them for future leverage."

"Future leverage for you? Against what or who?" Iya Lode demanded to know and then burst out laughing.

"Take him away!" Balogun shouted to the guards. Ake was dragged off, hollering.

Finally, the palace became quiet and we had the King's attention again.

"On behalf of the Ẹgba people, I apologize for the reception you have received since your arrival here. I would like to make amends. Is it still your wish to remain in Abẹokuta?"

Dare and I looked at each other. *Where else was there to go?*

"Yes, your highness," I said.

He nodded. "Madame Titilayo?"

"Your highness."

"Are you willing to keep them with you? A stipend will be given you to take care of them."

She smiled. "With all due respect my King, I do not need a stipend to take care of them. They are no trouble at all. It would be an honor."

"So be it then. However, I will still stretch out a hand of love by sending some things back with you today. You may arise and go."

HELPING HANDS

c. 1896 – c. 1897

"Since you have been indoors for a while, would you like to go and see Jumokẹ and her children today?"

I looked across at Madame Titilayo who had just returned from trading at the market square. "Don't you ever get tired? You just got back from the market!" I exclaimed.

She laughed. "There's much to do and so little time. If it's me you're worried about, don't be. Would you like to go?" she asked again.

"Yes, that would be nice," I said, looking behind me at Dare, who had his head buried in a book. He had been trying to teach himself how to read Yoruba for many days, at times with the help of Madame Titilayo.

"Dare, are you coming?" I asked.

He looked up, his eyes faraway. "What?" he asked.

Madame Titilayo giggled, shaking her head. "Let's leave Dare alone. He is too busy learning how to read," she said, waving to me to come. I got up, slipping into my sandals.

Dare's head sprung up. "I would like to learn some more. This just has the alphabets. I would like to start reading sentences and stories," he said excitedly.

"Aah, Dare, I've never seen you this excited. Mama," I paused, liking the way the word sounded on my lips. "You really must get Dare more books," I said.

"Now that I know what Dare likes, I will make sure to stop by and get some from the missionary school," Madame Titilayo giggled again, taking my hand.

My head jerked sideways to stare at her. "There's a missionary school here?" I could barely speak, my heart beating faster. I felt Dare's eyes digging holes into my back.

"Yes, of course, the Church Missionary Society established a school a long time ago. Are you all right?" she asked, taking my hand.

"Me? Oh, yes. Can…can we walk by the school sometime?" I asked.

Madame Titilayo looked surprised. "What for? Are you interested in going to school there?" she asked.

I shrugged nonchalantly. "I'm just curious," I said quietly. We walked to the doorway. "We will be back soon, Dare," I said, turning around to wave to him.

Dare's eyes bored into me, his face unsmiling. "Don't be long," he said softly, and turned his head back into his book.

∽

The people smiled and greeted us as we walked by. I could imagine mama growing up close to this place.

It was wonderful to be out and to be free. Madame Titilayo called to a young girl who walked ahead of us with a tray of covered food. "Come here. Give me six of your bean cakes."

We waited as the girl put down the tray on the side of the road and deftly wrapped up the bean cakes in large leaves.

"Give it to her." Madame pointed to me as she gave her a cowry.

"Thank you, ma," I said.

"Why are you holding it? Please, start eating. You barely ate anything before we left."

So she had noticed that I had played with the food. I could not understand why the food refused to stay down. I ate in silence, walking a step behind Madame Titilayo.

"Oh, look, over there, Amelia." She tapped my arm, pointing across the street to a large compound. The little speck looked like a building. "That is the Missionary school. It's been there for a long, long time...I think about the time I was born."

"You didn't attend the school?" I asked, not sure if to venture into the story of how Mama was also from here.

Madame Titilayo looked at me like I was crazy. "You did not know my father, better yet, my mother. "

"What do you mean?" I asked.

"My parents were ifa worshippers. I dare not be seen even looking in the direction of the school growing up," she said.

"Then how did you become a Bible worshipper?" I asked

Madame Titilayo threw her head back, laughing.

"Did I say something wrong?" I asked.

She finally stopped laughing. "Amelia, you are too funny! Bible worshipper? Oh, is that what you call a Christian?" she asked.

I looked away.

"Oh, I'm sorry, my child. Don't feel embarrassed. Do you know someone with a Bible? Someone from Danhomè?" she asked.

I nodded. "Yes. My mother. She also read the Bible," I said quietly, watching her closely.

Her eyes widened. "Your mother? That's interesting. Did she ever read to you?" she asked, lifting her head to look at me.

"No. Mama enjoyed her Bible on her own," I said, my voice trailing off, feigning disinterest.

She was quiet, watching me. "Tell me, Amelia, what did you like to do when you lived in Danhomè?" she asked.

"Oh, I loved to weave on the loom. I was very good."

"I see. You weave. I can get you a loom if you like," she said thoughtfully.

"Yes, I was quite good, taught by the very best in the kingdom. If you can get one, that would be nice," I said loudly.

"Oh, we are here already. We must continue this conversation later, Amelia," Madame Titilayo said as we approached the entrance to Ake's compound.

It was quite different from the last time Dare and I were there. The children were in the front yard playing and laughing loudly. Jumokẹ, Ake's wife was also outside, sitting on a bench outside her hut. She had a guest. It was Balogun from the Alake's palace. He got up slowly as we arrived.

"Aah, aah, Balogun. Is it you we see so late this evening? I hope there is no problem?" Madame Titilayo greeted him, looking curiously at both of them. Her sister shifted from one foot to the other.

"No problem, Madame Titilayo. I just called on the family to make sure that they are doing well, especially now that there is no husband or father to look after them," Balogun said. His fat face reminded me of a pig's. He was staring intensely at Ake's wife.

"Ẹgbon mi, I am happy to see you. Do you know I was meaning to come over today as well?" Jumokẹ hugged her sister. She was at least a good five inches taller than her.

"Hmm, I am sure." Madame turned her full attention on Balogun. "Please, greet your wives for me. I am sure you have a lot of business to attend to in the palace," she said.

"Yes, yes of course," he stumbled over his words as he bade Jumokẹ goodbye.

Once he left the compound, Madame Titilayo turned to her sister. "Adejumokẹ! Adejumokẹ!" I watched Madame Titilayo pull her sister's head close, and whisper in her ear. Jumokẹ laughed and whispered something back. Madame Titilayo shook her head slowly. "Just be careful. He's only after acquisitions.

So rather than go and look for Baba, as I asked you to, you are here fraternizing with that man?"

Jumokę gently clasped her arm round her sister. "Sister! Don't say that! I went to look for him as you asked, but he has been away visiting with his daughter in Bini. You know Adeola, his daughter, married a Bini man? I was told he would be away for several moons, if not more." She finally looked in my direction. "Aah, Amelia, how are you faring? Where is your brother?" She hugged me, touching my face.

Several of the children looked up from their play and ran to us. "Isn't this Amelia? Where have you been?" They surrounded me. I laughed, holding their hands. It had been a long time since I had played with young ones. They reminded me of my many siblings.

Someone took my hand. It was Kemi. She smiled and pulled me from the crowd. "Come with me. Let's go and talk," she said. I followed. She took me to the front of their hut. "How have you been?" she asked.

"Very well. Madame Titilayo has been very good to us. Your mother too."

She nodded. "You will be staying with Mama's sister then?" she asked.

My surroundings began to spin, just like it had the past few days. I clung to the wall to steady myself.

"Are you all right?" Kemi held my arm and pulled me down gently to the floor. "I have to call Mama. You don't look all right."

I heard her rush away. Everywhere was spinning. If only I could just lie down and go to sleep. I heard footsteps coming toward me.

"Amelia! Amelia!" Madame Titilayo put her arm around my shoulders and sat me upright. She called for some water. Almost immediately, I felt wetness on my face and chest. My eyes flew open. The spinning was slowing down.

"Ẹgbon mi, how long has this been going on?" Jumokẹ asked.

"It's been over a week—she hasn't been eating or sleeping well, but she has never done this," I heard Madame Titilayo say.

"All of you, leave now!" Jumokẹ shouted.

Madame Titilayo stood over me. "What is it Jumokẹ? Is she dying? Has that stupid witch called Iya Alata done something that we need to counter?" Madame Titilayo asked. She pulled her wrapper tighter around her waist as if to jump into action.

Jumokẹ placed her hand on her sister's shoulder gently. "No. It is not that serious." She sat down on my left, staring down on the ground and then up at me. "Amelia, have you been feeling sick for some time? Like you want to throw up?"

I nodded slowly.

"How long has this been going on?" she asked.

"Ever since I got to Abẹokuta. The first time it happened was when I was living with Iya Alata," I said slowly.

The sisters exchanged looks.

"What is wrong with me?" I asked, my voice shaking.

Madame Titilayo stretched out her hand to take mine. Her sister patted my shoulder. "Nothing is wrong with you, Amelia. It's just that there is a possibility that you might be pregnant."

I felt dizzy again.

"How is that possible Jumokẹ?" Madame Titilayo asked, chuckling

"Ẹgbon, please don't be naïve! You mean to tell me this girl does not know about such things? Come, Amelia, have you been with a man before?" Jumokẹ asked, peering into my face.

"Amelia, did you not hear what Jumokẹ said?"

Madame Titilayo shook me gently. "Amelia?"

I felt the gush of water over my head, drenching my body. "Please, stop. I heard you," I said, my voice drawling. I wiped my face with my hands, and closed my eyes briefly.

"Answer her, please!" Madame Titilayo asked, her voice shaking.

"Amelia, did anybody touch you? Did…did my husband touch you when you lived with us?" Jumokẹ asked, her voice faltering.

I shook my head.

"Then who did?" Madame Titilayo asked, touching my hand gently.

I looked up at the two sisters, sighing. "My husband," I said.

They stood still, unable to speak. Madame Titilayo finally did, touching my forehead, and then dropping her hand. "You were married?" she whispered in disbelief.

I nodded, the tears springing to my eyes.

"For how long?" Jumokẹ asked.

"It was not long enough," I said slowly, looking down at my hands.

"You were a newly wed?" she asked.

"Yes. We were married barely three moons before war started," I said.

The sisters looked at each other.

"I think she has been pregnant for almost five moons, if my calculations are correct." Ake's wife said.

"She looks so small! I would never have known, except, her hips looked wider than when she first arrived. Her breasts also…"

Their voices buzzed around me, even as my heart leapt for joy. I *was* carrying Dossou's child.

∽

My hands wandered to my flat stomach again, finding it hard to believe that a baby—Dossou's baby—was growing inside me. I had stopped lying on my stomach for days now, afraid that the baby would be crushed if I did. Looking up into the thatched roof of the room Madame Titilayo and I shared, thoughts of home clouded my mind again. I closed my eyes for a brief moment, the tears springing up again.

I must have dozed off. The next thing I felt was a trickle of spittle flowing down the side of my mouth. Part of the bedding was thrown over my face, one hand over my head. I looked from under heavy-laden eyes, and noticed the room was very dark. Though the wooden window was wide open, the evening shadows had taken over.

I heard a shuffling noise, which stopped suddenly, and then silence. Someone had come into the room. The person tiptoed to the opposite end of the room where Madame Titilayo had her things folded neatly in the corner. A ruffling noise ensued, followed by a clinking sound. I lifted my chin, looking through the space in my elbow. I gasped. Dare was bent over in the corner, holding jewelry, a lot of it.

His head turned swiftly in my direction and he dropped them on the ground.

"What are you doing?" I asked, holding my breath.

He immediately shoved the jewelry back, getting up.

"I didn't know you were awake," he said quietly, walking over to where I lay.

I sat up. "What are you doing Dare?" I whispered, watching as his eyes bore holes into me. I pulled my wrapper over my thighs, thankful that I had decided not to take the buba off before I lay down. He shrugged

"Nothing, Amelia, I was doing nothing." He had a strange light in his eyes as he walked out of the room.

∽

Madame Titilayo forbade me to work. She stressed the fact that this was my first pregnancy and I needed to be careful. Moreover, she did not know much about being pregnant or caring for a pregnant woman. She catered to me, hand and foot. Her motherly care was so overwhelming for me that sometimes I cried in secret.

Dare began going to Madame Titilayo's farms with the laborers, and in the evenings he attended the adult education class the missionary school held. Most days, I would be the only one at home with Atinukẹ. Madame Titilayo would go to the farm to oversee what was happening or to the market. A few times, she traveled to Lagos.

I was now seven moons pregnant. I felt it as I waddled across the room. The fact that I had not even known I was pregnant for five moons was still a shock to me. Granted, my monthly period had never been regular in the first place, but at least I should have *known*. I felt the baby move as I sat down on the stool. He was kicking me constantly now. I smiled. It was funny how I always referred to the baby as he. I just knew it was a boy. Dossou would like that.

I had heard little about the ongoing war. I suspected Madame Titilayo was keeping vital information from me in order as not to alarm me in my *delicate condition*, as she called it. The fact that I never left the house these days made matters worse.

In my spare time, I wove new tapestries on the loom Madame Titilayo had bought for me. After making several tapestries, I got tired and resorted to making myself a new bocie. I carved out the figure from wood and added personal pieces—a strand of my hair, eyelash, a gold bead—and tied them around the sculpture. I planned to ask Madame Titilayo—now that it was complete—if she knew any native priest I could go to.

I waited patiently for Madame Titilayo to arrive. With so much time on my hands now, I knew the exact time of both Madame Titilayo and Dare's arrival in the evenings. She was always in the house just before sunset, while Dare would get home about half an hour later, right before dinner.

I heard her footsteps outside the front gate.

"E kabọ ma," Atinukẹ greeted as Madame Titilayo she came in. Atinukẹ took her basket and sandals.

"Mama, welcome back," I said from where I sat on the mat.

"Amelia, my dear, how are you feeling? Hope no problem with the baby?" She pulled out a stool and sat beside me, smiling.

"No problem, I am doing well, and so is the baby. How was the market today?" I asked.

"Well, it was a bit slow. You know we have had some drought for some moons now, so there's not much to harvest." Her voice trailed off as she looked down in my lap. She picked up the bocie. I was very proud of my handiwork.

Her mouth turned down at the sides. "Amelia, what is this?" she asked. Her voice was grave. This was the first time she had ever looked angry with me.

"It's my bocie, ma. My protection. I just made this new one," I said slowly.

She held it up to her face. "Is this supposed to be an image of you?" she asked. The fact that the sculpture had breasts and hips like a woman had not escaped her. I nodded.

"And you say it's *protection?*" she asked.

"Yes, ma."

She looked at me, putting the figure back in my hands. "Protection from what, Amelia? What is scaring you?" she asked.

I stared at her, unable to speak.

"I cannot tell you what to believe in Amelia, but one thing I can tell you that is tried and true is that these idols *cannot* save you. I have done all these things when I was younger. They didn't save me from a lot of things that have happened to me. It did not save me from this." She proceeded to pull up her buba, exposing her round, small breast. Under it was a large, dark scar. I looked in her face, still unable to verbalize my thoughts. She had a peaceful look on her face. "That, my daughter, is the mark of the beast. My father felt that he had to protect us from evil and had a snake bite us—Jumokẹ and I. If we survived the bite, then it was proven that nothing else could ever harm us. I can remember when I was younger, going every year to sacrifice to his gods. They never helped me." She pulled down her buba and got up to go into the inner room.

She came out almost immediately, holding a black book. It looked familiar. "Amelia, what is in this book is what helped me."

It was the same book she had held up to Ake. It was just like mama's book, I could tell even before she opened it. I listened as she talked about her faith in the one true God. How God had helped her to break free from the bondage of sacrifices and pain. I could not understand the joy in her face as she spoke, but I could feel it.

༄

"Mama, where are you going?" I moved closer to where she was packing some clothes in a bundle. Mrs. Oladele sat close by on a stool. Both looked up in surprise.

"What do you mean, child? I have been telling you for almost a fortnight that I am going to Lagos to deliver some foodstuffs to my vendors. This is a very big shipment and I have to be there to supervise the unloading. Moreover, I am looking at setting up a stall there," Madame Titilayo said.

Mrs. Oladele giggled, her thick arms shaking.

"This your daughter, has grown too attached to you Titi! She won't even let you out of her sight." Her eyes looked me over, pausing at my round stomach.

I moved closer and sat on the floor. "Mama, you know the baby will be coming soon. I don't want you to miss the delivery." I waited for her response.

She dropped the wrapper in her hand and turned to me. "Amelia, I know, but don't worry. I'll be gone for only seven days. The baby must wait for me to get back!" she said, rubbing my stomach gently.

I smiled. "He will try to wait," I said.

Madame Titilayo laughed, returning to folding her clothes. "How are you sure it is a boy, you silly child?" she asked.

"I just know," I said quietly, running my hand over my stomach, feeling another kick.

Mrs Oladele began to fold the wrapper and sing softly under her breath.

"Oh, maybe after the baby is born, Amelia, we can see about you joining my trade?" Madame Titilayo asked, her head still bent over her work.

My heart skipped. "I would like that!" I said excitedly.

Mrs. Oladele looked up. "Titi, are you serious?" Her voice was low.

Madame Titilayo looked up, surprised—as was I. "Of course. This child is too young to just be doing nothing. Her mind is sharp and she needs to be doing something with her hands." Madame Titilayo said,

I watched Mrs Oladele's nose flare up, but she said nothing. We were all quiet, waiting for the other to speak.

Madame Titilayo shrugged wearily and turned toward the door. "Atinukẹ! Come and get this load from me!" Madame Titilayo shouted, getting up. "I will be back before you know it. Please, make sure you rest. I have told Doyin to check on you every evening," she said.

"Thank you," I said.

"And of course, Dare is there," Madame Titilayo said.

My heart fluttered. It had been doing that more frequently now anytime Dare was around or his name was mentioned.

The mention of his name must have conjured him up, for he soon appeared in the doorway, his books in hand. "Ma?" he asked.

Madame Titilayo turned to him, smiling. "You're the son of your father. I was just telling your sister here that she need not fear—you will be around to take care of her. Is that not so?" she asked, smiling broadly, looking from Dare to me.

He looked at my face, unsmiling as usual. I shrunk within myself, looking away.

"Is that not so, Dare?" Madame Titilayo asked again.

"Of course," he said quickly. "Are you leaving for Lagos tonight? I thought the ferry left first thing in the morning?" he asked.

"You are correct. Except, I will be staying with Doyin tonight. Her place is very close to the ferry stop. I want to get there early so I don't miss it."

"All right, ma. Journey mercies," Dare said, prostrating.

"Thank you, my son. Go and get some food in your stomach." She patted his shoulder as he rose to go. She came over to me again and hugged me "I will be back soon. Oh, before I forget, I have taken those beautiful tapestry works you did all these past weeks. I'm sure I'll have sold all of them by the time I get back," she said.

I smiled. "Thank you! I'm sure it'll make little sense to anyone. because it's all about Danhomé landmarks," I said.

She waved her hand downward dismissingly. "Who cares. They look wonderful," she said

"Thank you. Journey mercies, ma. Until we see again," I said.

Atinukẹ appeared to pick up the bundle and followed Madame Titilayo and her friend through the door.

༺ঔ

The next few days passed with Mrs. Oladele stopping by every evening as promised. She always came with a delicious stew to eat with pounded yam or garri, which Atinukẹ had readily available. On the seventh day, Madame Titilayo's expected day to arrive, I was sitting outside waiting for her to appear in the horizon.

I had turned away for only a brief moment to kill a mosquito biting at my ankle when footsteps sounded on the ground. I looked up to see a figure approaching. "Amelia!"

I jumped up, only to feel the disappointment wash over me as Mrs. Oladele approached, a small pot of stew in her hands.

"Good evening, ma," I said, feigning some cheer.

"I know. It is not your mother, only me. So, how are you doing today?" she asked.

I sat down. "I am fine. How was the market today?" I asked.

"The usual, but we thank God." She looked around. "Where are Atinukẹ and Dare?" she asked.

"Atinukẹ went to get some food stuff from the market, and as for Dare…" I shrugged.

Mrs. Oladele smiled. "Ah, that your brother. He is a strange one," she said.

"Won't you sit down?" I asked, attempting to get up for her, my protruding stomach almost hitting the ground.

"Please, don't bother yourself. I can get a stool inside," she said, and then walked in. An approaching figure in the distance caught my eyes. I focused my gaze to see Atinukẹ running toward me, her hands raised and shaking. As she got closer, I realized she was crying.

I sprung up, meeting her before she reached the doorway. "What is it Atinukẹ? What has happened?" I shouted, grabbing her hands

"Yeh! Yeh!" she yelled.

"Is it Dare?" I screamed, shaking her furiously.

Mrs. Oladele ran out. "What is it?" she asked, grabbing the hysterical girl.

Atinukẹ flung herself on the floor weeping bitterly. It was hard to breathe as I clung to the wall.

"Dare? What happened to him?" I heard Mrs. Oladele ask.

"It is not Dare o! The ferry from Lagos capsized!"Atinukẹ shouted, rolling on the floor.

"Ferry? What are you talking about Atinukẹ?" I screamed, running toward the rolling figure. By now, her body was covered in sand. Mrs. Oladele held me back.

"No, no, Amelia. Sit down," she said calmly, pushing me down gently on the ground. She went to Atinukẹ and held her down, looking into her face.

"Now, stop screaming and tell me what you know," she said slowly.

Atinukẹ's screaming stopped immediately, replaced by hiccups.

"Tell me!" Mrs. Oladele screamed in her face.

"Yes, yes. I will!" Atinukẹ whispered, sitting up, her hands resuming their shaking. "The ferry capsized this evening, the ferry from Lagos bringing Madame…it capsized. Many did not survive," she said, breaking down again, her body shaking.

I got up and held on to the wall. I had to go and see what had happened. Madame Titilayo might still be alive. A sharp pain spread from under my abdomen to my inner thigh. I let out a scream and fell back against the wall.

"Amelia!" They crowded around me, pulling me down to the floor.

"Let me go!" I screamed, fighting them off as they held me.

"Amelia, please stop this!" Mrs Oladele shouted over my noise.

"I have to go and find her! Let me go!" I felt something warm against my thighs.

"What is this on her leg?" I heard Mrs Oladele ask. She laid me on the ground. I felt everything spinning around me.

"Amelia, wake up! Wake up!" Someone slapped me lightly on the cheeks, and my eyes opened again. "Atinukẹ, stop your crying! Can't you see Amelia's water has broken? Get me some hot water now!"

Someone ran out. "Dare! Is Dare at home?" Mrs. Oladele shouted. I heard Atinukẹ return. "Let's take her in quickly."

The pain hit me again as I walked into the hut, slowly flanked by the two of them. I cried out. It was an unbearable, wrenching pain that wracked my body. I couldn't think. The pain had taken over every nerve. Tears streamed down my face as I called for Dossou and Mama. In the midst of the pain and noise, I heard Mrs. Oladele speaking to me calmly, holding my hands and wiping my face.

By the time the wave of pain subsided, I felt like dying. Mrs. Oladele felt my stomach, speaking soothing words. The pain came over and over again, and each time it was with increasing frequency. My body could not handle it anymore.

"Try and relax, Amelia. Let the baby come out in its time. Relax," Atinuke hovered, dabbing on my face with a damp cloth.

"She has to push now," I heard Mrs Oladele whisper.

"I know it's hard, Amelia, but you have to push now. When you feel the pressure, push as hard as you can," she said, gripping my hand. Atinuke wiped my face down and nodded encouragingly. The pain became so bad, I began to pull out my hair.

They tried holding me down, but strength came from nowhere and I lashed out. I heard myself calling for Dossou. I cursed at whatever higher power had brought me to Abẹokuta. The time stretched as their voices faded in and out. I even thought I heard Dare in the midst of it. I was imprisoned in my world of pain and regret.

Suddenly, I felt an urge to push—the hardest push I could muster—and then I felt a release. Flesh brushed against my inner thigh. I could feel him coming out.

"Another push, Amelia. The baby is coming!" Mrs. Oladele said excitedly. The pressure came immediately and I hunched over and pushed again. This time, he came out fully. Someone picked him up. I felt water between my legs as I was cleaned thoroughly. It was finally over. I turned to my side, wishing they would leave me. I heard them hitting the baby softly, and then harder.

"What is it?" someone asked. "What is it?" someone else asked again. I was drifting off.

"Amelia? Amelia?"

Blissful sleep—I escaped into it.

༄

It was quiet when I opened my eyes. I didn't know how long I had been asleep. I turned around slowly, still feeling pains in my lower body. *Had I really had the baby?* I felt my stomach. Someone moved beside me. "Amelia?"

Madame Titilayo peered into my face. Her eyes were blood red. She had been crying for too long. Then it all came back. I pushed myself up and looked around. It was just the two of us in the room. I turned to search her face, unable to utter my question.

"Mama. I thought you were dead. They said you were dead," my speech drawled.

She took my hand. "I know. It was a false alarm. I was not even on that ferry. I took a later ferry. I just got in the early hours of today." She paused, looking uncertain. "Don't you want to know about the baby?" she asked.

"Yes of course. How is the baby? It is a boy, right?" I asked.

"No, I was told it was a girl. But, Amelia…" Her voice was shaking, her hands too. "She did not survive, Amelia. She was too weak."

I felt her holding my hands tighter. "Amelia! Amelia! Did you hear me?" I heard her calling me, but it sounded so far away.

I turned to her again. "Please what about my child, my son?" I asked.

Madame Titilayo was staring at me strangely. Then she leaned over and seized me by the shoulders.

"Amelia, your baby is *dead!*" she said firmly.

I broke out of her grip and looked directly in her face.

"He is not! Please bring him to me now!" I shouted.

She sat, transfixed, and then seemed to make up her mind. She got up and left the room.

I rolled to my side and lifted myself up on my hands. They had changed my outfit. I was now in a new blouse and wrapper. I searched around for my sandals. Just as I saw one hiding in the corner, Madame Titilayo retuned with Mrs. Oladele.

"Do you see what I told you? Look at her!" she said.

Mrs Oladele came closer to me, and touched my shoulder gently. "Amelia, you can't be moving around like this, you just had a baby."

I eyed her in disgust. "And where is he?" I asked. Pointing to Madame Titilayo, I said, "I asked her to bring him to me, she refused."

They looked at each other. Mrs. Oladele turned back to me. "Amelia, just sit down, please sit down," she said.

"Only for a minute, because I have to go and get my baby since you have decided not to bring him," I said.

She motioned for me to lie down, but I refused. I sat down on the stool and waited for them to bring my baby. Madame Titilayo drew closer, her eyes were sparkling with tears. "Amelia…" she whispered. "I would have brought her, but please understand that she is not here anymore."

"Please, just bring him to me." I cried, as my heart shattered with every second they kept us apart.

They were whispering to each other. Mrs. Oladele got up slowly and left the room. "Is she getting my child?" I asked.

Madame Titilayo sat down by me, weeping softly.

"Amelia…" she said. I stared at her blood shot eyes. "Your baby is gone. She did not make it," Madame Titilayo said softly. It was in her eyes. She spoke the truth. Her hand opened up and I gazed down at a curl of black lustrous baby hair.

I touched it, feeling its softness, and then grabbed it to my nose, imbibing the smell. "God, no! Where are you, God?" I screamed. Madame Titilayo held me down as I screamed over and over again. The tears were running down our faces, but she didn't let go as my world shattered.

LAGOS

South-Western Nigeria

c. 1902 – c. 1903

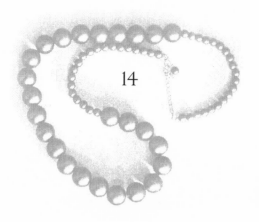

14

FREE SPIRIT

The hustle and bustle of Eko—Lagos as it was popularly called—never failed to amaze me. The people were a wonder to watch. They never grew tired, shouting their wares up and down the street. Neither did they take no for an answer when it came to pushing their goods on passersby. It was a melting pot of cultures and ideas. There were people from different parts of the new world everywhere I turned.

There were the Aworis. Stories passed down claimed that they were direct descendants of Oduduwa, father of the Yorubas. They migrated from Ile Ife and were the first to settle on Lagos Island. Olofin, son of Oduduwa, had been given a plate by his father when they parted ways. He was told to place the plate on the river and follow it. It was only when the plate stopped and sank to the bottom of the river that they would finally rest and make that location home. The plate finally stopped and sank at Idumota.

Soon after came the Bini people. They named Lagos Eko, which means cassava farm. The Amaros— freed slaves from Brazil and Cuba—with names like Fernandez, De Souza, and Alfonso to name a few, migrated next. They are known for their architectural acumen. They introduced the two-story buildings and bungalows. The Saros—descended from the Yoru-bas—were freed slaves from Sierra Leone that arrived years ago and made Lagos mainland home.

Lagos, colonized by the British for the past forty odd years, was flourishing under foreign rule. It was the commercial center of the west coast. Having taken over most of the trading from Madame Titilayo, since her health began to deteriorate a few years ago, I'd had the opportunity to see how Lagos flourished. I traveled as far as Port Harcourt, not minding the fact that very few women brave the unknown territories. I enjoyed my new life. It was a far cry from what it had been when I had first arrived Abẹokuta.

The loss of my baby had been the last straw for me. I sank into depression. I lost all motivation to live. I refused to eat, almost on the brink of death. Dare— who would have helped to bring some normalcy— decided that he had enough of Abẹokuta and moved to Lagos. Mrs. Oladele was the one that surprised everyone the most. She came early one morning and announced to her good friend that she would be mov-ing to Ibadan. In a few days she was gone.

The *constant* in my life became Madame Titilayo. She sat by my side daily for many moons. I would hear her praying over me at odd hours of the night. She forced me to drink beef or chicken broth when I could no longer swallow solids. Sometimes, I would hear her crying over my skeletal body.

Then she started to read her Bible in my room. She would tell me what book she was reading from, and then begin in low tones. It soothed me, calmed me down. I would watch her smiling as she read. She had a peace about her. She refused to travel. Rather, she sent her laborers, knowing that they would cheat her. I begged her to go, and told her that I would be fine, but she refused. "You are more important than that," she would say repeatedly and touch my cheek.

When I came around fully, I asked her what she had kept chanting over me all those moons. Madame Titilayo had smiled and said, "It is Psalm 23 in the Bible." Her constant chanting had caused me to memorize it.

One day, sitting at my bedside, Madame Titilayo said out of the blue, "You must release every false god, Amelia. It is time to let go and start afresh. Promise me you will at least try."

I gazed into this wonderful woman's face. "I promise, Mama. I have nothing more to lose. Everything of importance has already been taken from me," I said.

Madame Titilayo shook her head emphatically. "Not so, Amelia. God still has need of you. He wants to use you for His glory." Her eyes radiated with hope and joy.

"Use me?" I asked.

"Yes. He wants you to surrender yourself, so that through Him you can be made whole again," she said. "Will you give Him a chance?" she asked.

I studied her face again, wondering at her source of constant joy. I nodded.

The smile that appeared on Madame Titilayo's face was one that I had never witnessed before. Her arms appeared around me and pulled me close. "You will get a new start, Amelia. Somewhere you can begin afresh. God will be there for you. You will see."

৽

Madame Titilayo expanded her stalls to Lagos and I asked her to send me. I was determined not to look back or feel sorry for myself. I wanted to make something out of my life. That is what my parents would have wanted for me. I made up my mind to make that my legacy to them—alive or dead.

Now I managed two stalls—one at Ereko market in Isale Eko, Southern Lagos Island market, and the other at Oyingbo market in Ebute Metta, Yaba on the Mainland. Getting from one stall to the other was easier now that the new bridge had been built. I employed two young girls, one in each stall, to oversee sales when I traveled, but I always made sure if I was in town, that I was present. We sold food stuffs—cassava flour, yam, and plantain—which we brought from Abẹokuta. I realized that food was one commodity that would always be needed, and convinced Madame Titilayo to shift from luxury items, of which demand was prone to be unstable. The shift to food products had been a good one. Madame Titilayo could not praise me enough and she encouraged me to move to

Lagos while she stayed most of the time in Abẹokuta to coordinate the farmers.

Dare was already settled on the Mainland, working as an accountant trainee at the Government Department of Railways. Often times, we would meet to reminisce about home. Once, I had asked him if maybe we could go back.

"Go back for what? The whole kingdom has been destroyed by the French. Our family has been captured and exiled. Let us not go backward, Amelia. God has made it possible for us to move forward."

My mind would not stop wondering, hoping that *maybe* someone survived. Walking through the market sometimes, I would see a face that looked familiar—a friend from Abomey, one of my brothers—but I was always wrong. My heart still yearned for home.

For now though, Lagos was my home. The people were friendly and warm. They asked all the time where I was from and why I spoke the way I did. Especially Maria, my neighbor who lived in the same apartment building in Ebute Metta. She had migrated from Brazil with her family several years ago. Her parents were freed slaves who wanted a better life for their children. They were in earnest search of their roots. Knowing that they were descended from the Yoruba, they felt the best thing was to be among their people and made the decision to come.

When I first moved in, Maria had knocked on my door to welcome me. She explained that she was also new to the city and was curious about learning the culture. I told her that, though I spoke Yoruba, I was not originally from Lagos.

"I know," she had said and smiled. Her hazel brown eyes twinkled with mischief. She looked no older than thirty. From her complexion and curly hair, it was apparent she was of mixed blood. "I was told you were the Danhomè lady by way of Abẹokuta." Her smile deepened when she finished.

I must have looked surprised, because she laughed. My neighbors had given me a befitting name. I gathered myself and responded. "I can tell you what I do know about the culture. I can see you already speak Yoruba very well."

"Yes, yes, my parents made sure we learned it growing up so that we did not lose our identity." She said.

My mind went straight to mama. That was what she had been doing too.

"Maybe we can sit and talk sometime in the evenings when you return from work?"

I had agreed, and that was how we began our evenings of tea and biscuits where we talked about everything. I learned from her that in Brazil there was still an active Yoruba community where freed slaves still practiced their indigenous religions.

"Do you know my parents practice voodoo? In fact, they hold ceremonies in the room every week!" she whispered to me as we sipped tea one evening. My eyes widened in shock. She nodded in confirmation.

"Is that the reason for the crowd I see standing outside your door a few times each month?" I asked.

"Yes, Amelia. I have *begged* them to give it up. Do you know they practice it *with* Catholicism? I think that is just being hypocritical. I am one hundred percent catholic! I believe in Mary and Jesus, and that is all I need." She slapped her hands together to make her point and then burst out laughing. "Anyway, forget about that. How is business?" she asked.

"Fine. I am traveling to Ibadan in a few days," I replied.

Maria rolled her eyes in mock exasperation. "Travel here, travel there, when are you going to be still and have time for *yourself?*" she asked.

"I have time for myself! What about you? You're never at home," I said, laughing.

"That's because I am always in *church!* There's a difference. So when are you going to get married?" she asked.

I burst out laughing in disbelief. "Maria, *I* should be asking *you,* not the other way around...When are *you* getting married?"

She smiled sweetly. I had a feeling this had all been a set up.

"Well, there is this man, tall and handsome. He is always at the church..."

"I see...no wonder you keep going," I said.

"Yes, of course. He seems to be uninterested, but I know that with my charm, he will come around."

"Ummhmm. And?"

She shrugged nonchalantly. "Well, once I make him see reason that he can defrock and *still* be a child of God, *then* we can get married," she said, biting her lower lip mischievously.

I sat up straight in my chair. "Maria, you have to be joking! Father Duncan *cannot* get married. He's already married to God!"

I watched her lean over and pick an English biscuit from the row on the tray as calmly as ever. She dusted the crumbs off her blouse and finally looked at me. "Amelia, as you get closer to my age, you'll realize that happiness is going after what you want and making sure you get it. I intend to have Father Duncan as my husband. God said to *ask and you will receive,* and that is what I am doing."

I shook my head, unable to respond. I was not catholic. I attended the St. Jude's Church in Ebute-Metta, an Anglican church. Most of our neighbors were members. I enjoyed the service and the choir. Reverend Jaiyesimi had taken a keen interest in me when I joined. Madame Titilayo had personally introduced Dare and me, asking him to take care of us now that we were living in Lagos.

"Maria, I can't tell you what to do. I just don't want you wasting your time when some young *eligible* men are presently waiting for *you* to notice *them.*"

The plump woman before me looked unperturbed, like she had heard it all before. "Please my sister, stop all that rubbish. These young men are not serious. They want to have fun and not marry. I am looking for a God-fearing man, someone just like Father Duncan."

"Maria, that would be hard. You need to lower your standards. See, for instance, Mr. Caulcrick down the hall. He is unmarried with a fine paying job as a clerk in the Court. He isn't even *that* young—I would guess in his early forties. Is he not good enough?" I asked.

Maria wrinkled up her noise, looking puzzled.

"You don't know Mr. Caulcrick? The man who lives at the end of the hall? He's always opening the door for you every time we go out," I said, surprised at her puzzled look. It was impossible for her not to notice Mr. Caulcrick, the Saro immigrant. We saw him often hovering around the front steps of our building in the evenings when we went for our walks. On weekends, his gramophone would be placed close to the window, loud enough for the rest of us who didn't have one to listen. He was a kind soul.

"Well, pretend like you don't. He is pining away for you. I'd suggest you at least say hello to him one of these days. He may not look like what you want, but he could probably surprise you," I said.

Maria looked sharply at me, and then sighed. "Look, Amelia, I admit, I have noticed him, but he is not exactly what I'm looking for. He looks dull and boring. I need some excitement, you know." She rocked her plump self from side to side.

I laughed, trying to understand. Though she was older, I felt more mature than Maria. I had seen too much in my short period here on earth. I had never disclosed to her who I was, only that I was born in Abomey and had lived in Abẹokuta with my benefactor. "How is Father Duncan more exciting than Mr. Caulcrick?" I asked.

"Well, first and foremost, Father Duncan is *British!* He's lived in England and other parts of the world. He saves souls. What has Mr. Caulrick done?" she asked, turning her nose up.

"Why don't you ask him? Give him that chance, Maria."

She sniffed and bit down on another biscuit. "And you? Why haven't you given any of the young men a chance either?"

"Maria, there are *no* young men." I was surprised that she was turning the tables on me.

She looked ready to burst. "Indeed! So how about the choir master who walks you home from church?"

"He is a *married man!* Reverend Jaiyesimi asked him to walk me home *once!* That was it," I said, taken aback that she had even noticed.

She sat back. I could see her thinking, and waited for her to continue. "You have never had any relationship with anybody?" she asked.

I shook my head. It was easy to lie now. That part of my life was over.

"That is very strange, but that would make Marcos very happy."

I laughed so hard, I was afraid the neighbors would come knocking. "Marcos, your older brother? The one who works with the Brazilian architect?" I asked—his curly brown hair, green eyes, and olive skin materializing before me.

"Yes, so you noticed? He has been asking about you," Maria said.

I laughed again. "Tell him you got nothing. I'm not interested in any relationship at the moment," I said.

She shrugged. "Suit yourself. Just know that any girl that my brother likes and marries will enjoy life!" she shouted, raising her hands up.

I clapped my hands, laughing. I enjoyed Maria's company, because she didn't know my past and accepted me as I was. My life in Lagos was a content one.

❧

I was on my way to see Dare today. It was a Friday. Most of the markets were closed early, because of the weekly clean up exercise, which commenced at 4 p.m. I picked up my bag, turning to Saidat, my help. "I am leaving now. Please make sure you count all the money properly. We will go over the accounts tomorrow."

"Yes Madame…Madame?"

"Yes, Saidat. Hope all is well?" I had noticed her trailing after me as if there was something on her mind. She nodded, shifting from one leg to the other.

"A man came looking for you today."

My heart stopped. "A man? Did he say who he was?"

She shook her head. "He is not from these parts. He talks just like you."

"Did he say when he was coming back?"

"He did not say. He just said he wanted to see Amelia, and that he will return."

"Thank you. If he comes again, tomorrow before I get here, tell him he must wait for me. Do you hear?"

"Yes, Madame. Good night."

"Good night, Saidat. Please give your daughter some of these oranges on the shelf."

She knelt down, thanking me. My mind wondered as I shoved through the moving crowd. Almost everyone had closed and headed home. Fortunately, I was at the Ebute Metta market, and I would soon be at Dare's place, which was only a ten-minute walk.

He wouldn't believe it when I told him someone from Abomey had come looking for me. I am sure he would not be interested. Dare had all but shut his mind from that time in his life. His accent had even disappeared in the process. It was as though he was making every effort to erase all the memories of home.

As I stepped over the gutter, I felt myself tripping. Someone in the crowd steadied me. "Thank you!" I looked up to see a bespectacled man in a suit, still holding my arm. He held it until I made it across.

"You are welcome, Madame," he said. He looked scholarly, with a bow tie, a crisp white shirt, and a dark suit. His hair was parted in the center. He was holding a black suitcase.

"I am Fred Bodunrin. How do you do?" he asked, holding out his hand.

"How do you do? Amelia Sodipo," I replied, taking his hand. I had since taken Madame Titilayo's last name as mine.

"Are you new in the city? I pass this way all the time, and I have never seen you," he said, smiling.

"No, I have lived here for six years now. I live in Ebute Metta actually, on Jebba Street."

"Jebba Street? I am but a street away from you!" he said.

"I see. The reason we probably have never met is because I'm a trader and travel often." The words rolled out of my mouth effortlessly.

"A trader? That must be a lot of work for someone as young as you," he said, eyeing me curiously.

I felt the laughter bubble out of me. "That is very kind of you Mr. Bodunrin," I said.

By now, the crowd was pushing past us impatiently, and we began to walk again.

"Please, call me Fred. Not a kindness, I speak the truth," he said.

I glanced at him. "I may look young, but trust me; I have years of experience trading up and down the coast."

He nodded thoughtfully. I looked up to see that we were approaching my street. The crowd had thinned to a large extent and I could recognize the usual faces I saw daily on the street—except for one.

A man was standing across the street, watching as we drew closer. He was leaning against the wall of a house. Though he wore a European style shirt that fit across his wide chest tautly, and a fitting pair of khaki pants, he looked out of place. It was his eyes—they darted around like a caged lion.

Fred cleared his throat.

"I'm so sorry. Did you say something?" I must have appeared very rude.

"Do you know the man over there? He seems to be staring pretty hard."

"I was just wondering that myself."

By now we were walking right past him. He nodded his head in a form of greeting as we walked by. There was something about him. He looked...familiar. It wasn't his face though. I couldn't explain it. We had reached the beginning of my street. "Oh, I must go and see my brother, Dare, first. He lives two streets down from here. Thank you for walking with me."

He smiled, pushing back his glasses. "Dare? Is it the same Dare that works at the Railways?" he asked.

"Yes, do you know him?" I asked,

He laughed loudly. "Of course! He works under me as a trainee in the accounts department! I work for the Railways as the accountant," he said.

He looked young to be an accountant. He seemed no more than thirty-five years old. He was obviously very educated. He probably had been sent to the United Kingdom to study or attended the Fourah Bay College in Sierra Leone. Those were the likely places most of the educated young men attended in order to attain a higher social status. They returned to take up positions of authority.

"What a small world. Thank you again for saving me back there," I said.

"It was my pleasure. Hopefully, we will be chanced to meet and walk again sometime." His eyes twinkled.

"Yes, hopefully."

We bid each other good night and I hurried off to see Dare to give him the news.

∞

Dare was reading the day's papers when I stepped into his room. His tall stature was hunched over the table. "Dare."

He turned around and smiled. "Sister, sit down, please."

I pulled out his other chair and sat facing him. He was dressed in his usual French suit. He had every color imaginable.

"Guess what happened today?" I asked.

His eyes searched mine briefly, and went back to his papers. "Amelia, I cannot guess. Where would I start from?" he asked dryly.

A sigh escaped me. I was tired of how Dare had become self-absorbed of late.

"What now?" he mumbled, not looking up.

"Someone from Abomey came looking for me today."

He looked up.

"He did not leave a name. I assume that he will return tomorrow," I said.

Dare sat back, tapping his fingers on the table. "Do not speak to this person," he said, his voice hard as steel.

I felt my eyebrows rise up in surprise. This was the last thing I had expected from him. "I cannot do that, Dare. This person may have news!" I shouted.

He shook his head adamantly. "News? What news? Any news we want, we get right here!" He pointed at the papers. "Don't let anyone betray you to the enemies. Maybe they have come to kidnap you? Who knows? My advice to you, go into hiding for a few weeks," he said.

I got up angrily, grabbing my bag.

"Amelia! Did you hear me?" he asked.

I swung my bag on my shoulder and stepped toward the door. "Please remember this, Dare, I do *not* report to you, so you have no right to tell me what to do."

"I am only advising you!" he shouted.

"Stop right there Mr. I-can-care-less-about-my-home. Now that you are a bonafide Lagosian, see where that gets you. Go ahead and forget home!" I slammed the door after me, not waiting for a response.

〜

I pulled out the first drawer and picked out one of my many lace camisoles, smiling softly. This one was soft pink. Something fell to the floor, making a clinking sound as it bounced off three times. It sparkled as it lay on the floor.

I gasped, picking it up—a gold bead. That was all that remained of my beads. I had lost the beads many years ago before moving to Lagos. This single bead was the forgotten piece that had remained in Grandmother's pouch. I picked it up, marveling at the intricate circular designs on it. Glancing at the window, I noticed the sun was already coming up.

I placed the bead back in the drawer under my camisoles. I stuffed my pink camisole in the bag and headed out through the door. I locked the door and began to walk out slowly, hoping the creak in the middle of the floor would be silent this time. The hallway was quiet. It was too early on a Saturday morning for neighbors to be up. They had worked too hard during the week. Saturday was the day to lounge around. I walked quietly past Maria's door and the family of seven whose baby cried constantly. I was about to open the front door when it sprung open. A tall, skinny man stood on the stairs and smiled. I stepped outside.

"Mr. Caulcrick, how are you?" I asked.

He smiled broadly, his eyes resting on the floral bag on my shoulder. "Good morning Amelia. Are you traveling?" he asked.

"Yes, just for a few days. I am on my way to Ibadan."

His face fell. "That is a pity. I was just going to come over to your room and ask you something today," he said.

I tried not to smile. "What about Mr. Caulcrick?" I asked, feigning ignorance.

He moved closer, looking a little shy. "Well, there is this social that my office is having next week Saturday. It's going to be an evening social…er…" He began to stammer.

"Oh, not a problem. I can be of help. What time is the event?" I asked excitedly.

His face broke out in a smile. "7 p.m. It is a black tie event, really. It's our annual dinner. You can wear anything black."

My mouth went dry. There had to be a mistake. "Mr. Caulcrick…I…I…" It was my turn to stammer. He looked confused.

"I'm sorry, I thought you wanted to invite my friend, Maria…I didn't know…" My voice trailed off. I felt very uncomfortable standing beside him now, so early in the morning. Any passerby might think something more of it. I shifted the straps of my bag, feeling the weight.

"Oh, I'm sorry…" he said softly, hurrying to the door.

"Mr. Caulcrick, please wait!" I shouted, running to him.

He held on to the door, and waited for me to continue.

"I was just surprised. The thing is, I am too busy at this time to have much of a social life," I said softly.

He nodded, but still looked defeated.

"Look, why don't you ask Maria? She's a *very* nice girl," I said.

He smiled wryly, as though it might have crossed his mind.

"Just try, you might be surprised. One thing though…" I paused.

He looked up.

"She *loves* English biscuits," I said, smiling.

"English biscuits?" he asked in confirmation. I nodded. "I must hurry now. The train is bound to leave me behind if I don't," I said, waving as I hurried down the steps.

"You said English biscuits?" he called to me again.

"Yes! English biscuits!" I shouted, happy to see him smiling again as I ran down the street.

∽

Ibadan was not like Lagos. That I had concluded the first time I set foot there. The people were very simple and took life as it came. I missed the fast pace of my new home. I planned to be there for a few days, trading with the local farmers for some palm kernels. It was a commodity in high demand. I usually stayed with Mrs. Oladele. I was obligated to spend time in the three-bedroom mud house every time I was in town, but I always accelerated business matters in order to leave quickly. This time would be no different.

I arrived that same Saturday evening and made my way down the road to the house. The kids played outside as usual, and a few adult neighbors waved to me as I walked by. A boy was playing outside Mrs. Oladele's house as I approached. He looked up.

"Aah, aunty! You are welcome!"

He was Mrs. Oladele's ward—Ifẹmi, a niece's child born out of wedlock. She had taken charge of the child the moment she had arrived Ibadan years before. The boy ran to me, taking my bag.

"How are you, Ifẹmi? Is Mama home?" I asked, touching his soft hair.

"I'm fine," he said, hugging me around the waist.

"So, where is she? Is she home?" I asked.

"Yes, she is inside...but... " He seemed reluctant to say more.

"What is it? Is something wrong?" I asked.

Ifẹmi had a tight smile. He shrugged as if dismissing something. "No, Mama is in her room. You can go in. I will put your bag in your room." He entered the house, disappearing into the first room in the hallway. I walked further down to the end to Mrs. Oladele's room. I could hear two muffled voices talking as I stood at the door.

"It will work, don't worry!" Mrs. Oladele whispered

I cleared my throat to announce my presence before knocking. There were sudden movements in the room.

"Who is that? Ifẹmi, is that you?" Mrs Oladele asked.

"No, ma, it is Amelia," I said.

There was a pause, and then whispering. "Amelia?" she asked. I heard her get up and come toward the door.

"Yes. Good evening."

The door opened revealing a disheveled Mrs Oladele. Her blouse was crumpled, her wrapper almost falling off her waist.

"Aah, Amelia, you should have sent a message that you were coming!" she shouted, trying to close the door behind her, but her wide hips were in the way. A shadow moved behind the door.

"I have to oversee some transactions tomorrow morning. It was a last minute deal set up by Madame Titilayo," I said, cranking my neck to see who stood behind the door.

She nodded, bumping into me as she finally closed the door behind her. "I see. That's fine. Come, let me call Ifẹmi to bring some dinner." She walked with me down the hallway.

"No, ma, I am all right. I brought some food with me. I just want to retire for the night," I said.

"Is that right?" she asked, eyeing me suspiciously. It was times like this that she made me feel uncomfortable. I managed to smile, reaching for the handle of the door of the guest room.

"Yes. I am not hungry. I will be leaving very early for the farm tomorrow," I said.

"You said this was another deal? You are something else, Amelia! Deals left, right, and center! You're definitely cut from the same mold as Titi!" she said, her voice tinged with envy.

I laughed awkwardly. "Seven years under Madame Titilayo's tutelage must pay off. Good night, ma!" I said, finally able to lock the door behind me. I leaned against the door to listen as she walked down the hallway to her room. She closed the door firmly behind her. It was quiet after that. I listened closely for most of the night, eventually falling asleep.

∽

I woke up just before daybreak to take my bath in the backyard. As I took the back door out into the backyard, a tall figure turned the corner of the house leading to the front yard. I hurried after, getting to the front yard in time to catch a tall dark man dressed in a French suit disappear down the road. My heart stopped, the bucket in my hand dropping to the ground. "Dare! Dare!" I shouted.

I waited, hoping that he would retrace his steps back, but there was nothing, only silence.

Movements sounded behind me. I turned to see Mrs. Oladele appear, wide-eyed. "Why are you shouting Amelia? What is the matter?" she asked.

Ifẹmi walked out of the house, rubbing his eyes. "Aunty Amelia, are you all right?" He peered up at me, his brows knotted in concern. My heart steadied, and I managed a smile for him. "Don't mind me my dear. I thought I saw someone I knew. Go back inside." His wise eyes held mine. "It is all right Ifẹmi. I'm sorry for alarming you and your mother," I said, patting his shoulder. He looked sideways at Mrs. Oladele.

"You heard your aunty, go in now," she said softly. We watched him enter the house.

"Amelia," Mrs. Oladele said, hands on her hips.

"Ma," I said, picking up the bucket.

"Why were you shouting?" she asked.

"I saw someone who looked like Dare leaving *this house*," I said quickly.

Mrs. Oladele's mouth dropped open. "Dare? He hasn't been here. Dare hasn't been to my house in years!" she said in astonishment.

"I saw someone who looked like him," I whispered.

She shook her head even before I finished speaking. "No! No! No! Amelia, I do not know what you are trying to say, but I will stop you right now!" Mrs. Oladele's face was contorted with anger.

I stepped back. "Ma, I didn't mean to get you upset, but I can almost bet my life on it. That was my brother!" I shouted above her hissing.

She lifted a finger. "Amelia, I have not seen your brother, all right? It's best you go about your business for the day," she hissed, and then turned around, slamming into the bench that stood in her way disappearing into the house. A chill went through me as I looked down on the ground next to the fallen bench. Sandal prints as large as a grown man's were embedded into the wet ground going all the way to the road.

∽

I picked up another sample of the palm kernel and then glanced up at the farmer. "That is my last price! I cannot go any higher than that!" I said.

"Madame Amelia, the price is too low for me! I still have to pay the laborers!"

"And I still have to transport this to Lagos, Baba Gbolahan. This is not easy on both sides!" I said, knowing that we may have to go a few more rounds of bargaining.

We stood eyeing each other across the table, neither of us unwilling to yield. He tapped his feet on the ground, looking down briefly. I glanced at the laborers who were waiting to hear whether to proceed with the loading.

"Well, that's the most I can pay." I stepped forward, appearing as though I was leaving.

"Madame!" He held my arm, holding me back. This was a tactic that never failed me.

"Aah, aah, Baba Gbolahan, why are you holding me? You have refused, so it's best I leave now," I said, feigning surprise.

He let me go, wiping his face agitatedly. "Don't be angry, Madame. The price is all right. I will take it like that," he said quickly.

"Are you sure? Maybe it would be better for you to find another customer?" I asked.

He shook his head. As I had suspected, he had over-priced the goods. "For you. madame, I will sell it at your price," he smiled, waiting for me to respond.

"Good! Please tell them to load the cart."

He called out the order to the men standing about. My work here was done. I had completed it in a day. I would be on my way back to Lagos tomorrow. I paid immediately and watched them load the sacks of kernels. The deal was a success. Madame Titilayo would be happy to hear about it. I handed Baba Gbọlahan another bag. He took it, and then looked at me curiously, feeling the contents.

"What is this for?" he asked.

I smiled, swinging my bag on my shoulder. "That is for your trouble," I said.

I wished him a good evening, walking away quickly. I heard him yelling happily and smiled. Baba Gbọlahan needed the extra money. He had three wives and multiple mouths to feed.

༦༠

Ladi, Mrs. Oladele's foreman at her farms was sitting outside with her when I returned. They watched me from afar, and I gathered my wits about me.

"You're welcome, my dear," Mrs. Oladele said sweetly, shifting on her stool.

Ladi didn't move. He was staring unabashed.

"Thank you, ma," I said.

I glanced at Ladi who hadn't said a word.

"Good evening, brother Ladi," I said.

"How are you Amelia? How is Lagos?" he asked, leaning his head on the wall as he watched me from under half closed lids.

"Lagos is fine," I said, walking toward the entrance of the door.

"Wait, Amelia, sit with us. I need to speak with you," Mrs. Oladele said.

I walked over slowly to her and sat on the stool closest to her. She moved her stool closer. I glanced at Ladi, expecting him to leave.

"Oh, Ladi can stay. He is actually a big part of what I want to discuss," she said.

I waited for her to continue.

"You see, there is this new business that Ladi told me about—" She nodded to him to continue.

He leaned forward, placing his hands on his knees. "Amelia, I just got back from the border.," he said

"Border, what border?" I asked sharply. My mouth was drying up fast. His eyes were watching me closely.

"Kotonou. Are you not from there?" he asked.

"I am from Abomey, not Kotonou." I said.

"Oh, Abomey? Where Gbèhanzin was King," he said matter-of-factly.

"What has that got to do with the new business?" I asked.

"Well—" He rubbed his hands and leaned in again. "As you may know, Kotonou is a busy commercial center. There's a large port there that ships goods directly to Europe. There's a viable market for cotton there. We can mass produce it solely for the foreign market—"

"What demand have you seen to prompt this interest, brother Ladi?" I couldn't help interrupting him.

"Well, like I mentioned, I was in Kotonou recently, and I noticed the vast shipment of cotton and asked around. It appears the Europeans have a high demand for it," he said.

I remained quiet.

"Amelia? Did you not hear?" Mrs Oladele asked, smiling from ear to ear.

"Hmm? I heard," I said softly.

"Wouldn't that be a good business, Amelia?" she asked.

"That is hard to say, ma, since we have never produced cotton," I said.

An angry looked flashed across her face, and then she seemed to compose herself. "Why not discuss with Titilayo and come back and tell me what she thinks?" she asked coldly.

There it was again. She always reminded me of whom I was—an employee and not the one with final authority.

My smile was tight. I picked up my bag. "Of course, ma."

"Are you leaving already?" Ladi asked, looking surprised.

"Did you have something else to say?" I asked, getting up.

He did the same, towering over me. "No, I think everything has been said. Are you leaving tomorrow?" he asked.

"Yes," I replied.

"I am also traveling to Lagos. I will come by so we can travel back together. What time do you leave?" he asked.

"In the afternoon," I lied.

"Good. I will come by then." He smiled, but it did not reach his eyes.

"All right, thank you. I will surely discuss with Madame Titilayo. Good night," I said, excusing myself.

I entered the house. The door to Mrs. Oladele's room was opened at the end of the hall. The light from the lamp caught my attention as it glowed from within. A little head looked out and there appeared a visibly shaken Ifẹmi.

"It's only me, my dear. Why are you shaking like that?" I asked chuckling as I held on to his skinny arm. He reminded me of Akaba, sometimes.

He remained mute, his eyes round and fearful.

"Come. Come to my room. What are you doing in here anyway?" I pulled him slowly into my room and closed the door. His hands remained firmly behind his back as I watched him closely.

"What are you hiding Ifẹmi?" I asked, smiling and shaking my head.

He shrugged.

"I know there's something there. You can't fool me," I said.

Leaning forward, I pulled his stiff hand from his back. His strength was no match for mine and he finally succumbed. His hand opened, revealing gold beads threaded together. I looked up sharply at him, picking up the beads. "Where did you get this? I have been looking for this for a very long time!" I whispered.

His bare chest heaved up and down.

"Ifẹmi, I asked you where you got these from!"

He slowly took his other hand from behind his back and opened up his palm.

"There are *two* of them," he said.

The two sets of gold beads were identical, with the same circular designs. I recognized mine threaded with black thread. The other one Ifẹmi cupped in his hand was with cream thread. I looked up at him. "Where did you find them?" I whispered.

"In her room," he said.

"Where in her room?" I asked.

"In the bundle where she keeps her secrets," he whispered, his eyes almost bulging out of his sockets.

I touched his chest, feeling his heart racing. "Ifẹmi…" My heart was beating as fast as his.

"Yes?" he said.

"Are you afraid of your mother?" I asked.

He nodded his head slowly as my heart sank.

∾

"Mama, I must speak with you." I sat across from the petite woman.

Her face was lightly lined with wrinkles. Her almond shaped eyes still twinkled with laughter as she gazed at me. "Amelia. You have not even had a moment to clean up and eat," she said.

"There is time to do that later, Mama," I said, leaning forward.

Her eyes grew concerned. "What is the matter, Amelia?" she asked.

"Mama…" I paused, searching her face before speaking.

"Tell me what bothers you," she said, taking my hand across the table we sat.

"I was at Mama Ifẹmi's house in Ibadan," I said.

"I know, and I did not expect you here in Abẹokuta, happy as I am to see you," she said.

"It was important that I came to tell you what I saw...and to bring what was found," I said quickly.

"You speak in riddles, dear child," she said.

I took my hand out of hers and dug into my bag, pulling out the two sets of gold beads.

Madame Titilayo's hands froze. "Where did you get these? I have been looking for it, for mine, for a long time. Is this Jumokẹ's? She didn't tell me she found her—"

"Mama, what are you talking about?" I whispered, suddenly short of breath.

Her eyes darted to my face. "These are my gold beads. My father gave them to me, to me and my sisters, when growing up. I thought Jumokẹ lost hers years ago," she said slowly.

I shook my head, lifting up the beads with the black thread. "This is *mine*. My mother gave them to me when I was about to get married." I lifted up the other one with the cream thread. "Ifẹmi found both of them in your friend's room. I have been looking for mine ever since I moved to Lagos. I thought I must have lost them when I was packing," I said.

She opened up her palms. I put both sets of gold beads in them. I watched as she put them close to her eyes and study them one at a time. Eventually, she raised her eyes to meet mine.

"You are right. This one is not mine," she placed mine on the table.

We were silent, looking at each other, afraid to speak.

"Mama," I finally said, my voice shaking.

"Yes, my child," she said.

"How come we have identical beads? I asked.

She was silent.

"Who are you?" I whispered, the tears welling up in my eyes.

She leaned back in her seat, her eyes steadily looking back at me. "You know me already. I am your mother who has taken care of you for over seven years now," she said.

I shook my head. "No! Explain how we have identical beads, with the same designs on them!" I said, my breath labored.

She smiled. "Amelia, you know all about me. It is I that need to do the asking," she said.

I stared at her, waiting.

"Where did you get your beads from?" she asked.

"I told you already. My mother gave me the beads," I said.

"A Danhomè woman with the same beads as one from Abẹokuta?" she asked.

Shame washed over me, as I now regretted never telling my new mother my complete story. "No mama..." I said, looking into her face. "A young girl from Abẹokuta who was given the beads by her father..." I said slowly. Madame Titilayo's face lost all color. She slumped, closing her eyes. "Mama! Mama!" I screamed, rushing to her side.. "Atinukẹ!" I shouted.

"Ma," Atinukẹ answered. She came out of the back door into the backyard where we sat. "Mama!" She screamed, rushing to her side.

"Get some water!" I shouted. She ran back. I pulled off my wrapper and began to blow air on her. Slowly, her eyes opened and focused on me. "Mama!" I sank to my knees beside her again. She took my hand.

"What was your mother's name? Wait, did you not say it was Ajo?" She whispered.

"Ajo, yes, but her full name was Ajokẹ," I said quickly.

Madame Titilayo had a strange look in her eyes. She sat up slowly. Hurried footsteps sounded. We looked up to see Atinukẹ running with a pot of water on her head.

Madame Titilayo raised her hand. "No, I do not need that. Take it back," she said, her voice steady.

Atinukẹ stood, looking confused.

"Go," I said, waving my hand. We watched her go back, saying nothing.

Madame Titilayo turned to me. "Your mother's name was Ajokẹ and she grew up in Abẹokuta?" she asked.

"No, she grew up in the outskirts of Abẹokuta. She had a stepmother and...and she had..." I stopped, realizing the enormity of what I was about to say.

"Two younger sisters," Madame Titilayo said softly, touching my face.

"Ajokẹ was the name of my older stepsister. She disappeared. The rumor was that she had been captured by the Minos—the female warriors of the Danhomè army. Her mother died of a broken heart. Baba didn't last longer after her."

The tears flowed down my face. "Mama was your sister? My mother was your...your sister?" I whispered.

Madame Titilayo sat upright, opening her arms to me. "Yes. Amelia, you are my sister's daughter."

I screamed falling into her arms weeping.

"It is all right my dear. It is all right." She rocked me back and forth, raising one hand to the sky.

"I praise You, my God, for allowing me to see this day. Thank You for Your mercies. Amelia has returned home, even though we did not know it. She returned to her family. I praise You, Lord! I give You all the glory!"

15

FESTERED WOUNDS

I shifted on the wooden bench, trying to cushion my tired back as the choir stood up to sing. It was another Sunday morning at Cathedral Church of St. Jude's Church. I glanced across at Reverend Jai-yesimi, seated on the podium. He had asked me to see him unfailingly after church. I tried to think of any reasons why he would want to see me, certain that Madame Titilayo would not have told him of our recent discovery.

As the choir began to sing, I singled out Dare on the second row. He looked every bit a member of the choir in his brown robe. He looked at me briefly and continued singing. We had not spoken since I returned from Ibadan and Abẹokuta a week ago. Life had resumed its normal pace. Madame Titilayo had sworn me to secrecy, not to tell even Dare what we knew now.

"When it is time for all to be revealed, you will know," she had said.

As the last verses of *Will Your Anchor Hold* swept through the congregation, I looked up from the hymnbook and caught someone looking at me from the next aisle. His glasses were almost falling off his nose as he leaned back to catch my attention—Fred Bodunrin. He waved at me and I did the same, wondering why I had never noticed him in church.

As I walked slowly behind the crowd leaving the church, I waited patiently in line to shake the Reverend's hand. "Good afternoon Reverend," I said.

He took my hand, his eyes lighting up. "Amelia! How nice to see you this Sunday! Did you get my message to see me after church?" he asked.

"Yes, Reverend. I will wait in your office," I said.

"Very well, I will see you shortly."

I walked toward the office, waving to neighbors and acquaintances. I sometimes felt like an outsider. I had still not been able to make any lasting connections in church. My closest friends were Maria's family. In the beginning, I had been invited to baptismal and confirmation parties, but had declined to go.

"Miss Sodipo! Miss Sodipo!" I turned around to see Fred Bodunrin walking up to me, his Bible clasped firmly under his left arm. He had a nice middle parting in his dark hair that matched the perfect cut of his dark suit.

"Fred! What a surprise to see you here. How are you?" I asked, smiling.

He smiled, holding out his hand. I shook it warmly. "I am fine, how are you?" he asked.

"Very well, I didn't know you attended this church too," I said.

"Oh yes. This is my family church. I had not been attending regularly until recently." He paused awkwardly for a second, and then continued, "Enough about me, how is business?"

I smiled. "Things are moving along pretty well. How is the Railways these days?" I asked.

He nodded. "Good. We are expanding out to the Northern protectorate. These are exciting times for the Railways." We stood smiling at each other, lost for words.

"So—" I said

"Have you—"

We laughed.

"I'm sorry, ladies first," Fred said.

"I was just going to ask how long you've worked there," I said. Out of the corner of my eyes, I saw the Reverend walking toward us.

"Well, it's been two years…" he said.

"Fred, Amelia!" Reverend Jaiyesimi sounded elated. He could hardly hold his excitement as he bore down on us.

"Reverend, that was a good sermon." Both men shook hands.

"How is the family Fred?" Reverend asked.

"Everyone is fine. Mama is visiting with her family in Abẹokuta," he said.

"I see. Please send her my warmest greetings," Reverend said.

"I will. You must have a meeting with Ms. Sodipo?" Fred asked, looking at both of us.

"Please, call me Amelia," I interjected.

He smiled, and bowed slightly. "Of course. I will leave you to it then. A pleasure seeing you again, Amelia. Have a good day, Reverend."

"Bye," I said. We watched him walk to a group of young men.

"Now that is a very fine young man," Reverend said quietly.

After a few interruptions along the way to the office from the congregation, we finally made it in. He sat down behind his desk. "Sit, my dear," he said,

I did and waited for him to continue. His maroon-colored cassock was immaculately starched and pressed, fitting his stature perfectly. A distinguished older man with many years of experience in the Anglican Church, he had a reputation for leading his congregation with ease and servitude. He looked at me from under his half-moon glasses. "Amelia, I would like to discuss something of immense importance with you," he said.

I was praying under my breath, a habit I had picked up from Madame Titilayo. "Yes Reverend," I said.

He leaned forward, smiling slightly. "The church as you know has a number of societies."

I nodded.

"Well, we realize that there is still a void for a group of people that needs to be filled. Speaking with the curate, and a few senior people, we would like to nominate you as the founder of the single women's ministry."

I tried everything possible to stop the laughter, but it still came out. "Me? Leader of the single women's ministry?" I asked, laughing.

He nodded. "Reverend, I'm sorry, but I just think it's a little bit funny. I can't lead that ministry!"

He smiled. "But why? Are you not young and single?" he asked.

"Yes, but that's not enough qualification to lead," I said.

He leaned back in his seat. "Every team, ministry, or group needs a leader who they can look up to, learn from, emulate. Amelia, you have all of these strong leadership skills. You have accomplished feats that others your age cannot even dream of, and that to me is a definition of a leader."

I looked across at him in disbelief. "Thank you Reverend. Can you please give me some time to think about this?" I asked.

"Of course. How about we talk again next week Sunday?" he asked.

I agreed, getting up quickly before he threw another unexpected proposition at me.

I was almost at the door when he called to me. "Amelia."

"Yes, Reverend?"

"That young man, Fred Bodunrin…"

"What about him?" I asked.

"He is a very smart fellow from a very good home. It would not be a bad idea to give him an opportunity to know what a smart young lady you are too."

By the time I raised my eyes in surprise, he had buried his head in a large file.

‿⁀

I crossed the street quickly, just in time, before the old civil servant, Mr. Obi, in his khaki shorts and white shirt almost hit me with his bicycle. We all knew the day he bought that bike it would only be a matter of time before someone got hurt. So far, there had been three accidents, and this was just the third month since the purchase.

"That was a close call," someone said as I walked by. I looked sideways to see Marcos, Maria's brother, sitting down under the umbrella shade with a friend. I smiled and waved as I climbed up the few steps home.

My building was as noisy as ever. The baby, who was now a toddler, was shouting at the top of her lungs. Her mother was outside, holding her. She smiled as I came closer.

"Madame Amelia, how was work today?"

"It went well, Mama Ola. How was your day?" I asked.

She shrugged, looking bored. "Quiet as usual. You know that Ola's father has refused that I work. So every day, I stay home, watching the children. I wish I was like you, able to go out and do something worthwhile."

I searched her face, completely taken aback by her comment. "Mama Ola, you *are* doing something worthwhile—taking care of these children. Don't you ever think you're not," I said, touching her lightly on the arm.

She smiled slightly. "If you say so," she said.

"I say so! Have a good evening," I said, tickling baby Ola's fat cheeks. She giggled as I walked up the front steps. I opened the front door just in time to see

Maria and Mr. Caulcrick coming out of Maria's apartment. They were laughing softly and holding hands. I almost dropped my bag.

"Amelia! So good to see you home a little early today," Maria said, hugging me excitedly.

"Are you both going out?" I asked excitedly.

Mr. Caulcrick nodded. "Yes, just to Sakajojo cinema on Simpson Street. Would you like to come?" he asked.

"No, please, go and have fun!" I said. Turning to Maria I said, "And you, when you come back, you give me the details. No wonder I haven't been seeing you for some time now," I said, winking at her.

They both laughed, holding hands again. They looked happy.

"I will stop by later, my dear. Enjoy the rest of your day!" Maria called to me as they went out.

I watched them walk away, hands clasped together, in love.

❦

It was a beautiful morning. Fluffy white clouds floated freely along the skyline and birds chirped softly in the trees. It would turn out to be a lovely day. I whistled under my breath as I made the final steps to the stall. Saidat was just setting up the food-stuffs, her back turned to me.

"Good morning Saidat. How are you?"

She curtsied, "Good morning, Madame."

"Do you remember what I always tell you?" I asked, placing my bag on the empty chair.

Saidat's hands went to her mouth in embarrassment. She turned facing the street. "I'm sorry, Madame. You said never back the customers. You always have to have your face to them otherwise, you might lose one," she said, looking shamefaced.

I had to smile. "Good. What can I help you with, since I'm here so early?" I asked.

"Aah, no, ma. Please sit down and let me get you some breakfast," she said.

By now, our neighbors on both sides had arrived, and they shouted across their greetings.

"What brings you to the market today, Amelia? I thought you would be in Ereko?" That was Peju, my neighbor on the left, poking her head out of her stall.

"I just wanted a change, and of course, I missed seeing your face!" I shouted across to her.

She laughed, clapping her hands. "Indeed! Hmm, you, this Abẹokuta woman by way of Danhomè, you never do anything *just because*. There *must* be a reason why you are here."

She danced over to me and gave me a hug. I laughed, hugging her back. I had known Peju for as long as I had been in Lagos. When I first arrived, she had taken me under her wing and taught me how to deal with customers, not minding that we were competitors and selling the same foodstuffs.

"Regardless, it is good to see you more often, Amelia." Peju smiled again, the dimples on each cheek carving her face into four.

"Thank you," I said.

"Do you want anything to eat? I am just going down the street to get some bean cake and pap."

"No, thank you. I'll probably get something later," I said.

"All right, see you shortly," she said, walking away. I watched as she wished good morning to everyone as she went by their stalls.

I sat down to do some accounting, knowing that I had to report to Madame Titilayo in a few days. By the time I looked up, the sun was already high up. It was almost midday.

Saidat leaned out, and then turned to me. "It is a little girl. I think she's one of your neighbors."

I went out to see who it was. She looked familiar, about twelve years old with cropped hair framing a narrow face. She had her hands behind her back and waited patiently. She knelt down quickly upon seeing me.

"Madame Amelia, it is me, Iya Alakara's daughter," she said.

"Yes, I know you. Did your mother send you to buy some food stuff?" I asked.

She shook her head. "No, ma. I was sent by Mama Maria. She said you should come *kia kia!* You have visitors!" she said.

"Maria's mother wants me to come because I have visitors? Describe the visitors to me," I said.

She shrugged, holding up her slender hands. "I don't know, ma. I never saw them." She knelt down to say goodbye. I wondered why she was in such a rush, and then realized there were three girls waving to her across the street impatiently.

"I have to go, ma. Please, they are waiting for you. If you don't go now, Mama Maria will think I never came," she said in a pleading tone.

"Don't worry, I'm on my way," I said. I would go for her sake. "Saidat, I must go back home now. I won't be able to go to the other stall today, probably on Monday. Lock up well."

ॐ

I arrived home in half the time it usually took me. I rushed down the hall to Maria's door. It opened before I could knock. Maria smiled and hugged me.

"Amelia, I thought you would stay home today. Come in. You have a wonderful surprise in here!" She pulled me by the hand and immediately found myself in the presence of Madame Titilayo, Mrs. Oladele, Ifẹmi, and Anita. I stopped in my tracks, dropping my bag on the floor. Ifẹmi looked like he had been crying. I opened up my arms and he ran to me.

"How are you Ifẹmi? Is everything all right?" I asked.

He shook his head, sniffing noisily.

"That is what we have come to find out," Madame Titilayo said slowly from her seat.

I looked up at her, my heart racing. The day had come. Mrs. Oladele shifted in her seat, silent.

"Mama, how are you? Mrs. Oladele, you're welcome," I said as calmly as I could.

Mrs. Oladele gave me cursory look, but said nothing.

"Come, sit down, Amelia. We have a puzzle that we need to solve. Your name is in the center of the whole matter," Madame Titilayo said.

"Let me get you another seat in the room," Maria said, already hurrying in. She came out immediately carrying a plastic chair. I glanced at Anita, Maria's mother, who had this knowing look on her face as she sat on a chair behind me.

"Thank you, Maria," I said. I pulled Ifẹmi on my lap, patting his back reassuring. He winced as I touched it. "What is wrong with your back?" I asked.

He sniffed. By now, Mrs. Oladele was tapping her sandal-clad feet on the floor and hissing under her breath. Anita shifted slightly in her seat and smiled. Her eyes didn't miss anything as she looked at the fidgeting Mrs. Oladele.

Madame Titilayo sighed heavily and walked away to the window, talking softly to herself. I was almost sure she was praying.

Anita got up. "What can I offer you? I was just about to make lunch."

Both friends waved in dismissal, stating they were not hungry. Anita disappeared out of the door. I assumed to the backyard where we had a communal kitchen.

I looked at Ifẹmi again, who seemed to curl into himself anytime his mother looked at him. My hands felt his back again as he winced. I felt long gashes through his soft cotton shirt. Immediately, I pulled his shirt up and gasped at what was before me. "Who did this to you?" I screamed, looking at the deep scars down his back. He trembled, looking in Mrs. Oladele's direction.

"She knows I took the beads," he said slowly, wincing in pain.

I jumped up, pushing the boy down in haste as I went for Mrs. Oladele's throat. "You, this useless, *shameless* woman!" I screamed, grabbing her by the shoulder.

"Get her off me!" she screamed.

Maria and her mother pulled me back. Madame Titilayo was standing between her friend and me.

"It is enough, Amelia. Please," Madame Titilayo said calmly. She had Ifẹmi beside her now, holding his hand reassuringly.

Mrs. Oladele was looking around, for the first time, fear in her eyes.

"I'm all right, I'm all right," I said to Maria and Anita as they still held me down. Every bone in my body wanted to jump on the large woman across from me.

"Are you sure, Amelia? Are you sure we can leave you?" Anita asked, her voice low and knowing. I looked into her green eyes.

"Yes," I whispered.

She searched my face for the truth and finally let go. I sat back in the chair, my fingers laced together.

Madame Titilayo stood by the window and then turned to Ifẹmi. "Go into the room and close the door. When we are done, I will call for you," she said.

Ifẹmi looked in my direction. I attempted a smile and nodded. He went in and closed the door.

"Doyin, I brought you here today, because I had something important to ask you," Madame Titilayo said.

"Why we had to meet here for you to ask me, I don't know," Mrs. Oladele said heatedly.

"The same reason why I have asked Dare to also meet us here," she said.

I gasped, sitting up. "Dare's coming here? What has he got to do with this?" I asked, a dreadful feeling washing over me.

Someone knocked on the door.

"That must be him. Can you open the door, Maria?" Madame Titilayo asked.

Maria ran to the door, opening it for my brother. He stood carrying his worn out briefcase by his side.

"Come right in, Dare," Madame Titilayo called. He paused. "Come in Dare. "It is obvious my request that you and your sister make amends is not the only reason I called you here," she said.

He glanced at me. We had still not spoken since we had our argument.

"I felt you also needed to be here since your name has come up several times during my attempts to bring light to this matter," Madame Titilayo paused, as she brought out the two sets of gold beads.

"Aww!" Anita exclaimed beside me.

"Those are beautiful!" Maria said.

"Ifẹmi found these in your room, Doyin. One belongs to me, the other to Amelia. How did they get there?" Madame Titilayo asked.

Mrs. Oladele looked shocked, unable to respond.

Madame Titilayo turned to Dare. "Dare, you were in my friend's house the very day Amelia visited Ibadan. What were you there for?" she asked.

Dare looked back at her, his eyes blank. I stood up, my mind reeling from what could be.

"Amelia, please sit," Maria said softly, pulling me back down.

"Dare, I am waiting for your answer," Madame Titilayo said quietly.

He placed his brief case on the floor, his light blue French suit wrinkling slightly as he straightened up. "I was there on business," he said.

I gasped, falling back into my seat. "I am not crazy after all! I saw you, Dare! I saw you that morning!" I shouted, jumping off my seat before Maria could restrain me. My hands grabbed his shirt. He stood there, emotionless. His eyes were a dark pool of nothingness as they stared back at me.

"What business have you with Doyin here? I thought you never left Lagos?" Madame Titilayo asked.

I held on to his shirt, waiting.

Dare looked down at me, for the first time, smiling. Only, his smile did not reach his eyes. "It's *always* been about Amelia," he said, his voice rising.

"You tell me, Dare," Madame Titilayo said, lifting up the beads again.

He glanced down at me again. "Amelia was never meant to know you were related. That was the whole essence of hiding the gold beads I found in your room many years ago," he said.

I gasped, letting go of his shirt and stepping back. "You stole Mama's beads that night you crept into the room, Dare?" I shouted, putting my hand over my mouth.

"I took them, and yours as well, and handed them to mama's best friend," he continued, glancing at Mrs Oladele.

"Dare!" Mrs Oladele shouted.

"What? You should recognize when you've been caught, Doyin. That's the difference between us," Dare said harshly.

All of us looked shocked as he continued.

"You were already doing too much for Amelia without even knowing you were related. Imagine what you would do if you knew she was your sister's daughter?" he asked.

Anita and Maria gasped. Tears flowed down my face as I touched his chest, feeling his heartbeat. "You knew? You knew and you didn't tell me? Dare!" I shouted, crumbling to the floor.

"I went to the only other person who had a lot at stake, and who I knew would help me," he said, looking again at Mrs. Oladele. She had her head bent low, looking at the floor.

"Continue," Madame Titilayo said calmly.

"I was surprised at first, but she consented to keep the secret, and *many* secrets after that," he said smiling slyly.

I looked up at him, the vision of him standing over the dead guard appeared before me. This was the Dare I feared then and had forgotten existed.

"He lies!" Mrs. Oladele shouted.

Dare chuckled. "I don't lie. I have done every other thing *but* lie," he said.

Madame Titilayo came forward and stretched out her arms to me. I got up slowly with the help of Maria and Anita. All three helped me back to my seat. Madame Titilayo stood by me, gently holding my shoulder. "Doyin, why did you do this?" she asked her friend.

There was a deadly silence. I turned to see Mrs. Oladele smiling to herself, and shaking her head. "Titilayo, my good friend," she said. "How long have we known each other? Fifty-two, fifty-three years?" she asked, not waiting for an answer. She turned to me. "Then this little *runt* came into our lives to mess things up!" she shouted.

Madame Titilayo stepped back in surprise. "Doyin!" She exclaimed.

Mrs. Oladele got up. "Yes, this girl was not supposed to be the one you handed over the business in Lagos to. *I* was supposed to be the one!" she shouted, hitting her chest.

"Doyin, you never told me you were interested…" Madame Titilayo said in barely more than a whisper, her mouth dropping open.

Tears welled up in Mrs. Oladele's eyes and dropped like pellets on her cheeks. "I didn't think I had to. I thought we were too close for me to ask you that." She looked at me with daggers in her eyes. "But you decided I wasn't good enough," she said.

"And so, when I went to your bosom friend here with my discovery—" Dare said, smiling. "—She was only too happy to take the gold beads."

Mrs Oladele nodded. "And why not? Like Dare said, Madame Amelia here already had the *world* at her feet," she said, hissing.

"Dare! Dare! Why? You are my *brother!*" I shouted.

"I am not and will never be. Your father killed mine and that is all I will ever know. We can never be kin," Dare said coldly.

I fell back, clutching my chest. Anita leaned forward, pointing her finger at Mrs. Oladele. "You are hiding something very, very bad," she said in her thick accent.

A look was exchanged between Dare and Mrs. Oladele. They remained quiet.

"What are you still not telling us?" Madame Titilayo asked, beating the gold beads against her palm.

I saw the sweat trickle down Mrs. Oladele's temple. She entwined her hands nervously and then finally stole a glance at Dare. Her eyes traveled to the door where Ifẹmi had gone through earlier.

I took in a deep breath, realizing it was true. "What is it?" I whispered, shifting my gaze between the two accomplices.

They remained quiet. My heart raced faster as Dare's eyes remained on the door. I shot up, flinging myself on him and pulling on his shirt before anyone could stop me. "What have you done, Dare?" I screamed.

This time no one held me back as I clawed at him. He stood there as I unleashed my rage, screaming murderously.

"Stop, Amelia. Do not waste your breath," Mrs. Oladele said. I stopped, turning in her direction. She pointed to the door. "In there is your dead child. The one you lost seven years ago," she said slowly.

Madame Titilayo staggered back. Maria caught her just before hitting the floor. "Doyin, what have you done?" she murmured sinking to the floor with Maria.

My hands shook as I moved closer to the bearer of the news. I felt Anita beside me. "What did you say?" I asked.

Mrs. Oladele looked at me with steady eyes. "Ifẹmi is the child I told you was dead. I have raised him from birth."

My hands shook as they went to my face, clawing down the length of it to wake myself up. I turned to Dare. "She lies Dare. Tell me she lies!" I said quietly.

He looked at me and shook his head. "She speaks the truth. *That* is the other secret," he said.

My hands clawed down my neck, the smell of blood instantly filling my nostrils. "My baby was a girl and she died at birth!" I screamed.

Anita pulled my hands from neck. Dare chuckled and then started laughing crazily.

"Favored, *beautiful* Amelia. I beat you at this one, didn't I? No, your child was a boy. We lied to you. Mrs. Oladele has raised him all his life!" he shouted.

Madame Titilayo sprang up from the floor and slapped Mrs. Oladele across the face. "You useless, good-for-nothing! I never knew your heart could be so deep and dark! Why would you tear a mother from her child?" She let out a sob.

Mrs. Oladele held her wounded cheek. "Titilayo! So you *slapped* me because of *this girl*? I should not be surprised, though. Your whole life, you have lived for yourself alone, not caring for my feelings, choosing others over our friendship."

"When Doyin? When?" Madame Titilayo screamed back at her.

"How about my husband?" Mrs. Oladele shouted.

"Your husband? How can I choose your husband over you? He married *you!*"

Mrs. Oladele shook her head sadly. "O ma şe o! What a pity! He chose me, but only after *you* rejected him!" she shouted back.

"Yes, I rejected him, but only because I knew you loved him!" Madame Titilayo retorted.

"But he loved you instead!" she shouted back.

Madame Titilayo's sighed. "That doesn't matter," she finally said.

"Yes, it matters, Titilayo. Throughout our marriage, you were the elephant in the room. Do you think I don't know you lent him money several times and never asked for repayment?" She nodded. "Oh yes. I know all about the *secret* meetings."

"I did nothing with your husband! Nothing! He just needed some assistance, that was all," Madame Titilayo said vehemently.

"And that's exactly what I mean. You were *my* friend, not his. If he needed assistance, he should have come to me, not you!"

"What has this got to do with Amelia then? This was between the two of us," Madame Titilayo said.

Madame Titilayo was not seeing what everyone else in the room was seeing—including Maria's father who was peeping from the crack in the door. Mrs. Oladele was obsessed with her friend. Nobody could come too close to Madame Titilayo.

"Exactly! This had nothing to do with Amelia until she began to feel she could be an intermediary between the two of us. You should know by now that I should not be the last to know what is going on." She glanced at me, hissing. "You forgot the oath we took that we would never leave each other, always protect one another? You did not keep to your side of the bargain!" Mrs. Oladele asked, her eyes wild. I noticed Anita was now planted firmly beside her, ready to spring into action.

"So you wanted to destroy Amelia and Ifẹmi's lives with your lies? You and this…and this *useless* boy I took into my home!" Madame Titilayo was beside herself as she pointed her finger at Dare, who stood there. Her head tie flew off her head, her arms flaying above her head. She was held back by Anita and Maria. Mrs. Oladele cackled. She kept on, for five minutes, not stopping even for a breath.

"Look," Anita said softly, pointing at Mrs. Oladele. We watched Mrs. Oladele begin to unwrap her head tie and drop it on the floor. She proceeded to take off her buba, and then dropped her wrapper on the floor, exposing her slip.

"Mama, what is this?" Maria asked, stepping forward to pick up the wrapper. She leaned forward to tie it around her, but Mrs. Oladele was faster. She skipped on one leg, headed in the direction of the front door.

"Stop her!" Anita called.

Mrs. Oladele giggled, throwing back her hand and dancing around, her large flat breasts bobbing up and down under the cream slip. "Titilayo, let us go! We still have to get to Abẹokuta tonight. Baba said we should not be late," she turned and ran for the door, closing it behind her.

"Catch her before she gets to the market!" Anita shouted to Maria. "Call your brothers to catch her now. Don't let her get to the market!"

Maria ran after her, calling to her brothers down the hall. Madame Titilayo was transfixed.

"You took an oath with your friend," Anita said matter-of-factly, looking at Madame Titilayo.

Madame Titilayo nodded. "It was a playful thing. We were just twelve-years-old. It was done in jest…," she said quietly.

Anita smiled sadly. "But blood was involved?" she asked.

Madame Titilayo nodded.

"That's all that's needed. You can't take blood oaths lightly," Anita said. She beckoned to us to sit down. "Don't worry. We'll take care of her."

I looked at Dare who still stood, looking into space. "Dare, how could you?" I whispered, my heart breaking into pieces all over again.

He looked at me and then picked up his brief case. "I'm not sorry for anything I did. I'm only sorry that you were able to see this day and have joy come back into your life again," he said and walked out of the room.

"Stop! Call the police!" Madame Titilayo shouted as the door slammed behind him.

Anita patted her hand. "Leave him. He will pay for his sins very soon," she said, her lips turned downward.

I broke down, pounding my fists on the ground.

"Amelia, stop. Please, don't hurt yourself. Please," Madame Titilayo begged, holding my hands. She pulled me close and rocked me gently until my weeping subsided.

"Amelia." I looked up to see Anita pointing to the inner door. The small frame of Ifẹmi stood there, his eyes round with fear.

I gasped, sitting up. I was seeing him for the first time—the soft curly hair framing beautiful light brown eyes, those lips, why hadn't I noticed them sooner? They were Dossou's lips. He had my honey colored skin—just like Mama, just like Madame Titilayo.

I got up slowly. He still stood there, waiting. Finally, I reached him. I knelt, looking into my beautiful son's face. "I knew you would be a boy," I whispered, crushing him to my chest. "You're my little boy," I cried over him as he held me tight.

∽

I poked my head out of the doorway again searching until my eyes laid claim to Ifẹmi as he played with Atinukẹ's little son and daughter.

"Stop worrying your head, Amelia. He is not going anywhere," Madame Titilayo's voice said behind me.

I turned around, smiling. "I'm not worrying. I was just making sure he was all right," I said softly, walking back into the room to sit on the chair opposite her.

She smiled, looking at me. "I'm happy you decided to come back with me for a while. Just to get away from the city, and everything that has transpired there will do your heart good," she added.

"Yes, but like I said last night, Mama, it is time I returned—" I said, looking up. "—with my son."

Her eyebrows shot up. "With Ifẹmi...I don't know," she said with concern.

I leaned close, touching her thigh. "We can't stay away from reality any longer, Mama. We have had almost a month of this. It is time to face life," I said.

Madame Titilayo's eyes welled with tears as she looked at me and nodded. "I understand. Life must, after all, go on," she said.

I grabbed her hand and squeezed. "We will leave tomorrow," I said firmly, even as the tears flowed down.

She nodded and drew me close.

∽

My hand wrapped tighter round Ifẹmi's tiny one as we walked by Dare's street. I had not seen or heard from him since the day he confessed. Returning back to Lagos today brought back the memories of his unrepentant face. I glanced briefly at the white washed building he occupied—a four-bedroom bungalow shared with three other families. I gasped, seeing the mob outside. A woman ran past me and I quickly pulled her back. She hissed, eyeing me up and down.

"Sorry, but what is going on there?" I asked.

Her body stiffened against my touch and I dropped my hand quickly. "Are you not Madame Amelia?" she asked, eyes narrowed.

I nodded. "What has that got to do with what is going on?" I asked, my mouth already going dry.

She shook her head sadly. "Where were you when your brother was killing himself?" she shouted.

The mob turned in our direction. I felt dizzy. Ifẹmi shook my arm agitatedly.

"My brother? Dare? What happened to him?" I shouted, grabbing her hand, which she immediately shook off.

She snapped her fingers and threw her hand over her head to ward off evil. "Please don't touch me. God's anger is upon you and your family for what he has done." She hurried away into the crowd. I looked around and noticed the numerous eyes on me.

"Amelia?" Someone shook my shoulder. My eyes finally settled on Maria who looked happy to see me. "You're back!" She hugged me.

"She...she said Dare..." I stammered.

"Sssssh!" Maria said, looking down at Ifẹmi. "Not now. Let us talk about it when we get home. It is a pity what happened, but we cannot do anything about it now," she said calmly, already guiding us away.

"How?" I whispered.

She leaned over and cupped her hand over my ear. "He hung himself with a rope Amelia. He did not leave a note, nothing," she said.

I gasped, looking into her face. She nodded.

"Where is the body?" I whispered.

She shook her head sadly. "The church would not take him. His body has already been taken away this morning to an unmarked grave site."

I sobbed, covering my mouth.

"No, no, Amelia. Your son needs you now. He must see that his mother is strong for him," Maria whispered in my ear.

I glanced down at Ifẹmi whose eyes had grown to twice its size by now. I fell to one knee and pulled him close. "I'm all right, Ifẹmi. You are safe. I won't let anything happen to you ever again," I said.

He nodded and I saw the first hint of a smile.

16

NEW BEGINNINGS

I hurried past the two women who alternated as they pounded the boiled yam in the mortar. Each held a long, thick wood, and waited their turn before smashing it down, as though it weighed nothing. Next to them was Mama Ola, who sat stirring a large black pot over burning firewood. She was making her popular delicacy of catfish stew. I finally got to where Anita sat stirring a pot of jollof rice.

"Do you think this will be enough?" I asked, showing her the bowl of snails I had just cleaned. She checked it and nodded. "Yes, that is sufficient. It's going in the vegetable with other delicacies, so that should be all right."

"I hope you are keeping some, especially for Marcos. You know fried snails are his favorite!" Maria walked up to us, smiling brightly. Ever since her engagement to Mr. Caulcrick, she was even more jovial than normal. Her face shone with unexplainable joy. Her laughter rang so loudly it could be heard three streets away. The joy couldn't even be tempered by the fact that today was Marcos' going away party. He was going back to Brazil to learn architecture and construction. All of the neighborhood women were scattered all over our backyard hovering over bubbling pots. We were all happy to be sending off our Marcos. He was a son of the community and we were all proud to see him advancing in life. Tonight, we would dance and laugh together, and tomorrow, we would cry as we bade him goodbye.

༄

The young ladies rocked their bodies against the almost immovable chunk of muscle. Marcos was barely moving to the beat of the drums. He seemed to be deriving enjoyment as the three ladies each tried to get his attention. I shook my head as I walked by to sit with Maria and Mr. Caulcrick under one of the canopies lining the street. I had finally succumbed to Madame Titilayo's plea that Ifẹmi stay with her for a few days and didn't have to be turning around to look for him every second.

"Your brother has a very big head. I hope it will deflate before he boards that ship tomorrow!" I shouted over the noise.

Maria giggled, leaning across the table to whisper to me. "He is only making a show. He's trying to make you jealous!"

I made a face, wagging my finger. "Stop this nonsense, Maria. If any one of these ladies hears you speaking like this, they might think something was going on between me and Marcos! Do not spoil his fun!"

People sitting nearby laughed, shaking their hands.

"But it's true Amelia! Marcos has gone loco for you!" someone cried out.

I shook my head, my new, drooping earrings jiggling. I had made an effort to dress up for the party. I had my hair woven up in şuku, an upswept style that sat in the middle of my head. I had on a flowery pink midi dress and new white sandals. My gold beads jiggled as I moved my arms about. I was raising my cup of palm wine to my mouth when I heard a sound behind me. I turned around to see Marcos boring holes in my back. Laugher erupted from the crowd around us. I kicked Maria under the table. Her twinkling eyes told me that I was already betrayed.

"Marcos, is it not true that you would rather dance with Amelia than with these butterflies floating about you?" Maria pointed to the three ladies who eyed us from the dance floor. He glanced back at the ladies, his hands folded across his chest in his usual pose and chuckled.

"Tell them please, Marcos!" I shouted back, putting down my cup.

"Please clear this rumor we've been hearing!" someone shouted, followed by supporting cheers.

He dug his hand in his pockets, looked down on the floor, and then looked across the table at me. His curly brown hair with gold highlights seemed to shine even brighter. "Well, if you insist…" He paused, a tell-tale smile played around his lips. "Amelia is like a sister to me. How could I *think* of her in any other sort of way but as a sister?"

The crowd began to grumble. I noticed it was his group of friends who were making the most noise. I could also tell they were getting very drunk.

"But—" His middle finger went up. "Amelia—" He walked slowly to the table, and placed his hands on it. "Since you are *not* my sister, I would like to dance with you."

His friends jumped off their seats, shouting, and raised up their cups.

Mr. Caulcrick—who now insisted that I call him John—started clapping. Maria had her mouth hanging open. I giggled, a little tipsy from the palm wine.

"You have always been too funny, Marcos. You're not serious—me and you?" I clapped my hands and laughed. By now, the drummers had drawn closer, the talking drum beating loudly.

Marcos held out his hand to me.

"I'm very serious. Can I have this dance, Madame Amelia?"

"Yes!" His friends hollered, and the crowd surrounded us.

"Come on, I'm still waiting." Marcos still held his hand out, swaying slowly to the beat. Maria started clapping with the rest of the crowd.

I got up slowly and took the out stretched hand. His large hands were warm as he pulled me closer. He leaned close to my ear and said, "Finally. It had to take my going across the ocean to dance with you."

I pulled back to look in his face.

"I'm not drunk, Amelia," he said, moving slowly, holding on to my finger tips. I swayed slowly, trying to play it off.

"I know. So what has brought all *this* on? It's quite embarrassing."

He chuckled again. "Not as embarrassing as everyone knowing I'm pining away for someone who doesn't know that I exist."

I looked up at him. "What do you mean, Marcos? I know you exist!" I shouted above the music.

"Do you mind if we walk away for a little bit? I can hardly hear you," he said. He stopped dancing and waited for me to answer. I nodded. Immediately, I felt relief wash over him, as though he'd been expecting a refusal.

"Where are you both going? We thought you were going to the dance?" the crowd called to us, but we ignored them, walking away from the canopied party.

We stopped in front of the makeshift stall of Iya Alakara four houses away. The party noise was not so loud now.

"So, what were you saying, Marcos?" I asked. My hands were on my waist and my legs apart, ready to hit him if he said anything out of line. Our only source of light was the oil lamp burning outside the house, making it difficult to read his face.

"Amelia, my intention is not to make you feel uncomfortable or embarrassed," he said.

"That's too late Marcos! Everyone thinks there's something going on between us, when there's nothing," I said slowly for emphasis.

He shoved his hands deeper into his pockets and kept looking at me, almost sadly. He started to open his mouth and then stopped.

I hit him playfully on the chest, laughing. "Say something, Marcos! You're scaring me."

He placed his hand over mine before I could remove it. His heartbeat was steady against my hand and I didn't want to remove it. "Marcos?" I heard myself say softly. His brown eyes finally blinked and he dropped my hand, stepping back. "Marcos, are you changing your mind and not telling me what it is you brought me here for?" I asked. I could not cover my anger with laughter anymore.

He sighed, looking down at his feet. "I'm leaving tomorrow Amelia."

"I know that…"

"I'm going to miss you," he said.

"I'll miss you too—"

"But not as a friend, Amelia," he interrupted.

I couldn't speak.

"I wish I had summoned up the courage to tell you before now. Maybe things would have been different," he continued.

My heart was wrenching watching him push himself to release his pent-up feelings.

"I've loved you since the day you moved next door. You are so beautiful and so smart too. I wondered how you could manage two stalls when some other women just sat home all day counting their fingers and toes."

I smiled, and waited for him to continue.

"I was resigned to the fact that you were not interested in anyone when no man ever came calling."

I shrugged. "I don't need a man. I have my child to think of." I gulped, feeling the tears dart to my eyes.

"I'm sorry about what happened to you. I wish I could protect you from everything that's happened in your life," he said softly.

"No, Marcos, it was meant to be. It was all meant to happen," I said softly.

"You didn't deserve any of it. Especially from that one you called a *brother,*" he said through clenched teeth.

"Please, don't let's talk about the dead like that," I said slowly, reluctant to discuss Dare.

"A good thing he killed himself, or I would have had to."

"Please, I beg you to stop talking about him!" I said again.

"All right, I'm sorry," he said, turning away, his hands clenched.

I stared, dumbfounded at his straight back. "Marcos, let's go back." I said.

He stood still. I walked two steps closer to him, not sure what to do. I touched his back hesitantly.

"I don't bite, Amelia," he said, chuckling in his characteristic manner.

I smiled, relieved to see him not so serious.

"I will miss you, *Madame* Amelia. You are one special woman I could never forget," he said, holding out his arms.

I hugged him back and said, "Marcos Alvarez, you will never be forgotten either."

"And when I do come back, and you're not married, then it goes without saying that you will be mine," he whispered in my ear.

I laughed, throwing back my head.

"Is that a deal?" he asked.

I looked into his eyes. "Marcos, you need to stop joking around!" I said.

Breaking apart, we looked at each other and laughed again, not an uncomfortable laugh, but one shared by two people who had experienced something that could only be understood by them. We clasped hands and began to walk back to the party.

17

JOY AGAIN

I looked across at Ifẹmi playing on the bench beside me. He had grown so much in the past six months. He smiled a lot now, always rushing to me to give me a hug, or throwing me a glance to make sure I was not far away. My fellow market women called him my handbag and I enjoyed it.

"How can I help you, sir?" Saidat asked a customer.

"Is your madame here?" a male voice asked.

I sat up, recognizing the voice.

"Yes, who is asking for her?" Saidat asked.

"Fred Bodunrin. Is she here?" he asked.

I stood up. Ifẹmi looked up instantly. I patted his shoulder. "I'm just going out there to say hello to someone, all right?" I said quietly.

His brown eyes smiled back at me as he nodded. I smiled back and then walked out to the front of the stall. "Good afternoon Fred," I said, surprised to see him in the midday.

He looked relieved. "Amelia! My goodness, I was afraid I had come to the wrong place," he said.

I laughed. "How did you know my stall?" I asked.

"Oh, you are a very popular lady around here. I only asked for you by name, except they corrected me by adding *Madame* to your name," he said.

I giggled. "Oh, will you like to come into the back. You can sit down for some time if you wish," I said, opening the little path for him to come through.

"Thank you, that would be nice," he said.

"Saidat, we will be back there. Call me if you need anything," I said guiding him just a few feet to the back where I had a table and a chair and the bench where Ifẹmi played.

"Who is this handsome little man?" Fred asked, smiling.

Ifẹmi looked up and smiled at him.

"That's my son, Ifẹmi," I said with pride.

"S-son? H-h-how?" he asked.

I smiled, watching his obvious discomfort. "Yes, my son. I was married before and he is the product," I said calmly, watching as the emotions washed over his face.

Fred glanced at the two of us. "That...that's really a surprise."

I smiled, watching his continued discomfort. "Why have you come?" I finally asked.

"Well, I had not seen you in church for ages. The last time was at the burial of Dare. What an unfortunate incident. Poor boy, why he would hang himself is beyond me. And of course, Reverend Jaiyesimi also asked that I check on you," he said.

"Oh, I see," I murmured, remembering that since having Ifẹmi come to live with me, I had not attended church.

"So, this is the reason why," Fred said.

"Yes, it is," I said.

He picked up his briefcase, reminding me of Dare. "Well, I wouldn't want to keep you from your...er, duties," he said, moving toward the front of the stall.

"Of course, thank you for checking on me," I said, releasing him from his obligation and discomfort.

He hurried out of the stall, turning around only when his feet landed on the busy market street again. "See you in church, Ms. Sodipo," he said quickly and disappeared into the crowd.

Saidat looked after him. "What is wrong with that man Madame? Is he feeling all right?" she asked.

I looked at her, shaking my head. "I really don't know Saidat."

༄

I walked slowly down the hallway with Ifẹmi in tow. It had been a long day at the market. Ifẹmi, since starting school, would be picked up by Saidat on closing and brought to the market. He would stay with me until the end of the day. Today, like every other day, was tiring. Unlike other days though, today we heard music coming from Anita's apartment as we entered the building. The door was wide open and people were talking outside and crammed all the way in.

"Mama Ola!" I called over the music. She was holding a cup.

"Ah, Madame Amelia, you are back. How was work today?" she asked, smiling listlessly.

"Fine. What is going on?" I asked.

"You haven't heard?" she asked.

"Heard what?" I asked.

"Marcos is back!" she said, laughing.

A group of men standing by the wall looked up. I recognized them. "Amelia! Marcos has been asking of you all day!" one of them said. They were Marcos' friends from the going-away party.

I pulled Ifẹmi after me into the crowded room. There he was, sitting in the midst of his friends and family. His hair had grown out, now touching his shirt collar. His skin seemed a deeper tone, probably from being in the sun a lot. His eyes fell on me as he spoke. He stopped in mid-sentence, his hands still in the air. I smiled, holding on firmly to my son's hand.

"Has it been a year already?" I asked, laughing.

Marcos got up, and waded through the crowd to me.

"No, it's actually been eight months. I decided it was time to return. There was nothing more they could teach me," he said, smiling.

"That is so typical, Marcus," I said, shaking my head.

He held out his arms, laughing. "Where is my hug Madame?" he shouted.

I hugged him, letting go of Ifẹmi.

"Ouch!"

Marcos released me immediately, grabbing his ankle.

What was—" His voice trailed off as we both looked down at a very upset Ifẹmi. "Oh, this must be Ifẹmi. Maria told me all about you," he said, smiling at a very mean looking face.

"I certainly did!" Maria called from her seat. She was six months pregnant and looked like delivery day was a few days away.

Marcos crouched down to Ifẹmi's level. "I'm so sorry, little man. I should have asked for your permission before hugging your mother," Marcos said.

Ifẹmi nodded, the lines on his forehead disappearing slowly.

"My name is Marcos," he said, stretching out his hand.

Ifẹmi looked up at me and I nodded. He placed his hand in Marcos' and they shook. Marcos got up, smiling at me.

"Welcome back," I said, genuinely happy that he was.

"Thank you. Will you be staying for a while?" he asked.

"I can't. It's been a very long day for us, and there's school tomorrow," I said, looking down at Ifẹmi, who looked like he could drop any minute.

Marcos nodded. "I understand. What time do you leave the house?" he asked.

"At about seven," I said.

"All right. I'm glad to see you're doing well," he said.

"Thank you Marcos. Enjoy the party!" I said. He began to follow us out. "No, please stay. We can find our way out. We live just next door, remember?" I teased.

"How can I forget?" he called out.

I smiled. Marcos was back. Why did my heart race at the thought?

❧

"Ifẹmi, we have to leave now!" I called from the front door. I waited to hear his little feet approaching, but they didn't.

"He's already trying to play the little truant?" I turned to see Marcos coming out. Clean-shaven and neatly dressed in a white shirt and black pants.

"Good morning! You are up so early!" I said, wondering why my heart was beating fast.

"I'm early because I'm walking my two favorite people to school and work," he said standing close to me, his face looking down at me.

"You are?" I asked, smiling.

Ifẹmi appeared at the door. A smile lit up his face when he saw Marcos.

"Big man!" Marcos said, picking him up.

Ifẹmi laughed, holding on as he was lifted above Marcos's shoulders. I followed them as they made for the exit.

"How nice of you to do this," I said as he opened the door for me.

I heard the door close behind him. "Well, since you decided not to stay for the party, I thought this was the next best way to catch up," he said.

I watched him carry my little boy effortlessly.

"What are you thinking about?" he asked.

I blinked, realizing I had been staring at him the whole time. "Oh, I'm sorry, that was rude," I said, looking away.

He chuckled. "No, I actually enjoyed it," he said.

"I don't do that, trust me," I said, waving to a neighbor.

"I know," he said, his voice light with laughter.

Ifẹmi's school was not far away. The children were hurrying past us.

"Ifẹmi, get down from Uncle Marcos now. We're at your school," I said.

He scrambled down, excited to go. "Bye, Mama!" He said, hugging me around the waist.

I rubbed his close shaven head. He turned and flung his arms around Marcos' legs and then turned and disappeared with his schoolmates.

"He likes you," I said, watching his little head disappear into the classroom.

"Good, I was a little worried about that," Marcos said.

We began to walk in the direction of the market.

"Worried about what?" I asked, giggling.

Marcos looked down at me. "About the child of the woman I am going to marry not liking me," he said quietly.

I burst out laughing. "Marcos! I thought this madness would have left you by the time you returned! Did you not find any beauties over in Brazil, or were you just working too hard?" I asked.

He shoved his hand in his pocket and continued walking. This was characteristic of him when he was lost for words.

"Marcos!" I said, laughing again and touching his arm.

He stopped in his tracks and I paused beside him. "You take me for a joker all the time Amelia, but I am really serious," he said.

I gulped, looking into his face. Beads of sweat had formed over his upper lip. "I came back earlier than planned, because I was afraid you would have taken a liking to someone else," he said.

My mouth dropped. "That was stupid of you!" I shouted.

He looked surprised, and then burst into laughter. Passersby glanced at us curiously. "See, that was what I missed. You speak your mind. Not a lot of people, women, do that," he said.

"So, you missed me speaking my mind and decided to throw your career away?" I asked. I began to walk again and he followed.

"More than that—" he paused, waving at someone.

"Marcos! You're back!" the man shouted from across the street.

"Yes!" he replied, smiling broadly.

"We need to talk my good man!" the friend shouted.

"Sure, let's meet say about six today at the usual place?" Marcos asked.

I glanced up at him.

"All right!" the man said, waving back at him.

We walked in silence for a while.

"Amelia, Good morning!" Peju called as she ran past me.

"Peju! Good morning. Where are you rushing to?" I asked.

Her feet barely touched the ground. "It's that useless Ireti. She is at it again!" she shouted, disappearing around the corner.

I shook my head.

"What's happening?" Marcos asked.

"It happens every month. Ireti is Peju's stall neighbor on the other side. She has been trying to expand her stall by any means necessary. There were rumors that she's installing a new structure that will take up some of Peju's space. I think it just happened," I said, watching as the other market women began running in the direction of my stall.

Marcos took my hand, stopping me in my tracks. "Let's wait until the craziness is over," he said quietly. We looked at each other silently. Then he smiled. "As I was saying, Amelia, I came back because it was time. I did complete the apprenticeship, I just did it at an accelerated pace. My supervisor saw that I was motivated by something—or someone—so he worked with me." He smiled.

"What are you saying Marcos?" I asked.

"I'm saying that I want to court you and I want to marry you," he said quietly.

I shook my head slowly.

"No Amelia, don't do that," he said

I shook my head again, looking up at him. "I am not who you need Marcos," I said.

"How do you know that? I know what I need," he said, touching his chest.

"I am too broken for you," I said, my voice shaking.

He squeezed my hand gently. "You are just right for me. I love you," he said.

My eyes swelled with tears. I brushed them away hurriedly, angry with myself. His hand came up to brush the tears off one cheek. I sighed heavily. "Can I think about it…please?" I asked.

His eyes flickered. "Yes, but I give you just a week. That's already too long for me, but I know how you women are. You'll probably have to talk to all the women in your life," he said.

I burst out laughing. He had spoken the truth.

"Is that fair?" he asked.

"Yes," I said, my heart getting lighter.

"Good." He smiled

"I have to get to work now; I'm starting work with the new construction company Souza and Sons."

"You are? I heard about them. Isn't that where Baba Ola now works too?" I asked.

"Yes, he actually made the contact for me before I got back," he said, stepping back.

"Congratulations!" I said.

He nodded, smiling. "Have a good day at work," he said quietly.

"You too," I smiled and started walking away. I took about ten steps and turned around. He was still standing there watching me, his hands in his pockets. He smiled and raised his hand. I waved back and continued walking. I felt his eyes follow me until I turned the corner.

∽

I looked across the table at Madame Titilayo playing with Ifẹmi on her lap. Her face was transformed as she watched him playing. She looked up. "What is on your mind, Amelia?" she asked above the noise he made.

"Nothing," I said quickly, looking down at the untouched plate of food.

"You are not a good liar. Tell me what is on your mind," she said quietly.

I looked at Ifẹmi, who was also looking at me now. He had an overprotective nature that he got from his father.

"Ifẹmi, please go to the backyard and play. Did Atinukẹ bring her children with her today?" I asked.

"Yes. Ifẹmi, go and play with your friends," Madame Titilayo said. We watched him run out happily. "Now, what ails you, my daughter? What can I do to help?" she asked.

I smiled, loving her even more if that were possible. "You can't do anything to help the situation," I said quietly, feeling embarrassed.

She chuckled. "Why? Do you think it's something I've never experienced?" she asked.

I looked up sharply at her. "Mama," I murmured under my breath.

"Is it man troubles?" she asked, chuckling.

"I wouldn't say troubles, but definitely man *issues*," I said.

She leaned forward. "Has someone propositioned you?" she asked.

"Yes. Marcos," I said.

Her eyes lit up. "Anita's son," she said.

I nodded.

"He is a good man," she said

I smiled. "How do you know, Mama? You met him maybe once or twice," I said.

"I am a good judge of character...for the most part anyway," she paused. The topic of Mrs. Oladele was a bitter one for us still.

"How is she?" I asked

"She is still the same. The hospital says she cannot be released. Her mental state is still too delicate," Madame Titilayo said sadly.

I leaned over and took her hand. "God is still God, Mama. He will take care of her, and He will also heal your heart," I said softly, squeezing her hand gently.

The tears sparkled in her eyes but did not drop. She patted my hand over hers. "Thank you, Amelia. Thank you," she smiled. "Now back to you!" she said, her mood changing instantly.

I smiled, waiting for her to continue.

"Marcos is a good man, and I know he loves you." She had this look on her face.

"How do you know?" I asked, looking around. "Has he been here?" I asked.

Madame Titilayo smiled.

"He's been here? When?" I asked, pulling my hands back into my lap.

"Yesterday," she said.

"I haven't seen him in five days! He just left!" I said in disbelief.

"He said he wanted to give you some space, some time to yourself to think things through," she said.

"That he did! I was worried. I thought maybe something had happened to him," I said quietly.

Madam Titilayo smiled. "So you care for him after all," she said.

I looked back at her, as it dawned on me. "It seems so, ma," I said

Her smile was consent enough.

༄

"A re you ready, Amelia?" Marcos called to me. "I'm coming!" I shouted, pulling up the zipper on my dress. I walked to the mirror. The face that stared back at me was not mine—it was Mama's. I looked so much like her as the years went by. It was the same long, full hair under my cream and pink hat. My eyes, just like hers, were almond shaped, light brown. I pressed my lips together, the light grease smeared on giving them some shine.

"Mama, let's go!" Ifẹmi shouted.

I giggled, picking up my handbag. My heels resounded on the floor as I walked out to meet them in the living room.

"How do I look?" I asked, looking down to flick off a strand of hair on my dress. I looked up when there was no response. They sat side-by-side, mouths open. "Why aren't you saying anything?" I asked.

Ifẹmi got up in his little three-piece suit and walked over to me. He put his hands around my waist and hugged me.

"Mama, you look beautiful," he murmured against my stomach.

My hands touched his head. "Ifẹmi! You are so sweet, my boy!" I hugged him closer. Satisfied, he broke free and ran to the door.

"Where are you going? We have to leave for church in a few minutes," Marcos asked, getting up.

"I know. I'm going to Grandma Anita," Ifẹmi said quickly, slamming the door behind him.

Marcos and I looked at each other and shrugged, chuckling.

"You are beautiful Amelia," he whispered.

I smiled, staring into eyes that adored me.

"Are you nervous?" he asked, looking at me intently.

"A little bit," I said.

He came closer, taking my hand. "But you said Reverend Jaiyesimi is a very approachable man, so why worry? We're just telling him of our intentions to marry in the church," he said.

I nodded. "Yes. I don't know why I'm nervous, I just am."

He pulled me close for a hug. "I guess it's just getting used to the idea," he said.

"Yes. You look so handsome," I said, stepping back to look him over.

He straightened his tie. "You think so?" His smile was infectious. I laughed, taking his hand.

"Let's go before your head gets too big to go through the door."

Today, we would announce our engagement. In two months we would be married.

18

FAMILIAR STRANGER

I walked quickly after the disappearing Saidat through the market. I could barely see the large tray she had on her head. Today was especially busy, because the market was closing two hours early for the weekly sanitation clean-up. It was even busier for me, because in two days time, I would be married to Marcos.

"Saidat! Can you wait for me at the junction there?" I shouted, hoping she would hear me above the noise.

She did and waved her hands at me. "Madame, we have to hurry. You know that we still have to distribute these aṣo ẹbi tonight!" she shouted.

"That's true. You have the list? Okay, go ahead. I have to get something in the stall before I go home!" I shouted back.

She nodded and continued on her way. I crossed over the plank toward my stall. The women were sweeping and packing up their merchandise. As I approached my stall, which was already cleaned and empty, I saw a tall man standing there, talking to Peju.

"Ah, there she is," she said, pointing to me.

The man turned around. He looked familiar. "Princess Amelia?"

I peered into his face, and staggered back.

"Amelia!" Peju ran from behind her stall. Arms caught me before I fell to the ground.

"Who are you and what do you want?" Peju shouted, pulling me away from the stranger.

The other market women looked up. He stepped back, his hands behind him.

"I apologize. I didn't mean to startle you." His Fon accent was thick.

"I'm all right, Peju," I whispered, straightening up.

"Are you sure? Why is he calling you *Princess*? Amelia?" Peju whispered.

I looked up at the man before me. "Dokpe, you are alive?" I whispered. My hand reached out and touched his arm.

He bent to his waist in salutation and raised his head again.

"Yes. So it is true. The princess is alive," he said.

I grabbed his hand and pulled him after me into my stall.

"Amelia! Amelia!" Peju shouted, running in after us.

I turned around, bumping into her. "I know him, Peju. Don't worry, I am *safe* with him," I said calmly, though my heart raced.

Peju glanced at my face and then Dokpe. She sighed heavily, wagging her finger at him. "I know your face, mister man, if anything should happen to Amelia, hmm!" she said under her breath and then turned around and marched off.

Dokpe chuckled, and then put on a serious face. "My princess!" He fell to one knee.

I pulled him up. "Get up Dokpe! We are no longer in Danhomè. We are now equals," I said quickly.

"You will *always* be Princess Amelia of Danhomè," he said.

"How did you find me?" I asked.

"With this." He pulled out my tapestry work. One of many I had made while pregnant, years ago.

I gasped, touching it. "How?" I asked.

"My wife bought it from a trader, who said she bought it when she visited Abẹokuta. Apparently the trader had bought it from a Madame Titilayo on a ferry trip."

"That was such a long time ago!" I said.

"Yes. My wife had packed it up with her things and never had the chance to use it. She only brought it out by accident when she was cleaning up the house a few months ago," he said.

I gazed at him in disbelief. He had changed in many ways, but still remained the same. His dressing was modern—the cotton shirt and pants popular amongst the men worn with leather shoes. He looked well to do.

"And you knew it was mine?" I asked.

"Of course. You remember that you used to sew in your little symbol of three dots on the edge of each tapestry?" he asked.

I nodded, gulping. "Where is everyone?" I asked, my heart in my throat.

His face was stoic. "Gone. The only ones who got away were your father, who was exiled with your mother and Ma Hwanje. A few of the children went. Francine was the youngest. Adandejan, your uncle, also left with your father. Ouanilo went abroad to study law."

"Grandmother?" I asked.

"She...she..." He paused.

"What happened to her? Is she dead?" I whispered.

"She is dead, but..."

"But what?" I asked.

"She sacrificed herself for...for the King."

I gasped, clutching my chest.

"The King sent word to her that her sacrifice would be the only one that the gods would hear to save Danhomè. To save *him*."

"But it did not," I whispered.

"No, it didn't," he said, watching me closely. I was quiet, waiting for him to tell me more.

"I hear you are getting married," he said.

"Yes, in two days," I replied.

"I am happy for you. You waited a long time. He must be worth the wait," he said.

I smiled. "Will you still be here? It would be nice if you could come for the wedding," I said.

"Of course," he said, smiling, but his eyes looked sad.

"Tomorrow is the engagement ceremony. It's at the town hall just a few streets from here."

"At what time?" he asked.

"Four o'clock," I said.

"Will your wife be coming too?" I asked.

"Oh, no," he chuckled.

"Why do you laugh?" I asked.

"Well, my wife has actually never had the opportunity to leave Kotonou. She's afraid of the water."

I laughed along with him. "I see. Thank you for finding me, Dokpe. Thank you!" We hugged briefly. Drawing apart, he quickly dabbed at the corner of his eye. I smiled. He was not so hardened after all.

Someone entered the stall. "Mama! Where are you?" Ifẹmi shouted, appearing in his school uniform. His eyes quickly grew accustomed to the shadows.

"Ifẹmi, what are you doing here? I told you to go straight home to Grandma Anita!" I said, going to him.

"Folusho hit me on the head Mama!" He rubbed his head.

"Why does this silly boy play so rough?" I asked, feeling the contour on his head.

Ifẹmi stared at Dokpe. "Oh, Dokpe, meet my son, Ifẹmi," I said smiling.

Dokpe was silent, his mouth wide open.

"Good evening sir," Ifẹmi said, prostrating on the floor.

Dokpe immediately pulled him up. "Please, don't do that. Royalty does not bow to commoners," he said quickly.

Ifẹmi's eyes widened.

"It's okay Ifẹmi, I'll explain to you later," I said.

"Can I go now?" he asked.

"Yes, go to Grandma Anita now," I said, watching him run off.

"Princess—" Dokpe said softly.

I looked at him, noticing the line of sweat over his upper lip.

"Is that…is that…" he stammered

"Yes, that's Dossou's son," I said, smiling.

"You were pregnant?" he whispered.

"Yes. Is everything all right?" I asked, noticing that his hands shook.

He wiped sweat from his face. "Yes, yes. I must go now." He turned around.

"Wait! Will I see you tomorrow?" I called after him.

"Unfailingly," he said, and disappeared into the crowd.

∾

"Amelia, this outfit suits you so well," Madame Titilayo said.

"Won't you sit down with me for a while?" I asked over the noise of the music.

"I must see to our guests, Amelia. Look, your cousins are here to make sure you are all right," she said, patting my hand. She leaned closer and kissed my forehead. "I am so proud of you, my daughter," she whispered.

I smiled through the tears and finally released her.

"Let Aunty go, Amelia. Aah! Aah!" Kemi shouted, bending down to my level. Her ever-smiling face peered at me through the veil.

"Are you all right?" she asked.

"Yes, but when am I going to be called? I'm getting tired of waiting." I looked around the small room within the hall set aside for the bride. Surrounding me were my other cousins— Kemi's younger siblings.

"Marcos just arrived with his family. It should take another half hour before you're called," Kemi said.

The door opened and Maria came in holding her baby.

"You're not allowed in here! We haven't handed over our sister yet!" Kemi shouted, getting up to obstruct Maria's way.

I laughed, straining my neck to look at my friend. Maria made a face, side-stepping her.

"Please, please. This is my sister too. I can shift sides anytime I want. For now, I am from the Şodipo family," she said, bending down to hug me.

Everyone laughed.

"So, how are you feeling? Still nervous?" Maria asked.

"No, I'm actually not. How's the baby doing?" I asked, touching little David's face.

"He is eating, sleeping all day, and staying awake all night!" Maria shouted above the music, which got louder.

I laughed. "You look so happy Maria. Motherhood suits you," I said.

Her eyes danced as she gazed at me. "You look happy too, Amelia. For the first time, you really look happy," she said.

"Maria!" someone shouted from the door.

"I must go, Amelia! They must be calling the family forward for introductions." She bent and kissed my cheek.

"I'll see you later!" I called to her.

The door opened again. Aunty Jumokę came in, still as tall and commanding as ever. The only difference was the gray hair that peeked from under her elaborate head tie.

"Mama, I thought Aunty Titilayo said the ceremony had started. What are you still doing here?" Kemi asked.

Aunty Jumokę walked by her daughter, eyeing her playfully. "My dear, I just came to check on you," she said, touching my arm.

"Thank you, Aunty," I said, smiling up at her.

Her lips twitched at the sides.

I giggled. "What is it?" I asked.

She slapped my cheek playfully. "*Never-been-touched,* that should be your other name," she said.

Everyone laughed.

"Aunty, what does that mean?" I asked, looking at all of them.

Kemi shook her head. "Amelia, you mean to tell me you don't know what never-been-touched means?" she asked.

"If I could swear, I would," I replied.

Aunty Jumoke hugged me. "Let them educate you then. I must go and support my sister outside." She walked off quickly, closing the door behind her.

Kemi sat down opposite me, grinning. "You that have seen a lot more than we have, yet you don't know never-been-touched means a *virgin*. What she means really is that you still look young and innocent," she said.

I laughed so hard, holding my belly.

"Me? Aunty is funny. One look at Ifẹmi and you will know otherwise," I said, looking around.

"And where is that boy by the way? He was here a few minutes ago," I said.

"Eh! That boy is so confused right now he doesn't know whether he belongs to the Alvarez side or the Şodipo side," Kemi said, turning up her nose.

I chuckled. "You are right. I'm sure he's with Marcos. Can you help me check?" I asked.

She got up just as the door opened. *Alaga joko*— the intermediary representing my family for the engagement ceremony—entered dressed to the hilt. She wore the uniform orange head tie all the female family members of the bride-to-be wore.

"My young beautiful maidens, it is time to get ready to dance forward. Soon, your sister here will be called upon. Come on!" She waved to my cousins to come. They ran quickly to her disappearing through the door.

Kemi hugged me briefly. "I will come and get you shortly," she said and followed them.

I pulled the chair Kemi vacated and placed my feet on them, happy to free them from the dainty shoes. Finally able to have some few minutes to myself. Praises to God poured from my heart.

A knock sounded on the door. When I looked up, the door was already pushed open.

"Princess Amelia," Dokpe's head appeared.

"Dokpe?" I asked, springing up.

He looked unsure of himself.

"Come in, is everything all right? Did you not find a seat?" I asked, walking up to him.

He came in, but left the door cracked open. "Princess Amelia, congratulations again," he said, smiling slightly.

"Thank you," I said.

His hands were behind his back in that military style that I remembered.

"What is wrong Dokpe?" I asked, my heart starting to race. His eyes had not looked directly at me since coming in.

He looked at me now. "This was not how we had planned it, Princess Amelia, but when I saw your boy— *his* boy—I knew that the truth had to be told. Forgive me." He bowed slightly and stepped away from the door.

"Dokpe, what exactly are you saying? You're not making any sense!" I whispered.

The door opened wider and there stood Dossou. His eyes met mine and I stood transfixed. Nothing else mattered. His mouth opened. "Amelia," he said.

I took a step. Then another. My hand reached up and touched his face. He had grown a beard laced with gray strands. His hand covered mine and held it there. Dokpe bowed and left the room.

I looked up into his face and he smiled. We fell into each other's arms unable to speak, content to just touch.

"I finally found you." His voice was rough, laden with tears.

Tears flowed freely down my face as I clung to him. "I thought you were dead!" I whispered.

He pushed me back gently and looked into my face. He pulled me close again, showering kisses on my face.

"Dossou," I whispered, touching his face.

"My heart," he whispered, the tears swimming in his eyes.

"I'm supposed to be getting married tomorrow," I said.

He nodded. "Dokpe has explained everything. Moreover, it is the talk of the city," he said.

"I didn't know! I didn't know you were alive. If I knew, none of this would have even come to be," I said.

He took my hand and raised it to his lips, closing his eyes. "I know, Amelia," he said softly. "You look so beautiful."

I smiled, burying my face in his chest. I inhaled his maleness, filling my senses to the brim. "We have a son, Dossou," I said, looking up at him.

His lips parted slightly in a smile. "You always said you wanted a boy first," he said.

"God gave him to us," I said softly, touching his chest through his lace buba.

"He did. Just when you thought He had forgotten," he said.

My head jerked up in surprise. "Dossou, are you a Christian too?" I asked, holding my breath.

He smiled. "Yes, my love," he said.

I burst into tears, overcome with gratitude and sorrow at the same time. I pushed myself away. Dossou held out his arms, but I shook my head.

"I can't do this to Marcos. I love him too!" I whispered, my heart breaking.

"I understand, Amelia. I do," he said as tears washed down his face. "But imagine what I have felt not having you these years. Imagine dreaming of you all night and waking up to loneliness," he said, his hands reaching for mine.

"Dossou, please," I whispered.

My hands grabbed his and I was pulled into his embrace again.

"I will fight for you, Amelia. I have searched for you, and now that I have found you, I won't let go," he whispered in my ear.

There was a knock at the door. We pulled apart as it opened.

"They are coming for you, Princess," Dokpe said.

I heard the singing getting closer.

"You must go now," I whispered to them. I looked into Dossou's face. His eyes devoured me. "If you ever once believed in our love, meet me outside the ferry station. I will wait for you the whole night, Amelia. I will wait for you and my son," he said.

They left immediately, closing the door quietly after them.

☙

Marcos's hands clasped mine as we were prayed over by our families. The congregational prayers resounded throughout the hall, finally coming to an end with the alaga joko saying "Amin."

Marcos looked at me. "Are you all right? I felt you tremble just now," he whispered in my ear.

I looked into his eyes, my heart fluttering and smiled. "Yes of course. It must have been someone walking over my grave, nothing serious," I said, laughing nervously.

He studied me for a few seconds. "Something is wrong, Amelia," he said calmly.

The music started again. We turned to see our families hit the dance floor.

"Come and dance for us again handsome couple," someone called to us.

Marcos looked away and back at me, his cap still firmly positioned on his head. He got up, and held out his hand. "Come, my love. Let's talk," he said.

I placed my hand in his palm and he pulled me up gently.

"Where are you going now?" Madame Titilayo asked, dancing toward us.

"You know I won't see Amelia until tomorrow?" Marcos asked.

Madame Titilayo nodded.

"Well, I just wanted to have her to myself for just a few minutes before you take her away," he said.

She laughed. "I understand, but just a few minutes. We will still enjoy our daughter until tomorrow," she danced off again.

He squeezed my hand gently as we walked back to the room where I had stayed—the room Dossou had come to me. Marcos closed the door behind him and turned to me. He touched my cheek and let his fingers run down my neck. "Tell me what's wrong, Amelia," he said.

I looked down, trembling. His hands came around me, and pulled me to him.

"What is it? You can tell me anything." His voice was shaking.

I shook my head.

"I will still love you, Amelia, no matter what. Tell me," he said softly. "Tell me," he pleaded, kissing my forehead.

I closed my eyes tight as the tears escaped from under my eyelids. I opened my mouth. "He's alive," I said.

Marcos' body became still. He pulled me away from him. "Who is alive?" he asked. His eyes already told me he knew.

"Dossou," I said.

He was silent, watching me.

"He came here to see me," I said.

"He came here to *get* you," he said calmly, his hands took mine. "Does he know about Ifẹmi?" he asked.

I nodded.

He sighed heavily, looking down into my face. "He sees the same thing I see," he whispered.

I looked back at him.

"He wants what *he had,* and what *I want,*" he whispered again. His eyes glistened. "I don't blame him," he said, crushing me to him.

"Amelia, Marcos! It's time to go!" Madame Titilayo shouted from behind the door.

We pulled apart. Marcos lifted my chin up. "I love you, Amelia. I will love no other. I will wait for you to come down that aisle tomorrow." He bent and kissed me slowly. The door opened.

"Enough of this!" Madame Titilayo said, pushing us apart and chuckling. "You can continue tomorrow night," she said, pulling me after her.

"I will wait for you, Amelia," Marcos called to me

I broke free from Madame Titilayo and ran to Marcos, jumping into his arms. We clung together, crying softly.

"What is wrong with both of you? Behaving as if this is the last time you will see each other! Come here now, my young lady!" Madame Titilayo said, her voice rising with every word she spat out.

"You better go now before she says we can't get married," Marcos whispered in my ear, releasing me.

I chuckled, walking back to a disgruntled Madame Titilayo. She took my hand, and dragged me after her. Marcos had that crooked smile on his face as I waved.

$\backsim$

My eyes had gotten used to the dark as I lay on my bed, tossing and turning. From the sound of the cock crowing, it was almost dawn. I had not slept all night. I looked across at my son as he slept. His long dark lashes sharp against his honey-colored skin. His smiling lips a replica of his father's. My heart beat faster as Dossou's face flashed before me. He was alive. I sat up, placing my feet on the floor. I looked at the window. It was daybreak. He would have left by now. The tears washed down my face. I placed a hand over my mouth to muffle my cries.

"What can be so serious to keep you up this late Amelia?"

I stood up. Madame Titilayo's head appeared behind the door. She had slept in the living room last night.

"Mama," I murmured.

She entered the room. "Sit down and tell me," she said calmly.

I sat, brushing my tears hurriedly away.

"Tell me, Amelia," she said.

"Mama…" I burst into tears.

"Sssh…my dear, tell me," she said, holding my hand.

I hiccupped, trying to control my emotions.

"My husband is alive. My husband has come for me," I whispered.

Her eyes widened.

"What do you mean, Amelia? Marcos is not your husband yet…"

I shook my head.

"Dossou, the husband I thought was dead *is alive*," I said.

Madame Titilayou gasped, dropping my hand. I nodded. She looked down on the floor. "Aah, aah, aah. This is serious, Amelia," she said.

We were silent. Finally, she turned to me.

"Dossou is your first love, is that not so?" she asked.

I nodded.

"Marcus is your rekindled love, your second chance," she said.

"Yes. He is my hope restored," I said softly, his beautiful face appearing before me.

Madame Titilayo sighed heavily. "I cannot make this decision for you Amelia. You know your heart… follow it," she said.

"*My heart*," I murmured.

"Your heart can never lie to you. It knows the right thing to do," she said.

I closed my eyes, praying. Madame Titilayo got up. "Let me give you some time to yourself," she said.

"Thank you, Mama," I said, standing to give her a hug.

"I will support you *whatever* decision you make," she whispered and left the room.

"I know," I murmured to myself as she closed the door.

∽

My sandal-clad feet stomped the ground harder as I approached the ferry station. The whistle was blowing for passengers to board the ferry. My throat was choked with tears as I pushed through the crowd.

"Miss! Miss! Are you blind? Can't you see the line?" someone shouted at me.

Another pulled at my dress and I heard a tear but didn't stop. "Excuse me!" I shouted to the cashier at the window.

"I saw you, young lady! I saw you jump the line. I don't cater to people who disregard rules!" the bespectacled cashier said.

"Please, has the ferry to Kotonou left already? Did a foreigner stop by here? He is Fon, very tall—"

"Young lady, did you not hear me? I will not cater to someone who disregards rules. Get in line!" he shouted, getting up.

The crowd shouted in agreement. The tears streamed down my face as they pushed me out of the line. I staggered to the side, almost falling off the side of the wooden plank into the water. A hand grabbed me, pulling me from the edge.

"I received the very same treatment from them."

I gasped, looking up into my beloved's face. "You didn't leave!" I shouted, falling into his arms. He pressed his face into my hair, inhaling deeply.

"My legs would not move. I could not imagine leaving the soil that you walked on," he whispered in my ear.

I trembled in his arms. "I love you, Dossou."

He pulled me back, looking into my eyes. His eyes danced with laughter.

"I have waited to hear you say that to me since you left, since I lost you." His voice shook as he spoke. I wiped his tears with my hand.

"Amelia! Amelia!" We looked up to see Madame Titilayo running toward us with Ifẹmi, a bag swinging from her shoulder.

"Mama!" I ran to them, followed closely by Dossou.

Ifẹmi hugged me. His eyes were still heavy with sleep.

"Ifẹmi, my love. I'm sorry Grandmother had to wake you so early, but I had to bring you here to meet someone special," I said slowly.

Dossou stooped down to where I knelt by our son. He caught his breath. Ifẹmi turned his gaze on Dossou.

"This is your father, Ifẹmi," I said.

Ifẹmi looked at me quizzically, and then at Dossou. He looked up at Madame Titilayo. She nodded. He looked back at Dossou and then held out his hand. Dossou leaned forward and opened up his arms. Ifẹmi took one cautious step. Dossou picked him up, holding Ifẹmi to his chest. I cried, feeling the years of hurt and loss wash away. I didn't realize Madame Titilayo held me until I felt her hand rubbing my back. Dossou got up with Ifẹmi in his arms and turned to Madame Titilayo and I. He held out his hand for me to get up with her. He then bowed to his waist in respect.

"Madame Titilayo, thank you for taking care of my family," he said, raising his free hand to his chest. The tears flowed freely down his face.

She looked up at him. "You know me?" she asked, surprised.

Dossou smiled. "Yes. I began my search for Amelia in Abẹokuta, and I know you were her benefactor," he said.

Madame Titilayo smiled. "Then you must also know that she is my niece, my sister's daughter," she said.

Dossou turned to me, surprised

"Yes, she is Mama's sister," I said, touching his arm.

"You knew?" he asked.

"Not immediately. It was this." I held up my wrist, showing off my gold beads.

Madame Titilayo raised her arm too, revealing hers. "It was the beads that brought her home," Madame Titilayo said.

Dossou looked into my face, a smile spread on his lips.

"Yes, it was the gold beads," I said, smiling back.

The whistle sounded. Dossou looked up. "We must go now, that's the final whistle for boarding," he said soflty.

Madame Titilayo handed me the bag. "Take this Amelia. It has the necessary things for now. I can send more when you are settled," she said.

"Mama, what...what will you tell Marcos? His family?" I asked anxiously.

She touched my shoulder. "Have no fear, Amelia. I will take care of it. You have made the right decision," she said, looking at Dossou and Ifẹmi.

I hugged her one last time. Ifẹmi flung his arms around her and quickly went back into the arms of Dossou. Madame Titilayo held her arms out and Dossou hugged her.

"Thank you, Mama. Thank you," he said.

"Go now! God go with you. God keep you!" she called to us, tears streaming down her face.

The whistle sounded again, and we ran toward the ferry, not looking back.

The End

ACKNOWLEDGEMENTS

Words are not enough to convey my gratitude to everyone who assisted me with weaving the tale of *Thread of Gold Beads*. To many of you, it was a labor of love. My thanks go out to all including:

My family, Patience Modupẹ Coker and Frederick Douglas Sorunkẹ Coker, my maternal grandparents who through telling me about their lives and generations before them, planted the idea to write this novel. I enjoyed every moment spent listening as you told me of your life experiences, your parents' and grandparents'. They were life lessons that have shaped me into the person I am today.

Tunde Fatoki, my husband, who has supported me in every way. You never got tired of my updates and sleepless nights on the laptop. For reading my very first draft and sticking to it until the end. That can only be true love. My three boys - Babajimi, Babafemi, and Babatoye - I did this for you too. Follow your dreams, pursue your passion. You can do whatever you set your mind to and see it come to pass by the grace of God.

Dr. Busola Campbell, my mother who shared all that she knew. You never said no to any request to get historical information. You epitomize the selflessness in every loving mother. Dr. Mobola Campbell-Yesufu, my sister and friend. You were the first reader of my hand-written work. Even then you encouraged me to write. Thank you for being an eager reader who provided honest feedback. My brothers, Seyi and Yinka Campbell, who supported me by always asking how the book was going and believing in me. Iyiola Yesufu, my brother, who made a comment that you were waiting on my novel three years ago. It was the challenge I needed - thank you.

Anwuli Ojogwu, my editor, who was patient enough to work with my very rough drafts. Our meeting was not by chance in Nigeria. I believe everything happens for a reason. I appreciate your tutelage. Simi Dosekun, who introduced me to my editor. You were a crucial link in the chain. Tugdial Kpekpe, my first helper in understanding the culture and traditions of Benin.

Wale Ajao, my illustrator and photographer, for seeing what I envisioned the book to look like and creating it perfectly.

Pastor Ghandi Olaoye of Jesus House DC, Redeemed Christian Church of God, Washington, DC, for your prayers, words of encouragement, and the helping hand you gave.

The Embassy of the Republic of Benin, Washington DC, for the warm welcome given me at our first meeting and several meetings after. Thank you for the precious time you took to sit with me to understand the rich culture of your country which I have also embraced as mine.

Made in the USA
Lexington, KY
30 December 2012